Unwanted Truths

To Viv
Enjoy the read

Unwanted Truths

Tricia Haddon

TRICIA HADDON

Copyright © 2015 Tricia Haddon

The moral right of the author has been asserted.

Apart from any fair dealing for the purposes of research or private study, or criticism or review, as permitted under the Copyright, Designs and Patents Act 1988, this publication may only be reproduced, stored or transmitted, in any form or by any means, with the prior permission in writing of the publishers, or in the case of reprographic reproduction in accordance with the terms of licences issued by the Copyright Licensing Agency. Enquiries concerning reproduction outside those terms should be sent to the publishers.

This book is a work of fiction. Names, characters, places and incidents are either a product of the author's imagination or are used fictitiously. Any resemblance to actual people, living or dead, is purely coincidental.

Matador
9 Priory Business Park
Kibworth Beauchamp
Leicestershire LE8 0RX, UK
Tel: (+44) 116 279 2299
Fax: (+44) 116 279 2277
Email: books@troubador.co.uk
Web: www.troubador.co.uk/matador

ISBN 978 1784621 575

British Library Cataloguing in Publication Data.
A catalogue record for this book is available from the British Library.

Typeset in Garamond by Troubador Publishing Ltd
Printed and bound in the UK by TJ International, Padstow, Cornwall

Matador is an imprint of Troubador Publishing Ltd

Dedicated to my parents and with grateful thanks to my family and friends for their help and encouragement.

Always tell the truth. That's what we are told as children. But do we tell the truth to someone who hasn't asked the question? Truth is final; no room to manoeuvre; the damage is done.

PROLOGUE

November 1981

She opened her umbrella as she picked her way across the green towards the church. In her hand was a single red rose. Feeling strands of damp hair sticking to her forehead, she drew the umbrella closer to her head and stepped up to the gate. A sycamore, its branches stripped of leaves by the tail-end of an Atlantic hurricane, separated the lichen covered stones from recent memorials. She noticed that three more graves had been dug since her last visit and glanced down at the shiny brass plaques, but didn't recognise any of the names. Bending down she placed her rose in front of a wooden cross and whispered, 'Happy birthday, Mum.' Tears streamed down her face, mingling with the drizzle. She wiped the sleeve of her coat across her cheeks, and wondered why she hadn't thought to bring any tissues. She sniffed hard and stood up. Moving to the end of the mound, she stared at the light brown soil interspersed with chalk. '*You'll miss me when I'm gone,*' her mother's words that she had dismissed with the casualness of youth, now seemed a just retribution. She would have to decide about a memorial stone soon. Someone, she couldn't remember who, said that you had to wait a year for the ground to settle.

'Excuse me.'

She jumped and spun round, lifting her umbrella. A man stood in front of her, the tip of his jacket collar touching the lobes of his ears.

'I'm sorry if I startled you, but I think you've left your lights on. Is that your Morris Minor outside?' He frowned and looked down at the cross.

'My God, it's Jenny — Jenny Porter, isn't it? I don't believe it.' A broad smile stretched across his sharp features. He held out his hand, but then let it drop by his side.

Is it him? she thought, her heart banging against her ribs. *No, it can't be. Not here.* As the man turned his head slightly, she noticed a mole that interrupted the line of his jaw. 'Martin.'

'I'm sorry, I shouldn't have disturbed you.' He turned to go.

'No, no — it's alright.' Her chest tightened. She swallowed. 'I never expected to see you again. You moved away. You don't live here any more.'

'Yes, we did, and I don't. But my parents moved back about ten years ago. They always liked it up this way. That's their house down there.' He turned and pointed in the direction of a red tiled roof.

'Yes, it is nice here. But not today — I mean with the

rain.' She blinked several times to refresh her eyes, thinking how awkward she must sound.

'You were crying the last time I saw you,' he said softly.

So he remembers. It was here by the windmill. But I'm years older now. She flicked her head back and ran her fingers through her hair, pushing it off her face. 'I'd better go – my lights. I'm always doing that when it's dark during the day.' She didn't move.

'Yes, it's easily done.' He gazed at her. 'It's great to see you again, Jenny. I can't believe it.'

'Yes, it's great to see you too,' she said. Words that she had always imagined saying had vanished. 'I must go – my lights.' She drew her umbrella closer and started walking towards the path. She knew he was watching her, and it took all her strength to place one foot in front of the other.

'I'm sorry about your parents,' his words carried across the churchyard.

She turned and nodded. He was still standing at the foot of her parents' grave. A pied wagtail bobbed out of her way as she met the solidness of the path. She shut the gate and, glancing back to check that she was out of sight, ran across the green towards the faint yellow beams. Balancing the umbrella against her body, she leant on the car and fumbled in her coat pocket for the key, her hand trembling as she tried to force it into the lock. *For God's sake, go in. Why won't it go in?* She removed it and tried again, it turned. Relieved, she threw her umbrella onto the passenger seat and sank behind the wheel. *Why is he here? He must have lost someone too*, she thought. *I should have asked. I must go before he comes out. He can't see me – not looking like this.* She pulled the choke out and turned the ignition. The engine groaned. *No, not the lights, please start, come on, don't let me down.* She adjusted the choke. On the third attempt the engine fired. She released the handbrake and drove away.

Jenny thought of nothing else for the rest of that afternoon. She now had a new image of Martin. It would take some getting used to; she had been comfortable with the old one. His words replayed in her mind as she stared at her son, who was twirling a sausage around with his fork in a pool of tomato sauce. She slammed her hand on the table. 'Stop playing with your food, Nicky.'

'I'm not hungry. Look, it's a helicopter.'

'You're not hungry because you've been stuffing your face with chocolates,' said his sister, leaning over the table towards him.

'You said you wouldn't tell.'

'Well, you shouldn't have hit me then, should you?'

'She had some too,' Nicky turned towards his mother.

'But I've eaten all my dinner.'

'For God's sake, stop it you two,' Jenny said, irritated that her thoughts were being interrupted. She glanced up at the clock on the kitchen wall. 'Lorna, finish your pudding, then go and get ready for Brownies. You'll need your coat, it's still drizzling. No pudding for you, Nicky. I should be able to trust you not to eat sweets before dinner.'

'Jen, let it go, what's the matter with you?' Robert, her husband, stopped eating and looked up. 'He's eight years old. He's going to eat sweets if they're around. Did you do anything today?'

Jenny winced as she spotted a sliver of cabbage stuck between his front teeth. 'I went to the churchyard. I told you I was going. It's Mum's birthday; she would have been seventy-four today.'

'I'm sorry, Jen, I should have remembered.' He reached for the tomato sauce. 'I thought I'd never get home tonight; the A23 was a bloody nightmare.'

'But, Mummy, why did you go to the churchyard? You said Granny's gone to heaven.'

'She has Nicky, and so has Granddad. I go there to feel close to them.'

'Is that because they lived near there? Why don't you go to their flat?'

'Nicky, that's enough. Just get down,' said Robert.

'I miss Granddad.' His lower lip quivered as he slid off his chair.

'I know Nicky, we all do, come here.' Seeing him hesitate, Jenny pulled him towards her and hugged him.

'You must have been the only person there on a day

like this,' Robert said as he pierced a sausage with his fork.

'Yes, I was,' she said, thinking that this was the first time she had lied to her husband.

PART ONE

1

January 1953

Jenny Porter was bored. Dropping her book to the floor, she threw the bedcovers back and knelt at the window, dipping her fingertips in and out of the pools of water that lay on the sill. Lifting the net curtain she peered out, hoping to spot her friends as they returned to school after lunch. But the pavements and roads were deserted. Above the frosted roofs she could see the sails of the windmill that stood on top of a flint barn. Miss Bruce, who she thought was the prettiest teacher in the whole world, had said that years ago it had been a landmark for ships; and that a famous painter – Jenny couldn't remember his name – had painted a picture of it.

The smock windmill, a manor house and a church were all that remained of the downland village of West Blatchington; one of several that surrounded Brighton and Hove. The farm labourers' cottages had been demolished at the end of the Second World War, to make way for the housing estate. Jenny remembered how excited she had been when she was told they were going to live in a new flat with a bathroom. Homes for heroes, her father had called them.

Jenny coughed and fell back onto her bed. She was convalescing from measles. On the fourth day of her illness, a plethora of scarlet spots had appeared, making it difficult to tell whether she was red with white spots, or white with red spots. She winced. Sliding her hand under her pyjama bottoms, she dug her thumbnail into the largest and meanest spot, and watched as blood oozed through the angry skin. She basked in the satisfaction of self-injury. Reaching across to the bedside table, she grabbed a brown fluted bottle and pulled a tuft of cotton wool from a roll. Soaking it in the cold liquid, she dabbed the swelling, until it resembled a fluffy pink cloud. The ritual was complete.

Her mother was in the sitting room. The painful sound of metal on metal, as she scraped yesterday's ashes, had ceased; so had the crunching of newspaper into loose balls for tinder. Jenny listened for the familiar crackle as the fire burst into life, but it didn't come. She thought she could hear someone crying. But there was only the two of them in the flat, and mums don't cry. She stiffened. There was shuffling on the lino outside her room. She relaxed, thinking that her mother was returning to the kitchen, and how she always made tea after she lit the fire. She listened for the rush of water from the tap, the clank of the kettle settling on the gas ring; but the flat lay heavy with silence.

Jenny wriggled to the end of the bed and peered

around the edge of the door. She could see along the landing and into the kitchen.

Her mother was kneeling on the floor, her calves encased in brown wrinkly stockings. Jenny thought they looked like thick worms. On her feet was a pair of scarlet slippers.

That's why it's so quiet. She's cleaning the oven. But she did that on Sunday, Jenny thought. *Why is she doing it again?* She heard mumbling, and felt guilty that she was spying on her mother. *What's she doing? Something's not right. Where's her head?* Her heart pounded as she tried to make sense of what she could see. The rest of her body no longer existed; no spots, no itching, just a drum thumping inside her head. An icy wave washed over her. She scrambled from the bed screaming. 'Mummy, Mummy, Mummy!'

Her mother was sitting on the floor with legs outstretched, and her head drooping onto her chest. 'Help me up Jenny,' she croaked, reaching for the open oven door, 'help me up.'

Jenny's nose wrinkled and her eyes watered as she heaved her mother to her feet and away from the smell, supporting her as she staggered to the edge of the wooden draining board. Her mother reached over the sink and rattled the metal catch on the side window. It flew open, sucking out one half of a pair of blue gingham curtains, which billowed like a flag in the wind. She gasped three times and retched into the sink. Grabbing a towel from the rail on the larder door, she wiped it across her face, and leaning on Jenny, lurched towards the nearer of two matching stools that stood either side of the gas stove.

'Mum. Are you alright? You frightened me,' her voice wobbled.

'Go back to bed, Jenny. Go back to bed. I'll just sit here for a bit. I'll be fine. I just left the gas on too long.'

Jenny didn't move, but stared at her until convinced that what she said was true. She turned to go and knocked her right knee against the oven door. Numb to physical pain, she stumbled along the landing and flopped down on her bed. She started to cry, her nose and mouth buried in the eiderdown. The gaps between her sobs lengthened, until she fell asleep. Ten minutes later, she woke shivering. Looking along the landing, she saw her mother sitting at the kitchen table holding her head in her hands, with a glass of water at her elbow. Jenny crawled to the top of the bed and slid underneath the covers.

Her bed was moving. It was dark. Jenny squinted and rubbed her hands across her eyes. Her mother had pushed her bed away from the window, and was drawing the curtains.

Alice was forty-six years old and no more than five foot two inches in height. Her thin-lipped face was framed by tight dark curls.

Jenny's lower lip trembled and tears trickled down her cheeks as she remembered. Her mother pushed her bed back against the wall, and sitting beside her, stroked her damp hair away from her eyes and kissed her forehead.

'Don't cry, Jenny,' she whispered. 'I'm feeling better now. I'm sorry I frightened you.' She patted Jenny's shoulder and stood up. 'I'm going to light the fire in the sitting room now. Do you want me to put your light on?'

Jenny didn't reply, but rolled over onto her side and lay on the far edge of the bed, her back to her mother, and the tip of her nose touching the ice-cold wall.

Barring illness or injury, Charlie Porter's key turned in the lock at six o'clock every weekday for fifty weeks of the year.

A stocky man of average height, he would fling his trilby hat onto the hook on the cupboard door in the hallway, exposing a shock of snow-white hair. Hanging his coat under his hat, he would whistle his way up the stairs to the landing. Entering the kitchen he would plant a kiss on Alice's cheek, and begin a diatribe on the day's events. Today was no exception.

Hearing her father's footsteps, Jenny shuffled to the end of her bed and listened.

'Do you know what Alfie Moore said today, Gal?' His wife's Christian name was a mystery to most people, as Charlie always called her Gal to her face, and Missus to everyone else.

'He told Bill Gardner that he would move the sacks, I tell you, Gal, that man hasn't got the bloody guts to stand up to anyone. You know what that means don't you? We'll all have to lug bloody sacks about now, even though there are lads there half our age. That Alfie's a bloody yes man if ever there was one.'

Charlie had worked in the baking powder department of Green's Cake Mix factory since 1946. For him, life had ended the day he had been demobbed after twenty-five years of regular army service. When anyone asked what he did for a living, he would tell them that he had reached the rank of Regimental Sergeant Major in the second battalion of the Duke of Wellington's Regiment. He would then add 'West Riding Division', as if worried that he hadn't provided quite enough information. He endured a domestic life now. In Charlie's eyes his fellow workers weren't real men. They lacked backbone. Real men would never be satisfied with a nine to five existence.

'You look terrible, Gal. Your face and your eyes, they're all red. Have you been crying?'

'Charlie – for God's sake, don't you know the date? It's the 14th of January, as if I could ever forget. My ulcer's been giving me gyp as well. The pain's been unbearable, even with the tablets. You'll have to help me with the dinner.'

'Don't – don't upset yourself, Gal.'

'I can't help it Charlie. I did something terrible today – unforgivable. I don't know what came over me. I just couldn't help myself.'

Jenny waited open-mouthed for her father to ask

what it was. *What would she say?* She strained her ears.

'You'll hear from the hospital soon, Gal, then you'll be fine. What's for dinner?'

Alice had never been fine. All her teeth had been removed on her twenty-first birthday in an attempt to cure her stomach pains. By twenty-five, she had been in every hospital within a five mile radius of her home, for ailments ranging from diphtheria to in-growing toenails, and everything in between. 'Mile End Hospital, Bethnal Green Infirmary, London Hospital Whitechapel, oh, and I nearly forgot St. Bart's. I've been in them all,' she would say as if listing holiday destinations. Then after a full description of the ailment which had led her to each one, would add, 'But there's always someone worse off than yourself, that's what I say.'

Alice had lived with her parents and younger brother, in three rented rooms; part of a terrace that lay to the south of Roman Road. At fourteen, she was working fifty hours a week as a pattern cutter. 'There's many a time I've seen rats as big as cats, and bigger, in that factory at Aldgate,' she told Jenny on numerous occasions, stretching out her arms as if her words weren't enough of a description.

Charlie's family occupied the whole of a house that stood directly opposite Alice's. Whenever he returned home on leave, he would see her sitting squashed between his half sisters and brothers, eagerly anticipating his latest tales from the empire.

By 1934 Alice's health had improved. With a group of fellow Sunday school teachers, she went on a five day holiday to Brussels, bringing home a brass paper knife with the *Manneken Pis* shaped as the handle. In 1940 at the age of thirty-three, she married Charlie Porter.

'He's been all over the world, but he came home and married me,' Alice would say.

Charlie would then add wistfully, 'Mind you, those Anglo-Indian girls, with their pale skin and dark almond eyes, beauties they were, beauties.'

Jenny scrambled to the top of her bed.

'How's my girl today?' Charlie poked his head around her bedroom door.

'Better. I'm getting up for dinner.' Jenny wanted everything to be normal again, how it was before this afternoon.

'That's my girl.'

Jenny slid into her slippers, and attempted to tie the cord of her dressing-gown around her waist; but her earlier strength had deserted her. She picked her book up from the floor and shuffled into the sitting room.

The armchair under the brass standard lamp in the corner was either empty or occupied by Charlie. The ceiling above was the colour of strong tea. Charlie sighed, sank into the cushions and lit a cigarette. Jenny sat at his feet and undid the laces on his shiny leather shoes. Usually, she only needed one tug to remove each shoe. But today several were necessary. She toppled backwards with the second shoe in her hand.

'That's better,' sighed Charlie lifting his feet onto a leather *pouffe*. Jenny replaced his shoes with slippers, and stretched out on the rug in front of the fire. She supported her head with her hands, and waited. *Any minute now*, she thought, until what she looked forward to every evening, would begin.

Charlie cleared his throat. 'Nepal,' he said.

'Kathmandu,' she answered.

'Burma.'

'Rangoon.'

'Fiji.'

'Suva.'

'Jamaica.'

'Kingston.'

Suddenly, Charlie reversed the order.

'Vaduz.'

'Liechtenstein.'

'Ankara.'

'Turkey.'

'Seoul.'

'South Korea.'

'Colombo.'

'Ceylon.'

Their duet continued until Charlie ran out of countries or capitals. He said that Jenny was the only child in her school, and probably in the whole country, who knew the name of every capital city from Australia to Zanzibar. If dinner was delayed Charlie would relate one of his army exploits, which Jenny relished long after Alice had grown impatient of yet another tale. They were usually sparked by a word, which reminded Charlie of a person or event. Each story embellished with the name and rank of the soldier involved.

'Charlie, would you pierce this tin for me.' Jenny looked up from her book. Her mother was leaning against the door surround holding a tin of peas.

'Captain Pearce, now he was a man who knew how to command, I remember when we were out on patrol one night. There was a rustling in the undergrowth. We all thought it was bandits, but no, it turned out to be a black panther didn't it? Killers they were – even took kids. We saw its eyes burning like hot coals in the darkness. Ready to spring it was, but quick as a flash Captain Pearce drew his revolver and shot it dead. By God, we had some good times back then.'

'Charlie, the tin,' said Alice wearily.

'What's that book you're reading Jenny?' Charlie asked as he returned to his chair.

'It's about Rome. We've been doing Romans at school, so Miss Bruce dropped it off for me. I'll read you some… *the boys grew up to be very strong and clever and they decided to build a town on the spot where the shepherd had found them. But they had a big fight about who should be in charge. Romulus overpowered his brother Remus who died. So Romulus became the first king of this town which he named Rome.*' Jenny looked up. Her father was asleep.

A wooden table covered with a check tablecloth and laid with three dinner plates, was carried from the kitchen, by Alice at one end, and Charlie at the other. They placed it in front of the fire.

'That was lovely, Gal,' said Charlie when he'd finished soaking up the gravy on his plate with a chunk of white bread. He pulled a large handkerchief from his trouser pocket and with one wipe removed the drips from his mouth and chin.

Jenny watched her mother like an anxious parent, as she picked at a tiny piece of liver in the centre of her plate.

'Can't you eat any more, Gal?'

'Not today, Charlie.'

From the wireless that stood high on a table behind the standard lamp. Wilfred Pickle's voice was loud and clear.

'What's on the table, Mabel?'

2

February 1953

A blanket of smog surrounded them as they emerged from Whitechapel Underground Station and turned left into Brady Street. 'I can't see, Dad.'

'Put your scarf over your nose and mouth, and tie it tight,' Charlie's muffled voice came through the suffocating gloom. He tightened his grip on his daughter's hand.

They strode in silence through green-tinged swirls. A dark shape collided with Charlie, the woman muttering her apologies. An amber halo of light appeared, suspended in the darkness. As they walked closer they could see it was a lamp attached to an even blacker arch. Their footsteps echoed in the tunnel. Jenny wished that someone else would bump into them, as it seemed that they were the only people alive in the whole world. A whistle screeched and wheels thundered overhead, obliterating everything.

Re-entering their silent world, indistinct lights flickered in mid-air. As they strode nearer, they heard muffled voices, and the tinkling of a piano. A door was flung open, illuminating the pavement, and releasing laughter. A man stumbled in front of them, reaching out to steady himself on a lamppost.

'Joe, Joe Carberry,' said Charlie.

The man straightened himself, lifted his cap and placed one hand on Charlie's shoulder.

'Good to see you again, mate. I heard your old man's sick.'

'I got a telegram this morning. He's been going downhill for a while.'

Jenny saw her father mouth a word to the man, who said, 'My old man had it in the gut. It always gets them in the end.'

'It does that,' said Charlie.

'Best drayman we had at Mann & Crossman, he was. No-one had his touch with the horses. Well, you look after yourself, Chas.'

'Who's that?' asked Jenny as they walked away.

'Granddad worked with him at the brewery for years.'

'Are we nearly there?'

'Not far now.'

At the corner of a bomb site, dark shapes huddled together, leaning against the remains of a wall. Men's voices, indistinct in the murkiness, shouted across at them; a woman's laugh and the smash of a bottle. Jenny bit her lower lip and gripped her father's hand. The dark mass of a tenement building loomed. A left turn brought them into Finnis Street and up the steep steps of number 132.

'Hello, Cis,' said Charlie as the door opened. Jenny put her hand above her eyes against the brightness.

'Alice not with you?' the woman said.

'She's not been so good lately.'

Jenny recalled her parents' conversation earlier that day.

'We'll have to go up there pretty sharpish, Gal, according to Josie. I'll leave work early.'

'I'm not well enough to go, Charlie. There'll be enough of your family there, as it is. It's Friday, so you could take Jenny with you. Dad would love to see her if he's not too far gone.'

From the tone of her mother's voice, Jenny had thought that bad health was not the only reason for her staying behind.

Unburdening themselves of coats, hats, scarves and gloves, they were ushered up two flights of creaky stairs into a dimly-lit room. Another woman sat on a stool in the corner, and a dark cloth covered a lampshade in the centre of the room.

An old man lay propped up on pillows on a wooden bed. An enamel bowl sat on a table beside him. He turned his head.

He's not Granddad Albert, Jenny thought. Her granddad was a smiley man with a prickly moustache, who smelt of stables. She remembered the last time she had seen him. He had hoisted her onto his shoulders, pretending she was on a horse. 'Gee up, gee up,' he had said, as he thrust his shoulders into the air. *This man was not Granddad.*

Charlie pushed Jenny forward. 'Kiss your granddad. Kiss your granddad,' he repeated. Jenny bent forward. Her lips brushed his yellow skin. A skeletal hand reached out and touched her hair. The man's toothless mouth opened slightly, but no words came. She drew back.

'You'd better go downstairs, Jenny,' the woman spoke softly from the shadows. 'I want to talk to your dad.'

Jenny turned and ran from the room.

'Here she is.' Four pairs of female eyes looked up as Jenny hesitated in the doorway of the sitting room crowded with unfamiliar relations. Three men stood huddled together in a cloud of smoke around a table covered with beer bottles. In the fireplace stood an electric barred fire, and a black cloth was draped along the mantelpiece. In the centre was a marble clock, with a framed sepia photograph of a man in uniform, on each side.

'Sit down here, Jenny, I won't bite,' said the woman nearest the fire, patting the sofa beside her. Jenny sat sandwiched between two sturdy women, each wearing identical wrap-over blue floral aprons.

'You know who we are, don't you?' asked the woman to Jenny's left.

'Yes, you're my aunts,' she whispered.

'I'm Aunt Josie and that's your Aunt Cissy,' she nodded to Jenny's right. 'We remember when you were a baby, don't we, Cis?'

'Yes, and look at her now.' Jenny felt the first aunt's eyes looking her up and down. 'Must be all that sea air.'

Two more women were seated opposite. Jenny assumed they must be more aunts. They started whispering. They were dressed the same as the other pair, except for lines of metal curlers peeping out from under their headscarves. Jenny thought it must hurt to have them pinned to their heads, and smiled as she imagined what would happen if she was to put the large magnet in her "special box" near them. She bent her head, stared at the buckles on her shoes and strained her ears.

'Charlie and Alice are so proud of her; she's got lovely dark curls.'

More whispers from the opposite sofa, too indistinct for Jenny to decipher. She looked around. She assumed that the three men around the table were her uncles, but they didn't ask her if she knew who they were. The one with a moustache was speaking.

'I've heard the twins have scarpered again.'

'You should leave well alone there, Ernie. They're trouble those Krays; always have been, always will be,' said the one with his back to Jenny.

'Charlie's been good to me; always uses my cab; tips well too.'

'We know why, don't we?'

'Not now, Stan. Give it a rest,' said the third, taking a step forward and raising his arm.

'Remember Eric, he should be here with us now, not

buried on the other side of the bloody world. Jap bastards, they might just as well have killed Ma as well.'

Jenny watched as Ernie took another swig of beer and wiped the back of his hand across his moustache.

'Cat got your tongue?' asked the aunt called Cissy.

Jenny was saved from replying by a sudden fit of coughing that rattled down the stairs. The whispering and laughter ceased and the talk turned to funeral arrangements.

Her father filled the doorway. Jenny noticed that his face was red and puffy. She looked down at her shoes once more.

Ernie stepped forward and placed his arm around Charlie's shoulders. 'Glad you could make it, Chas. How's Alice?'

'Not that good. She's waiting to hear from the hospital. But you know the missus, she's a fighter.'

'She's always been that, bruv. How old's Jenny now?'

'Seven – she started junior school last year.' Her father then chatted to his brothers about people she didn't know for what seemed like hours. Her aunts had forgotten about her losing her tongue, and had moved on to more interesting matters.

'Who does she think she is sitting upstairs? Madam High and Mighty; she wouldn't let me in earlier today. We are his daughters after all. We have a right.'

'Of course we have; thinks she's better than us, just 'cos her old man owned a shop.'

'I must say. I'm not a bit surprised that Doris hasn't

turned up. She's only ever been interested in a good time. It's a good job Ma's not here, it would break her heart.'

Jenny stared at the ashtrays balanced on the sofa arms, thinking they looked like miniature bonfires.

Charlie pulled Jenny to her feet. 'Come on, it's time we were going.'

Huge hands patted her head. She heard a jangling of coins. 'That's for you,' her uncles said in turn, as they pressed cold metal into her hand.

'Mind how you go, you can't see a hand in front of you,' a woman shouted as they stepped over the doorstep and tightened their scarves around their faces.

Their footsteps echoed along the street as they strode towards the railway arch. They were the only people in the world again, and Jenny tightened her fingers around her father's hand.

'Who was that woman upstairs with Granddad?'

'That's Nanny May. She's Granddad's friend. She's looking after him.'

Jenny thought that her father had been unusually slow in answering. She remembered postcards arriving from Margate and Southend, addressed to her parents, and signed Dad and May.

'Look Dad,' said Jenny as they passed under a lamppost. She opened her right palm and several coins slid out from under her glove. She held three silver half-crowns under her father's chin.

'You're a lucky girl, come on, we'd better hurry if we're going to catch that train.'

They settled in an empty second class compartment, under posters showing yellow sands and azure skies; tempting travellers to spend their annual holiday in Bognor and Littlehampton. Charlie turned to Jenny as the train clattered over Grosvenor Bridge.

'Indonesia.'

'Jakarta.'

'Togo.'

'Lome.'

'Chile.'

'Santiago.'

'Oman.'

'Muscat.'

'Cuba.'

'Havana.'

By the time the train drew in to East Croydon, Jenny was asleep.

Two days later a further telegram arrived. Charlie reached into the back of his wardrobe for a black armband which he wore around the sleeve of his coat. Jenny wondered about Nanny May. The last time she heard her name mentioned was the day after Granddad Albert's funeral. She was reading… *there are seven gates that provide an entrance to the old city of Jerusalem. The most important are the Jaffa Gate and the Damascus Gate. The city is holy to three religions…* when she heard her father's voice from the kitchen. Instinctively she put her book down.

'You know, Gal, the girls aren't happy about May keeping some of Dad's things. You ought to have heard the things they were saying about her after the funeral. I couldn't repeat them.'

'That doesn't surprise me, one bit. The poor bugger's hardly six foot under and they're arguing. That's your sisters for you. They'd fight over the cat's dinner.'

Jenny thought it mean too; after all, she had been his friend.

3

April 1953

Jenny peered anxiously out of the window as the coach nosed into Victoria. She spotted two black feathers poking out of a bright red hat. Doris was the oldest of Charlie's half sisters and the closest in age. A large boned, energetic woman of forty; she had escaped the East End through hard work and a quick brain, and now owned a Victorian house in Woolwich. As well as working full-time in a local department store, she rented rooms to overseas students from the local polytechnic.

The coach station bustled with activity. Children bored with waiting chased each other around their parents, while smartly dressed older couples stood patiently by their cases.

Jenny hesitated at the bottom of the coach steps as her aunt hurried towards her.

'Don't I get a kiss then?' smiled Doris, and then, after looking her up and down, 'You'll be company for Alan. Did your dad give you any money for me?'

Jenny handed over the crumpled brown envelope she had been clutching since Charlie had put her into the care of the coach driver. She stood on tiptoe and brushed her aunt's rouged cheek.

Doris stuffed the envelope in her coat pocket and grabbed Jenny's hand.

'My case,' muttered Jenny.

'Well, run back and get it then. Be quick, it's quite a way for the bus; then we've got to change at Elephant and Castle.'

Jenny's case bumped against her legs as she was pulled along the pavement.

'Come on,' said Doris.

Jenny was relieved that her mother was in hospital, as she could stop worrying about leaving her on her own when she left for school. Her eyes would moisten whenever she thought about that day in January, and she had to blink to stop her tears. She had begged her parents to let her stay with Mrs Walters, a widow, who lived in the flat below. She could visit her mother, and be company for her father in the evenings; but was told that six weeks was far too long to stay with a neighbour. She was to stay with Aunt Doris.

Jenny eyed her cousin shyly across the kitchen table. Doris's husband Jim hovered over her as she nibbled a fish paste sandwich. He was a slight man, who worked at the local gas works. Doris told her family that she only married him because he kept pestering her and she felt sorry for him. 'Poor Jim, he has to do what he's told,' was the usual comment by Alice, at the mention of his name.

Alan, also an only child, was eighteen months older than Jenny. He was wearing a red check, open-necked shirt and dark brown corduroy shorts which ended just above his scabbed knees. His straight dark hair was struck through on the right-hand side with a white parting. He spoke first. 'Are you coming to school with me on Monday?'

'I'll have to ask Aunt Doris,' said Jenny. She hadn't thought about school. She was more worried that she might have to drink all the milk that was in her glass. It had a sickly sweet taste.

'Well, you can't ask her now. She's getting ready.'

'Ready for what?'

'It's Saturday night, Mum always goes out on Tuesday and Saturday nights.'

'Goes out? Goes out where?' asked Jenny, forgetting her shyness. She had never known her parents to go out in the evening together, never mind separately.

'She goes dancing, of course.'

Jenny sat cross-legged on the floor beside Alan, mesmerised by the flickering television in the wooden cabinet. The door opened. She looked over her shoulder and stared at her aunt who occupied the doorway. She thought she looked like a film star. Her dark wavy hair was styled close to her head, and her lips glistened with scarlet lipstick.

'Desmond and I are off now, so make sure you behave yourselves,' she said, smoothing black satin gloves along her lower arm. 'It's Saturday, so you can put yourselves to bed. I've made up the camp bed in Alan's room for you, Jenny. Don't forget to brush your teeth – that means you too, Alan.' She turned sharply on high heels; her black taffeta skirt swishing draughtily behind her. Her perfume lingered for the rest of the evening, as if to compensate for her absence.

A door slammed. Jenny woke in a panic. Where was she? She bit her lower lip. She needed the toilet. Suppose she wet the bed? She felt the struts of the wooden camp bed digging into her ribs through the blanket and sheet. Raised voices travelled along the landing. Turning over she could just make out the humped outline of Alan as he lay in the bed alongside her own. He was fast asleep and breathing noisily. She stared into the blackness and wished she was at home. There were witches dancing on the curtain rail, their evil faces mocking her. She turned over and lay on her stomach, her need for the toilet disappeared. More raised voices; she recognised her aunt's.

'The dance didn't end 'til one-thirty, I certainly wasn't going to leave before then. Anyway, you know I'm with Desmond. Get back to sleep, for God's sake. What's the matter with you?'

Then her uncle's voice, louder than usual; 'I've told you before Dori, it's not right you coming home this late. It's two o'clock in the morning, I don't like it.'

'Don't like what? You don't like me enjoying myself. What am I supposed to do, stay in with you every night?'

'You enjoyed yourself before, and look what happened then.'

'For Christ's sake; trust you to bring that up.'

Their voices trailed as Jenny fell asleep.

Jenny was halfway through eating a slice of toast when her aunt appeared wearing a cream silk dressing gown, covered with pink roses. Jenny waited for her to say something, but she ignored both herself and Alan. She perched on a high stool by the cupboard and pulled out a cigarette from a packet in her pocket, tapping it on the Formica surface. She put it between her lips, flicked a lighter and drew deeply. Jenny noticed that she still had powder and lipstick on from the night before.

'Has Desmond been down yet?' she asked, as Alan and Jenny piled their breakfast plates in the sink.

'Yes,' they both answered.

Desmond was one of three West African students who lodged at the house. He had been eating his breakfast when Jenny and Alan had come down. Jenny hadn't been able to stop staring at him. She had never seen a black man before, only pictures in the *The Peoples of the World* section of her encyclopaedia. She was fascinated by his hair. She wanted to touch it, and wondered how he washed and combed it.

Aunt Doris sighed, and looked out of the kitchen

window at her husband who was digging a patch of earth at the end of the garden. She drew deeper on her cigarette. Alan bent down to pull up one of his socks, which lay like a concertina around his ankle. Doris stubbed her cigarette in an ashtray. 'Leave the washing up, I'll do it. Go and play in the garden – both of you.'

The sound of Frankie Laine bellowing "I Believe" from the radiogram drew Alan and Jenny downstairs.

The sofa and armchairs had been moved back against the wall. Desmond was leaning on the mantelpiece, his left foot tapping to the rhythm. Another student was twirling Doris around the lounge. Jim leant back in an armchair, his eyes tightly shut and a pained expression on his face. An open newspaper lay across his lap, and a pair of glasses hung from a cord around his neck.

'Jenny, don't stand in the doorway. Come in and let me show you how to dance.' Desmond's deep voice invited her in.

'Just follow me round, little one; put your hands on my shoulder and stand on my shoes, I'll soon have you dancing like your aunt.' He gripped Jenny under her armpits. She was enthralled. She stood on tiptoe on his shoes, her head against his chest and followed his movements, thinking that nothing like this ever happened at home.

'Why are your teeth so white Desmond?' she ventured.

'I've brought this special twig all the way from Nigeria. It keeps them clean and bright. I'll show it to you later.'

'I know the capital of Nigeria.'

'Do you?'

'Yes, it's Lagos. Did you live there?'

'Fancy you knowing that now. No, my village is hundreds of miles to the north. But I studied there before coming to England.' The record slowed on the turntable. 'Shall we have another dance, little lady?'

Jenny beamed up at him and nodded.

Doris poked her head around the bedroom door at eight o' clock. 'Goodnight you two,' and with a flick on the light switch she disappeared. Five minutes later, Alan whispered across to Jenny.

'Come into my bed. I've got a torch; we can read my comic.'

Jenny slipped out of the camp bed and squeezed in beside him. They read a page and then giggled as they tried to turn it with tangled arms. Alan lifted the blankets and shone the light under the bedclothes.

'Look,' he said nodding downwards and opening his pyjama bottoms, 'you can touch it if you like.'

Jenny stared down and shook her head vigorously.

'It's your turn now.'

'There's nothing there,' she said.

'There must be, come on show me.'

'No, I don't want to.'

'You've got to. I've shown you mine.'

She wriggled out of her pyjamas trousers. The beam illuminated a circle of white skin at the top of her legs. Alan peered hard and long.

'I told you, there's nothing there,' Jenny said, pulling up her pyjamas. 'I'm going back to my bed now.' She felt she had been tricked into revealing herself and it smarted, but she couldn't have said no. He had done it first – so it was only fair. But she wouldn't fall for it again.

'Open wide.' Doris thrust a large teaspoonful of malt into Jenny's mouth. 'I won't be here when you get home. But Alan's got a key, and Uncle Jim will do some tea for you.' Screwing the lid back on the large black jar she returned it to the cupboard. Moving in front of a round mirror by the side of the sink, she started to remove a line of rollers from her hair. Jenny wondered how much longer it would be before the line of ash, that drooped from the cigarette in the corner of her mouth, would fall to the floor.

'Don't stare at me like that Jenny. You're always doing that. It gives me the creeps. Off you go, or you'll be late for school. Alan will look after you.'

Jenny wore a pair of black wellington boots and a belted gabardine raincoat. On her head was a hand-knitted bonnet, with a pom-pom dangling from the back. Alan was dressed exactly the same, except he had a grey balaclava wrapped around his head and neck.

'You'd better keep up,' he said, pausing momentarily from kicking a tin can along the pavement.

They walked past terraces of identical houses. Each one with a postage stamp sized front garden edged by a wall. In some of the windows were taped cardboard signs covered with uneven black writing:

NO DOGS
NO CHILDREN
NO IRISH
NO BLACKS

'Is she your girlfriend?' shouted a boy with metal-rimmed glasses as he ran alongside them.

'No, stupid, she's my cousin.'

The boy tugged at Jenny's pom-pom, pulling her hat back from her head.

'Al's got a girlfriend, Al's got a girlfriend,' taunted the boy, now joined by another.

Alan ran headlong into the first boy sending his glasses flying. The second boy hurled himself at Alan and all three fell to the pavement, their fists pummelling each other, until Jenny couldn't make out which arms and legs belonged to which boy. Satisfied that justice had been done Alan stood up, dusted himself down and grabbed Jenny's hand.

'Come on, we'll be late,' they started running.

'Nigger lover, nigger lover; bugger off to Notting Hill, there's plenty more there,' shouted the first boy picking up his glasses from the gutter.

The red-brick school surrounded by high railings stood like a prison at the top of Plum Lane. Instead of the brightly-coloured tables and chairs that Jenny was used to, there were battered wooden desks, their lids scarred with the names of past occupants. In the top right-hand corner was a hole that held a cracked china inkwell filled with deep blue ink. *They write with pens here*, thought Jenny, worried that she wouldn't know how to use one. The pupils were more boisterous than she was used to. Rough, her mother would have said. She hoped that she wouldn't be ignored at break time. Alan wouldn't want to play with her.

The first postcard from her mother, showing an aerial view of Brighton's two piers, arrived fifteen days into her stay:

Dear Jenny,

I've had my operation now, which went well. I'm still feeling tired and sleeping plenty but gradually getting stronger. Be a good girl for your aunt and uncle. Dad has visited me every day after work and sends his love.
Love Mummy x

P.S. Dad has put some postal orders in the post for Aunt Doris.

The second postcard arrived two weeks later, and had a Tunbridge Wells postmark. On the other side was a black and white photograph of a large country house. It showed nurses in starched uniforms with head coverings that, Jenny thought, made them look like nuns. They were standing on a veranda, alongside a line of bed-ridden patients:

Dear Jenny,
I'm feeling a lot better now, and have been sent to this lovely place for two weeks for a complete rest before I go home. Don't forget to thank Aunt Doris for looking after you, and tell her that Dad has put some more postal orders in the post. See you soon. Love Mummy x

Jenny thought that her aunt hadn't done very much looking after to be thanked for. That had been left to her uncle, and whichever student happened to be around. She might just as well have stayed with Mrs Walters. But then, she wouldn't have met Desmond, or experienced Sunday afternoons, when she would perch on top of Desmond's shoes, stretch her arms around his neck, and with his arm around her waist, they would glide around the lounge to the sounds of Perry Como and Frankie Laine. She wished those afternoons could last forever.

4

May 1953

'I haven't got all day you know,' said the shopkeeper as Jenny's eyes darted around the penny box. Her fingers closed around the pink flying saucer.

'Anything else?' he said, peering over his round spectacles.

'Twenty Weights, please,' Jenny looked up at him and added, 'for my dad.' But he was already slapping the packet down on the counter.

'That will be two shillings and seven pence.'

The small parade of shops stood in the centre of the estate, halfway between the school and Jenny's home. It was late May, and the Whitsun school holiday. Jenny dawdled down the hill sucking the sherbet from its outer casing. The semi-detached houses that lined both sides of the road were occupied by families; a father, a mother, and two or three children. One prolific couple, with ten children, were allocated two semi-detached houses with a connecting door. The flats lay on the perimeter of the estate. First-floor flats were for families with one child. The ground-floor flats for older couples, or widows. Jenny stood and watched as a girl turned a skipping rope tied to the lamppost. It was Pamela Edwards, who was in her class. Another girl, who Jenny recognised as being in the year below, was breathlessly counting her jumps. With each leap her dress billowed like a tiny parachute, her thin legs hanging like cords.

'Hello,' said Jenny.

'Do you want a go?' asked Pamela.

Jenny shook her head and continued to suck her sherbet.

'Eighty-one, that's my highest so far,' the younger girl gasped; the rope slack between her legs.

Pamela turned to Jenny, the handle clattering onto the pavement. 'I've got to go in now. Do you want to help me bathe my baby brother?' She was the second eldest of a family of six. Her sister Patricia was in the year below, and her brother Philip the year below that. There was also an older brother of around twelve called Peter. All the children's names began with the letter P and Jenny imagined that they would continue multiplying until they ran out of names.

Jenny followed Pamela as she walked up the garden path dragging her left leg behind her. She wore a heavy high laced leather boot. Attached to the boot was a pair of metal callipers that reached to her knee. She had told everyone that she had polio when she was younger, and had spent a year in a long box like a coffin, that breathed for her.

Screams bombarded Jenny's ears. The younger

children were laughing and chasing each other around the kitchen table. The toddler was naked from the waist down. They ignored the screams from the large black pram beside the boiler. Pamela nimbly avoided a full potty and the coloured play bricks that lay scattered across the floor. She went over to the pram. Jenny followed and peered inside. 'Does he always cry so loudly?'

'Only when he's hungry; and that's quite often.'

Paul, the latest addition to the family, lay red-faced and kicking, clad only in an off-white nappy and vest. Pamela scooped him up and thrust him into Jenny's arms, before disappearing through the side door and returning with a galvanised tin bath. Placing the bath on the Formica table she began filling it with jugs of hot and cold water. Jenny thought that although they were the same age, Pamela appeared years older; a housewife in miniature. She lay the baby on a threadbare towel, deftly undid the buttons on his vest and unpinned his nappy. Jenny's nose wrinkled. Once cleaned, Paul was lowered into the water. He immediately stopped crying. Huge blue eyes focused on Jenny as Pamela rubbed him with a bar of soap.

'You can wash the soap off now if you like?'

'Like this?' Jenny scooped up the water in her hands and splashed him.

'Yes, that's fine.' Another towel appeared as if by magic, and Paul was wrapped and dried in seconds. Pamela's sister appeared clutching a curved glass bottle of milk. She grabbed Paul and sitting down in a threadbare armchair began to feed her brother. Jenny watched as his tiny hands grabbed the bottle and he began to slurp noisily on the teat. She compared Pamela's busy family life to her own quiet existence.

'I do this every day to help Mum,' Pamela said, as if reading Jenny's thoughts. 'Mum's giving Pearl her tea in the other room.' Pearl was the toddler.

Wanting to appear more grown-up in Pamela's eyes, Jenny considered telling her about what Alan had shown her, but was too embarrassed. Also she thought that in this house, it would probably not be worthy of amazement. Instead she blurted, 'I can write with pen and ink now. They used them at the school I went to in London.'

'Miss Bruce said that we'll be using ink next term,' said Pamela as her friend came through the side door into the kitchen, her skipping rope trailing behind her.

'I've been taught to dance, just like the grown-ups. This black man showed me. He's the son of an African chief from Nigeria.' Jenny played her trump card.

'Where was that?' said both girls, staring open-mouthed at Jenny.

'In London of course; at my cousin's house.'

Jenny left the two girls re-tying the rope around the lamppost and continued down the road. She could hear Pamela shouting, 'two, three, four, five…' until there was only the sound of her own footsteps. In the distance the sails of the windmill rose above the roof of the church. She thought they were like ladders leading to heaven, and imagined angels climbing them. She lingered at the road junction and turned left, not wanting to go straight home; there was no one to play with. Gail, who lived opposite, had chickenpox. Wandering to the edge of the estate, where a grass verge bordered a field of ripening wheat, Jenny walked across and flopped down, watching the house-martins flash their white rumps at her, as they flew back and forth to their nests under the eaves. A ladybird landed on her cardigan. She encouraged it onto her finger, and counted the spots as it crawled up her hand.

'Ladybird, ladybird fly away home
Your house is on fire and your children are gone.'

Bored by the ladybird, she picked a stem of plantain grass. Making a loop around the square stalk she catapulted the seed head, repeating it, again and again, trying to beat her previous record. As the sun sank behind the houses, she drew her cardigan around her chest and wondered what time it was. She hadn't intended to stop this long. Standing up she brushed the grass from her dress, and looked around for the packet of cigarettes and change. She flattened the tall grass at the edge of the field with the edge of her sandals, exposing only scurrying insects. She wondered if she had left them at Pamela's house. She couldn't go back, not with all those children staring at her, anyway, she must go home. She retraced her steps to the road junction, her eyes searching the pavement and gutter, willing the missing items to appear.

'Where on earth have you been? I was just about to come looking for you.' Her mother seemed taller as she spoke in the tone that Jenny dreaded. She hated upsetting her; she might be ill again, and it would be her fault.

'I stopped off at Pamela Edwards' house.'

'What, all this time?'

Jenny slipped past her mother and ran up the stairs.

'Come here. Have you got Dad's cigarettes?' Alice said following her.

'No, they didn't have any.' Jenny stopped outside the kitchen, feeling her cheeks redden as she stared at the squares on the lino.

'Didn't have any? They've never been out of stock before. Well, give me the money back then.'

Jenny could feel her mother's eyes boring into her, seeking out her secrets. Why hadn't she thought about that? 'I've lost it.'

'Lost it, how can you lose money? You must have left it at Pamela's house. You'd better go back and get it.'

Jenny panicked. If she did that, her first untruth would be exposed.

'No, I can't,' she cried. 'They've gone out.'

'What all of them?'

'Yes. I can't remember where I left it anyway.'

'I don't believe you, Jenny. Have you spent that money?'

'No.'

'If I find out you're lying, you'll be punished. You know that, don't you?'

Jenny nodded.

'We've always brought you up to tell the truth. Never tell lies, Jenny; you'll always be found out.'

A key turned in the front door. 'Gal, you know what Ernie Moore said today?' Charlie's voice echoed up the stairs. 'He said that he'd go in on Saturday morning. That means we've all got to work now, I was hoping to have this Saturday off. I tell you Gal, I've had enough of that man. If only he'd keep his big mouth shut. Phew.' Charlie was out of breath by the time he'd reached the landing. 'There's my girl.' He smiled at Jenny. 'What have you been up to today?'

'Something she shouldn't have, if you ask me,' said Alice. 'Don't forget what I said Jenny.'

She ran into the sitting room, and lay along the sofa, supporting her head with her hand. Charlie followed, picking up the *News Chronicle* from his chair before sinking into the cushions. In her anticipation, Jenny forgot about the missing cigarettes.

'Ethiopia,' he said.

'Addis Ababa,' said Jenny.

'Albania.'

'Tirana.'

'Finland.'

'Helsinki.'

'Luxembourg.'

'Luxembourg – see you didn't catch me out.' Jenny grinned at her father.

'Persia.'

'Tehran.'

'Afganistan.'

'Kabul.'

Charlie fumbled down the inside of his chair and produced his reading glasses. 'I remember when we were up at the North West Frontier, wild tribesman up there you know Jenny; no trees, nothing except rocks and scrub. Then before you could say Jack Robinson, a bullet whistled past me – Pathans. By God we moved quick. You couldn't trust those tribesmen farther than you could throw them; one minute friendly as can be, next shooting at you. Mind you, they were good-looking men; never saw any women up there though. They weren't allowed out; all kept indoors; purdah they called it. Murder I'd call it, not purdah.'

5

August 1954

'And how are you today, Jennifer?'

'Very well thank you.' Jenny answered exactly as Alice had instructed, but didn't look up from her library book... *Peking – is also called the Forbidden City, because for five hundred years it was inaccessible. It has the best preserved buildings in China, and was the home to the Ming and Qing dynasties...*

'I hear that you're doing well at school.' Mrs Rowland pulled a pair of cream gloves over her manicured hands, pushing the material down between each finger. 'Now, where did I put my handbag?' she muttered, looking around the room.

Jenny knew the handbag was on the chair next to her, hidden by the green chenille tablecloth. She bent her head lower over her book... *the traditional entrance was the Wumen gate where important ceremonies where held...*

'So, what do you like doing during the holidays, Jenny?' Mrs Rowland asked as she looked behind a cushion on the *chaise longue*.

'I like watching the birds.'

Charlie had inherited a small pair of brass

binoculars from his father and Jenny spent hours kneeling on a chair at the window identifying the birds that landed in their back garden.

Mrs Rowland turned and gave Jenny a surprised look. 'Oh, that's nice.'

Earlier that year, Alice had recovered sufficiently to apply for a cleaning position on two mornings each week. Mrs Rowland lived in a detached Edwardian villa to the north of Hove Station. On a glass panel above the front door was written the name BEAULIEU in large black letters. Alice had never met Mr Rowland, telling Jenny that he was 'something in the city,' Jenny thought that he sounded like a building. He commuted to London Bridge early each weekday morning, and remained a moustachioed figure; one half of a wedding photograph that stood on the sideboard in the dining room.

'Can I play with Mandy, Mrs Rowland?'

Mandy was a miniature French poodle with white powder puffs on her head and tail, and a jewelled pink collar around her neck. She was the only reason that made accompanying her mother bearable for Jenny. She hated seeing her mother cleaning someone elses house, it always made her tired.

'Yes, you can, but make sure you take her into the back garden.' Mrs Rowland tipped the dining chair back. 'There it is,' she tutted, as the handbag appeared from under the folds.

'Why can't we have a dog? I could play with it, and

take it for walks.' Since the age of five, Jenny had pestered her parents for a sister, a brother, a kitten or a puppy. But since helping Pamela Edwards bathe her brother, the first two had dropped off her list – their answer never varied.

'You know we can't, not in a flat, it wouldn't be fair on the animal. Anyway the council don't allow it.'

'But I would take it out before school, and when I get home. It wouldn't be any trouble.'

'And how long would that last? No, we can't.'

'Isn't it time to go yet?'

'Just give me five more minutes. Put that book down and take this coal scuttle into the lounge for me.'

Jenny sighed and slid down from her chair.

Alice untied her overall, revealing a navy-blue calf-length dress. She kicked her old slip-ons into the hall cupboard and replaced them with a pair of black court shoes, completing her outfit with a cream jacket and matching hat. 'Come on, Jenny. Let's go and buy your shoes.'

They walked hand in hand towards a footbridge over the south coast railway line that separated the residential areas of the town from George Street. As she jumped over each join between the pavement slabs, Jenny muttered, 'If I touch a crack – I'll get a whack.' The aroma of freshly ground coffee wafted up the street and led them into the shoe shop. The interior was dark and smelt of polished leather. Jenny ran over to a dappled grey rocking horse – that to her chagrin she had now outgrown – and pushing its head forward, watched as it bounced to and fro. Alice pointed the assistant to a pair of brown lace-ups in the window, and after they were fitted and prodded, Jenny was led to a large machine standing benignly in the corner. She put her feet in the gap at the top of the steps and looked down into the eyepiece. The machine whirred and her metatarsals glowed luminous green.

'They're fine, plenty of growing room,' said the assistant.

'You can hold them.' Alice passed Jenny the brown paper bag as they left the shop. 'If we hurry we'll have time for a sandwich in De Mario's before the bus comes.'

Jenny returned to jumping over the pavement cracks, knowing that a sandwich in De Mario's also meant ice cream.

The bus swung around the northern edge of Hove Park. Jenny sat by the window on the upper deck swinging her legs and looking down into the gardens, imagining herself chasing her puppy around the lawn: they would be inseparable. She stared into the distance, thinking that her mother was unusually quiet. A road ran along the top of the Downs, an occasional vehicle breaking the line of the horizon. She wondered if Gail would be at home. She might be her very best friend, but she was a goody-goody, always saying she had to be home on time, and never keen to explore. Although this holiday she had managed to persuade her to play in the manor house that stood opposite the church. It was being demolished, and the rooms were exposed to the sky; like a giant doll's house. Every day they would run from room to room pretending that they lived there and playing hide and seek amongst the rubble. Once when she was crouching behind a fallen door, she had found a glass perfume bottle complete with a puffer spray, and had taken it home for her "special box".

'I know you would have liked a brother or sister Jenny,' said Alice.

'No – it's alright. I'd rather have a dog – a poodle like Mandy.' She had already decided on a name, "Bella".

'You had an older brother,' said Alice.

Jenny froze. Her right foot suspended in the air. Pamela Edwards' baby brother, red faced and screaming flashed before her. Her heart raced. *What did "had" mean? Had he disappeared?* Should she be upset, or pleased that she had a brother?

'Where is he?'

'He died soon after he was born, Jenny. It was freezing cold in Bradford that January. I thought everything was normal, being my first, but by the time the doctor came it was too late. Of course it would never happen nowadays.'

'No,' Jenny whispered. 'What was his name?' It was important to know.

'Christopher Charles. It was 1941, so he would have been thirteen now, a young man. That's why we moved down here. I couldn't go back to London after the war, not with all your father's family there. Anyway, there was nowhere to live; most of the houses had gone in the blitz. Then you came along and we could smile again.'

Jenny knew that her parents had lived in Yorkshire during the war. Charlie had lost his right eye in an explosion in India, turning his hair white overnight and rendering him unfit for active service. Instead, he became a regimental instructor at Catterick barracks. Alice was always reminding Jenny – whenever she complained of the cold – that compared to Yorkshire, Sussex was virtually sub-tropical. In Yorkshire, she said, 'They had to wear several sheets of newspapers under their clothes to keep warm.'

Her mother didn't say anything else, but stared straight ahead. Jenny glanced up. Her mother's cheek glistened in the sunlight. She thought she ought to say something, but didn't know what to say. It seemed unkind to change the subject. Shocked at what her mother had told her, she suddenly hated her for providing this unwanted information. She stared even more intently out of the window. A combine harvester was creeping around the contours of the field. They sat in silence.

The sails of the windmill appeared above the semi-detached houses. As Alice stood up, Jenny rushed past her and down the stairs of the bus. She had to get away from her mother and the weight of unwelcome knowledge.

Gail was standing in her front garden waving her

hands above her head. It was a signal that she could come out. Jenny returned a low wave, from left to right across her chest. There would be no play today.

Pulling the front door key through the letterbox, she opened the door and ran upstairs into her parents' bedroom at the rear of the flat. Lifting the binoculars that she had left on the windowsill, she trained them on the deep pink breast of a male chaffinch, as it pecked at the ground beneath the apple tree. She stared at the bird until it flew away, trying to replace the picture that filled her mind, of a baby with her father's face and white hair.

6

Summer 1955

Charlie's glass eye sat staring and forbidding on the bathroom windowsill. Jenny hated seeing it, and normally refused to go into the room until Charlie had finished washing and shaving. But today an early start was necessary. Aunt Doris was coming.

Jenny opened the bathroom door warily, her eyes shut and her face crinkled and distorted. Groping her way to the wash basin she splashed her face and hands with cold water, and dabbed them with the towel from the rail under the sink. She then felt along the windowsill for the toothpaste and toothbrush that stood in a blue plastic mug by the wall.

'Argh!' Jenny stiffened and recoiled. She had touched it. It was cold, hard and in the wrong place. As her heart slowed, she peeped through one eye. There it was, sitting next to the mug, the pale blue iris gleaming, a shade lighter than her father's intact eye. It stared at her, daring her to touch it again.

There's a one-eyed yellow idol to the north of Kathmandu – her father's quotation repeated in her mind as she ran from the room.

* * *

'When your dad asked if you could stay with us again, I thought, it's summer; why don't I come down and collect you? I love Brighton. There's something exciting about being beside the sea. We can have a day out together and then go back,' said Doris. The turnstile clanked behind them and they stepped onto the wooden slats of the Palace Pier. A red and white striped kiosk, its skirts flapping in the wind, stood to one side. 'Would you like some candy-floss?'

'Yes please.'

'Your dad's given me some money, so get me a choc ice as well.' Doris pressed some coins into Jenny's hand.

They sat on a wrought-iron bench that faced the sea and watched a speedboat tearing through the waves. Doris took several deep breaths. 'Sea air is so bracing, I always feel better for a day at the seaside.' She turned to Jenny. 'You're quite a young lady now aren't you? I prefer children when they're older. I'm no good with small children. I wish I was, but I don't have the patience, not like your mum.'

Jenny thought how much friendlier her aunt seemed, compared to before. 'Do you still go dancing with Desmond?' she ventured.

'Not with Desmond.' Doris continued to stare out to sea.

'I can still remember the dance he taught me. I practise it all the time at home.'

'He'll be thrilled to hear that. He's still staying with us.'

'Good,' Jenny looked forward to dancing with him again.

'I expect you find it hard, with your mum being ill so much?'

'No, no it's alright.' Jenny looked down and stared at the waves foaming beneath the gaps in the boards. She wasn't going to admit that she worried about her mother, and how she longed for her to be like other mothers who never seemed to be tired.

'Sometimes I wish…' Doris paused. 'I always wanted a daughter. Boys are no fun – all grazed knees and noise – at least not until they're grown up.'

Jenny scrutinised her aunt. Boy's games were exciting, not like some of the games girls play. How could they be more fun when they're grown up?

'Don't stare at me like that Jenny, you're always doing that, it's rude. You know, I could style your hair for you, while you're with me. It looks a bit wild. That page-boy style would suit you – like Audrey Hepburn.' She handed her ice cream wrapper to Jenny. 'What do you think?'

Fruit machines clanked rhythmically in the arcade behind them as Jenny thought that she didn't want her hair cut, and she knew that her mother would not be happy about it. 'It's only the wind making it untidy. It's better when I do this.' She licked the sticky pink sweetness from her fingers and smoothed her hair back behind her ears.

'Well anyway, we can go up the West End – Regent Street, Oxford Street – it will be lovely to have some female company. You'd like that wouldn't you?'

Jenny didn't reply, she was thinking about seeing Desmond again and showing him her dance steps. Doris leapt up and shook her head vigorously as if trying to rid herself of her thoughts. 'Let's go and look at the helter-skelter, we can walk around the top of the pier, then when we've had enough sea air we can have lunch. I'll have to watch my heels in these slats though. I won't be able to dance if I break my ankle, will I?' she laughed.

'There's a café in the gardens across the road. Mum and I go there sometimes; we could have our lunch there,' Jenny said as she turned and pointed at the onion domes of the Royal Pavilion. She always imagined she was in India when she was there.

Two weeks later, Charlie came to visit. After their initial greeting, Doris asked Jenny to go to the corner shop to buy her some cigarettes. She lingered in the hallway and heard her father say to her aunt and uncle, 'She's had it all taken away you know, huge scar right down her front. The doc says she needs to take it easy for at least three months, and if we can afford to go away for a week somewhere, we should.'

On her return home, Jenny abandoned her travel books for the medical section of *Pears Encyclopaedia*. Every night before going to bed she would scan her body. Any spot was now smallpox; a galloping rash that would cover the whole of her body, leaving her scarred for life. Every stomach ache meant an immediate admission to the accident and emergency department at the children's hospital; where she would emerge six weeks later, with a scar from hip to hip and an empty stomach.

One evening a few days before they were due to leave for their one week holiday in Guernsey, Jenny was in the sitting room reading the encyclopaedia. There had been a cluster of polio cases reported locally and she was worried about pins and needles in her left foot. She saw her father open the door to the cupboard on the landing and pull out a step ladder. That meant only one thing. She jumped up, the encyclopaedia dropping to the floor. Charlie climbed the wooden steps and pushed up the hatch to the loft. The space was empty, apart from a deep brown trunk with leather straps and rusty buckles. It was ceremoniously lowered to Alice and Jenny who waited below with outstretched arms. They laid it on two spread newspapers on the settee. The lid of the trunk was covered with faded coloured labels – Gibraltar; Aden; Colombo and Bombay – Jenny had never seen it before and was impatient to see what exotic treats lay inside. She fumbled with the stiff leather straps and released the buckles. She lifted the lid. A musty smell crept into the room along with clouds of dust. The trunk was empty.

'I can never understand why your dad didn't bring

back any souvenirs of all his years abroad,' Alice said. 'I asked him once. I said a pair of ivory elephants would look really nice on the mantelpiece – one at each end. All he said was, he didn't need to bring anything back. I mean what sort of answer's that?'

Jenny looked at her mother. Since that day on the bus she felt uncomfortable whenever her mother spoke to her about her marriage. She didn't want to hear any more revelations. She might mention her dead baby again.

'Dad's always talking about India, isn't he?'

'Yes, that's what I can't understand. Everybody brings something back if they go abroad. I mean one of those Indian rugs with tassels on the end would really suit our landing. Mrs Rowland has one that her husband brought back from somewhere. You know, the red patterned one in their hallway?'

Jenny nodded as she remembered her mother cleaning it.

Charlie slapped his hands against his trousers releasing more dust. 'That's given Bill Gardner something to think about Gal. I told him today we're going abroad for our holiday. He's always going on about owning his own house, thinks he's a cut above everyone else 'cos he's got a mortgage. He's never been anywhere or done anything. He's never been out of the country in his life. I remember in Peshawar, there were these Pathan tribesmen, tall, good-looking men with turbans and long beards, some of them had blue or green eyes. They were fierce. Kill you as soon as look at you. Brilliant marksmen though, you could never see them. Little Johnny Parr got killed by one. We were out on patrol one day when he needed a crap…'

'Charlie, language,' said Alice.

'The silly bugger thought he'd go behind a rock, didn't he, sitting target with his white topee. He should have gone behind our truck like I told him to – right, are you ready Jenny?'

'Iceland.'

'Reykjarvik.'

'Sudan.'

'Khartoum.'

'Hungary.'

Jenny looked up. 'That's too easy – make it harder.'

'Yemen.'

'Sana'a.'

'Venezuala.'

'Caracas.'

'Zanzibar.'

'Zanzibar City.'

Jenny imagined the uniqueness of each capital city, and longed to visit every one. In New Delhi, she would see white domes and bejewelled women in brightly-coloured saris. In Cairo she would hear the call of the Muezzin from the minarets, and smell the spices in the souk. In Paris she would climb the Eiffel Tower, and from the deck of a riverboat she would gaze at the Notre Dame, and have her first romance.

7

Summer 1957

Jenny failed the eleven-plus. Alice said that there were two reasons why; the first was the attack of mumps that Jenny had caught earlier in the year; and the second was the emergency appendectomy six weeks later, that caused her to miss the mock interviews. Charlie said that they had made a big mistake. 'How could they not want my girl – who knows every capital city in the world?'

Jenny thought differently. She had been thrilled that trawling through the encyclopaedia had finally produced results. She had known she would fail from the moment she had been ushered into the interview room at the local grammar school. Two women had sat on either side of a fair-haired young man. They faced her across a large desk.

'Don't be nervous, Jennifer. We just need to have a little chat with you,' said the man, smiling, but she knew that when grown-ups wanted to talk to you, there was good reason to be nervous, even if they smiled when they said it. The younger of the two women fiddled with some papers. She had fluffy hair, and wore a gold tulip brooch pinned to her beige jumper.

Jenny fixed her eyes on the brooch, travelling along the edge of the leaf and stem, then up and across the bloom and down the opposite edge and leaf.

'Tell us about your hobbies, Jennifer. What do you like to do in your spare time?' said the fair-haired man. The jumper under his corduroy jacket was decorated with a Fair-Isle pattern that Jenny recognised from her mother's knitting book.

'I enjoy watching the birds in our garden. I love reading, especially travel books, and I know the name of every capital city in the world.'

'That's very interesting,' the young man sounded surprised. 'What's the capital of Egypt?'

'Cairo.'

'And Uruguay?'

'Montevideo,' Jenny thought that he looked impressed.

'What would you like to do when you grow up, Jennifer?' It was the turn of the older woman. She looked fierce and spoke in a gruff voice. She wore a grey suit that matched her hair, which was short and coarse like a Brillo pad. Jenny panicked. She should have known they would ask this. Grown-ups always ask this. She usually replied 'I don't know' which always seemed to satisfy them, as they never asked anything else. But she realised this answer would not do for today. She panicked and glanced out of the window to the playing fields that stretched into the distance. A ginger cat scampered past.

'I think I'd like to work with animals.'

'Do you mean you would like to be a veterinary surgeon?' The young man's voice sounded hopeful.

She couldn't remember her parents ever discussing her future. Even if they had, she doubted that veterinary surgeon would have been on the list.

'No, I don't think so,' she said.

'Which school subjects do you enjoy, Jennifer?' It was the turn of the fluffy-haired woman.

'English, nature study and geography are my favourites; and I know the name of…'

'Thank you, Jennifer,' the woman interrupted.

The man leant towards the elder woman and spoke quietly; his hair flopping over his forehead. He scribbled something on the paper in front of him. Jenny heard the elder woman whisper something that sounded like, 'But she wouldn't benefit.'

'That will be all, Jennifer, you may go now.' The fluffy-haired woman smiled, stood up and walked her towards the door.

Three weeks later a small brown envelope dropped through the letterbox, informing Charlie and Alice that a place had been allocated for Jenny at the nearest secondary modern school.

Two bull-nosed coaches stood in the school drive. It was the annual fourth year day trip to the Tower of

London, and additional help had been enlisted from six willing parents, who were assigned to the children from class 4B. According to the deputy head, children from 4A were too intelligent to misbehave; and the children from 4C too stupid. But first there was the obligatory photograph of pupils, teachers and helpers who lined up in rows in the playground according to height. Then pandemonium, as the children jostled and clambered onto the coaches in their hurry to sit with their friends. No one wanted the humiliation of an empty seat beside them.

The children cheered as their coach pulled away and negotiated the roads to the edge of the estate. It passed the flint barn that carried the weight of the windmill, and with a sharp turn rolled downhill. Leaving behind abandoned farm buildings, the coach lumbered up a steep incline, lined on one side with a field of barley. The panorama at the summit stretched from the sharp chalk face of Seaford Head, to the mystical dark circle of Chanctonbury Ring. To the children it was the top of the world, their very own Tibetan plateau. The coach sped down the other side, under the railway tunnel, and finally onto the main London road.

'Look Miss, fifty miles to London!' shouted the boy sitting opposite Jenny, who had already eaten his round of cheese sandwiches, a packet of crisps and an apple.

'When are we going to get there, Miss?' Jenny recognised the voice of Spencer Whittacker, a puny boy with glasses and a perpetually runny nose. He was always ignored by his classmates and sat on his own at the rear of the coach.

'There's a long way to go yet, Spencer. Just settle down and enjoy the trip.'

The children began to name call between the sexes, their voices rising to a crescendo.

Miss Bruce stood up at the front of the coach. 'Be quiet, all of you.'

Jenny sat next to Gail; their dark heads, one straight and one wavy haired, conspiratorially close. In the seat behind them sat Wendy Nowak and Pamela Edwards, who, with a third girl formed a superior clique in the fourth year. Wendy, who was destined for the grammar school in September, looked and acted at least two years older than her classmates. Jenny put this down to her father being an American. Wendy had told her, 'Actually he comes from Canada; he came to England for D-Day and stayed on to marry my mum.' But for Jenny and her friends, this distinction was unimportant. He spoke with an American accent, so he was American.

'Guess what? I caught my brother with his hand up his girlfriend's skirt last night. They were on the sofa and didn't hear me come in,' Pamela said loud enough for at least half the coach to hear. 'They were slobbering all over each other and I heard him say, "When can we go all the way?" Soon as she saw me, she pulled her skirt down and tried to pretend nothing was happening.'

'What does that mean?' Gail said, turning her head to peer between the seats at the two girls behind.

'What does what mean?' said Pamela.

'Go all the way. What did he mean?'

The coach fell silent. Gail had managed what Miss Bruce had failed to do.

'Surely you know that,' said Wendy, spitting the last word. A small sliver of saliva landed on the headrest in front of her.

The coach was heavy with anticipation. No one wanted to appear ignorant in front of Wendy Nowak. Jenny was as eager as her friend to know what the words meant, but wasn't going to admit it.

'No,' said Gail, her face now scarlet.

'It's how babies are made, you dummy,' Wendy giggled.

'Yes, the man puts his thing inside you, and wiggles it around,' Pamela added.

'But she doesn't want a baby, does she? Anyway I don't believe you, that's disgusting,' said Gail.

Jenny changed colour in sympathy with her friend. She also thought it was disgusting, but she believed them. She wondered where his thing could be put. She certainly wasn't going to ask Wendy Nowak. She decided it must go into the girl's belly button; because that's where babies grow.

8

Summer 1960

'Guess what? We're moving. We're buying a house near my cousin's. Mum's been left some money by my nan,' Gail had said. She had also started going to a youth club near her new home, and every Wednesday morning Jenny rushed to school to meet her friend before lessons began, and to hear what progress Gail had made towards her goal of going out with Steve. It was like having a boyfriend herself, but without the anguish that seemed to accompany it.

'He was there again last night. He kept looking over at me. I'm sure he's going to ask me out soon. He's just got to. I'll just die if he doesn't.'

'Of course he will, Gail,' said Jenny. 'He's bound to. I tell you what; I'll come with you next Tuesday. I can't have you dying for love of this Steve.'

'Will your mum and dad let you?'

'Even if they don't, I'll find a way to come.'

'Dad, can I join a youth club?' Jenny chose her moment carefully.

Charlie lifted his eyes briefly from the television. 'Better ask your mother.' His eyes drifted back to the U.S. cavalry galloping across the screen. Since the set had been delivered it had become the main attraction in life for Charlie. Jenny thought that with each flicker of the screen he seemed younger. She went into the kitchen.

'Mum, can I join a youth club? The one Gail goes to, down in the town.'

'But you start your O levels next term, there'll be lots of homework to do. We didn't agree to you staying on at school for nothing,' said Alice, who had wanted Jenny to leave as soon as she turned fifteen.

'What's the point of her staying on?' she had said to Charlie earlier in the year. 'She'll only get married. She can get a decent office job without these O levels.'

'I think she should stay on, Gal. The head says she's capable of getting good results. It's only one year more.'

'I can easily finish my homework before I go. It's only one evening; and anyway school finishes in two weeks. If I start now, I can get used to going before next term.' As she spoke Jenny was already planning how she could leave the flat next Tuesday evening without her parents noticing.

'Anyway it's too far away. If you went to one at all, it would be better if you went to the one at Hangleton; it's much nearer.'

'But nobody I know goes there. Everyone goes to the other one.'

'I don't know, Jenny. How will you get back?'

'I can walk, or get a bus. It doesn't get dark until nearly ten o'clock. Gail said she'd leave if I don't join.'

'Well, I suppose you could, it is summer. Alright then, you can go. But I want you back by nine-thirty. If you're one minute late, there'll be trouble.'

Jenny returned to the sitting room where to her surprise the television had been switched off.

'What did Mum say?'

'She said I could go.'

'Oh, she did, did she? Well that must be alright then. Ecuador?'

'Quito.'

'Madagascar.'

'Antananarivo.'

'Somalia.'

'That's enough now Dad. I'm going to my room now.'

'But, we haven't finished.'

'I've got things to do.'

'Things?' said Charlie with a puzzled look. 'What things?'

The following Tuesday Jenny cycled home from school, bolted her dinner and disappeared into her bedroom. She peered into the mirror, examining her face for any fresh eruption. With "it will only make it worse" ringing in her ears, she squeezed the offending spot, until the white head burst onto her handkerchief with a satisfactory pop. She spent the next thirty minutes deciding what to wear, and a further five minutes tying her now shoulder-length hair into a pony-tail. At seven o'clock, she was ready.

'I'm off,' she shouted after checking that her parents were still behind the closed sitting room door. She rushed down the stairs, a brown paper bag in her hand.

Gail was leaning against the brick wall of a ladies' toilet in the local park. They marched inside, immediately swapping their flat shoes for the heels in their bags. Standing in front of the mirror, they applied a thick layer of foundation, a curtain of mascara, and pale pink lipstick. They emerged like butterflies from their chrysalises; two inches taller and ready for action.

The Shirelles thumped out their agonies from a record player in the corner of the hall. Behind a rolled up metal blind was a galley kitchen, where an older girl in a tight jumper served soft drinks in paper cups. Two table-tennis tables and a pool table stood on one side of the hall. Jenny noticed that only boys were playing. The girls stood around in twos and threes watching and giggling. Wooden chairs lined the walls. They sat down in the middle of the row.

Gail nudged Jenny in the ribs. 'He's over there. He's such a hunk.'

'Where?'

'By the toilet, I really dig him,' Gail sighed.

Jenny gathered that the tall fair-haired lad must be Steve.

'Come on let's jive. He'll notice me then.' Gail pulled Jenny up and they joined some girls dancing in the middle of the floor.

Jenny remembered how she used to dance with Desmond. He had returned to Nigeria a couple of years before. Alice had said that, 'it was not before time', and that she thought, 'he was never going back'. Although she hadn't seen him for three years, Jenny felt that she had lost a friend. The record finished and Gail walked towards Steve. Feeling self-conscious by herself, Jenny went into the girls' toilet, stood in front of the mirror for a minute and then came out again. Gail was still talking to Steve and seemed oblivious to anything or anybody else.

Jenny picked up her bag and walked over to the hatch. As she stood sipping her drink the swing doors to the hall burst open and two boys entered laughing. They were both dark-haired, but one was slightly taller than the other and wore a blue jumper. She stared at him. Both boys looked at her as they walked past; the taller one's eyes meeting her own. Her cheeks turned red as she returned to her chair.

Gail ran over and sat down. 'Steve's asked me what I'm doing at the weekend. I know he's going to ask me out. I just know it.' Her head shook excitedly.

It was Jenny's turn to nudge Gail. 'Who's that?'

'Where?'

'Over there by the pool table; the taller one, he's just picked up the cue.'

'Oh, they were here when I first started coming, Martin someone, I think. My cousin knows him. She's over there. I'll go and ask her.'

'No don't!' she called out, but Gail was already halfway across the floor.

'Yes, that's Martin Barretti,' Gail said breathlessly arriving back at Jenny's side. He lives next door to her. 'Do you fancy him then?' Her blue eyes demanded an answer.

'No, of course not.'

'Oh yeah – you're all red.'

Jenny was conscious of Martin for the remainder of the evening. As she danced with her friend she kept glancing over to the pool table. She couldn't stop herself from looking at him. When the boys had finished their game, they stood talking and drinking, pretending not to be interested in the girls dancing in front of them. But Jenny was sure he was looking at her.

Two weeks later, Jenny stood between Gail and her cousin, keeping one eye on the doors. *There they are*, she thought, *bang on time*.

Gail put her hand over her mouth. 'He's coming over, give me your drink.' She pushed Jenny into the middle of the hall. Suddenly she was standing in front of him. She couldn't look him in the eyes, so looked over his left shoulder.

'It's Jenny, isn't it? You're new here, aren't you?' he said.

'Yes, this is only my third time.'

'I'd buy you a drink, but you've already got one.'

Jenny nodded.

'Are you doing anything this Saturday?'

'No,' Jenny answered, although she knew that her mother would be expecting her to go shopping.

'Would you like to come for a walk then – say Saturday afternoon?'

'OK,' Jenny blushed.

'Where would you like to meet?'

Knowing that he didn't live near her, she said the only place that she was sure he knew, 'I could meet you in Hove Park.' She caught his eyes for a second and looked away.

'By the miniature railway?'

'Yes, that's fine.' She smiled.

'OK. I'll see you there then, two o'clock on Saturday.' He left her and walked over to where his friend was waiting by the pool table.

Gail pulled Jenny into the toilet. 'Come on, what did he say?'

'He asked me out on Saturday.'

'And?' said Gail.

'And what?'

'What did you say?' Gail emphasised, as if talking to a small child.

'I said yes of course.'

'There you are.' Gail smiled at her cousin, who was standing behind her.

Jenny stared at Gail, and then her cousin. 'You didn't tell him I wanted to go out with him did you?'

'Of course I did,' said Gail, adjusting her hair in the mirror. 'It's obvious you fancy him like crazy. You can't stop staring at him.'

'That's so embarrassing,' said Jenny, wishing that she hadn't made her attraction so obvious.

'No it isn't. He fancies you too. He's looking over here now,' Gail said as they opened the door and went back into the hall.

Jenny spotted his blue jumper first. He was standing at the end of the miniature railway track. Her heart leapt and she quickened her step.

'Hello,' said Jenny as she walked up behind him. She had decided to wear the same blouse and skirt she had worn when he had asked her out. She was not normally superstitious, but had thought it might be a good omen.

He turned and smiled. 'Hello Jenny.'

'Have you been waiting long?'

'No, not long. Shall we go for a walk?'

'Good idea.'

'I used to love going on this train when I was a kid. I was always pestering my parents to bring me up here. Have you been on it?'

'Only once; I think it only runs on Sundays and Bank Holidays,' said Jenny.

They walked side by side in silence, crossing the old drover's road that sliced the park in two. Stopping by the swings they watched as some children were pushed higher and higher by their friends; their screams filling the air.

'I used to push my sister like that until she cried; that was down in Stoneham Park,' said Martin. 'Did you used to play here?'

'Yes, with Gail sometimes. She lived opposite me before she moved. I preferred the roundabout though,' said Jenny.

'You live near here then?'

'Yes, up by the windmill. Gail said you live next door to her cousin.' Jenny reddened as she imagined what Gail must have said to him.

'Yes, I used to play with her when I was young, but not anymore.' He gave Jenny a wry grin and reached for her hand. They stood watching as a young boy tied the free swings to the struts, until the shrill whistle of the park keeper made him run away.

'I used to do that too,' Martin laughed. They walked slowly towards the tearoom. 'Do you fancy a drink? We could sit down for a bit.'

'Yes, that would be great. There's a table outside,' Jenny worried whether she should let go of his hand first.

'What would you like?' asked Martin, dropping her hand as they stepped onto the veranda.

'A lemonade if they've got one, otherwise a Tizer.'

Jenny sat down. Two couples were playing a game of doubles on the tennis courts opposite. She felt shy in Martin's presence; but not uncomfortable. She remembered how awkward she had felt whenever she had been to Gail's house and her older brother was there. She hadn't even been able to say hello to him.

'You're in luck.' Martin placed the bottle of lemonade in front of her. 'Tizer for me and I've bought a Wagon Wheel. I thought we could share it. Hope you like them.'

'I love them.' Jenny's stomach rumbled at the sight of food. She had been too excited to eat before she left home, saying that Gail's mother wanted to talk to her about exams, and that she was late and hadn't got time for lunch. 'I heard you work in a bank. Which one do you work in?'

'The Midland Bank in Brighton, I'm a trainee bank clerk. I only started four weeks ago. I'm enjoying it so far. What do you want to do when you leave school?'

'Haven't a clue. I start my O levels in September.'

'I didn't know either. Dad wanted me to get a steady job with prospects. He runs a café near the seafront. I used to work there in the school holidays. He said he wanted something better for me though. That's what they all want isn't it?'

'Yes, all my parents say is – I've got to get a job in an office.'

'Do you want that?'

'I don't want to work in a factory or a shop, and I know I want more out of life than just being a housewife.' She thought of her mother charring for Mrs

Rowland, coming home exhausted and then having to clean her own flat. Her life wasn't going to be like that.

'What do you enjoy doing?'

'I like reading – especially about foreign countries, I enjoy the countryside and cycling, but I don't expect any careers advisor is going to think much of that.' She decided not to mention the capital cities; he might think it odd.

'I like the countryside too. Perhaps we could go for a ride sometime?'

She blushed.

As they left the tearoom, Martin reached again for her hand and they strolled to the southern edge of the park.

'I'm fascinated by this stone. It's enormous,' Martin said as they stood and read the metal plaque at the base of the Goldstone, a twenty-ton sarsen stone that gave its name to the surrounding area.

'Yes, it's huge,' but today Jenny was only interested in the boy at her side. They continued around the edge of the park, stopping at the tennis courts to watch a father teaching his son how to perfect his serve. They crossed back over the drover's road.

'I expect you like Cliff Richard, don't you?' Martin asked.

'No, not much; I prefer Paul Anka; The Everley Brothers; and Neil Sedaka.'

'They're all American.'

'It's not because they're American. I like their sound.'

'I prefer instrumentals; The Shadows and Duane Eddy. I've got all their records. I'm saving up to buy a guitar. I reckon I'll have enough by Christmas.'

'Do you fancy joining a group?'

'A couple of mates have, but I've a way to go yet.'

They continued in silence. Jenny tried to think of something else to say, but the harder she tried the more the words retreated. She spotted the tracks of the railway through the trees, and hoped that he would want to see her again.

'It's my sister's thirteenth birthday next Saturday afternoon. She's having a special tea for a couple of friends from school. Would you like to come?'

She thought it was as if he knew what she was thinking. 'Won't your parents mind?'

'I'll tell Mum you're coming; one more won't make any difference. She's very easy-going. Dad won't be there, he'll be at the café. It's more relaxed when he's not at home. It would be good if you could come.'

'Yes, I'd love to. Have you just got one sister?'

'Yes, she's enough. She's so annoying. What about you?'

'No, I'm an only child,' she said, then adding, 'but I don't mind, I have some good friends.'

'What you never have, you never miss.' Martin smiled at her. 'Not that I'd miss Anna; the house would be a lot quieter. She's a pain in the backside. Well, it looks as if we're back where we started.' They stood staring at the engine shed.

'I'd better go,' said Jenny.

He turned to face her and taking both her hands in his, dipped his face and briefly touched her lips. 'I won't be at the club on Tuesday, my uncle's coming down. So I'll meet you at the end of my street next Saturday, about three o'clock?'

The area to the south of the railway was known locally as "Poet's Corner". At the end of the nineteenth century, a councillor with a literary bent decided to name all roads built surrounding the town's hospital after poets. Jenny leant her cycle against the wall of the house in Byron Street and looked at her watch: five to three. The ride down had not taken as long as she'd thought. She peered into the distance. Someone that looked like Martin was coming out of a house at the far end of the street, as he came nearer she saw that he was holding something in his hand. She should have bought a present for his sister. It was too late now.

'You came on your bike then?' Martin said as he approached her. 'This is for you.' He passed her a brown paper bag.

'For me?'

'Yes, look inside.'

'It's Neil Sedaka, his latest,' she said, her face breaking into a wide smile.

'Yes, you said you liked him.'

'I do, thank you. I should have bought a present for Anna.'

'Don't worry about that. She's got loads, and her friends will bring some more. You better put it in your saddle-bag,' he nodded towards the record.

'Are you sure it's alright me coming? I mean with your mother.' Jenny took hold of the handlebars.

'Course it is. Come on.' Martin draped his arm around Jenny's shoulders and they walked along the street.

'Have you always lived here?' Jenny asked.

'We used to live in the centre of Brighton. But I don't remember it. I think we moved here when I was about five. You can leave your bike here, behind mine.' Martin led Jenny through a side door, to where a bicycle with drop handlebars stood against the wall of the house. Jenny positioned her front wheel so that it lightly touched the rear wheel of Martin's bicycle. 'Don't look so worried,' Martin said as Jenny bit her lower lip. He took her hand and led her through the back door and into the kitchen.

A slim dark-haired woman, wearing an apron with a frill around the edge, looked up and smiled at Jenny. She was turning a jelly upside down on a plate. 'So you're Jenny?'

'I hope it's alright me coming today, Mrs Barretti?'

'Yes, of course it is. Martin hasn't stopped talking about you all week.'

'Mum, for God's sake. Come on Jenny.' He took her hand and pulled her through the doorway.

'Yes, take Jenny into the front room. I don't know

if Anna's in there, her friends haven't arrived yet. I'm setting the food on the table in the dining room.'

'We'll go in there first then,' said Martin, throwing a grin at his mother.

'Don't you dare,' she laughed.

Jenny relaxed, picking up on the easy atmosphere, and followed Martin along the hallway and into a neat sitting room.

'Well, Anna's not in here, that's good.' Martin sank into the sofa. 'Sit down here,' he patted the seat beside him. 'I'll put some 45s on the record player in a minute. That will get us into the party mood.'

'I like you in those trousers. They suit you.' Martin looked down approvingly as Jenny sat beside him.

'They're Capri pants. I always wear them when I cycle.'

There was a thundering of feet on the stairs. The door burst open. 'There you are. Where's my money?' A girl with straight dark hair and a fringe faced them, with both hands on her hips.

'What are you talking about?' said Martin.

'You know what I'm talking about; my birthday money. I had five pound notes, on my bed-side table. Now I've only got three. You've taken them. No one else would.'

'No I haven't,' Martin said.

'You're a liar and a thief.'

'And you're a rude brat. We've got a guest, and all you can do is scream and shout. Aren't you going to say hello?'

'No I'm not.' Her dark eyes flashed from under her fringe. 'Not 'til you own up and give me my money back.'

'Anna, Anna, what on earth's going on? It's your birthday.' Mrs Barretti stood behind her daughter in the hallway. Her hands were white with icing sugar.

'I don't care. I want my money.'

'Martin, did you take it?'

'No, of course I didn't. She's just lost it. It's probably lying in all that mess under her bed. She never cleans her room.'

'We'll sort it out later Anna. You don't need it now do you? Just calm down, and go and get ready. Your friends will be here any minute. I'm sorry about this Jenny. Your first visit, what must you think of us?'

'It's alright,' said Jenny, thinking that she had never experienced the rough and tumble of family life. She remembered Pamela Edwards' house, and then thought of her dead brother. He would be nineteen now; her own childhood would have been very different had he lived.

'I'll get you later.' Anna flashed her eyes at her brother.

'Don't bet on it,' said Martin mockingly as his sister ran back up the stairs. He turned to Jenny. 'She takes after Dad, always exploding at the slightest thing.'

'Martin, there's no need to say that,' said his mother.

'Well, it's the truth.'

'Can I help you with the tea, Mrs Barretti?'

'Thank you Jenny. That would be nice. I'm even more behind now. My husband's at the café this afternoon; Saturday's always their busiest time. Mind you, he wouldn't help if he was here. Italian men,' she sighed, 'more trouble than they're worth.'

Jenny followed her into the kitchen.

'Martin said that you live up at West Blatchington,' she said as she placed silver balls onto the circles of white icing that capped the tiny sponge cakes.

'Yes, opposite the windmill.'

'It's nice up there; near the Downs. I used to live near the New Forest, just outside Southampton. My sister still lives there. Unfortunately, it's all houses and traffic round here. I prefer the countryside. Right, that's the fairy cakes finished. There's just the butter icing for the birthday cake to do, then I'll be finished.' There was a ring on the doorbell. 'Anna,' she shouted, 'answer the door, your friend's here. Jenny, would you mind taking this jelly through to the dining room?' She passed her a strawberry mould in the shape of a rabbit. 'I expect your mum used to make these for you?'

'Yes, she did.' Jenny remembered the bright green jellies and pink blancmanges of her childhood.

Jenny placed the jelly in the centre of the table decked with paper plates and serviettes. She thought what fun Martin's mother seemed. She imagined her laughing and dancing and contrasted her with her own mother.

'So, how old are you Jenny? I can never tell with

young people these days.' She picked up the baking tray of fairy cakes. 'Could you pass me that plate, the one with the cherries round the edge?'

'I'll be fifteen in February,' she said, worried that she might think her too young to be going out with Martin.

'Martin's birthday's in February, the second. I can't believe he'll be seventeen next year.'

'Oh, mine's not 'til the end of the month – the twenty-eighth.'

The doorbell rang once more and the baking tray clattered to the floor, throwing fairy cakes everywhere. 'Oh, no, look what I've done now, the tray just slipped out of my hands.'

'I'll pick them up for you.' Jenny bent down and began picking up the cakes that lay scattered like pebbles under the kitchen table.

'I can't throw them away. They'll have to be alright.'

'They'll be fine, Mrs Barretti, they're in their cases. I'll put them on the plate,' said Jenny, concerned that she might be blamed for chatting to her.

'What's going on out here?' Martin leant against the doorpost smiling. 'Two women in the kitchen; always a bad idea.'

'It's just me being clumsy,' said his mother in a shaky voice. 'Anna!' she shouted.

'Did you enjoy this afternoon?' Martin asked later as he closed the back door behind them.

'Yes, it was great,' said Jenny.

'What, even with Anna throwing a tantrum, and her friends screaming and running wild?'

'Yes, even with Anna and her friends. It was fun.'

Martin pulled her towards him and kissed her softly. Jenny wished that moment could last forever.

The following weekend Martin was waiting by the gate to the farmyard that adjoined Hangleton Church. Jenny braked and stood down from the pedals.

'Do I get a kiss then?' Martin grinned.

Jenny hesitated and then leant towards him and pressed her lips to his. She drew back, unsure how long she should keep them there.

'He's a big boy, isn't he?' Martin nodded in the direction of a bull with a ring through its nose that was standing in a patch of shade in the yard.

'Yes, he is.' Jenny squinted at the animal, his tone made her think he wasn't referring to the animal's bulk. 'I've brought some lunch for us.'

'I thought we might take the track of the old railway to the Dyke, what do you think?' Martin kicked his pedals round and threw his leg over the saddle.

'As long as we can go to Poynings afterwards – I like it there. Don't forget you've got gears, and I haven't. You better wait for me on the hills.'

'I might, or I might not,' he turned and grinned.

Breathless, they stopped at the top of the hill. To their right lay the hamlet of Saddlescombe. A pair of tile-hung cottages fronted the road, behind them sat a large pond. The muddy brown water had shrunk from the cracked edges to form a shallow puddle in the middle. A few ducks waddled and quacked in the midday heat.

'We can have our lunch over there.' Jenny pointed to a grassy bank opposite the pond.

The tall grass was interspersed with light blue scabious flowers. Jenny reached into her saddle-bag and with a flick of her wrists patted the check cloth as flat as she could on the grass.

Jenny passed Martin a sandwich wrapped in greaseproof paper. 'They're cheese and tomato, hope you like them?'

'I eat anything. I've even been known to eat cardboard.'

'I don't believe that.'

'True – you can ask my mum.'

They sat side by side eating. A lone swallow skimmed over the water chasing a meal. 'I've brought two apples to finish off with, or we can save them for later,' said Jenny.

'Let's save them for later.' Martin leaned back in the grass, his arms folded to support his head. 'You – you are my girlfriend, aren't you Jenny?' his voice wavered.

Jenny brimmed with happiness. 'Yes.'

'Good, I can really talk to you. Not like some of the other girls at the club. I knew that as soon as I saw you. It's just that…'

'Just what?' asked Jenny, immediately thinking he must have another girlfriend.

He pulled her back beside him. 'It doesn't matter.'

'No – tell me.'

'I'll tell you later. I'm not going out with anyone else,' he said, as if reading her thoughts.

Jenny relaxed and shielded her eyes from the rays of the sun that pulsed down. Half a dozen swifts circled above, like tiny anchors cast adrift in the sky. 'They'll be gone soon,' she said.

'What will?'

'The swifts, I hate it when they go.'

Martin slid his arm under her neck and shoulders; his fingers briefly touched the swell of her breast. He quickly pulled his arm away and sat up. 'Let's look around. We can leave our bikes here.'

An Elizabethan farmhouse lay behind the pond. It was built of flint, but part of the frontage had been faced with grey concrete; underneath a large gable, was a clock, its hands stuck at six thirty-five. Jenny wondered if it had been morning or evening when time had stood still. She wished that time would stand still today. She had never been so happy. They wandered hand in hand past the house, lingering as a dozen brown and white Sussex hens scratched in the dry earth, supervised by their ever-watchful cockerel.

'We'd better go if we're going to make Poynings,' said Jenny.

They paused on the brow of the hill to eat their apples; the twin towns of Brighton and Hove spread beneath them, with the sails of the windmill a tiny cross in the distance.

'I love this view,' said Martin. 'Look, we don't have to go back to Hangleton, we can go back down Snaky Hill, if you like. We'll be closer to your place then.'

Jenny looked at her watch – five-thirty – her parents should be indoors. Mum would be preparing tea. 'Good idea; but let's stay here a bit longer.'

Fifteen minutes later they stood under the windmill, and leant their bikes against the barn doors. Martin took hold of Jenny's hand. 'I've got something to tell you. I've been putting it off. I didn't want to spoil our day out.'

'What is it?' She felt cold, although the sun was still burning her bare arms. His assertion that he hadn't got another girlfriend had pushed his earlier words from her mind.

'I've got to go away for a while.'

'Go away? What do you mean?'

'It won't be for long. Just for a while. That's why I wanted to know if you were my girlfriend.'

'Why?'

'My mum's got a twin sister. She still lives in my grandparent's house just outside Southampton. She's not married and she's ill. Apparently it's serious. That's what Mum said, cancer I suppose. I heard Mum whispering to her on the phone, she's been doing that a lot lately, she only told us yesterday.'

Jenny stared at him; his words bouncing inside her head. There was a pricking at the back of her eyes.

'She's got to go down to look after her, and me and Anna have got to go with her. Dad will stay here for a while because of the café. I kept telling her that I didn't want to go, that I could stay with Dad, but she wouldn't have it, said she needed me there to help them. I said what about my job, I've only just started. She said that I can get a transfer to a branch in Southampton. So I'm going to have to ask at work on Monday. Anna had a terrible tantrum. Tears and screams all last night and this morning. She doesn't want to leave her friends. Mum said she'd been thinking about going down for a while, but was waiting 'til the summer holidays, so Anna can start school down there in September. Jenny, I don't want to go, but I've no choice. I've got to help Mum. It won't be for long; then I can come back. You'll wait for me won't you? We can still see each other 'til I go.'

Tears trickled down Jenny's cheeks. Martin picked up the edge of his tee-shirt and wiped them away. Her chest felt tight. She couldn't breathe. How could she carry on seeing him? Each meeting would bring them closer, only for it to be snatched away, leaving her lonelier than before. It would probably be for weeks – even months. No, she couldn't do it; best to leave now. She grabbed her handlebars.

'What are you doing?'

In a mist of tears she kicked the pedals into position and pedalled away.

'Jenny! Jenny – what are you doing? Come back!'

When she was sure she was out of his sight, she stopped. Panting, she leant over the handlebars and rested. Then, when she had recovered, she pushed her cycle home.

'I don't know what's come over you lately,' said Alice. 'You're always disappearing into your room. Not speaking to me or your father. You pestered us to let you go to that youth club, and now you don't want to go. I give up trying to understand you, I really do.'

'Well don't bother. You never did anyway,' said Jenny slamming the bedroom door behind her. Gail didn't understand either. She didn't tell her about Martin going away, it was too painful. She kept pestering her to go to the club, saying that Martin was asking where she was. But she always made an excuse.

9

March 1961

Jenny was not looking forward to being a bridesmaid. She thought she ought to, but she couldn't see what there was to celebrate about staying in every evening with the same person for the rest of your life. However, it was not worth the effort of rebelling. She would suffer in silence; the token family bridesmaid.

'All your family will be there, arguing and showing off,' Alice said to Charlie when the invitation arrived. 'As for Doris, I just feel sorry for Jim.'

'She's alright, Gal,' said Charlie.

'Yes, alright when she's getting her own way.'

'I don't know why you're so hard on her.'

'You don't know? Well you should do. Ernie will be flashing his money around, and we all know where he gets it from. He doesn't fool me with all his talk about doing well with his taxi. You don't get what they've got from fares to the West End and back, and the rest of them will be drinking as if there's no tomorrow.'

Charlie's elder step-brother Stan was a compositor in Fleet Street, and the only one of his brothers and sisters to resist the diaspora and still live with his family in Bethnal Green. The East End was in flux. Slum clearance had relocated the poorer families to either high rise blocks nearby, or council estates in Harlow and Basildon. Full employment meant that many families could manage to save the deposit to buy a small semi in Essex. There was an unwritten rule that if you had been brought up north of the Thames you never moved south of it, and visa-versa. Although his parents were content to remain where they had been born, his son Leslie and fiancée Carol had grander ideas. They planned to start married life in a rented one-bedroom flat nearby, but would move north as soon as possible. In March 1961 they took the first step on their journey.

'Stand still Jen. I can't fix this if you keep fidgeting.'

Jenny marvelled how Carol's mother, like her own, could speak and not swallow the pins that were stuck like metal cigarettes between her teeth. She decided that it was a skill that came with middle-age like moaning. Once the blue dress had been adjusted to fit tightly over her figure, it was removed and hung on a hanger until later. She was then squeezed into a taxi between Carol, and Yvonne the other bridesmaid. At Luigi's in the Mile End Road, Jenny's dark hair was teased, tweaked, smoothed and then backcombed into the latest bouffant style. Finally, it was enveloped in hairspray until it became a solid mass incapable of independent movement.

The wedding ceremony was at St. John's Church, where Stan and most of his siblings had been married a generation before. As the first of the cousins to marry, all Leslie's relatives – with the exception of Doris – were at the church. Ernie was dressed in a bespoke Italian suit, with his wife Betty – who all the family agreed, was a dead ringer for Elizabeth Taylor – draped on one arm. A grey fur stole warmed her shoulders, and her collarbone was hidden by two rows of glistening diamonds. Everyone loved Betty, saying that 'she had no airs and graces', and 'had a lot to put up with being married to Ernie'. She had brought up three young boys, having had to cope on her own when Ernie was 'away for a while'. Talking to Betty was Jean, Eric's widow from Dagenham. Their son had grown up never knowing his father, who watched him from a wooden frame that stood on his bedside table. Every night before sleeping, John would whisper the day's events to the smiling young man in uniform.

The buffet reception was held in a large room above The Crown public house, and no expense had been spared in order to put on a good show. After the guests had eaten, the chairs and tables were pushed back along the edge of the room. A black and white clad five-piece band was in full swing when Doris, Jim and Alan arrived. Jim was soon running to and fro to the bar, providing his wife with a never-ending supply of dry Martinis, while Doris took to the dancefloor.

'I wonder how many practice sessions she's had with

her lodgers,' Jenny overheard her mother say to Jean who was sharing their table.

'Doris has always enjoyed dancing though, hasn't she?' said Jean.

'Yes, amongst other things.' Alice put her glass of stout on the table, her lips disappearing, as she threw a look of disapproval towards the dancefloor.

'I think I'll go and sit with Yvonne and the others,' said Jenny, picking up her glass.

'Yes, you should be over there with the other young people, not with us oldies,' said Jean. 'It's lovely to see you again Jenny, it's been so long.'

Jenny pulled back a chair and sat between Yvonne and Leslie's younger brother Keith. She fingered the stem of the glass; her first Babycham. Alan sat opposite smoking. He ignored her, preferring to brag to the other boys. Jenny thought he was trying too hard to impress. The last time she had seen him he was in short trousers, now he was sixteen with acne. Keith introduced her to his friend, Phil Goldstein, who Jenny thought was the image of Elvis, and wondered if he played the guitar. He leant back in his chair, a beer in one hand and a cigarette in the other and blew smoke rings into the air.

'Another drink?' Phil asked as soon as she placed her empty glass on the table. 'Same again?'

'Yes please,' she said, flattered that he had spoken to her. Her heart quickened as she watched him amble over to the bar.

'So, are you another cousin then? I haven't seen you

around here before; I would have noticed,' he said, placing her drink in front of her.

'Yes, we live in Brighton. We don't come up here as much as we used to. Not many of our relatives live around here anymore.' She twirled the cherry around the bowl of the glass causing more bubbles to surface.

'Your aunt's a bit of a goer, isn't she?' He sat down opposite and nodded to where Doris was twirling a barman around the floor.

'She's only enjoying herself. That's what people are supposed to do at weddings, isn't it?'

'Take it easy. I didn't mean anything,' he grinned. 'Mind you, I like girls with a bit of fire.'

As if realising she was the subject of discussion, Doris came and sat down on the empty chair next to Jenny. 'I didn't recognise you with that hair-do.' She waved Jim over. 'Look at our Jenny, she's a bridesmaid. Go and get me another Martini will you?' She nodded towards Phil. 'I think he likes you. You can always tell by the way they look at you.'

Jenny blushed.

'Have you got a boyfriend?'

'Not at the moment.'

'Well, you will have soon, I'm sure. Let me give you some advice. They might look casual, but inside they're just as nervous as you are; more so probably. It's hard for them always having to make the first move. Not that I waited. I didn't care. If I liked someone I made sure they knew; none of this playing hard to get nonsense.

You'll find they don't often turn you down. Mind you, you've got to be careful. Enjoy yourself, but make sure you don't get into trouble. That's the important bit.' She downed the last few drops of her Martini and whispered in Jenny's ear, 'I expect your mum's told you everything, now that you're a teenager.'

'Told me what?' She stared at her aunt, then deciding that she meant the facts of life, blushed, and added, 'Oh, yes.'

'We've got a special bond you and I, haven't we?' Doris slurred, patting Jenny's arm as she stood up.

Feeling braver, she held Phil's gaze as she sipped her third drink.

'It's a bit stuffy in here, d'you fancy a walk?'

Jenny glanced at her watch – nine-fifteen. She looked over at her mother who was still talking to Jean. Over at the bar, her father was surrounded by his brothers. He had a beer in one hand and was waving the other around expressively. *He's probably halfway up the Khyber Pass by now.*

'Why not?' she said picking up her bolero from the back of her chair. She lifted her dress as she followed Phil down the stairs and through the fug and noise of the packed saloon bar. Meeting the evening chill, she caught her breath, and crossed her arms across her chest.

'This area's changed so much in the last few years. A lot of my friends have moved away. We're moving soon. I work in my dad's shop in Roman Road. He's buying another one out at Chingford, and we're going to live above the shop. It will be much nicer for us than round here. I'll miss Keith though. We've been mates since infant school. How old are you?'

Jenny wondered whether to say sixteen, as she guessed he was about eighteen.

'I'll be sixteen in a few months.'

'Have you got a boyfriend?'

'I did have last year, but he moved away.'

'What did he do that for?'

'He had to, there were family reasons.'

'They would have to be pretty serious to leave you behind.' He grinned at her.

'They were.'

As they crossed the bridge over Regent's Canal, Jenny discovered that he didn't have a guitar, and that his hand was sweaty. But she didn't mind. They continued alongside the railings that surrounded Victoria Park. When they reached a tree that spread its branches low over the pavement, Phil suddenly stopped, and pulling her towards him, kissed her hard on her lips. Manoeuvring her against the railings, he forced his tongue into her mouth. Gail had told her about French kissing, and Jenny had wondered why anyone would want to do something so unhygienic. She found herself responding, and wondered if she was supposed to do anything. She decided there was no need, as Phil seemed to know what to do; anyway she might do the wrong thing which would be embarrassing. She remembered to keep her eyes closed, as that was what girls did in films. Phil's breathing became heavier as he rubbed his hands over her breasts. He tried to push his fingers inside the bodice of her dress, but Carole's mother's adjustments defeated him. He pressed his body against her and she felt his hardness. The iron railings dug into her back and head. Phil drew his head back and looked to either side. Jenny copied him. 'There's no one about,' he said, bending down and putting his hand under her dress. He stroked her bare thigh above her stocking top. His fingers crept under her knicker elastic until one was inside her. She didn't stop him, and no longer felt cold. His breathing changed as he removed his hand and she heard a zip unfasten. He looked around, lifted her dress once more and tugged at her knickers.

'Don't let boys touch you, they won't respect you; a lifetime of misery for a few moments of pleasure.' Her mother's words on her fourteenth birthday interrupted the moment; Jenny hadn't understood them then, but she did now. She was enjoying what Phil was doing. It took all her resolve to push him away.

'Don't stop me now Jenny,' he panted, forcing himself between her thighs.

'No, no, I'm sorry, I can't risk it.'

'Yes, you can, I'll be careful; just keep it between your legs then.' He started to thrust against her, pressing her harder against the railings.

'No, no, I'm sorry, stop.' She pushed him back,

thinking how easy it would be to let him continue. She had only met him this afternoon and she wanted him – here – against the railings. She adjusted her underwear and straightened her dress.

He sighed. 'You're a cock-teaser you know, it's difficult for men to stop when we've gone so far. Didn't your boyfriend tell you that?' He tugged at his zip. Taking a packet of cigarettes from his jacket pocket, he said, 'I need this. Do you want one?'

'No, it's O.K. I don't smoke.'

'That's not all you don't do is it?'

He drew deeply on his cigarette. 'I suppose we'd better get back. They'll be wondering where you are.'

They walked back in an uneasy silence. He didn't hold her hand. Phil's words smarted. Jenny couldn't believe how easily one thing had led to another. Aunt Doris had said you had to be careful. This must be what she meant. She couldn't wait to tell Gail about it first thing on Monday. Then she wondered why she was so keen to tell Gail about tonight, but hadn't wanted to tell her anything about Martin. She remembered their last date, nothing like this had happened.

They squeezed through the crowded bar, and back up the stairs. Charlie was still at the bar, only now he had both arms outstretched. *He's probably face to face with a man-eating tiger now*, thought Jenny. Doris was still dancing, and her mother didn't look up as she cradled her glass of stout.

10

Autumn 1962

Exams were over, and after the painful post-mortems, immediately forgotten. Gail had missed the art O level, preferring instead to meet a boy who she claimed was 'a dead ringer for Adam Faith'. There was the option of transferring to the sixth form at the grammar school, but no girl took up the offer. Gail wanted to train as a teacher, saying how much she enjoyed bossing her young cousins about, but to earn money, had accepted a job as junior secretary for a local solicitor. 'This is just for now, so I've got something behind me,' she told Jenny. 'What about you?'

'I know what I *don't* want to do. It's just that I don't know what I *do* want.' So Jenny continued with her Saturday job on the nuts and bolts counter at Woolworths, where she thought that the entire male population of Brighton must be do-it-yourself fanatics.

'I'll have six of the half inch screws, ten of the inch ones and sixteen nuts to fit.' She would pick them out of their square wooden boxes, pour them into small paper bags and attempt to come up with the correct price.

* * *

'Have you heard about that job with the electricity board yet?' Alice asked as she carried a pile of folded washing into the bedroom.

'I didn't apply, it didn't sound very interesting.' Jenny carried on reading… *Bangkok lies on the Chao Phraya River twelve miles from the Gulf of Thailand. It is a city of seven million people founded by Rama 1 in 1782 and within the Grand Palace lies The Emerald Buddha…*

'What on earth has interesting got to do with it? It sounded like a good job to me. You can't hang around here any longer with your head stuck in a book. I'm going to arrange an appointment for both of us, at the youth employment office.'

'I see you took five O levels Jenny,' said the woman in a tweed suit looking down at the slip of paper between her fingers.

'Yes, but I failed art by one grade.'

'But the others are good passes in academic subjects. I think I know of a vacancy for you.' The woman lifted the receiver of the black Bakelite phone and dialled. 'Can I speak to Mr Winstanley please?'

Jenny watched as the woman drummed her fingers on the desk.

'Hello, Miss Gardner here. Yes, I'm well thank you. I have a school-leaver with me who can start straight away if you're interested.'

The woman continued to drum as she held the receiver to her ear. 'Yes, I realise that. I'll tell her, thank you very much.' She replaced the receiver and looked at Jenny.

'There's a vacancy for a clerical assistant at The Ministry of Pensions and National Insurance, in Church Road. If you had five passes you could have started as a clerical officer, but that doesn't matter. You can always take the civil service internal exams; or an extra O level. You'll find there are good opportunities for promotion there if you're interested. So, you're to report to Mr Winstanley's secretary; nine o'clock sharp, on Monday. I'll write the address down for you.' The woman scribbled on a notepad, and passed the sheet to Alice. 'Do you have any questions?'

'No, that will be fine, won't it Jenny?' said Alice.

Jenny ignored her, thinking that the office sounded the most boring place on earth.

'Thank you very much.' Alice turned and smiled at the woman as they left her office. 'Jenny?'

'Yes, thank you,' Jenny said, thinking that the only plus side was that she should be able to save enough money to visit some capital cities. She would start with Paris.

The Ministry of Pensions and National Insurance stood solidly on a corner opposite the floral clock that was bright with burnished autumn blooms. The outside walls were beige, flanked by dark brown marble columns that gave the building an air of authority. The high windows were opaque, conveying to the public the confidential nature of the work undertaken inside.

Jenny followed the arrow on the "staff only" sign and, walking under an iron fire escape, rang the bell on the back door. She rang again. The door opened and a short middle-aged woman faced her.

'You must be Miss Porter? We're expecting you. I'm Mr Winstanley's secretary. If you hang your coat on the stand over there, I'll show you around.'

Jenny stared at a narrow mahogany telephone exchange which sat just inside the door.

'Yes, this is our exchange. It's not quite up to Post Office standards I'm afraid, but it does the job. Follow me.' She walked along a gloomy corridor and pushed a door open. The morning sun brightened their faces as they walked through. 'This is the main enquiry room.' Jenny looked around. Two hard chairs stood in front of a counter that stretched the length of the room. Perched on the end were two racks of official leaflets. Two more chairs stood on either side of the main entrance.

The door closed behind them, shrouding them in darkness once more. The woman started to climb a narrow stairway. 'You'll find Miss Porter that the civil service is strictly hierarchical. Each section has its own grades. Clerical assistants and secretarial staff do the routine work; then there are two higher grades, and at managerial level, executive officers and managers.' On the first floor, they entered a large office containing about twelve people. Jenny looked down as two men turned and stared at her. 'This is the busiest section – contributions.' A slim blonde girl entered the room behind them, and the woman looked at her watch. 'Diana, I've got to go now, would you continue showing this young lady around for me? There's some paperwork that needs completing Miss Porter, so would you bring your passport or birth certificate in sometime this week?'

Jenny stared at the girl.

'I hope you're not going to work in here,' the girl said. 'No one I know likes it; or the pensions department – much too boring. Most people want to work in death grants, maternity or family allowances; that's because bereaved people are too upset, and new parents too busy, to pester us. But I don't think there's a vacancy, they're usually filled internally. I'm secretary to the tax inspectors, on the top floor. We're there because we're superior.' She grinned and bent her head towards Jenny. 'They're rumoured not to exist because they're glimpsed so rarely.'

After showing Jenny the rest of the building she left her outside Mr Winstanley's office.

'Good luck – I'll see you around.'

Jenny realised that she hadn't said a word since entering the building.

'I've had to sign the Official Secrets Act,' Jenny said in a conspiratorial tone to Gail as they dipped their straws into bottles of Tizer at the youth club.

'I thought only spies did that,' said Gail, her eyes bulging. 'How exciting – you're not a spy are you?'

'Don't be ridiculous Gail, of course I'm not a spy. Anyway, I wouldn't tell you if I was, would I?'

Jenny discovered that she enjoyed the camaraderie and gossip of office life. But there was one exception – the telephone. The shrill ring jumped at her from the desk, and she ignored it for as long as possible, hoping that someone else would answer it. When she could no longer avoid picking up the receiver, she would turn bright red with embarrassment at having to speak within earshot of everyone, to an apparently invisible person. One of her duties included manning the telephone exchange. She would sit in front of the dark wood and the numerous plugs. The metal earphones fitted tightly over her head, obscuring any other sounds. She dreaded having to put calls on hold, especially if they were for Mr Golightly – one of the tax inspectors.

'What do you think you're doing girl, where's my caller?' he would shout down the line to her, if she had cut the caller off.

A few members of the public would call in person at the counter on the ground floor. Disputes were few. People accepted what they were told by the staff, and were grateful for whatever they were entitled to. Jenny was told that as far as anybody could recall, only one threat had ever been made against the counter staff.

A burly builder had been told the unwelcome news

that his contribution card was deficient in stamps. He had stormed out of the building, cursing and swearing, returning one minute later carrying an enormous plank of wood which he threatened to bring down over the head of mild-mannered Mr Faithfull. Five minutes later he was hustled out of the building struggling between two policemen.

During her first two months, Jenny enjoyed a peripatetic existence; working in whichever section she was needed. Three long weeks were spent in contributions – the boredom broken by a week in late October when everybody started snapping at each other and walking about with long faces. The only topic of conversation was Cuba. Jenny worried that there was no nuclear bunker under their flat – only deaf Mrs Walters. What would they do, and where would they go when missiles were launched at England?

In early December, a vacancy arose in family allowances.

'You're Jenny aren't you? I remember I showed you round. I'm Diana but you can call me Dido, not to be confused with Dodo, I'm not dead yet, nor do I intend to be, at least not 'til I've had more fun. Welcome to the bird's nest.' She walked over to the window. 'If you stand here, you can just see the sea.' Her grey eyes twinkled as she pointed, and Jenny knew that she would like her.

Jenny had glimpsed Diana around the office

occasionally, but hadn't dared speak to her. As the tax inspectors' secretary, she was endowed with a certain mystery. To Jenny she was the epitome of sophistication. She spoke in husky tones, and her natural blonde hair was back-combed into a beehive that added at least four inches to her height. A fringe swept to one side of her forehead, accentuated her flawless complexion. She was eighteen, but looked and acted with the assurance of a girl who already knew all there was to know about life.

'I'm so excited you're coming up here. It will be fabulous to have someone my own age – well nearly – to talk to.'

Jenny hoped that she could live up to Dido's expectations. But she needn't have worried, as Dido didn't need anyone to talk to her. She wanted a willing and captive listener to tell her adventures to, and guessed rightly that Jenny would fit the role perfectly.

Her adventures consisted of being driven around Brighton in a red MG sports car owned by her Iranian boyfriend. Ten minutes before the end of the working day, she would disappear behind the wooden door of the women's toilet, and would emerge with her make-up reapplied to perfection, and her bouffant hair solid with hairspray. The smell would still be lingering at eight-thirty the following morning when the tax inspectors would wrinkle their noses and remark on its pungency. At five o'clock, a car horn would sound. Jenny would look out of the window to see Dido elegantly positioning herself in the passenger's seat, and wrapping a scarf around her hair. With a wave of her hand she would disappear into the early evening and a good time.

'Guess where we went last night?' Dido said.
'The Two I's?' said Jenny.
'No.'
'Starlight Rooms?'
'No.'

Dido only allowed Jenny two attempts at the correct answer. Jenny would rack her brains for the names of Brighton's more notorious coffee bars, which her mother called "dens of iniquity", and had told Jenny that on no account was she to go anywhere near them. But Jenny was determined to visit one, once she found someone to go with. In the meantime she lived vicariously through Dido.

'We went to the Metropole for dinner, and then on to that jazz club by the aquarium; had an absolutely fantastic time. I can't wait to go there again.' She gave a large sigh and reluctantly removed the cover from her typewriter.

'Why don't you come with me to the Gondola after work?' Dido said one wet Wednesday lunchtime as they ate their sandwiches at their desks.

'Mmm, yes, OK. I'd like to,' Jenny said, the quickening in her chest belying her outward nonchalance. The coffee bar lay halfway along Church

Road, a short walk from the office. It was a popular haunt for the many foreign students studying in the area. Dido had told her that they were mostly Iranian. She also told her that they were all from wealthy families, which explained the sports car and seemingly unending spending money. On her way home from work Jenny would peer down into its smoky interior from the top deck of the bus, and think how stylish and different the students looked, in comparison with the teenagers at the youth club.

Jenny looked up at the clock for the tenth time later that afternoon. Her mother would be cooking dinner now, and there was no way of contacting her. But that thought was quickly dismissed: instead, she marvelled at her foresight in having her hair re-styled the previous Saturday, into a fashionable smooth bob.

They chatted and giggled in the evening drizzle as they wandered towards the neon gondola that hung incongruously above the pavement. The large window was opaque with steam. As they pushed the door open a coffee machine gurgled a welcome. Posters of the Colosseum in Rome, and canals in Venice, adorned the walls. Dido was immediately waved over by a group of students sitting at a table in the corner.

'This is Jenny, she sits opposite me at the ministry,' said Dido.

How does she do it? She even makes work sound glamorous and mysterious. It must be her voice, thought Jenny. She marvelled at her friend's ability to talk effortlessly with everyone in the group – male and female. Compared to the boys at the youth club, these were young men.

'This is Peter.' Jenny recognised him as the one who would pick Dido up after work.

That's not really his name, it's Perv… something or other, but I call him Peter.'

'Any friend of Dido's is a friend of mine.' He lifted Jenny's hand to his lips, and held her gaze.

'Hey, that's enough, are you trying to make me jealous? Go and put some records on the jukebox.'

'Cigarette?' a packet was offered from across the table.

Jenny took one and placed it between her lips as the man flicked his lighter. 'Thank you.' She then removed it and put it between her fingers. Occasionally she would raise it to her lips and give a gentle puff, terrified to inhale in case she started coughing. *This was another world*, she thought; one she desperately wanted to be part of. One cigarette and several coffees later, Jenny remembered her waiting meal.

'I'm sorry, but I must go. My friend's coming round.'

'You must join us again soon.' Peter smiled, his hand brushing her arm.

'Where on earth have you been? Your dinner's in the oven, what's left of it. We've waited over an hour for you. This isn't a hotel you know.' Alice faced her daughter at the top of the stairs.

'I didn't ask you to wait for me. Why don't you get a telephone like everybody else? Then I could phone you if I'm going to be late,' said Jenny, imagining future impromptu evenings in the coffee bar.

'We'll have none of your cheek here, my girl. While you live here you do as we say,' Alice said.

'I don't want your stupid dinner anyway.' Jenny stormed into her bedroom slamming the door behind her.

'I'm not having her behave like that, Charlie, go and do something.' She could hear her mother remonstrating outside her bedroom door.

'What am I supposed to do, Gal?' Jenny listened at the door knowing that her father hated emotional scenes. He would always retreat to his chair and carry on watching T.V.

'Well I don't get any help from you, do I? You're either still in the bloody army or watching T.V. It's no wonder I'm always ill.'

Mr Winstanley was the deputy manager of the Hove office; a benign, rotund man of middle age. He arrived each morning dressed in a dark pinstriped suit, matching waistcoat and a bowler hat. His presence went unnoticed until lunchtime.

'Quick Jenny, it's nearly one, he'll be leaving in a minute.' Dido left her shorthand translation in mid-sentence, and rushed across to the sash window.

Jenny stopped filing and joined her friend to peer at the road below.

'There he goes. He looks just like a penguin.'

'He waddles like one too,' Jenny dissolved into giggles.

Every day at one o'clock sharp, Mr Winstanley would leave the office and walk across to the floral clock, which sat on an island in the middle of the main road. With his furled umbrella tapping each step, he would cross the road and walk along the tall terrace of Regency houses that curved behind a public garden. He would then vanish from their sight. At one fifty-five precisely, they would watch him return by exactly the same route.

'Where do you think he goes every lunchtime?' Jenny said.

'To meet his boyfriend of course,' said Dido.

It was common knowledge among the staff that Mr Winstanley was unmarried and lived alone. Speculation was rife.

'He might just like to go for a walk along the seafront, or he might meet a woman,' said Jenny.

'What with a walk like that? He wriggles like Marilyn Monroe. He's a pansy. No normal man walks like that.'

Jenny had to admit he did have a strange walk, and so on that basis, Mr Winstanley's sexual preference was decided.

'What did you do at the weekend?'

Jenny looked up from the pile of family allowance applications. She couldn't believe that Dido was asking her something.

'Oh. On Friday evening I met up with some friends from school, at the youth club I used to belong to.'

'That sounds fun.'

'Not really, I've known them for ages. They always do the same old things. That's why I don't go there any more.' Jenny hadn't told Dido that she still went there, thinking that it would spoil her desired image. She wanted and needed to keep her two worlds separate. Apart from being interested in what Gail was doing, she also wanted to hear any news of Martin and his family. She clung to the hope that he would return. Gail told her recently, that she had heard he was still working in a bank in Southampton.

'By the way, I've finished with Peter.'

'Oh, I'm sorry,' said Jenny thinking that her friend didn't seem very upset.

'I'm going out with Reza now. He's as sharp as one too.' Dido laughed at her own joke. 'He's much more mature. Peter was so shallow, he's such a flirt. I got bored with him.'

Jenny recalled Reza. He was one of the group at the Gondola. She thought he looked much the same as Peter, but quieter, and with a larger sports car.

She now spent every Wednesday evening with Dido and her friends. She basked in Peter's flirtatious remarks. They helped her forget about Martin. She told her mother that she had been invited to spend Wednesday evenings at Dido's house. When she added that her father was a bank manager, it was never questioned.

It was Jenny's responsibility to open a new file for each family allowance application. The allowance was only paid on the birth of the second child, so Jenny needed to verify both children's birth certificates and the parents' marriage certificate. She enjoyed seeing the names that parents gave to their children. Mark, Kevin, Karen and Nicola seemed the most popular choices, with the occasional exotic Francesca and Sebastian. The naming of a Crispin or Hermione would reduce Jenny and Dido to giggles. To relieve the tedium they would fantasise about the names they would give their own children.

'I'm going to call my daughter Araminta,' Dido said grinning.

'That sounds like a Polo,' said Jenny. 'I'm going to call my son Peregrine.'

'Isn't that a bird?'

Jenny laughed until her side ached.

'The rain's stopped. Do you fancy going into Brighton this lunchtime?' said Dido as she walked over to the window to wait for Mr Winstanley to leave the office.

'No, I can't today Dido, I've got to go to the library.'

'The library – what do you want to go there for?'

'There's a book I want to read. I've got to reserve it.'

'A book – what's it about?'

'Tibet.'

'Tibet,' Dido threw her a puzzled look, as if she was trying to remember a long forgotten geography lesson. 'Doesn't that Lama person come from there? I always thought they were animals.'

Jenny had said the first word that came into her mind. She hated lying, but having promised Gail on Friday evening that she would meet her for lunch, she didn't want Dido questioning her, or worse still, asking if she could join them. Gail was from a past that she was trying to escape from.

As she left Jenny glanced up at the window to check that Dido wasn't watching, and then walked in the opposite direction to the library. She had arranged to meet Gail at one-fifteen, and wondered why she had been keen to meet again so soon. Thinking back to Friday evening she remembered that she had seemed quieter than usual.

'I'm so glad you've come.' Gail was already waiting outside her office; her shoulder-length straight hair contrasting with her pale face. 'Shall we go up the road to the Wimpy?'

'If you like, I can have one of their strawberry milkshakes. What will you have?' asked Jenny.

'Nothing, I'm not feeling well.'

'Why didn't you cancel if you're not well? You could have phoned and we could have made it another day.'

'I couldn't, I had to see you today Jenny, quick, let's get inside out of the cold. I'm freezing.' Gail rubbed her hands together.

'We can sit over in the corner,' said Jenny, wondering what was so important. She shuffled along the plastic-covered bench seat.

Gail sat opposite and fiddled with the lid on the large plastic tomato. 'Jenny – I'm pregnant.'

'What! You can't be.'

'Yes I am. I've been throwing up every morning before work, and I'm two months late. What am I going to do? Mum will kill me. I'm so scared. She's going to guess soon.'

'You can't be. How? What happened?'

'Stop saying I can't be. I tell you I am. I've tried doing loads of exercises, stretching, running up and down stairs. I've had hot baths. I've even drunk half a bottle of Dad's gin that he's been saving for Christmas. But nothing's happened. I have to tell somebody, or I'll go mad. I thought you would know what to do. You know lots of things, Jen. What am I going to do?'

Jenny panicked as she realised that she didn't know what to do either. She remembered Gail telling her a couple of months ago that she was seeing an older man who she'd met at a dancehall in Brighton. 'Is it Chris?' she said.

'Yes, it must have happened the first time we did it. We didn't use anything, I didn't think you could get pregnant the first time. It was late at night and I'd had too many drinks. How could I have been so stupid?' A tear rolled down Gail's pallid cheek.

Jenny sat in silence, fiddling with her straw. How

could this have happened to Gail? She wanted to be a teacher.

'Does he know?'

'No, I keep thinking I'll come on, and it will be alright, but I'm just kidding myself.'

'Do you want to marry him?'

'I don't know Jen, I'm only seventeen, I'd have to get Mum and Dad's permission, and I know they won't like him. He's not like the boys at the club, he's twenty-five. He's even done National Service. That's what attracted me. He's a man, not a boy. You'll still be friends with me won't you?'

'Of course I will,' said Jenny. But no sooner had she spoken than she thought of the embarrassment of being seen with her friend as she became noticeably larger. Then she thought of Dido. This would never have happened to her. She would never allow the undesirable consequences of passion to disrupt her life. 'We'd better go Gail. I've got to get back,' she poked her straw into the ice cream that still sat at the bottom of her glass.

'You'll meet me next week, won't you? You won't tell anyone?'

'No, of course not,' Jenny thought there was no likelihood of that. As she walked back to the office she veered between sympathy for Gail's predicament, and thinking how stupid she'd been. She remembered her walk with Phil Goldstein. *A few minutes*, she thought, *that's all it takes. A few minutes, that could decide a girl's future.*

She mustn't be hard on Gail. She'd been carried away in the heat of the moment, just as she had been. She wondered what she would do if she was pregnant, and decided that having to tell her parents would be a fate worse than death.

'Golly, you look so serious. I don't think you'd better go to the library again if that's how you look when you come back,' said Dido.

'Oh, I've just got cold that's all, it's freezing outside.'

'Well my girl, I'm the bearer of good news. There's a party on New Year's Eve. That will cheer you up. It's at Nick's house, well his parents' house actually, but they'll be away. He's a friend of my brother. You'd better come. He told me to bring a friend, the more the merrier.'

I am her friend, Jenny thought, thrilled to be asked.

The following Monday was the start of Christmas week. A new junior had made a half-hearted attempt to decorate the upstairs offices by draping paper chains around the filing cabinets and the few spider plants that were hanging onto life. Jenny thought continually about Gail and wondered what she could say to her when they next met.

'Have you told Chris?' Jenny bit into a beef burger.

'I hated having to tell him. I was dead scared; but he was good, said he'd stand by me. I was so relieved. I'm not sure about getting married. But I can't bring a baby up on my own, can I?'

'You could have it adopted. Then you needn't marry him if you don't want to, and once it's born you can carry on as if it had never happened.' Jenny felt pleased with herself to have come up with what she considered the ideal solution.

'I still haven't told Mum, I'm petrified she'll throw me out.'

'Well, whatever you decide, she'll have to know, Gail,' said Jenny with the conviction of someone not in the same predicament.

'I know you're right.' Gail picked half-heartedly at her burger. 'Let's meet again after Christmas? I can wait another couple of weeks until I decide what to do. It's been such a relief to talk things over with you. I'll phone you at work.'

'O.K.'

Jenny arrived at the door to the office at the same time as Mr Winstanley. 'I trust you enjoyed your lunch break Miss Porter?' He tapped his furled umbrella three times on the entrance step and removed his bowler hat, revealing a shiny bald head with a fringe of dark hair above his ears.

'Yes, Mr Winstanley,' said Jenny.

'Good, good, glad to hear it, glad to hear it. I like to think we run a happy ship here.'

11

December 1962

'I remember when we had to do all our Christmas shopping late on Christmas Eve,' said Alice. 'My poor dad had to work well into the evening before he was paid. Then we'd go up Green Street market. It stayed open 'til late, back then. There'd be hot chestnuts and bagels, and we'd search the stalls for our presents, not that we had much to spend; but we loved every minute.'

Jenny gave a large sigh, as she heard her mother's annual reminisces, and picked up her book – *Casablanca, principal city of Morocco and largest port of the Maghreb was enlarged by the French in the early twentieth century. The Old Medina is still partially walled and the vast Mosque Hassan 11 stands nearby, on a promontory overlooking the Atlantic…*

'Then, when we'd get home, we'd make paper chains and hang them. It was magical. On Christmas Day we'd find a tangerine and some nuts at the bottom of our stockings. If we were lucky there'd be crayons and a colouring book.'

Jenny didn't glance up from her book.

They opened their presents after breakfast on Christmas morning and once the wrapping paper had been scrunched away, Charlie opened a bottle of sherry – their annual aperitif. The kitchen table covered with a festive tablecloth was carried through into the sitting room. 'It's got all the trimmings,' Alice said, as they tucked into the roast chicken. Timed to perfection, they finished eating their Christmas pudding the minute the queen started her speech. Alice and Charlie raised their glasses and watched in reverential silence.

'Shhh,' they said as Jenny opened her mouth.

'Another good speech; I don't like those corgis though,' said Charlie. 'I remember Major, the Bull-Terrier I had in India. One man dogs they are, you know, wouldn't go with anyone except me, superb guard dog. Anyway, one of the natives had spotted a krait in the shrubbery by the barracks – deadly poisonous they are, small, mind you, and nowhere near as big as a cobra or python but they'd kill a man easily. The natives searched the bushes with sticks but couldn't find it. Anyway, Major hated snakes, he'd stand his ground against a leopard, but hated snakes. One morning, he started growling and barking. That was unusual, so I jumped out of bed to see what the commotion was about, and there curled up at the back of the toilet was this krait. Major had found it. I tell you Gal, I'd have been a goner if it hadn't been for that dog, saved my life he did.' He drew a deep breath and turned towards his daughter. 'Come on Jenny. It's Christmas.' His intact eye sparkled, while his glass eye stared solidly from its socket.

Jenny knew that apart from the obligatory games of whist and rummy, spiced up for Christmas by playing for money, the rest of the day stretched ahead. But she had the New Year's Eve party to look forward to, so could afford to be charitable.

'Saudi Arabia,' said Charlie.

'Medina.'

'Iraq.'

'Baghdad.'

'Damascus.'

'Syria.'

'Beirut.'

'Lebanon.'

'Jerusalem.'

'Israel.'

Charlie had kept to a biblical theme. 'We can do some more tomorrow.'

'I'm going to my room now.' Jenny left them watching television and lay on her bed listening to Elvis Presley. She thought of Martin, as she always did when she was on her own, then wondered whether Gail would find the courage to tell her mother. She imagined a scene from a recent film. Gail's mother would be crying, and her father would shout, 'Get out of this house, and don't darken our door again.'

The house stood in one of many roads that led from

the centre of Hove to the sea. Jenny approached with trepidation, realising that the only person she knew who was going to the party, was Dido. Why didn't she think of asking to meet her first, then they could have arrived together? She had been so thrilled at being invited, that the reality of turning up on her own, and ringing the doorbell, hadn't entered her mind. How would she know if Dido was already there? She wouldn't. She could only hang around and see who turned up. If a girl appeared, she would go in with her. It was bitterly cold, and loud music blared out from behind the drawn curtains. She walked up and down the road to keep warm.

'Are you going to Nick's party?' said a voice from behind, as she was on her sixth walk down the road. She turned, and saw a tall young man dressed in a corduroy jacket. Fair hair flopped over his forehead and a college scarf was wrapped around his neck.

'Yes. I was worried that I might be late.'

'Good God, you're not late.'

'I'm supposed to be meeting my friend there.'

'What's her name?'

'It's Diana but I call her Dido.'

He smiled at her, 'So do I. She'll be there already. In fact, I expect she's been there all afternoon, Nick's her brother's friend.'

'Yes, she told me.'

'I'm Mike by the way. What's your name?'

'Jenny.'

'Well, let's go in, little Jenny-wren.' His smile reminded her of Martin. The door was on the latch and they went through into the hall. 'We can leave our coats here.' He removed his jacket and scarf, and laid them on top of the pile draped over the banister. Jenny did the same.

'Look what I found outside,' Mike announced as they entered a darkened lounge heaving with people.

Jenny turned bright red. She didn't have time to wonder what she should do next, as Dido was pushing through the bodies towards her.

'Where've you been? I've been waiting ages for you. Don't take any notice of Mike.'

'What do you mean, don't take any notice of me. Let the girl decide for herself. She might want to take notice of me. Don't you go too far away little Jenny-wren. Remember I was the first to spot you.'

Dido led her away by the arm. 'Come on, let's get you a drink.' Scattered around the room were several white candles pushed down into the necks of round-bellied wine bottles. Streams of wax dripped down onto the straw holders. Jenny thought they looked very bohemian. She stayed glued to Dido for the first hour, being introduced to person after person. Alcohol and cigarettes were passed around along with witticisms. Chubby Checker 'twisted the night away', from a record player in the corner until someone shouted, 'Let's have some jazz.'

Jenny perched on the arm of a sofa and held a

cigarette and a glass of rum and coke. Below her sat Nick, the host. He wore a baggy jumper with leather elbow pads, his brown hair combed back from his forehead. He turned to Jenny, 'I'm off on a demo next week. I had all the posters prepared at college – ban the bomb, ban the bomb, no more old order, it's our turn now – that's what they say. Look at the mess the establishment have got us into. We don't even know if we'll still be alive next week, never mind next year. They've had their time, and we can do better. Are you coming?'

Before she could think of a suitable reply, the music changed and she was pulled into the centre of the room. Mike held her close and she placed both arms around his neck, her fingertips touching wisps of his hair as they rested on his collar. With three other couples they swayed to the slow tempo. They hung together for two more numbers and then collapsed onto the sofa next to Nick. Jenny turned and through the open lounge door saw Dido leading another friend of Nick's up the stairs.

'So how do you know Dido?' Mike put his arm around her shoulders.

'I work with her at the Ministry of Pensions. You know the building on the corner, near the floral clock.'

'I know the floral clock.'

'What do you do?' Jenny asked.

'I don't. Well not work as such. I'm at Reading University in my second year – reading history.'

'How long have you known Dido?'

'Ages, Nick and I were at school with her brother, so we all know each other.'

On the stroke of midnight those who remained in the lounge staggered to their feet to toast the New Year. As they finished shouting Auld Lang Syne, Mike turned and kissed her. *This is going to be a good year,* she thought.

The party was showing no sign of ending as Jenny reluctantly checked her watch under the light of a candle. 'I've got to go now,' she said.

'What already? It's only just getting going.'

'I know, I don't want to; but I've got to order a taxi.'

'I'll phone for you. But before I do, you're to promise me we'll meet up next week.'

'I promise,' she smiled.

Snowflakes the size of draught counters tumbled down outside, cloaking everything with a silent blanket. Jenny walked unsteadily down the path, leaving her footprints in the virgin snow. She walked away from 1962, and into the big freeze of 1963.

12

January 1963

The heavy snowfalls continued, disrupting everyone's journeys. Bus drivers manfully attempted to reach the end of their journeys in the outlying estates, but their vehicles jack-knifed and were abandoned. Jenny, with many others, had to walk past the church and the windmill, its sails heavy with snow, to where the buses now terminated. Although the pavements had been salted, they froze every night, and were treacherous in the mornings. She stepped gingerly, as she had slipped the week before, spraining her ankle. A frozen wall edged the pavement, which was added to by the council workmen following each fresh fall of snow. It now stood three foot high, with narrow exits shovelled out every few yards.

A collection of wellington boots, and a mountain of heavy coats and hats, cluttered the side entrance to the office. In an effort to boost the indoor temperature, Mr Winstanley had ordered electric bar heaters for every room.

Post was being delivered later than usual, but by ten-thirty, it had been opened, date stamped and distributed.

'Here we are Miss Porter, your very own population explosion,' said Mr Winstanley, laying four family allowance applications on Jenny's desk.

'I've bad news,' Dido said as soon as Mr Winstanley had left the room. 'Reza's parents are coming to England in six weeks. So I suppose I'll have to be on my best behaviour.'

'It doesn't matter what they think does it? You're not planning on marrying him, are you?'

'I haven't ruled it out. His parents are wealthy. I could have a good life, so I don't want to ruin my chances. Parents' opinions are very important over there. Reza's always going on about his family.'

Mr Golightly poked his head around the door. 'Miss Worboys, would you take down some dictation please?'

'Here we go again,' Dido sighed, and after whispering, 'back soon,' walked out of the room carrying her shorthand notebook, leaving in her wake a waft of Midnight perfume. Jenny started unpinning the two birth certificates from the first application. She noticed that Virginia's, the elder child's certificate was slightly different from the younger child's – a boy named Alistair. It was exactly the same size and shape. But instead of two lines at the bottom stating the registration district and sub-registration district; Virginia's had only one line that stated Country of Birth; after which was handwritten in black ink – England. Jenny read the short accompanying note.

'Please find my application for family allowance. I have now had my second child and enclose both short birth certificates as required.' The note had been signed by an Audrey Pattison.

Jenny wondered why Virginia's certificate should state country of birth instead of the registration districts. Every short certificate she had seen, had two bottom lines. She stared at it again. She had seen several certificates of children who had been born abroad, all of them differed, according to the country. But she hadn't seen one until now that only stated country of birth.

Jenny stood up, reluctant to leave the heat thrown onto her legs from the electric fire. She'd better check with the Bible. She had been told that if she was unsure of anything, she was to check it in "The Births and Deaths Registration Act 1947" – a copy of which sat on a shelf above Dido's head. Jenny pulled the slim volume down, wiping off the dust with the palm of her hand. She turned to a page headed "Birth Certificates". There in black and white pen drawings were examples of a full and a short birth certificate. The full birth certificate, gave full details of the child's birthplace, mother, father and their occupations. She had always enjoyed reading these when they landed in front of her. To liven her day, she often shared the information with Dido. The cheaper, shortened version, like Alastair's, gave only the necessary information. But of Virginia's certificate there was no sign. Jenny glanced out of the window. Heavy flakes were falling onto the already compressed snow. People dressed in dark coats and hats scurried as fast as they could in the icy conditions. She flicked over the parchment thin pages, thinking that she would have to ask Mr Winstanley, when on a right-hand page she saw a black and white pen drawing of a short certificate, that stated country of birth. On the opposite page was a drawing of a longer certificate. Jenny read the lines above the short certificate, *the short adoption certificate of which an example is printed below, provides no evidence of the child's adoptive state and place of birth and is valid for all legal purposes.*

'Adopted,' Jenny said the word out loud. *That's why I haven't seen one like this before. Virginia must have been adopted, but not her younger brother; that's why his is the usual type.* She ticked the verified box on their mother's application form, and pinning the certificates onto it, passed it for payment.

'You're concentrating especially hard today.' Dido had returned to her typewriter and was applying some more mascara, having given up deciphering a particularly taxing phrase.

'I was puzzling over one of my applications, but I've solved it now.'

'Good. We don't want any problems here. You're still going out with Mike then?'

'Yes, we had our third date on Saturday. He's gone back to Reading now, so I probably won't see him again 'til the end of March. I'll write though.' Jenny smiled as she remembered how Mike had stroked her hair and called her his little Jenny-wren as they had kissed goodbye. She liked him a lot, but was worried. He was nearly twenty, and part of another world in Reading; a world that didn't include herself.

'Can you come with me to the Gondola tonight?'

'What on a Tuesday?'

'Yes, Reza said he would be there.'

Dido and Jenny walked through swirls of cigarette smoke, to a round table at the rear of the coffee bar.

'I'm glad you've come.' Peter stood up and smiled at Jenny. His dark liquid eyes held hers until she was forced to look away. He put his arm around her, slowly removing her coat. 'When are you going to come out with me then, just the two of us?' Peter whispered the last five words, his mouth close to Jenny's cheek.

'I'm going out with someone now. Mike, he's a friend of Dido's brother.'

'Mike, Mike, who is this Mike? I don't see him here,' Peter addressed his query to the small group huddled around the table.

'Shut up Peter. Leave the girl alone,' Dido said, her right arm wrapped around Reza's shoulders.

'Never mind this Mike, you can still come out with me, I'll show you a good time, eh?'

'We know your idea of a good time.' Dido lit her cigarette.

'That's where you're wrong. I mean good

restaurants; cinema; drives along the coast, anything you want – anything.' Peter stared at Jenny as he emphasised the last word.

'I'll pay for these,' Peter said to the waitress as she placed two coffees on the table.

'I can pay for my own,' said Jenny.

'For heaven's sake, go and put that Beatles record on,' said Dido.

'Do I detect a jealous woman?' Peter said, rising from his chair.

'I've got to go now,' Jenny said, after drinking her coffee.

'But, you've only been here half an hour,' said Dido.

'I know, but my mother's not well, and they're expecting me home.'

'You didn't say anything earlier.'

'It's nothing serious; probably that flu that's going round.'

'I'll do the washing up tonight,' Jenny said as Charlie wiped drips of custard from his chin with his handkerchief.

'You did it last night.' Alice gave her daughter a surprised look.

Jenny knew that her parents would now watch television for an hour – they didn't seem to care what was on – then her mother would go into the kitchen to make a bedtime drink. Their routine never varied. She left the kitchen door open and turned the kitchen taps full on. Water gushed into the washing-up bowl. She thought back to last September. Her mother had gone into her bedroom, and Jenny had heard her pulling out the drawers in her dressing table. She came out and handed Jenny her folded birth certificate. She had only given it a cursory glance, before handing it to Mr Winstanley's secretary for verification, and had given it back to her mother that same evening.

Turning the taps off, she crept into her parents' bedroom and carefully lowered the light switch. Her heart thumped at twice its normal rate. Whenever she entered her parents' bedroom – which was always when they were out – she felt guilty, as if it was a forbidden city, like Llasa. Sometimes they would lock the door, but not always. She would open her mother's wardrobe, releasing the smell of mothballs, and place the soft fur of her fox stole – that she had never seen her mother wear – against her face. She always avoided looking at its head; those orange glass eyes staring accusingly at her. She walked over to the 1930's style dressing table with its large oval mirror and pulled out the top right-hand drawer revealing, a pile of clean stiff corsets. She put her hand underneath, nothing there. Her mother's smell wafted into the room. After listening for any movement from the sitting room, she opened the second drawer. Delving under the pile of brassieres and knickers, she found a dark-blue book, *Married Love*. She had seen it when she was thirteen, she had not been looking for anything in particular, but knowing that whatever she found would be something they didn't want her to see. She had been fascinated by the old-fashioned drawings, but shocked that her parents would have such a book at their age. She covered the book with her mother's underwear, and pulled open the third and bottom drawer. Underneath the pile of woollen vests, she felt paper. Removing a large brown envelope, she tipped out the contents. There were two ancient brown birth certificates, each one bearing the name of one of her parents; then their marriage certificate; and another piece of paper; her own folded certificate. She stuffed the others back in the envelope, and replacing it under the vests, hurried from the room.

In the safety of her bedroom she opened her certificate and stared hard at the last line; Country of Birth, and alongside, handwritten in black ink – England. It was the same as Virginia's. She stared at it for a further minute, then slipped it under her pillow and went back into the kitchen. *There must be another reason why mine's different,* she thought, *because I'm not adopted. If I had been, they would have told me, something as important as that. They tell me everything else; all those boring stories of years ago, that nobody's interested in. So they would have told me something as important as that.* A deep gurgle came from the plughole. *They even told me about...* a blurred baby's face floated before her – she didn't like thinking about it, and tried not to remember his name, as that made him real, and was upsetting. She was back again on the top deck of the bus. *'You had an older brother,'* Mum had said. So she couldn't have been adopted, her parents could have children. Her mother had given birth to her dead brother before her.

She returned to her room and tuned her transistor radio to Radio Luxembourg. A few minutes later, exasperated by the crackling that prevented her from enjoying her favourite record, she switched it off, removed the certificate from under her pillow and put it in her handbag.

Jenny's first thought on waking was the certificate. She was not unduly concerned. It was just something that needed to be explained. Plenty of children must have been given them. They'd probably run out of the others.

Arriving at the office she removed her boots, hung her heavy winter coat on the coat stand and went upstairs. She sat for five minutes on the iron radiator, until the undersides of her thighs turned bright red, then took a deep breath and went over to the shelf above Dido's head.

'I can't have this. That's the second time this week you've got your nose buried in that boring book.' Dido was repairing her make-up from the ravages of the early morning cold. Jenny wondered if she slept in her beehive hair style. It looked too complicated to re-arrange each morning.

'I thought you said that you'd solved the problem of that certificate?'

'I had, but I thought of something else last night.'

'Last night! What are you doing thinking about work? You're obviously not having enough fun in the evenings. I'll have to speak to Mike when he comes back.'

Jenny smiled at her friend, knowing she had her best interests at heart, even if their ideas of the amount of fun necessary for a happy life differed.

'Back to the grind-stone, I suppose,' Dido sighed and returned her make-up bag to her desk drawer.

Jenny took the certificate from her handbag and returned to page fifty-eight. Her heart raced. Although she had seen the example the day before, she stared at it again, as if seeing it for the first time, comparing every word with her own certificate. It was exactly the same. She turned to the index; there were no other pages dealing with birth certificates apart from the ones she had already read. She flipped a page back and saw "Adopted Children's Register – Schedule Six, page 256". She turned to the page and read, *A register of all adopted children under their adoptive names with the date of the adoption order is kept at Somerset House, Strand, London… which is open for public inspection.*

'How's your mother?' asked Dido.

'My mother?'

'Yes, you left early last night. You said she hadn't been well.'

'Oh, she's getting better.'

Jenny remembered a genetics lesson at school. They

were learning about Mendel and the Laws of Inheritance. For homework they were asked to produce a family tree showing eye and hair colouring. Jenny's grandparents were dead, so her tree was a spindly specimen. She had shown her mother's eyes as hazel/brown, and her hair dark brown. Her father, well, he only had one eye, and that was blue, so she had assumed that his other eye must have been the same colour. She remembered puzzling over his hair, which was white as a result of his accident. But a dark-haired, handsome man in his early thirties, dressed in his white and black mess suit, looked down at her from the picture frame hanging on the sitting-room wall; so dark hair went down on the tree. She had then added herself, a solitary short stem. She wrote against her name – green eyes and dark brown hair. She remembered proudly showing it to her mother. Mendel's theory had been proved correct in the Porter household. *If I had been adopted they would have told me then,* she reasoned. The next day at school her homework was returned with a heavy, black tick.

She reasoned that it must be that some children were given these, because they'd run out of the other certificates. But she hadn't seen any others, apart from Virginia's. She reached into her desk drawer and pulled out a leave request form – "I apply for… day's leave on …… January 1963" – she filled in the number 1 and 24th January, signed it at the bottom and took the form downstairs to Mr Winstanley's secretary. One hour later it was returned marked "agreed".

'I'm taking tomorrow off as a day's leave, Dido.'

'What an earth for? It's freezing cold.'

Jenny didn't reply. She couldn't think what to say. Of course Dido would want to know where she was going at such short notice.

'I know: you're pining over Mike, aren't you? I bet you're going up to Reading to see him, aren't you?'

Jenny didn't contradict her.

'That's why you look so pale. You're lovesick. Oh, that's so romantic. You'll be running away to Gretna Green next.'

Jenny woke early, pulling a woollen shift dress over her polo-necked jumper and went into the kitchen.

'You're up early this morning,' said Alice.

'Oh, I couldn't get warm in bed; so I thought I'd better get up.' Jenny scraped the sugar spoon distractedly around the bottom of the bowl. She looked closely at her mother's features, thinking it would be a lot easier just to ask her. No, she couldn't do it. She would be so upset. It might make her ill again. Anyway there was nothing to ask. It was just a doubt that would be assuaged by the end of the day.

'Stop doing that with the spoon. It's getting on my nerves.'

'Sorry, I'm off now.' Jenny jumped up from the table and plumped a kiss on her mother's cheek.

'Have a good day at work. Wrap up warm, it might snow again later.'

Jenny pulled a pair of woollen ankle socks over her stockings for extra warmth before putting her feet inside a pair of fur-lined ankle boots. A coat and hand-knitted scarf completed her outfit.

She picked her way along the slippery pavements, past the windmill, its sails looming threateningly in the leaden sky. The bus drove past the office and Jenny stood up to get off. She could say that she had changed her mind. Of course she didn't want a day off today; it was ridiculous. She sat down again. No, she had to go. She had to find out that it was a mistake.

She sipped a cup of tea in the station cafeteria, and waited for the nine-thirty train. Choosing an empty carriage she settled herself in the window seat away from the corridor. Once through the tunnels that had been carved through the Downs, the train rattled through an arctic landscape; thick snow lay on the roofs of the cottages, and obliterated any boundaries between the fields. *I could be in Russia or Poland,* Jenny thought, the capitals of Moscow and Warsaw springing into her mind. At Wivelsfield, two amply proportioned middle-aged babushkas wearing headscarves, and carrying boat-shaped wicker shopping baskets settled opposite Jenny. They left the carriage two stops further on, leaving Jenny alone with her thoughts once more. At East Croydon the carriage filled with dour, heavy-coated men, stragglers from the rush hour. Her early doubts had evaporated, and by the time the train pulled into Victoria she had relaxed.

Jenny knew this part of London well. On earlier visits with her parents, they had often caught the bus to the East End at Victoria. There was only a small amount of grey ice lingering on the pavements, so Jenny decided to walk along Victoria Street. It was still early. A bitter east wind funnelled down from Westminster, so after only half an hour of window shopping, she caught the bus to Charing Cross. Her stomach rumbled, reminding her to find somewhere for lunch and pleased that she had a reason to delay the final leg of her journey.

She spotted an Italian coffee shop in a side street and ordered a cup of tea and a round of cheese and tomato sandwiches. It was too cold to remove her coat, so she sat huddled in a seat by the window staring at the people hurrying along outside; each one wrapped up in their thoughts as well as their clothes. She ordered a second tea, and lingered for as long as she dared. Unable to delay any longer she left, leaving half of her sandwich on the plate.

Sleet started to fall, covering her coat with white dots. She walked down the Strand and looked up at the names of the streets; Ivybridge Lane; Carting Lane, the Savoy Hotel on her right, and across Lancaster Place. Turning into the driveway to Somerset House, Jenny gazed in awe at the imposing façade. Spotting the entrance she nervously followed the signs up a curved granite staircase and into a high-ceilinged room. A scene from a novel by Dickens greeted her. Shelves filled with enormous green, red and black ledgers covered the walls. People silent with purpose stood hunched over sloping desks, and stared intently at the open ledgers. Jenny hung her coat on a wooden stand, and after asking at the enquiries desk walked to the far end of the room. Under a shelf marked "Births Abroad – Colonies and HMS Services", stood three heavy black ledgers, each marked in gold lettering – "Adopted Children's Register". Her heart pounded, and her mouth felt parched.

She took down the volume marked "Adoptions 1945 to 1959" and turned to the letter P. Running her finger down the page she found Pattison. Alan; Jane; Madeleine; Richard; Susan – *plenty of Susans* – she thought; Trevor; Vernon; Virginia… Virginia Ann Pattison, date of Adoption Order – December 1954. *So that must be my Virginia.* Her breathing became shallower and she felt light-headed. Nothing else existed, just herself and this ledger. She turned the page; Pearse; Pearson; Platt – Porter. She ran her index finger down the names of children, all of them with one thing in common as well as their surname. Anthony John; Barbara Elizabeth: David Howard; Felicity Ann; Gerald Joseph; Jennifer: "Jennifer Jane… date of adoption order 3rd September 1946". She stared at the typewritten letters. Her legs weakened; they were about to buckle. Gripping the edge of the desk she crept over to a nearby chair and sat down. Jenny stared at the open ledger on the high desk where she had left it. *It doesn't have to be me though, it could easily be some other Jennifer Jane, born and adopted in the same year, but somewhere else – Birmingham – Cornwall – anywhere. It doesn't prove that it's me just because it's my name and year of birth.* Her breathing slowed and she felt stronger. She returned to the ledger. Above her name was a Jennifer Porter, no middle name... date of adoption order 1st August 1952, and below her name, a Jennifer Jayne Porter... date of adoption order 19th January 1949. *So, there are other Jennifer Porters, and they're not me, but Jennifer Jane is my full name.* She returned to the chair and sat for about fifteen minutes staring into space. She went back again to the ledger. After looking at her name for over a minute, she finally replaced the ledger on the shelf. She must leave before the rush hour.

Confused and worried she walked to the bus stop in the Strand. Sleet was falling heavier now, so she sheltered in a doorway. Her thoughts alternated between thinking that the name in the ledger must belong to someone else, and having to challenge her parents about what she had found. But that was scary. From the top deck of the bus she looked down upon a mass of bowler hats, as they crawled like black draughts counters into Charing Cross Station. Leaving the bus at the end of Victoria Street, she was carried along with the waves of early evening commuters washing into the station. She wished she had left earlier.

Disembodied, she carried out the actions of someone returning from a normal day out in London;

checking her watch for the time of the next train; hurrying along the platform and finding a seat in the nearest compartment. Her head spun. She was supported by a commuter on either side of her, both of them reading the *Evening Standard*.

Usually she would have bought a paper herself, or at least looked over someone's shoulders at the headlines. But today, she just stared into the darkness outside of the carriage. She had to know the truth. There was no alternative.

It was drizzling as Jenny waited for the bus outside Brighton Station. She climbed the stairs to the upper deck, her head buzzing. The bus passed the greyhound stadium, where her mother had told her about her dead brother. It had been high summer. She remembered there had been golden fields in the distance; but today there was only darkness. Her head felt twice its size as she came down the stairs. The conductor turned to her, his lips moving, but she didn't hear what he said.

Fuelled by adrenaline, she slammed the front door and ran up the stairs into the kitchen.

'You're home late.' Her mother was at the sink washing up.

'You've got to tell me the truth, I'm adopted aren't I?' Jenny cried, her words emerging in a strange squeaky voice.

Alice turned to face her daughter. Her face drained of the little colour it had. 'What are you talking about?'

'I'm adopted aren't I?' A tear rolled down Jenny's cheeks. 'Aren't I?'

Alice's hands gripped the large white sink. 'How did you find out?'

'It's true then, isn't it? Why didn't you tell me?'

Alice started to cry.

'How could you not tell me?' Jenny screamed at her mother.

'We… I was going to tell you, but it never seemed the right time. You were happy and so were we, we didn't want to upset you, and spoil everything. Then you were older and it seemed too late to say anything.'

'Well, I'm not happy now, am I? How could you let me think that you were my parents when you're not?'

'But we are your parents Jenny, we are.'

'No, you're not. You've lied to me. All my life you've lied to me.'

Alice wiped her eyes with the edge of the tea-cloth. Jenny fixed her eyes on the crumpled words. "A gift from Guernsey".

'No we haven't, we've loved you. No one else could have loved you more. We thought that when you were twenty-one, or married and settled, we'd tell you then, when it wouldn't upset you.' Alice moved towards her daughter to hug her. But Jenny, frightened at the intensity of her emotions, backed away.

'Who was my mother then?'

'She was just a young girl, she wasn't from around here. We'd just moved down and she couldn't look after you. She was on her own.'

'What about my father then, who's he?'

'He was a soldier. It was the end of the war. Things were different then.'

'How can I believe you? How can I believe anything you say ever again?' Jenny shouted, thinking about her dead brother.

'Jenny, Jenny.' Alice moved towards her daughter again. 'We thought it was for the best. We would never hurt you, you know that.'

'Well you have, haven't you? Don't touch me,' Jenny stepped back.

'Who else knows? What about Auntie Doris and everyone else?'

'No one else knows. Dad and I moved down here as soon as the war had finished. We didn't want to go back to living in London, not after losing Christopher, we couldn't anyway, everywhere was bombed. They think you're our daughter, and you are, Jenny, you are. We thought if we told them, they might treat you differently, we didn't want that. There was no need for them to know.'

Previous visits to relatives flashed into Jenny's mind. 'You're still lying to me. Aunt Doris knows, she said something once – at Leslie's wedding.'

'What did she say?'

'I can't remember exactly – I thought she meant something else. It just sounded a bit strange when I thought about it later.'

'Well, she doesn't know, it's just that she... she doesn't know Jenny.' Her mother started to weep again.

But all that mattered was that she wasn't who she thought she was. She wasn't their child. She didn't know who she was anymore.

'I'm going to my room.' Sobbing, she ran from the kitchen, slammed her bedroom door and collapsed on her bed.

Jenny heard her father's voice from deep inside the sitting room. 'What the hell's going on Gal?'

She heard her mother's low sobbing and a muttering of words.

'How the hell did she find out? What's happened? How does she know?'

'I don't know Charlie. I don't know.'

'You were going to tell her when she was older, weren't you?'

Then her mother said something she couldn't quite hear.

'No, leave her, Gal, leave her. Let her be for now. She'll calm down best if she's left on her own. You can talk to her tomorrow.'

Jenny lay on top of her bed still wearing her coat and boots, and stared through the bare window at the night sky. The drizzle had cleared. A few stars were trying to peep through the remaining clouds, like torch beams in a fog. She re-played her mother's words, again and again. How could they not have told her? She made a promise to herself that she would never lie to her children, if she had any. Her stomach rumbled.

Normally she would have eaten her dinner over an hour ago. She pulled herself up, leant back against the pillows and reached for a handkerchief to wipe her eyes. She didn't know anyone who was adopted. None of her friends had ever mentioned that they were. A knife twisted inside her gut. She must be illegitimate – a bastard. She had heard the word tossed about; a word that had nothing to do with her. Now it meant everything. She'd been given away – unwanted. There must be something wrong with her. Her mother's pleas that no one could have loved her more, were of no account. She felt only shame.

An hour later Jenny crept into the kitchen for a biscuit and some water; she opened the door of the oven. Two lamb chops lay shrivelled on a plate. She closed the door and started to hiccup. Back in her bedroom she removed her boots and coat and lay back down on the bed. Normally she would have kissed her parents before going to bed, but not tonight; they had lied to her. They were not her parents. She thought about work the next day. She didn't want to go, but if she didn't, she would have to phone and explain why. Then she'd have to stay at home, with her, just the two of them. No, that would be worse. She set her alarm clock, undressed and lay heavy-bodied under the weight of the blankets. She tossed and turned. The luminous hands on her clock showed five-thirty. She lay and stared at the icy patterns of frost on the inside of the windowpane and remembered. After falling into the deep early morning slumber of an insomniac, she woke to the shrill bell of her alarm.

Jenny staggered into the bathroom and splashed her face with cold water. A pot of tea and some buttered toast stood on the kitchen table. Her father had already left for work. She downed half a cup of tea and took three bites from a slice of toast. Her hiccups returned immediately, bringing her mother into the kitchen. Jenny glanced swiftly at her and noticing her red eyes, avoided meeting them.

'Jenny, can we talk?'

'No, I've got to go, I'm late already.'

An east wind whipped her face as she left the house. The concentration required to reach the bus without slipping on the ice distracted her. Safely on the bus, she wondered how she could avoid Dido's inevitable questioning about the previous day.

'Oh, I'm so glad you're back, Jenny. I really needed to talk to you yesterday. I'm so upset. Reza told me on Wednesday evening he couldn't see me any more; well not until his parents have gone home. He said he's been neglecting his studies, and that his parents won't approve of him having a steady girlfriend. What on earth am I going to do in the evenings for six whole weeks?' She stared at Jenny. 'Mind you, I suppose we could go out somewhere together, couldn't we?'

'Yes, I suppose so. We could go down the jazz club, and we can still go to the Gondola.'

'Your eyes look all red and puffy. I hope you haven't caught your mum's cold.'

'No, it's just the wind.'

'I'd even booked this afternoon off. We were supposed to be going to London for the weekend,' Dido wailed.

Jenny knew that she couldn't share the truth about her own visit to London with Dido. She felt too ashamed. There was nobody she could tell. She couldn't speak to her relatives and betray her parents. She would have to bear it alone.

'Miss Porter, are you alright?' said Mr Winstanley, as he placed two applications on Jenny's desk. 'You look very pale.'

'I'm fine, just tired, that's all.'

'You young people, you're all the same, burning the candle at both ends, I expect. Wouldn't you agree with me Miss Worboys?'

'Definitely, Mr Winstanley,' Dido raised her eyebrows; her grey eyes staring at him from behind blackened lashes.

Jenny managed to keep awake until Dido had left for her half-day. Then, exhausted, she lay her head on folded arms and fell asleep. Half an hour later she woke and went into the toilet. Staring at her unmade-up face in the mirror, she thought how terrible she looked. She splashed her face with water, dabbing it dry with the rough towel. She glanced at her watch; two and a half more hours to go.

Jenny stared out of the third floor window. A lunchtime snowfall now covered the already icy pavements and roads. Buses and cars slithered everywhere. The sky was a uniform dirty grey. *There's more to come*, she thought. Gail had phoned her a few days before, breaking the news that she had finally told her parents. She said that all hell had broke loose, and that she would tell her all about it soon. Jenny had been relieved that she hadn't wanted to meet. She couldn't face her friend at the moment. How nonchalantly she had suggested that she should have her baby adopted. She wondered what her own mother had done when she had realised she was pregnant. Panic, almost certainly, like Gail. Did her father – the soldier – know? Did he abandon her? He must have done. Did she try to get rid of her? There were safe options if you had money; but the fact that she existed, meant that she probably hadn't had any. Then, the worst thought of all. Had her mother been raped?

She looked up at the square calendar on the office wall. Blood red numbers stared down at her. It would be February soon – the twenty-eighth – her seventeenth birthday. Before this week, it was just that, her birthday – a day to look forward to. When she was younger there had been parties; but for the last four years, it had been just herself and a couple of friends for tea, and a trip to the cinema afterwards. Now a shadowy female figure intruded. She didn't want to think about her. She wondered if *they* thought about her real mother on her birthday; probably not. They would have been told to 'take her home, she's yours now. Her mother will never be able to claim her'. They must have blocked her out, just as she wanted to do. She wanted to enjoy her life, not to have these thoughts intruding – spoiling everything. She thought of Mike and was relieved that she had seen him at the weekend. She wouldn't see him again for several weeks. She wondered if she could tell him, but decided not to risk it. He might not want to know her. She decided that she would forget this week had ever happened. She certainly didn't want to talk about it at home. There was nothing else to say. Supposing Mum was ill again. She'd been so upset. She had never seen her cry like that even when she had been sick. *Dad won't say anything; he always leaves everything to Mum.* She remembered his words… *'No, leave her Gal, leave her. You can talk to her tomorrow.'* In her mind she was still calling them Mum and Dad, but then she thought, *they're not my mum and dad*, but what else should she call them? She glanced down at her desk. The two applications were in the same place where Mr Winstanley had left them earlier that day.

Jenny waited until everyone except Mr Winstanley had gone home before creeping down the stairs. After leaving the office, Jenny lingered in the snow looking into the dimmed interiors of the shop windows in

Church Road; her eyes misty with fresh tears. When she could bear the cold no longer, she walked to the bus stop.

'Jenny, Jenny, is that you?' her mother's words threatened her as she tiptoed to the top of the stairs. 'I'm in here, in the kitchen. Come in and we can talk.'

'I don't want to talk. Just leave me alone. I'm alright.'

As she passed the sitting room she heard a cough and splutter. She peered in. Her father was hidden behind the *News Chronicle*, only a shock of white hair showed above the headlines. Relieved, Jenny went into her bedroom, shut the door and went over to the pile of 45s by the side of her record player. Without looking at the label, she took the first one from its sleeve and balanced it on the arm of the turntable, then lay fully clothed on her bed and turned the volume higher.

13

February 1963

Her seventeenth birthday fell on a weekday. Nothing had changed, yet everything had changed. Jenny thought that it must be like the first anniversary of a loved one's death; a Sword of Damocles; looming ever closer, but once over, the next one wouldn't be so bad.

'I'm having something to eat with Dido after work. I won't be late,' she had said when Alice asked what she wanted to do for her birthday. Jenny had no intention of celebrating her birthday with anyone, only wanting to put the day behind her.

On the morning of the twentieth-eighth she rushed downstairs to collect the post. 'Yes!' she cried, when she saw the post-mark Reading on a square envelope. He hadn't forgotten. She could face the world and Dido.

Sitting on the upper deck of the bus, she turned the envelope over several times reliving the excitement of seeing Mike's handwriting. Eventually she pulled out the card, savouring the roses for a full minute. She smiled as she read the words inside and kept the open card on her lap.

'Come on then, pass it over. You can tell a lot from what's inside a boy's card.' With a flourish Dido flung the typewriter carriage across and waved her hands excitedly in front of Jenny's face.

'Oh, look, he's even put some kisses, that's a good sign; how romantic.' She smiled at Jenny as she handed the card back. Dido leant down and reached into her bag under her desk. 'Here's my card, happy birthday. Don't forget that you have to buy cakes for everyone. We must celebrate. Are you doing anything tonight?'

'No, I can't tonight. I've got to get home. But we could do something another evening?'

At five o'clock Jenny muffled herself against the wind by wrapping her scarf around her face, and picked her way along the icy pavements. The earlier winter sunshine had disappeared. Waiting for a gap in the traffic, she crossed the main road, and walked slowly down First Avenue to the seafront; the sea and sky now indiscernible in the darkness. She walked along one block and then turned up Second Avenue, returning to the main road. The evening traffic had thinned. She crossed the double width of Grand Avenue and turned down the next road. The curtains in a ground-floor flat had not yet been drawn. Children were playing in front of a fire, whilst a woman, presumably their mother, laid a table for tea. Jenny stopped and stared at the scene. She felt a pricking behind her eyes and walked on. Reaching the seafront for the second time, she stopped and rested against a lamp-post. She looked across to the line of beach huts and shivered. What was she doing here, in this unending blackness? Why hadn't she gone straight home? She should be with her parents in front of their fire; it was her birthday. She turned around and walked back to the main road. The Victorian Town Hall loomed above her as she stared into a children's clothes shop. There was a doll dressed in a white matinee outfit, she wondered if her real mother had bought something similar for her, and if she had kept it as a memento. Perhaps she hadn't bothered to buy anything; glad to be rid of her. No longer able to feel her fingers and toes, she peered through the steamy windows of the coffee bar. After checking that there was no one inside who she knew, she pushed the door, and sat down in the far corner where she usually sat with Dido, and ordered a hot chocolate. She warmed her hands around the glass and sipped the steaming liquid, making it last as long as she dared. At eight o'clock she left.

'Oh good, you're back. Did you have a nice time?' said Alice.

'Yes, it was O.K.'

'Where did you go?'

'Oh… a steakhouse in Church Road.'

'What did you have to eat?'

'Steak, chips, the usual,' *for God's sake stop questioning me*, Jenny thought.

'Well come and open your presents and cards.'

Jenny joined her parents in the sitting room, thinking that the fire had never seemed so welcoming. She opened her cards, and thanked them both with a kiss for the polo-necked jumper.

'We've got something else for you.' Alice smiled, and walked over to the bureau drawer, pulling out a flat brown paper parcel. A smile spread across Jenny's face as she ripped open the paper to reveal the record 'Love Me Do' – the same words that Mike had written inside his card.

14

Spring 1963

Snow had only recently disappeared from the centre of town. In the outlying estates, a dirty white covering still lay on the verges. Alice peered over the half net-curtain that stretched across the kitchen window and looked down onto the small rear garden. A sudden gust of wind caused the yellow trumpets of the daffodils to nod furiously.

As she stared out of the window Alice reflected that it was about nine weeks since Jenny had confronted her. She had thought about it every day, the same question going around and around in her head. How could she have found out? Apart from herself and Charlie, no one else knew. Doris wouldn't have told her — she might be lot of things — but she wasn't cruel. It must have been to do with her work; she thought, but the Ministry of Pensions and National Insurance did not sound a likely place. Anyway, what did it matter how she had found out — she knew. Her stomach, always a barometer of her emotions, rose and fell whenever her daughter appeared. She wanted and needed to talk to her. She had especially wanted to talk to her on her birthday, but that chance had now gone. Jenny didn't want to talk to her. She was deliberately avoiding being alone with her, preferring instead to shut herself in her room and play her records. She only spoke when necessary. She wasn't rude. She still called them Mum and Dad; still kissed them goodnight; still said goodbye when she left the house; but there was a coldness in her words and actions.

She remembered when Charlie had told her to *'let her be,'* and he had said it again later when she had spoken to him about it.

'There's nothing to be gained by bringing it up again. Let it be, it will only upset her, and you as well Gal.'

It didn't seem right not to mention it now it was out in the open. But Jenny didn't want to talk, so what could she do? *Charlie was probably right*, she thought. But then that's what Charlie would have said. She knew him well enough. It had been the same when their son had been born. Charlie had been devastated. She remembered the look on his face as the midwife ushered him into the silent bedroom in Bradford. He had been summoned urgently from the barracks and was still wearing his army uniform. Tears had filled his eyes, and the line of his mouth had almost disappeared in a Herculean effort to keep everything from bursting forth. It was the line of his mouth that she remembered whenever she thought back to that day. It must have been especially hard for him to lose the son he had always wanted, and their only chance of a family. 'No more I'm afraid, Mrs Porter,' the doctor had said. She had been too shattered by her three day labour to feel anything other than exhaustion; grief and loss had come later. She knew that Charlie was the most in need of comfort. The words he had uttered that day played again in her head.

'It doesn't matter, Gal. It doesn't matter.'

Later when she had recovered her strength, she had tried on numerous occasions to talk about their dead son. But every time Charlie would say, *'Don't upset yourself Gal, don't upset yourself.'* Then with a flick and a rustle Charlie would raise the newspaper in front of his face, or worse still. *'Did I ever tell you 'bout that time in Rawalpindi…?'* What had that to do with their son?

She had wanted and needed to talk. Christopher may have been born dead, but he had been born; a full term baby boy – their baby boy. Alice had a niggling feeling that she wasn't the one who would have been the more upset by speaking about him. So they never spoke. The pain of their loss had eased, when four years later they moved to Sussex and decided to adopt a baby girl. She had been pleased for Charlie's sake that Jenny had idolised him. They had been inseparable when she was younger, the pictures every Sunday afternoon, and Jenny never tired of hearing his stories. He was so proud of her. As for herself, she still felt ashamed when she remembered what she had tried to do here in the kitchen, all those years ago. But the pain from her ulcer had been unbearable that day. All she had wanted was to join her dead child, until Jenny's screams had brought her to her senses.

While Alice was staring out of the window, Jenny was sitting opposite Dido daydreaming. She was going to meet Mike. It had been ten weeks since she had last seen him. She had written every week, apart from the two week gap at the end of January. Mike had written back twice; she would have liked him to have written more frequently, but decided that he must be very busy, reading and essay writing. She had never visited Reading, or any other university, and imagined him hunched for hours over his desk, a bright desk light illuminating his writing and constantly referring to the books scattered around him.

Jenny knew on the day following her trip to London that the last thing she wanted to do was to talk about her adoption. It would be embarrassing and upsetting. She certainly didn't want any cosy chats with her mother. Dad hadn't said anything at all to her. It was as if he didn't know that she had found out. But he did know. She had heard them talking that evening. So why didn't he say anything? She had decided that day must be erased from the calendar; there were now only three hundred and sixty-four days in 1963.

'How much longer are you going to be in that bathroom? I want to get in and clean.'

'I'm just coming out,' said Jenny.

'About time too, anyone would think you're going to meet the queen.'

'I wouldn't take so long if I was,' Jenny shouted. In Mike's last letter, he had suggested they meet at his house this Saturday afternoon, and Jenny had replied by return of post. Then she started to worry. What would she wear? Should she change her hairstyle? No, best not to. Suppose it rains? Her hair always went frizzy in the rain.

Last weekend had been a trial run. She had pulled a heap of jumpers from the bottom of her wardrobe and discarded each in turn. It couldn't be too short; it had to be long enough to cover her bottom. It couldn't be too loose either, but tight enough to show the curve of her breasts. She had turned left and then right, and then back again in front of her bedroom mirror. What colour? Her trousers were mustard yellow, so the turquoise and lime green jumpers were cast aside, as was a light-brown one her mother had hand-knitted, it was the right colour and fit, but she didn't want Mike thinking that they made their own clothes. Eventually she decided on her green birthday jumper that had earlier been consigned to the bottom of the pile.

She couldn't face any food, so left the house as soon as she was ready, deciding to walk to use up the time. The verges were now clear of ice for the first time since Boxing Day, but the dirty grey remains of earlier snowfalls still stood in piles on the grass as she passed the windmill. A snowman, gradually disappearing in the sunshine smiled lopsidedly at her. Forty minutes later she reached the lagoon that lay behind the seafront. People were walking briskly up and down the promenade. Jenny checked her watch and joined them. The beach huts were still padlocked, their bright-coloured doors optimistically facing out to sea. She reached three fishing boats drawn up high on the beach and checked her watch again. Mike had said about two, but she remembered Dido's advice.

'Never be too keen. Boys don't like that; they like a challenge.' Jenny wondered why Dido didn't seem to practice what she preached; but she wasn't going to take any chances with Mike.

With renewed confidence she returned to the Lagoon, crossed the south coast road and turned into the first road on the left. Jenny wondered why all the houses had hydrangeas in their front gardens – badges of acceptability – she decided. Her stomach knotted as she pressed the doorbell. *Please let him be here – please let him be here.* She could hear footsteps behind the door, and then the latch being pulled down.

'Look at you, little Jenny-wren. Come in, come in.' He smiled, reminding her again of Martin.

He shut the door and drew Jenny to him, kissing her full on the lips. 'It's so good to see you. Have you missed me?'

'You know I have.' Jenny unwound her scarf and pulled off her gloves.

'I hope you've been a good girl, while I've been

away?' Mike lifted her handbag and placed it on the floor. He took her coat and hung it on the wooden coat stand.

'I haven't had much choice, have I?' Jenny said, thinking that she would never have asked him the same question.

'The parents are out. I was hoping they would be. I don't know for how long though.'

His words hardy registered with Jenny as he pulled her towards him again. She responded with a passion that surprised her.

'God, that feels good. What a welcome, I'd have come home before if I'd known.' Mike whispered the last few words and they fell against the wall. 'Wow, take it easy Jenny. Let's go to my room.'

They embraced and kissed their way to the top of the stairs.

'We'd better leave the door open.'

Collapsing together on the single bed, Mike reached around her and released the clasp to her bra. Pushing her clothes up, he kissed each breast in turn. Jenny pulled his jumper and shirt loose and caressed his back. He unzipped the side of Jenny's slacks and pulled them over her hips. Following his cue, Jenny undid his trouser belt and caught a flash of white underpants. He pressed his lips and body against hers and started to pant. 'I can't stop Jenny, sorry… ah… sorry…' he lay still, squashing her. She felt dampness seeping through her knickers onto her skin. After smothering her neck and face with kisses he reached across to the bookcase and grabbed a crumpled handkerchief. He wiped himself, dabbed Jenny's knickers and put the handkerchief under his pillow.

'Sorry about that Jenny, I just couldn't help myself. I wasn't expecting this to happen today; you know, for you to be so…'

'Eager?' Jenny finished his sentence, thinking that she hadn't expected this either, at least, not today. She couldn't believe she had wanted him so much.

She lay back on the bed and stared straight ahead. A picture of Che Guevara pinned lopsidedly on the wall opposite seemed to mock her. She stared at his bandana, thinking how she had imagined Mike and herself going for a walk, holding hands, kissing and petting like they had done on earlier dates. 'I suppose I must have really missed you.'

'I'm going to have to keep an eye on you, little Jenny-wren.' Mike leant over, his hair flopping against his forehead and kissed her gently on her lips, 'Cigarette?'

'Yes, please.' *I expect all the girls at Reading smoke*, she thought.

Mike reached across again to the bookcase and pulled two from a packet, placed one in Jenny's mouth and then one in his own and lit them with one flick of his lighter. He fell back on the bed, inhaled deeply and sighed. 'You certainly surprised me this afternoon, Jenny-wren. Let's get between the sheets, you'll get cold.' He sat up and balanced his cigarette on a black ashtray, then slipped out of his trousers and underpants. Jenny copied him, and embracing they lay side by side.

'Tell me what's been happening these past weeks? Do you still go to the Gondola with Dido?'

'Yes, only on Wednesdays though.'

'You haven't been out with any of those students, have you?'

'No, of course I haven't.'

'I know Dido does. She likes a good time. You're not like her.'

Jenny was unsure whether to take his remark as a compliment.

Mike kissed her on the lips. 'So tell me what's been happening lately. What did you do for your birthday?'

'I went out for a meal with Dido.'

'Just Dido?'

'Yes, just Dido.' Jenny desperately tried to think of something else to say, but the memory of her discovery smothered everything. 'I've been busy at work.'

'That doesn't sound very exciting.'

Mike sat up and stubbed his cigarette out in the ashtray and took Jenny's barely reduced cigarette from between her thumb and forefinger. 'Now – you're much more interesting.' He covered her lips with his and they explored each other's mouths. She felt him harden against her. 'Just a sec – don't move. I'll be back.' He went over to an antique chest and opened the top drawer. Jenny lay motionless, staring at his hand-knitted black jumper that contrasted with his white buttocks. Leaving the drawer open he returned to the bed and sat with his back to her. 'I've put something on. We can do it properly this time.' He slipped under the covers and stroked her between her legs. Jenny pulled him on top of her. He raised his body and pushed against her, felt the resistance and pushed harder. Jenny winced. They lay still savouring their closeness. He started to move.

'I'm not hurting you, am I?'

'No, it's fine,' she lied. Tentatively she began to return his movements. He thrust quicker and deeper and gave a low moan of pleasure. Jenny smiled, pleased that she was a woman at last.

'Oh, Jenny-wren, that was good – really good.' They lay together for a minute, and then he withdrew. 'I'll just get rid of this.'

So that's it. That's what all the fuss is about, Jenny thought as she lay on the bed. *I've done it. I wasn't expecting to, but I have. He enjoyed it more than me. He must have done it before, he was prepared.* She sat up and leant against the headboard. Lifting the bed covers she stared down at her nakedness, thinking that now she could remember today, instead of that day in January. She moved her legs apart. 'Oh God.' The scarlet stain assaulted her. She was still staring at the sheet when Mike returned from the bathroom.

'Oh shit.'

'What are we going to do?'

'I'll get it out, don't worry.'

Jenny jumped off the bed and together they tugged

at the sheet. Mike disappeared, dragging the evidence behind him. She heard a tap running.

'Look it's not too bad now. I can say I've cut my toe or something. We better get dressed, the parents will be back soon.'

'I feel terrible,' said Jenny as she struggled into her trousers.

Mike wrapped his arms around her. 'Don't worry. I'm pleased I'm the first.' Jenny reached under her jumper, refastened her bra and then ran her fingers through her hair.

'Go downstairs. I'll be down in a minute to make you a drink. Is tea O.K?'

'Yes, fine.'

Jenny wandered around the lounge, thinking that it was virtually a replica of Dido's house. Two bookcases filled with books stood either side of the fireplace. There was an open piano at the far end of the room with a sheet of music on the stand; photographs covered the sideboard. She picked up one of Mike in school uniform, thinking that he looked much the same, only older. Hearing him come into the room, she quickly replaced it.

'We can sit and relax for a bit,' he said, placing the tray on a side table by the sofa. As she sat beside him and drank her tea, Jenny couldn't imagine why he would be pleased that she wasn't like Dido. She sniffed, 'I can smell burning.'

Mike leapt up smiling. 'Oh God, I put the iron on it

to dry it quicker. See what you've done to me?' He laughed as he rushed from the room, 'Made me forget about everything else.'

He shouted down the stairs, 'There's a large scorch mark now as well as a stain. I'll have to throw it out otherwise it will be the Spanish Inquisition.'

A key turned in the lock. Jenny's hand trembled as she placed her cup and saucer on the tray.

'We're back,' a woman's voice called out. There was shuffling in the hall and a smartly dressed man strode into the lounge. A shorter fair-haired woman followed. She held out her hand.

'Hello, you must be Jenny. Michael mentioned that you might call round. My goodness, he's made you some tea? That's a first. Where is Michael?'

'He's just popped upstairs,' said Jenny, her voice wavering. She wished she hadn't said 'popped', it sounded so unsophisticated.

They seated themselves opposite Jenny in two armchairs. Mike's father's legs stretched out until they almost touched her own. He picked up a pipe and a leather pouch from the side table, and started to stuff his pipe with tobacco. Jenny though he looked like an older version of Mike. 'So, are you at college, Jenny?'

He even sounds like him, she thought incredulously. 'No, I work with Dido. Mike – Michael said that you know her.'

'Yes, we've known her since she was a baby, lovely

family. She did two years at Clark's secretarial college; always useful for a girl. Are you a secretary too?'

'No, I do clerical work – family allowance applications,' Jenny said, but added, thinking that it showed ambition, 'I hope to take the exam for a higher grade soon.'

'Good for you.' He leant back in his chair.

'Do you live near here Jenny?' His mother smiled.

'No, not really, I live up near the windmill.'

'Oh yes, I know. Mrs Jenkins lives up there, doesn't she Norman? Some of the roads up there are quite nice.' She crossed her legs.

'Yes they are. I like it up there,' said Jenny, immediately defending her patch.

'I expect Michael's told you that he'll be in his final year at Reading come September. We're pleased that he's finally decided to buckle down and do some work; so provided there aren't too many distractions he should get a good degree. Shouldn't he Norman?' she turned to her husband, 'Norman?'

'Sorry, what did you say dear?'

'I said that Michael should get a good degree.'

'Oh, yes... should do.'

Jenny wished he wouldn't keep staring at her jumper, and was relieved to hear Mike's footsteps on the stairs.

'So there you are at last. I hope you're not neglecting your guest?'

'No, of course not, Ma, don't fuss. We're just on our way out.'

'What so soon? That's a shame. I thought we were going to have some tea together now we're back. We were just getting to know each other, weren't we Jenny?'

Jenny nodded and stood up, 'Goodbye.'

'It's lovely to meet you. I'm sure we'll see you again.' His mother smiled.

Not if I can help it. She's alright, but he makes me shiver, looking at me like that. She followed Mike into the hall, where next to her handbag stood a brown carrier bag containing a crumpled white sheet.

'I've noticed that you're looking a lot jollier lately Miss Porter,' Mr Winstanley beamed as he placed the applications on Jenny's desk. 'I was getting quite worried about you. I like to think my staff are happy in their work.'

'Yes, I am happier,' said Jenny.

'Good, good. I don't know what you young people get up to these days, but sometimes I think that we had more fun when we were young; anyway, as long as you come to work with a smile on your face.'

Once he had left the room Dido leaned across her typewriter. 'Did you hear that? Mr Winstanley had fun. Can you imagine him doing the Charleston and wearing Oxford Bags?'

'No, it takes some believing,' Jenny giggled.

'I know why you're happier lately. It's because of Mike. You've been seeing a lot of him now he's back, haven't you? In fact I think you've seen rather more of Mike than you're letting on.'

Jenny blushed and picked the first application from the top of the pile.

'I knew it, well, well, well. Welcome to the club? Is it good?'

'Yes, I suppose so.'

'You suppose so. Don't you know?'

Jenny thought back over the past two weeks. She had been seeing Mike twice during the week and on Saturday evenings. He would borrow his father's Morris Traveller and call for her after dinner. At the sound of the car's horn Charlie would go over to the window, lift the net curtain and tut, 'Here he is again; 'bout time he got a job like everybody else. He wouldn't have so much time on his hands then.'

'Why don't you ask him up?' Alice would say.

'There isn't time.'

'But he's here three times a week.'

'I'm off, I'll see you later.'

In the remaining daylight they would drive up onto the Downs, and walk along the chalk paths overlooking the Weald. The house-martins advertised their return by swooping and diving on unsuspecting insects. When the lights in the cottages below flickered into life, they would return to the car, clamber into the back seat and, covering themselves with Mike's duffle coat, make love. Jenny enjoyed the closeness it brought, but couldn't relax. It was uncomfortable, squashed against the misted side window. She half expected a policeman to rattle the door handle. One evening a large dog leapt up and started clawing at the glass, barking furiously in Jenny's flattened ear. Afterwards Mike would ask her if she had enjoyed it. She always said yes.

'By the way, I've asked Nick if we can meet at his parent's house next week. They're away on holiday,' Mike said one evening as they adjusted their clothing.

'A warm and comfortable room; now that would be something,' Jenny smiled and squeezed his hand.

'Well we've got to make the most of our time together before I go back. There's a debate at the student's union next term. The motion is, "Should there be equal pay for women?" I've been elected to find a speaker.'

'I think they should if they're doing exactly the same job.'

'The problem is though, that men might be paid less, and they have families to support.'

'But a woman might have a family too. Suppose she's a widow, or divorced. She may even be single.'

'Usually their families support them, don't they?'

'Not always; what about the men who don't marry and have a family,' she said thinking of Mr Winstanley. 'Why should they be paid more than a woman for doing the same job?'

The following week, Mike collected Jenny as usual, but

drove back to a road parallel to his own. Jenny remembered the New Year's party, and could have sworn Nick's house was larger than it looked now. Nick opened two beers, one for Mike and himself, and then mixed a gin and orange for Jenny from the cluster of bottles that stood on a silver tray on the sideboard.

'We've got to support the Civil Rights Movement,' Nick said as he stood by the mantelpiece and pushed his black-framed glasses up over the bridge of his nose. 'We can't stand by and do nothing while coloured people are banned from travelling on the same buses, or going to the same schools as whites. People make a fuss about apartheid in South Africa, but look at the States – our closest ally. They're just as bad, if not worse.'

'I agree, there was a lynching in Alabama last week. They said he didn't even get a fair trial; guilty just because of the colour of his skin,' Mike said.

'I hope you two are going to join me on the CND march from Aldermaston this weekend?'

'Not this weekend, Nick. I'm going back. I'll come next time though.'

'You owe me, who's leaving the warmth and comfort of his fireside, so you two love-birds can be alone?'

'I'd do the same for you. You've only got to say the word.'

'I've got to find the girl first.' Nick grinned at Jenny. 'Well I'm off to the pub now. I'll ring the bell when I get back, so make sure you're not *indelecto flagrento*. I draw the line at voyeurism.'

'Two whole hours to ourselves, with drinks thrown in; what more could we ask for?' Jenny said, pulling Mike towards her, as the front door slammed.

Mike laughed and pushed her back onto the sofa, his hand already on her thigh.

'How am I going to manage without you, Jenny-wren?' Mike drew deeply on a post-coital cigarette. 'I'll pour us another drink. Nick won't mind. Have a drag.' He kissed her and placed his cigarette between her lips.

'I received the distinct impression that your parents would like you to.'

'Like me to what?' he turned to her from the sideboard.

'Manage without me.'

'Don't take any notice of what they say. Ma can be a bit of a snob, but she's alright when you get to know her. I'm pretty sure Dad's got a woman up in town. He's always coming home late.'

That fits, Jenny thought, trying not to look shocked. No one she knew had ever said that about their father. 'I think you'll manage better than me.'

'How's that?'

'Well you'll have other distractions. What will I have once you've gone back?' Jenny imagined weeks of empty evenings alone with her parents, worrying about what Mike was doing in Reading.

'Here you are, my lovely.' Mike handed her the glass and sat down. 'Don't worry, we'll make up for it when I come back, I promise. It's only eight weeks. My parents are going away in July. So we've got another empty house to look forward too.'

'Where are they going?'

'Touring round Switzerland; they like the Alps. I went with them last year. Have you ever been abroad?'

'Not yet. But I will. I thought I'd start with Paris.'

Pulling away from their embrace, Mike picked up his holdall and went through the ticket barrier.

'Bye, bye,' Jenny shouted after him. He turned, blew her a kiss and disappeared into the train carriage. Reluctant to leave, Jenny stood and stared at the passengers hurrying along the platform. At the sound of the whistle the train drew away. He had gone. She watched the train disappear and stared at the empty tracks, then went into the station café and ordered a tea, remembering the last time she had sat there. How worried she had been. Now life was good – he loved her. Of course he had to go away, but he would be back.

Gail sucked what remained of her banana milkshake through a straw. 'I was so pleased to speak to you last week. I'd phoned several times before, but the girl on your switchboard said she couldn't find you. I was starting to think you didn't want to meet up, that you were ashamed of being seen with me.'

'No, of course not, it wasn't that,' said Jenny, almost too quickly.

'I'm leaving at the end of the week, I'm seven months now.' Gail patted her swollen stomach and leant back on the seat. 'Make sure you don't end up like me, I was so stupid.'

Jenny found it hard to take her eyes from her friend's belly. It was enormous. How could this be the same girl that used to laugh, dance and gossip at the club?

'Your Mike sounds nice. No wonder you've been too busy to meet up. You make sure he's careful. You don't want to end up like me. Chris and I are going to the registry office next week when I finish work. Then I'll move in with him. He's got a bedsit near the station. I didn't want this, Jenny. I was dead set on going to teacher training college, wasn't I? I didn't want to be a typist. I never even made it to secretary. Now it's too late.' A tear trailed down her cheek. 'I couldn't have the baby adopted though, not once I felt it move. I couldn't give it up. I know lots of girls do – but I just couldn't.'

'No,' said Jenny softly, remembering how quickly she had suggested adoption to her friend. Would she do the same now? 'But at least you've got Chris,' she added, thinking of her mother's probable abandonment.

'I do worry that I'm doing the right thing in marrying Chris, but what else can I do?'

'But he's older, he can support you. At least you're leaving home. I wish I could.'

'Well, perhaps Mike's the one. Do you love him?'

'Yes, I think so. I really miss him when he's not around; more now than ever.'

'You've made some new friends at work haven't you? Do you think you'll stay there?'

'I'm thinking of taking the Clerical Officers Exam this autumn. I don't want Mike thinking that I'm just a clerk. You know, him being at university.'

'But you know all those capital cities. I always remember that. I thought you were so clever.'

'Maybe, but not in the same way that Mike is; he's involved in marches and protests, that sort of thing. He's always talking about policies and politics. I feel that I can't compete with his friends at Reading.'

'You don't need to Jenny. You're just as good as they are, probably better. Anyway I must get back; everything seems to take so much longer at the moment.' Gail stood up. Jenny noticed how she could only fasten her coat by the top button, her fecundity advertising itself to the world. 'You will come and see the baby won't you? I'll drop you a line.'

'Yes, I will,' said Jenny as they walked to the door. Ensuring she left first, she peered left and right along the pavement before turning to Gail. 'Well, bye for now then.' Not knowing what else to say they parted, each to their separate futures. Jenny felt the lightness of freedom in her steps as she walked away. *I should have said more to her. She's leaving work, getting married, leaving home, and worst of all, having a baby in eight weeks, and I didn't even say good luck.*

'Did you meet your friend?' Dido said as Jenny walked into the office. 'You haven't met up for ages.'

'Yes, it was good.'

'Well, perhaps I can come along next time?' Dido smoothed her blonde fringe across her forehead with her fingers.

'There won't be a next time; she's leaving her job at the end of the week.' *I was right in thinking she'd want to come*, thought Jenny. Before Dido had a chance to ask why and where Gail was going, she added, 'I'm thinking about sitting the exams.'

'What an earth for? You don't need to be promoted. You'll get married won't you?'

'Well, yes sometime, I hope. But I need something to aim for. I can't just carry on processing these applications forever. I'd like to earn more money as well, so I can travel.'

'I'd rather aim on finding a rich husband. It's more fun and the result's the same.' Dido laughed out loud.

'So, why haven't I seen you lately?' asked Peter, as Jenny sat beside him sipping her cup of coffee.

'Mike's been home, but he's gone back now.'

'Ah, the mysterious Mike, so he's the reason. How could he leave you alone again?'

'Don't be so obtuse Peter. He has to go back, to study, not everybody's like you,' Dido said.

'I know that. I was just teasing our little friend here.'

'He's working really hard. He didn't want to go back,' Jenny added.

'I'm sure he didn't.' He stared at Jenny until she was forced to lower her eyes to the forest of black hairs in the triangle at the top of his open-necked shirt. 'Well if you get bored with waiting, you know I'm here.'

15

Summer 1963

J enny applied to sit the exam in October. To pass the time and to feel closer to Mike she spent most evenings studying with The Beatles strumming their guitars and shouting their lyrics in the background. She wrote to tell Mike of her decision and four weeks later a letter lay on the doormat.

Dear Jenny-wren,

I miss you so much. The parents were quite right to worry about you distracting me. Every time I start to write an essay I think about our evenings together. Then I imagine you're here with me, and that's the end of any studying. Anyway, true to my word I'm joining Nick on his marches and demos. I spend most of my spare time making placards. If I keep him happy he might let us use his parent's house again in the summer…

'You'll be engaged by September,' Dido said breathlessly as she read Mike's letter over her typewriter. 'I can't have you beating me to the altar.'

'You think so?'

'Definitely, that's why I said you don't need to bother about those exams. He'll get a good job and you'll be married in a couple of years.'

Jenny thought that if she married she could leave home. She hated the atmosphere there now and remembered the previous evening.

The three of them were watching television when a programme came on about adoption. She was about to leave the room when her father had said, 'There's something I want to watch on the other side.' He then changed channels to a programme about gardening. He hated gardens. He only went down there to take the rubbish out.

A few weeks earlier her mother had cornered her and said, 'Jenny, I found out today that that family opposite have an adopted son,' and she had wanted to reply, 'oh, yes and I expect they told him he was adopted. Not like you, leaving me to find out.' But she didn't say anything, and had left the room.

She hadn't given marriage a thought until now, but the more she thought about it, the more it seemed the answer to everything. She even found herself peering in jewellers' windows. She was careful not to mention any of her thoughts when she wrote to Mike. She kept the tone light, but always mentioned Peter being at the Gondola, just to keep him interested.

Hello Jenny-wren,
Thank you for your letter. It's coming up to the end of

term soon. There's going to be an end of term ball, not sure if I'll go or not. I've been on some more marches with Nick and this girl he knows called Jillian. There's always a good atmosphere, everyone mucks in together. I've quite enjoyed them...

Then one week after his second letter Jenny was surprised to receive a third.

Hello there, hope the studying is going well. I'm afraid I won't be coming straight back home at the end of term as Jill has invited Nick and myself to stay at her parent's house near Bristol. I think I told you that she joined us on the marches. Anyway I'll let you know as soon as I'm back...

Jenny wasn't unduly concerned that Mike wasn't coming back immediately; but she was disappointed. She wondered what they would do at Jillian's house; whether it was large or small – and decided on the former. She would have to be patient. They would have so much to talk about when he returned. They might even arrange a holiday together. He did ask her if she had been abroad. For three weeks she remained buoyed up by memories of their time together and rushed down the stairs every morning to check the post. One day she received a card from Gail informing her that Mark Jonathan had weighed in at 6lbs 8 oz. and gave her new address near Brighton Station. Jenny decided to distract herself by paying her a visit.

The thermometer on the landing showed seventy-five degrees. Jenny wore a simple blue shift dress and clutching a paper bag caught the bus to the Clock Tower. She was walking towards the station when she noticed a young man with hair that flopped over his forehead standing outside a music shop. He was talking in an animated way to a shorter man with brown hair. 'He's back!' Jenny said out loud as she ran towards them.

'Mike, Mike you're back. Why didn't you let me know?'

'Well, well, look who it is?'

She held her face up for his kiss. She waited, her heart thumping. His face reddened. Nick took three paces back, leaving them facing each other.

'I'm sorry I didn't tell you I was back, Jenny. Only I'm going away next week to France for three weeks, and I knew you'd be disappointed. We only decided last week.'

'Oh,' Jenny panicked. This was not how she had imagined their reunion.

'I'll ring you at work when I get back,' he added.

'We could meet up this weekend. It's been so long, and I've really missed you,' she said softly.

'I can't Jenny; some people from Reading are coming down.'

'Well, I could come too. I can come with you to France. I can get the time off work.' Jenny knew that she sounded clingy, but couldn't help herself.

'I don't think so. You don't know anyone.'

'I know you, and Nick.'

'He's not going.'

'But…'

'Look, Jenny, I'll get in touch with you when I get back. I promise. You know I like you.'

'Like me, like me! I thought you loved me,' she screamed. The pavement moved closer and people swayed. Forcing herself to remain upright she caught her breath, turned and ran back to the bus stop, colliding with an elderly man.

When she reached the bus stop she found that the paper bag she was carrying was empty. She walked back a few steps. 'There it is,' she muttered. The blue matinee jacket was lying in the gutter. She picked it up and brushed it clean with her fingers. Gail was expecting her, she'd already let her down once, she couldn't do it again.

'I knew you'd come out with me eventually. That Mike didn't know how to treat you; he's just a boy.' Peter's dark eyes smiled at Jenny as he turned in the driving seat. 'I'll give you a good time, I promise.'

16

Winter 1963

JFK ASSASSINATED – the billboards screamed the atrocity at passers by.

The conversation that morning was of nothing else. Dido had even forgotten to back-comb her hair in her rush to come to work. Jenny thought that her aura of glamour had disappeared, as if in sympathy with the American people. 'I couldn't believe it. I still can't. I'd just got home from being out with Reza when my dad told me.'

'I was in my room when they announced it on the radio,' said Jenny. 'I couldn't believe it either. I couldn't sleep for thinking about it.'

Every possible reason for the assassination, and the subsequent shooting of the perpetrator was discussed and dissected.

'Of course, these things happen in America. That's what you get when the right to own a gun is written into the constitution. It could never happen here,' said Mr Winstanley, twirling the watch chain that threaded through his waistcoat. 'They're hot-headed, not like us British.'

Jenny decided to walk into Brighton at lunchtime. It had just started to drizzle. She felt uneasy. She thought that if the President of America – who was so young, handsome and popular – could be shot dead, anything was possible. Everything could change in a flash, like her relationship with Mike. Then she remembered her adoption and her legs weakened. She swayed and collided into a woman who was emerging from Hill's of Hove department store.

'Look what you've done. Why don't you look where you're going?'

'I'm sorry. I'll pick them up for you.' Jenny scrambled around picking up the packages that lay scattered on the pavement. She thought the woman looked familiar.

'Look they're all wet now. Haven't I seen you before? Weren't you a friend of my son – Michael? Yes, that's it, you came to our house, didn't you? I'm sorry I was sharp with you just now, it's been one of those days.'

'No, it wasn't me,' Jenny mumbled. She replaced the parcels in the stiff carrier bag, straightened herself and hurried away. Her heart raced. She felt dizzy. There was a sudden screech of brakes and a horn hooted loudly.

'Are you blind?' A man's head poked out of the driver's window.

She ran to the pavement. Her chest tightened. She was sweating. *I must go back to the office. It's safe there.*

'That was quick.' Dido looked up from reading her magazine. 'You look as if you've seen a ghost.'

'I've just had a funny turn, that's all,' Jenny said leaning back in her chair. 'I'll feel better in a minute.' Her heart gradually resumed its normal rhythm, as she sat in familiar surroundings.

'It's all that studying. It's affected you. I told you it wasn't a good idea.'

'The exam was over a month ago, Dido. I can relax now.'

'Good, because I've got something exiting to tell you. I would have told you earlier, but we were all so busy discussing the shootings. I'm thinking of going to work in Germany. There's a secretarial job going in Wiesbaden – working for the American army – if I get it, it would be the most amazing thing. You could come out and stay. Think of all those gorgeous men in uniform – Elvis Presley doubles – what a brilliant time we'd have. I can just see us both now, sitting in a Jeep being driven all over Europe – you'd like that – and I've heard that German night-life is something else.'

'Oh, no, you can't leave Dido. It won't be the same here without you.'

'That's why you should come out and visit. You can update me on all the news from good old Brighton and Hove.'

'What about Reza? You really like him.'

'Oh, I'm getting a bit bored with him – you know me.'

* * *

It was still drizzling when Jenny left. She waited in her usual place to cross the road and ruminated on Dido's news. Her heart thudded until it was all she could hear. She felt faint. Was she having a heart attack? Beads of sweat lay on her forehead, belying the November temperature. She sat on the low wall outside an estate agent's office. She couldn't cross the road. The bus stop was only ten yards away, but it might as well have been behind the Berlin Wall. Jenny panicked. *What is happening? Am I ill? I am going mad? If I can get halfway, I can rest there, and there won't be too large a space to cross.* She crept along for about a hundred yards, steadying herself on the walls that edged the pavement.

'Are you alright dear?' asked a middle-aged woman peering through misted glasses.

'I just feel a bit faint; I'll be alright in a moment.'

Jenny spotted a bollard in the middle of the road, just before the town hall. Her breathing became shallower as she wobbled on the edge of the kerb. There was a gap in the traffic. She ran across and clutched at the bollard, then took a deep breath and dashed to the other side of the road.

She leant against a shop window to steady herself until her bus appeared. Sitting downstairs she clutched the rail of the seat in front of her and tried to relax. She would soon be home. Relieved, she spotted the dark outlines of the sails of the windmill. Walking unsteadily to the bus platform she swayed and the conductor put his hand out to steady her.

'Too early for drinking,' he chuckled.

She ran across the road. Her hands trembling as she struggled to put her key in the door. What was happening to her?

By the time dinner was ready Jenny felt calmer.

'Yanks, what can you expect, always bloody trigger happy. There was that incident in France during the war, four of our men mown down. Friendly fire the papers said – not in my book – bloody carelessness I call it. No discipline that's their trouble, not trained properly – not like our troops.'

Jenny thought that her father's comments on John Kennedy's assassination were much the same as Mr Winstanley's, only blunter.

'Be quiet, Charlie, eat your dinner, we're watching the funeral.'

'I don't know why they're having it so soon. Bloody Papists I suppose, all that superstitious clap trap.'

'Charlie, that's no way to speak at a time like this. Look at that dear little boy saluting his father's coffin, poor mite.'

Jenny thought how glamorous Jackie Kennedy was, even when mourning her dead husband. She looked so composed under her black veil. She doubted if she could ever be like that. She was a nervous wreck just trying to get home from work.

The next day Jenny decided that what had happened to

her was a one off, and put it down to bumping into Mike's mother. That wouldn't happen again. But that evening as she tried to cross the road, the palpitations began. She was suffocating and was going to collapse in the street, and die. She sat on the low wall until she felt calmer, and then edged her way along the pavement until she teetered on the edge of the kerb opposite the bollard.

'Hello Jenny, I haven't seen you for a while, take a seat.' Dr Marks smiled at her across his desk.

Jenny took a deep breath and explained her symptoms. How for the past two weeks she had been terrified of leaving home, and when she did, she had the ordeal of getting back.

'Your mother's been a lot better these past few years, hasn't she? You're not worrying about her are you?' Jenny fastened the buttons on her blouse as Dr Marks folded his stethoscope and returned to his chair.

'No.'

'Has anything happened to you recently?'

'What do you mean?' Jenny thought that quite a lot had happened, but that was months ago. She couldn't tell Dr Marks; he had been their family doctor for as long as she could remember. Anyway she would need a lot longer than a few minutes.

'Well, have you had a shock, been upset about something; for example has a man, interfered with you?'

'No, no,' said Jenny.

'I'm glad to hear it.' Dr Marks smiled and scratched

his forehead. 'I expect you have a boyfriend now? It seems only a short time ago when you had the measles.'

'I did have, until recently.' A few weeks ago she had woken up one morning and realised that she had nothing in common with Peter. Their affair had run its course. She had told him that she wanted to concentrate on her coming exam. He wasn't upset or even surprised. It was as if he was expecting it.

'You're not in any trouble are you?' he spoke softly and leaned across his desk towards her.

'No, I'm not.'

'Good.' He ran his fingers through what remained of his hair. 'Well, I can't find anything physically wrong with you. From what you've described, they sound like severe anxiety attacks, but why they should start now, I don't know. There doesn't seem to be any reason. I don't want to prescribe you tablets, so I think I'll refer you to a colleague of mine at the County Hospital.' He scribbled a few lines on a writing pad, folded the paper inside an envelope and handed it to Jenny. 'Post this and you should get an appointment soon. In the meantime I recommend that you take a couple of weeks off from that job of yours. I'll give you a sick note. Please give my regards to your parents, won't you?'

'A psychiatrist, Dr Marks has said you have to see a psychiatrist. What on earth for?' Alice stared at Jenny in amazement. 'You're not mental. You've just had a few funny turns. Perhaps you need to see someone else, another doctor?'

'It was Dr Marks' suggestion, not mine. I can't carry on having these attacks, they're so frightening.' Once Dr Marks had reassured her that there was nothing physically wrong, she knew that his suspicions were right. The attacks were related to the events earlier that year.

'Goodness knows what your father will say.'

'Bloody load of rubbish. What good will going to see a shrink do? Your granddad, aunts and uncles all went through the war, not knowing if they'd have a house, or even be alive the next morning. Bombed out twice they were; lost everything. They never saw no psychiatrist,' Charlie sighed and picked up his newspaper.

A strong smell of disinfectant wafted past as they waited in the narrow corridor. Jenny hadn't eaten since nibbling a slice of toast earlier that morning, but she wasn't hungry.

'Miss Porter, Dr McCaffrey will see you now,' a brisk voice echoed down the corridor. Alice stood up. 'No, just Miss Porter please.'

A man wearing a white coat, his face half-covered with a black beard, sat at a desk and invited Jenny to sit beside him. 'I have a letter here from Dr Marks; now you tell me in your own words what has been happening.'

Tears streamed down Jenny's face as she described

how she felt whenever she tried to cross an open space.

'What else has happened to you in the past year?'

Jenny broke down. She poured out the discovery of her adoption to this stranger, and how she no longer knew who she was. How she couldn't face talking about it to her parents or anyone else. She told him about her mother's ill health and how she had always worried about her. Then after she had heard about the death of President Kennedy the attacks had started and she didn't know why. Dr McCaffrey handed her a tissue from a box on his desk and took her hand.

'What you've described, Jennifer, are panic attacks; caused by severe anxiety. They are usually triggered by a shock of some kind, such as the one you had. They don't always start immediately; sometimes, something quite trivial will trigger them. I don't think these attacks will improve while you remain at home with your parents. So, I would like you to stay for a short while in a hospital in Hove. It's not a hospital like this one; basically it's a large house. That will have the effect of removing you from surroundings that you are finding stressful, and enable us to talk in depth about what's happened. I'm sure you'll find that therapeutic.' He reached for a prescription pad. 'In the meantime I'll prescribe some tablets which will help, and you'll receive a letter from us shortly.'

'What! He wants you to stay in hospital, move away from home. Why?'

'I told you, I keep having these panic attacks every time I leave home.'

'Well, then, surely you need to stay at home, not go somewhere else?'

'He said it will only be for a short while. He said he can't help me properly unless I go.'

'You've got two perfectly good parents. You don't need to go anywhere else. I'm going in to speak to him, Nurse.'

Jenny sat in the corridor wishing that she had never been to Dr Marks. This wasn't what she had imagined would happen.

Alice's lips were set in a thin line and her face was ashen, as she emerged from the consulting room. 'Come on, let's get home.' They travelled home in silence.

Jenny strained her ears at the door of the sitting room.

'It might be something to do with that Charlie, but I've been trying to get her to talk about it for almost a year, she didn't want to. Perhaps we should have told her earlier, but I never thought she'd find out. I don't like to think this Charlie, but perhaps it's something in her blood. We don't know everything about her do we?'

Screams echoed along the corridor. Jenny stood at the tall window and looked across the frost covered lawns that stretched to New Church Road. Cars and the occasional bus made their way along, carrying people with lives outside the grey stone walls of Aldrington House.

It was Rosemary who was screaming. Her bed was next to Jenny's in a dormitory they shared with four other women. She was married and in her early twenties, and told Jenny she had become depressed after her baby had been born. She said that they had forced her to come here. Jenny wasn't sure who "they" were. Three times a week Rosemary was wheeled screaming into a small side room where wires were placed on either side of her head. She told Jenny that they gave her electric shocks to make her better, but Jenny saw the terrified look on Rosemary's face as the nurses held her arms down to sedate her. When they wheeled her back to their room, she would say her head hurt. Jenny would talk to her, but she couldn't remember things, and Jenny wondered if she would forget that she had a baby. Perhaps that was the idea. For the first two weeks of her stay Jenny had been petrified that she too would be wheeled on a trolley into a side room. She had wondered if that was what Dr McCaffrey had in mind for her – electrical currents to make her forget?

But Jenny wasn't wheeled into a side room. Instead she was given bright blue pills to swallow four times a day and spent her time weaving baskets of various shapes and sizes until she had enough to fill a small florist's shop. She attended relaxation classes, and twice a week would talk to Dr McCaffrey about everything that she had bottled up for years. She looked forward to these sessions, washing her hair, and applying mascara and lipstick before she went into his consulting room. Revealing her feelings and fears for the first time, she became – like his other patients – a little in love with him.

'What on earth are you doing in this loony-bin?' Dido said the first time she visited. 'I couldn't believe it when Mr Winstanley told me. I knew you had a few funny turns, but I thought it was all that studying. You're not mad are you?'

'No, of course not,' Jenny smiled at her friend as she sat on her bed.

'Thank God for that. I can't believe you're in here. I pass it every day on the bus, but I never thought I'd be visiting anyone here, especially a friend,' said Dido.

'It's not that bad. I'm just having a rest away from everything,' said Jenny.

'I didn't think you were that upset about Mike. You went out with Peter soon after, didn't you?'

'It's not just Mike. There were other things.'

'I've brought you some magazines.' Dido looked around the room. 'It looks very boring in here,' she cupped her hand around her mouth, 'what's wrong with that girl next to you?'

'She's depressed. She's just had a baby.'

'Now that I can understand – all those dirty nappies and staying in every night. Guess what? I've handed my notice in, I'm leaving for Wiesbaden at the end of February. You ought to have seen Mr Winstanley's face.

It was like a red balloon about to burst. I think he's quite fond of us really. It was a shock to him, coming so soon after you being on sick leave. That will give you something to get better for. You can come and visit me.'

'Yes, I'd love to.'

Alice visited Jenny every day in the afternoons, staying for about half an hour. Their conversation was stilted, and repeated on every visit.

'I really can't understand why you're in here. What's the point of staying here just to talk to Dr McCaffrey twice a week? You could be at home and still do that. I don't understand it. We're not told anything, after all, you're still under twenty-one, and we are your parents.'

'How's Dad?' Jenny would ask, knowing that he would never set foot inside the building.

'Dad can't understand it either.'

Nine months later Jenny returned to the small office on the third floor. A middle-aged woman wearing a pair of pink horn-rimmed glasses was sitting in Dido's chair. She stood up and offered her hand.

'I'm Mavis, you must be Jenny.'

PART TWO

1

Spring 1967

Mrs Jennifer Maynard – Mrs Jennifer Maynard, it has a ring about it, thought Jenny, smiling at her unintended pun. *I expect I'll get used to it in time.* A colleague had called her Mrs Maynard twice yesterday before she had realised he was talking to her. *This isn't the first time my name's been changed. A new name – a new life.*

Jenny stood up and tugged her mini-skirt down until it sat three inches above her knees and walked over to the sash window. The shower had passed. Below were scattered the red tiled roofs of the county town. They reminded her of a picture from *Grimm's Fairy Tales*. She relished the view. Instead of the sails of the windmill rising above suburban sprawl, there was beyond the roofs, the green turf of uncultivated downland. Between the steep escarpments, the River Ouse glinted in the late April sunshine – like the silver trail of a snail – as it flowed south to the sea.

She had been married to Robert for three weeks. They were renting a one-bedroom flat above a gentleman's outfitters, where square-jawed models in tweed jackets filled the window. A young couple with a baby lived in the flat that fronted the High Street. Jenny remembered when she had knocked nervously on their door to borrow some milk. The noise from the lorries as they trundled under their window, twisting and turning to avoid the medieval buttresses, had filled the room. She had been glad that they had taken the rear flat.

She smiled as she remembered Robert grabbing a sponge cake as he rushed to work earlier that morning. On waking, the closeness of their bodies had quickly led to lovemaking, and he easily dismissed the fact that he had to be at his desk by eight-thirty.

Jenny always called, and thought of him as Robert, although his family and friends called him Rob. She had tried to fall into line, but it just didn't sound right. *He's not a Rob or a Bob*, she had thought, they're too light, too happy-go-lucky. Robert sounded solid. He was her rock – dependable – she felt safe with him. It was fate she had told herself. She had only agreed to go dancing that evening two and a half years ago, because Sue in contributions had asked her. A square-jawed man with light brown hair and a ruddy complexion had stood in front of her as she sat cradling a rum and coke. Eighteen months later they were engaged. When Robert had asked her where she wanted to go to celebrate, she had answered immediately – Edinburgh. It was not too far away, and would be the first of many capital cities they would visit together. Once she had flashed her diamond solitaire in front of her mother, no objections were raised. They consummated their relationship on the night sleeper from Euston. With the security of commitment Jenny relaxed and experienced a pleasure that she was eager to repeat in the small hotel off Princes Street. Any doubts she had assuaged.

Jenny glanced at her watch. Ten o'clock. She moved away from the window and walked into their bedroom. Breathing in, she edged herself around the small gap on either side of the double bed and straightened the crumpled sheet. *Thank God for the pill,* she thought, as she pulled the top sheet over the damp patch on her side of the bed. She straightened the blankets and covered them with the candlewick bedspread – a wedding present from work. Moving the portable electric fire out of the way she surveyed herself in the small mirror that hung above a chest of drawers and combed a wing of dark hair back off her face, glad that she had decided on a shorter style for her wedding. She pulled on a pair of knee-high boots and lifted a suede coat from the hook on the bedroom door. She picked up the car key from the shelf in the hallway and left.

Today was only the second time she had driven the Ford Popular by herself. She was nervous, but bolstered her courage by thinking that the roads shouldn't be busy at this time. She would be fine. Pulling the choke out just far enough, she turned the ignition key. The engine groaned. She tried again, this time pressing lightly on the accelerator, 'Not too hard, not too hard,' she could hear Robert's words. The engine spluttered into life, and the car jerked forward several times, and then steadied. She manoeuvred out of the narrow lane and into the High Street.

Twenty minutes later Jenny reached the road to the Dyke. Below her she spotted the sails of the windmill, and thought how much she was enjoying driving; the freedom to go wherever she wanted. *Perhaps we could drive on the continent later this year, Brussels, Bonn – perhaps Rome? No, that's a capital too far.*

'It's strange to see you arriving by car,' said Alice as Jenny kissed her on the cheek.

'It feels weird to me too.' Jenny also thought it strange to be visiting her parents. Distance – and her new status, combined to make her more confident and comfortable with them.

'Is Robert well?'

'He's fine. Where's Dad?'

'Down the garden, I'll tap on the window, and he'll come up.'

For the past year, Charlie had been suffering from repeated attacks of conjunctivitis due to the high concentration of baking powder dust in the factory. On Dr Marks' advice he had taken early retirement and began gardening with a fervour that no one could have imagined. Before he had only mown the lawns under sufferance, saying that gardening was women's work, along with children, cooking and housework. But the day after he was presented with a gold plated carriage clock, he had walked down the stairs at nine o' clock sharp, pulled on a pair of wellington boots, and didn't climb the stairs again until lunchtime. Seven days a week he followed the same routine. Rain and wind made no difference.

'I'm pleased you're taking Mum in the car. It's still cold outside,' said Charlie. 'The pains have been getting worse lately, but she wouldn't go and see the doc, said she didn't want any hospital appointments 'til after the wedding.'

'It wasn't easy asking for a day off. I've only been at the Brighton office for a week.'

'I hope that husband of yours is looking after you?'

'Yes, he is.' Jenny smiled as she saw the gold plated Eiffel Tower on their mantelpiece next to the carriage clock. She picked it up and turned it in her hand, thinking of their honeymoon; the excitement of the boat train, and then emerging from the Gare de Nord into a different country. As they had sailed down the Seine with the lights of the city like stars flickering around them; Paris had lived up to her expectations.

Jenny twisted her wedding ring around her finger as she waited in the corridor. *It must be my fault that she's ill again. If I hadn't had that breakdown, she wouldn't be here.* She remembered how upset her mother had been, it had shown in her face when she had visited her. It was about a year afterwards that the stomach pains began.

'How did you get on?'

'Oh, he prodded my stomach, asked lots of questions. I'm to have a blood test and barium X-rays. I shouldn't have to wait too long.'

'That's good, I'll treat you to lunch, and then we can collect the photos.'

Jenny flipped the black and white photographs over on the counter. 'They've come out really well, haven't they? I love this one of us getting into the car. It's a pity they don't show the colours though, especially the red roses in my bouquet.'

'The ordinary snaps will. I'm picking them up tomorrow.'

'I think we ought to go back now Mum, I don't want to get caught up in traffic. Robert and I can bring these over on Sunday. We can see yours then, and you can decide which ones you'd like.'

Driving back through the centre of town, Jenny glimpsed the grey walls of Aldrington House. She couldn't believe that she had ever been a patient there, and decided not to come this way again. She wondered how Rosemary was getting on and whether she remembered her.

Well, I've made it back, Jenny thought, as she flopped onto the sofa and checked her watch – four-fifteen; time for another chapter before I need to think about food. She picked up the book on the coffee table… *Bonn – the capital of West Germany lies about twenty-five kilometres south of Cologne on the River Rhine. It was founded by the Romans and the materials used in the original fort were incorporated in the later construction of the city wall…*

'That was lovely Jen, my favourite dinner,' Robert smiled as he carried their plates into the kitchenette, 'just what a man needs at the end of a working week; talking about what a man needs; what about an early night?' He came up behind her as she was lifting the tablecloth and cupped both hands around her breasts. 'Saturday tomorrow, we can take our time,' he whispered, nuzzling the back of her neck.

'Let's have a quick look at the photos first; they've come out really well.'

'Oh, sorry, I didn't ask, how did your mum get on?'

'She's got to have some X-rays. She didn't look too good, though. I said we'd go over on Sunday.' Jenny collected the photographs from the chair by the door and placed them on the table.

'I love this one of us getting into the car. I think we'll get it framed. Look at Dido in this group one, wasn't her outfit fabulous?'

'I didn't take to that guy with her, Ed wasn't it?'

'Jed – he was just a bit brash that's all. Americans can be like that.'

'Yes, think they own the place.'

'They invited us over there. They're really keen for us to visit. I'd love to go. Perhaps we could later this year?'

'I thought we might go on the Settle Carlisle railway.'

'We can do both, Robert, it needn't be for long, we can drive over and stay a couple of days. It will be so exciting.'

Robert went over to the record player on the sideboard and lifted the needle arm, halting Bob Dylan in mid protest.

'Good idea, Mrs Maynard, but I've got an even better one.'

'That's odd. I haven't seen that car before,' Jenny said.

Robert pulled on the handbrake. 'I expect it's to do with a neighbour.'

Jenny slammed the car door and hurried up the garden path carrying the wedding photographs under her arm. Opening the door she glimpsed a pair of long suited legs ahead of her on the stairs.

'It's good of you to come, sir,' she heard Charlie say. 'The missus is in there with Dr Marks.'

Blood drained from Jenny's face. 'What's going on?' She faced her father on the landing. His white hair was dishevelled, and Jenny thought for the first time how old he looked.

'Your Mum's pains have got worse since Friday, doubled up she's been, and vomiting all this black stuff. She can't keep anything down. I had to call the doc yesterday evening. He took one look at her and said he'd ask the consultant to call.' Jenny stared into her father's empty socket. He hadn't even put his eye in.

'Mum saw him at the hospital on Friday.'

'Well let's hope he can do something.'

Jenny stepped back and collided with Robert. They huddled outside the closed bedroom door; straining to hear what was being said inside.

The consultant was the first to emerge, followed by Dr Marks.

'Can I have a few words with you Mr Porter?' Charlie followed the medics into the sitting room. Jenny and Robert remained on the landing, staring at each other.

A few minutes later Charlie said, 'Mum's going into hospital. They're sending an ambulance.'

'What now? I'll go and see her.' Jenny pushed the bedroom door open. Her mother lay propped on three pillows, beads of sweat strung along her forehead.

'Hello dear, this is a right welcome isn't it? We were going to look at the photos today, weren't we?' she managed a smile.

'Don't worry about that Mum. We can do that once you're better.'

'The pains started again on Saturday, but they didn't go away this time, like severe colic. Dr Marks even gave me morphine for the pain. The worse thing is I can't keep anything down…' her voice trailed.

'Get some sleep Mum. I'll make us some tea.'

Two days later Alice woke from the anaesthetic to see the consultant bending benignly over her.

'We found out what the trouble was Mrs Porter.

There was a growth in your bowel that was causing a blockage.' He then added in perfect bedside manner, 'But you're not to worry, it's all been taken away. Unfortunately, we had to remove quite a large portion of the intestine as well. But you'll be fine. Don't worry.' He smiled down at her, patted her on the arm and then moved on to the next patient.

2

September 1967

They travelled by train to Carlisle and spent an uncomfortable night in the valley of a mattress that had seen better days. The next day they bought two return tickets to Settle.

On her return Jenny called on her parents. It had been four months since Alice's operation. She had spent three weeks in hospital, and a further two in a convalescent home that was known locally as the French Home, due to the grey turrets at each end of the building, giving it the appearance of a chateau in the Loire Valley. The nurses wore grey uniforms, and the building had the air of a hospital during the First World War. When Jenny had visited, she half expected to see bandaged soldiers being wheeled in bath chairs.

'You're looking a lot better now Mum.'

'Yes, I'm feeling stronger. It's probably something to do with the bottle of Guinness I've been told to drink each day,' Alice smiled at her daughter, but Jenny thought that she was still painfully thin. She also knew that she had to rush into the bathroom after eating the smallest amount of food.

'So how was your trip?'

'Well it improved as the days went on. The hotel opposite the station was pretty dingy. Robert didn't care though. I've never seen him so excited.' Jenny pictured him as a small boy train-spotting in his cap and gabardine raincoat. 'I enjoyed the train ride. There were some spectacular views from the viaduct, I even saw a merlin.'

'A merlin – isn't that a magician?'

'No,' Jenny laughed. 'It's a bird, they're moorland birds mostly. We don't see them down here.'

'Well I'm glad you had a good time. Make sure you take care tomorrow. They drive on the wrong side of the road over there,' said Alice.

'No the right side,' laughed Jenny.

'These autobahns are amazing,' said Robert.

'Yes, but the other cars go so fast.'

'Well that's what autobahns are for. I wish this car would go faster. Everyone's overtaking us.'

That's true, Jenny thought, but she didn't care, she was thrilled to be anywhere other than England, but could sense Robert's impatience. 'The countryside's so different, isn't it? Those hills are completely covered with forest apart from a few squares of lighter green. The trees are a different shape too, and we've even seen vineyards.'

'Well, it would be different wouldn't it? It's abroad,' said Robert.

'That's why it's so exciting. It was good to visit Bonn though, wasn't it?'

'You and your capital cities, Jen. There wasn't much there, just a load of government buildings.'

'There was the old town. I loved all the architecture, and it was Beethoven's birthplace.' Jenny had to admit that Bonn wasn't the most exciting place on the tourist trail, but how could she have been so near the West German capital and pass it by? She picked up the road map that lay at her feet. 'It's not far to Wiesbaden now, and I can drive again when you've had enough,' she said, offering Robert encouragement. He had been reluctant to come, saying it was too far away, and that he would have preferred to spend longer in the north of England. But, they had agreed to split their holiday, and he didn't break an agreement. He did admit though, that he was impressed by the size of the Rhine, and the amount of river traffic.

Jenny fingered Dido's postcard, re-reading her confirmation that they could stay with her for two nights. She wondered why she now dotted her letter 'i's with circles instead of dots, and decided that it must be because she was mixing with Americans.

'Wow, look at you both, aren't you just the happy couple! I can't believe you've driven all this way in that cute car.'

'It only seems small over here. There are lots of these in England,' Robert retorted.

Jenny hugged her friend noticing that Dido's blonde hair now fell in a smooth bob that turned under at her jaw-line. She thought that she looked even more like a model than before.

'You found me easily then?'

'Well, only because you're just off the main street – *Rheinstrasse*,' Jenny corrected herself.

'Yes, I was so lucky to get this flat. It's easy to get to the base and Marlene's great company. She's from South Carolina, I can't get enough of her accent, and she can't get enough of mine – she says I speak like royalty. She's gone to stay with another friend, so you can have her room.'

'That's really kind of her,' said Jenny.

'Yes, Americans are really friendly, I stayed in accommodation at the base when I first came here and I never once felt homesick. Then last year I heard about this flat, sharing with Marlene. I'd only spoken a few words when she said she'd just gotta have me so she can hear my accent every single day, isn't that a scream?'

'Yes, it is.' Jenny smiled thinking that this could only have happened to Dido. 'Are you still seeing Jed?'

'You bet, he's joining us for a meal later. His leave finishes today so he's got to be back at the base by ten. We know this marvellous beer cellar round the corner. Come on, I'll show you to your room, you must be exhausted, all that way in that tiny car.'

'If she mentions the size of our car any more, I'm going to say something I'll regret,' Robert muttered under his breath as he closed the bedroom door behind them. 'I bet her Ed won't be able to resist a dig either.'

'Jed,' said Jenny.

The four of them sat awkwardly behind overflowing steins of local beer, and on Dido's recommendation ordered pork and sauerkraut.

'So how do you like working in the Brighton office?' asked Dido.

'Well its early days yet, the people aren't nearly as much fun as Hove. But the extra money's useful.'

'Of course you're a clerical officer now, aren't you?'

'Yes, I can actually make decisions of my own, and not keep referring to a higher grade all the time. Mr Winstanley's still at Hove. He'll be there 'til he's pensioned off,' Jenny laughed.

'Until he dies, more like it,' Dido giggled. 'I often think about him. Do you remember how he used to waddle across the road?'

'How could I forget, he still does, I'm sure.'

'Are Peter and Reza still in Hove?'

'No, they both went back to Iran about nine months after you left. They'd finished their courses. I saw Peter once in the Gondola, he told me they were going back. I expect they're both married by now to some second cousin.'

Dido leant towards Jenny and whispered in her ear, 'I really loved Reza, but I knew he wouldn't marry me. That's why I left.'

'Yes, I think I knew.'

'What are you whispering about honey?' Jed licked his lips as he placed his glass on the wooden table.

'Just telling Jenny that I'm crazy about you.'

Jed turned to Robert and grinned, 'That's my girl.'

'So what part of the States do you hail from Ed?'

'My folks live in Kansas, on the edge of a small town, near Wicheta. Have you heard of it?' Jed ran a large hand over his close-cropped fair hair.

'I know where Kansas is. It's the mid-west?' Robert said.

'Yep, corn for miles around. I really miss my folks. I'm hoping to take Dido back with me when I've done my duty.'

Jenny glanced at her friend. She couldn't imagine Dido in Kansas. Jed started talking about Vietnam. Jenny realised that for him and his friends it was much more than a background news item to be heard and then forgotten.

'Some families in Kansas have started tying yellow ribbons around the trees outside their houses while their boys are away. Everyone at the base is saying that more men might be drafted because of the progress of the Viet Cong, and there's going to be a big demonstration against the war back home.'

When he politely excused himself halfway through

their meal, Dido told Jenny that he was really worried that he might be sent to Vietnam; only the day before, he had heard that a school friend had been killed.

They stayed in the beer cellar until nine-thirty. As they were leaving Jed walked over to three off-duty soldiers who were shouting and swearing at the bar, 'Buddies from the base,' he said, as he joined them outside, 'the younger brother of one has been blown up; left both legs in a paddy field.'

'Ed seemed different this evening,' Robert said later as they were getting undressed, 'not at all brash like he was at our wedding. It was a bit of an eye-opener hearing about Vietnam, wasn't it?'

Jenny had given up correcting Robert. 'Yes, it was. I must admit I've never taken much interest before. I'll think about Jed now, whenever I hear it on the news.'

The next day they drove into the countryside. Dido took them on a route along the River Lahn, where they sipped mineral water from a metal cup. Jenny spat hers out, and Robert said it tasted so bitter that if you were ill, the thought of having to drink some would soon make you well again. They stared at the turrets of Marksburg Castle, perched on precipitous slopes above the Rhine, and then drove back to Dido's flat where they feasted on enormous slices of *apfelkuchen*.

'It's been great hasn't it? Just like old times, well almost,' Dido said looking at Robert. She hugged Jenny.

'So you beat me to the altar after all, didn't you?'

'He's right for me – just what I need.'

'I heard that Mike's working in London now. At Lloyd's I think Nick said.'

'So much for Che Guevara, then,' said Jenny.

'What?'

'Oh it doesn't matter.' It was Jenny's turn to hug her friend.

'Drive carefully. I want to see you both again, before I go to Kansas.'

'Not much chance to drive any other way in this car,' Robert muttered as Jenny climbed in beside him.

Jenny continued waving until Dido was a matchstick figure in the distance. She felt sad, and wondered if she would ever see Dido again. She picked the road map off the floor and unfolding it, searched for Berne. She had hoped they might have had time to drive there, but it was too far. They had to be back in Ostend for the ferry the following day. Jenny traced their return route with her finger. *We could stop in Brussels though*. She opened the glove compartment, pulling out a guidebook... *Brussels – the capital of Belgium and the largest urban area. It was founded in the tenth century by a descendant of Charlemagne. Although originally Dutch speaking, the main language is now French...*

Three days later after Alan and his bride had made the first cut into the top tier of their wedding cake, Jenny felt a tap on her shoulder.

'I'm pleased you and Robert could come.' Alan looked genuinely pleased to see her. She thought how much he had changed in the last six years. He was quite fanciable; perhaps it was the well-cut suit and carnation. Alan and Jackie had been at her wedding, but she had been in such a daze, she had no recollection of them ever being there.

'Congratulations, everyone seems to be getting married,' said Jenny, thinking of all the girls she knew who had either been married or engaged in the past year.

'Well, we're all in our early twenties aren't we? Girls are on the shelf if they're not married by twenty-four.'

Jenny thought his words made her sex seem like rows of baked bean cans in the cupboard, patiently waiting to be opened, but all the same, was glad that she was safely married.

'Then there's the tax advantage,' Alan added.

'There speaks a true accountant.'

'How's married life treating you anyway? You look very good on it. It must suit you.'

'Yes it does. We're very happy,' said Jenny, but she wasn't thinking about Robert. She was thinking, as she always did whenever she saw Alan; of being seven years old and in his bedroom at her aunt's house. She wondered if he thought it too. It seemed impossible to see him and not to remember. There had been nothing overtly sexual about their curiosity, but the memory surfaced every time they met, like a cork floating on water that refused to be submerged. Then another thought – they weren't even related, not genetically. They could marry. But Alan, like her other relatives, didn't know that. Only she and her parents knew – secrets that only they shared – like spies. There was a certain thrill at knowing something that other people didn't, and never would, unless she decided to tell them, it made her feel powerful. 'In fact, we've just got back from visiting my friend in Germany.'

'Germany – you always were keen on travelling, weren't you? Remind me, what does Robert do?'

'He's a draughtsman in the county transport office.'

'Look Jenny, I better go. I think the band's about to strike up. I'll catch up with you both later.'

Aunt Doris was enjoying her elevated status as the groom's mother. Uncle Jim had died two years before. Alice said that he had died of nagging. She also said it wasn't decent when Doris re-married a year later; adding that this proved what she had suspected all along. Alan's stepfather was Greek, with a name that ended in opoulos. He had been staying in Doris's house – it was always known as Doris's house even when Jim was alive – as a mature student, staying on long after his course had finished. Watching her new husband twirling her around the dancefloor, Jenny thought that her aunt certainly looked happy.

'You look lovely in that green dress.' Robert put his arm around Jenny's waist as she emerged through the fog of cigarette smoke.

'This outfit's come in really useful with all these weddings.'

'Very attractive, Mrs Maynard,' he stroked her thigh. 'How long do we have to stay here?'

'We can make a move at nine. It will take a couple of hours to get back and drop Mum and Dad off.'

'I don't know if I can wait that long.' His hand disappeared under the hem of Jenny's dress.

'Stop it, Mum and Dad are over there, they'll see you.'

'We are married. Anyway Dad's deep in conversation, he wouldn't notice if we were actually doing it.'

'Deep in India, more like it.' Jenny could see that Charlie had cornered someone by the bar, and could hear that he was treating him to a full description of a visit to the bazaar... 'Small boys were always coming up to you, offering you anything for money. Their sister, or brother if you were that way inclined, anything you fancied for a few rupees... couldn't trust any of them...' *It's so embarrassing, that man's just being polite. Why can't Dad see it?*

'Well, if we can't leave yet, I'm off to the bar, what can I get you?' Robert asked.

'I'll have a gin and orange, please.'

Jenny heard Doris's voice behind her. 'Georgie, come and meet my favourite niece. You didn't have much chance to speak to her earlier. You remember we went to her wedding?'

'Of course I remember.' He lifted Jenny's hand to his lips.

'You must both come up and visit us soon. It will be good to see you on your own now you're married. We've got such a lot to chat about. You could even stay with us overnight. I've had some work done to the house since Uncle died. He was never very keen on change. George has been a marvel. Couldn't do enough for me, could you Georgie?' she said, blowing him a kiss. 'I can inspect your husband properly then.' She turned to Robert as he returned with their drinks. 'Don't worry I don't bite. Come on Georgie,' she grabbed her husband's hand and led him onto to the dancefloor.

'Your aunt's quite a character, isn't she? I like her.'

'She certainly is. Let's join them. I love this record.'

'It must be nearly nine, Jen, let's go,' Robert said, getting up and leaving his third drink half drunk on the table.

Halfway through their journey home from Woolwich, Robert said, 'What do you think about us changing our car, Jen? We could buy a Ford Anglia, the 105 model, it's got four gears. I've been thinking about it ever since we came back from Germany. This journey today has really made my mind up, it's taking forever.'

'What about a Mini? It's more modern and it would match my dress.'

'I've got used to Fords now. I can manage the repairs myself. It will be cheaper than taking it to the garage.'

He put his hand on Jenny's thigh. 'They're asleep,' he whispered, turning his head towards her parents slumped on the back seat.

3

Winter 1963

'What a luxury having a heater at last,' Jenny enthused as they scraped a thin layer of ice from the windscreen, remembering how she had to wrap a tartan blanket over her legs in their Ford Popular.

'And four gears,' Robert added.

Robert's parents lived in a 1930's semi on the northern edge of Brighton. Maggie had suggested that they stay for dinner when Robert had phoned. As they drove up the hill towards their house Jenny wondered why Robert was so keen to show his parents the car. It was dark for God's sake, and he was always saying how unhappy he had been at home. When he had told her that, she had told him about her adoption. She had worried that once he knew he wouldn't want to see her again. So, when on their next date, she spotted him walking towards her, his face breaking into a smile; she decided there and then that she would marry him.

'It's turquoise, but it doesn't look like it under the streetlamp. Look at the bodywork, not a patch of rust on it.' Robert shone a torch along the sills of the car.

'You've got a good one there boy.' Reggie puffed on his pipe.

'I like the interior, it smells lovely. Not as big as Mr Hunt's car though,' Maggie withdrew her head and slammed the passenger door.

Jenny shivered on the pavement, crossing her arms around her body to keep warm and hoping that the inspection would soon be over. 'You do like it then Mum?' Robert threw a concerned look at his mother.

'Yes, but as I said it's not as big inside as Mr Hunt's.'

'His is the four-door model, the A60, that's why.'

Maggie was a tall woman with rosy cheeks and salt and pepper hair piled high on her head. Jenny thought that nothing Robert did seemed good enough for his mother, and wondered if that was why her first husband had disappeared. 'Ran off with a tart; we don't speak his name in this house any more,' Robert said he was told. He had a vague memory of sitting at a window, his father waving at him, as he walked down the path for the last time. He had been brought up by Maggie until he was nine, when he acquired a stepfather, Reginald, and later, a half-brother. Jenny liked Reggie, he was fun and easy going.

'You look a bit pale, Jenny,' said Maggie.

'Just a bit cold, it's freezing outside.'

'Oh, do you think so? I don't feel the cold.' Jenny thought that didn't surprise her, her mother-in-law didn't seem to feel anything. She worked as a receptionist at a doctor's surgery; a strange choice Jenny thought for someone who had no patience with sick people. 'I thought you might have some exciting news for us, coming round in the middle of the week?'

'We have,' said Jenny. 'We're excited about our new car.'

'Come on, let's have our meal,' Reggie said. 'I'm starving.'

Whatever her shortcomings, Jenny had to admit that her mother-in-law was a good cook, her meals were substantial. Two pork chops and the plate piled high with vegetables. She took it as a personal affront if anything was left uneaten. 'That was lovely Maggie, thank you.'

'Do you think Rob's lost a bit of weight?' Maggie looked at Jenny as if waiting for a diagnosis.

'I'm fine Mum,' said Robert.

'Yes, he's fine,' Jenny added.

'He looks better for being a bit thinner. It's healthier at his age,' Reggie said.

'Shouldn't you be promoted soon Rob? Three years is a long time to stay at the same level in local government. If you're not careful you'll remain there. I'm right aren't I Reggie?'

'There's a review shortly, Mum. I'm pretty confident I'll go up a grade. Mr Sutcliffe thinks I've done well since I've been there, and he's the man that counts. David's not here tonight then?' Robert quickly changed the subject.

'Out with his arty-farty friends,' said Reggie.

Robert looked relieved. Jenny couldn't believe that David was even Robert's half-brother. They were complete opposites – in looks and personality. She had noticed that Maggie favoured her younger son – he could do nothing wrong. It was left to Reggie to discipline him.

'He's just enjoying himself, he's only young,' Maggie added.

'Enjoying himself, my arse; at his age I'd been working for four years, and I'd had a haircut.' Reggie rubbed his hand over his shiny scalp fringed with ginger hair. 'Wish I needed one now.'

On their way home Jenny turned to Robert, 'I can't stand how your mother never comes out with anything directly. She always makes me feel uncomfortable. Look what she said about our car not being as big as so as so's.'

'Perhaps I ought to have a word with Mr Sutcliffe tomorrow.'

'No, not yet, wait for the review. As you said, it's not long.'

***

Gail had written to say that although the coming Saturday afternoon wasn't convenient, Jenny could visit the following weekend.

She squinted at the line of faded scraps of paper

next to the doorbells, but couldn't see Gail's name. She checked the house number that had been hand painted on the plastered wall. Gail had told her it was a first-floor flat in a converted house in Buckingham Road. She lifted the brass knocker, slammed it against the plate and waited.

'Jenny, it's so good to see you. It's been so long, come in.'

'We did bump into each other last winter, but you were in a hurry.'

Gail cast her eyes down and quickly turned away. Her dark hair had grown below her shoulders, and was loosely tied back with an elastic band. Her legs were bare and mottled blue under a brown skirt. Jenny thought she looked thinner in the face than the last time she had seen her.

'Come through, I'll put the kettle on, mind the pushchair.'

Jenny followed her friend down a dark musty hallway, past a paraffin heater and into the kitchen. A dingy net curtain half covered the sash window. A little boy jumped out from behind a clothes horse, brandishing a water pistol. A jet of water shot into the air and landed on her head. A little girl toddled over and clutched at the hem of her coat.

'Oh, I'm so sorry,' Gail said, grabbing a nappy from the clothes horse to wipe Jenny's hair.

'That's O.K. Don't worry about it.'

'Put that down Mark. Leave Auntie Jenny alone

Vicky, or she won't come again,' Gail threatened, as she cleared a pile of clothes from a chair. 'Sit down Jenny.'

Mark ran back to hide behind the clothes horse while Vicky, still clinging to her coat, stared up at her with china blue eyes. 'I've brought some presents.' She opened her bag. 'I hope they're O.K?'

'I'm sure they will be. You better give them to them now, or we won't get any peace, they seem to have a sixth sense about presents. It's my mum's fault she always brings something for them when she visits. I've told her not to. What do you say?' She looked at the little boy peeping around the nappies.

Mark whispered a thank you, whilst Vicky stuck her thumb in her mouth.

'So how are you doing Gail? You must be really busy.' Jenny looked behind her as Gail opened the door to a cupboard that hung lopsided on the wall. The shelf was bare apart from a packet of tea, half a packet of biscuits and a bag of sugar.

'Oh, I can't complain. It's hard with the kids of course. I never get a minute's peace, but I wouldn't have it any other way. Take those toys out onto the landing you two, you can play out there.' Gail put the biscuit packet on the table and sat down. 'I'll make some tea in a minute, Jenny. Take your coat off and put it on the chair.'

'Where's Chris?'

'He's down the bookies. He needs a break from the kids.'

'Did you go somewhere nice last Saturday? You said it wasn't convenient.'

'Somewhere nice? Yes we did. We went to Eastbourne on the bus for the day. The kids had a lovely time – there's a really good playground there.' Her face suddenly crumpled. 'Oh Jenny – I can't lie to you, of course we didn't go to Eastbourne, we don't go anywhere. I didn't want to tell you, but I'm so unhappy, if it wasn't for the children.' A tear rolled down her cheek. She sniffed, 'I'm sorry.'

Jenny reached out and patted her friend's arm. Gail sniffed again and reaching for a crumpled tea cloth wiped her cheek. 'Things have got worse since Vicky was born. Chris is out most of the time. He says he feels trapped. I wouldn't mind that so much, but we don't have any money – most weeks he gambles it away as soon as he's been paid – I don't know what to do. If I say anything he gets so angry and hits me, saying it's my fault for getting pregnant,' she sobbed. 'Jenny I'm so ashamed, I feel it's my fault, that's why I couldn't see you last Saturday. We'd had a row the previous weekend and my eye was still swollen. I didn't want you to see me like that.'

Jenny sat stunned. She remembered how relieved Gail had been when Chris had agreed to marry her.

'Chris says he's trapped, but I am too aren't I? Mark and Vicky have to sleep in our bedroom. I can never get away from them. I didn't think it would be as bad as this. The worse thing is that I'm frightened of Chris now. I never know when he's going to lose his temper.

The best I can hope for now is a council house. I wanted so much more than that.'

'Perhaps once they're both at school, you could go back to studying?'

'How could we possibly afford that? Sometimes I have to go without my dinner so there's enough money for Chris and the kids to have theirs. And that's ages away, in the meantime I'm stuck here without any money to do anything, or go anywhere.' More tears fell down her cheek.

'I'm so sorry Gail,' Jenny stood up and hugged her friend. 'I'll come and see you again soon, if you'd like me to?'

Gail nodded and wiped her face. 'That's enough about me, and my problems. Like Chris says, it's my own stupid fault. I'll make us some tea. How are you finding married life?'

'Good. We've just changed our car.' She decided she wouldn't tell her about their trip to Germany.

'Tell me all about Robert then. Oh, by the way my cousin's getting married.'

Jenny remembered that Martin's family had lived next door. 'Does she still live in Hove?'

'Yes, until she gets married.'

Jenny thought there was no point in asking Gail about Martin's family. 'Did you watch *Top of the Pops* last week?' she said, in an effort to cheer her friend.

'Yes I did.'

'Did you know that Spence Bartlett, the lead

guitarist with The Sinners, went to our junior school? He's Spencer Whittaker.'

'No, I didn't. I knew he came from Brighton though. I can't believe it's him. I remember him sitting on his own at the back of the coach; on that day we went to London.'

'I know, you wouldn't believe it was the same person would you?' Jenny said. 'He was tiny and always had a runny nose. He never had any friends, now he's got all those fans. If his life can change so much, yours can too.'

4

Summer 1969

For the third time in ten minutes, Jenny cast her eyes up at the clock on the kitchen wall and willed the hands to move faster. Robert's coming-home time was now unpredictable. His promotion had been later than expected, and he had started to search the situations vacant pages of the *Mid-Sussex Times* when fate intervened. Mr Sutcliffe collapsed and died of a brain haemorrhage. Robert immediately oversaw his projects, and his promotion had been confirmed at Christmas. Jenny thought it was a bad omen – dead man's shoes.

In the New Year they had scraped together the deposit on a two-bedroom terraced house, near the top of the High Street. The walls of the prison loomed large from their small lounge. 'You can catch the bus to Brighton now, instead of the train. It'll save you walking up the hills,' Robert had said.

Jenny beat the batter furiously with a fork, and looked up at the clock again. *It takes him longer to walk home, and he might have had to shelter from the rain. It's no good,*

I'm not making this. I can't concentrate. These sausages are going back into the fridge. We'll have ham salad instead. The front door slammed and she heard Robert say, 'I'm soaking wet Jen, it's pouring down out there.'

Jenny flung herself into his arms. 'Robert, I'm pregnant.'

'Are you sure?'

'Of course I am. I've just come from the doctors. I left work early.'

'That's fantastic!' he said kissing her on her lips. Raindrops slid from his face onto hers. 'You thought you might be didn't you?'

'Yes, but it seemed too soon after I stopped taking the pill.'

'I love you Mrs Maynard, I can start building that train set now.'

'Not so fast, it might be a girl.'

'I don't care. I'll still build it. Quick, who can we tell, your parents?'

'No, let's tell yours first.'

'Are you sure?'

'Yes.'

'Well this is a surprise,' Maggie said as she opened the door.

'Come in, come in, it's pouring down out there,' Reggie said, peering around the door to the lounge.

'Jenny's just had it confirmed Mum. We're expecting a baby. We just had to tell someone.'

'Well, it's not before time, is it Rob? Reggie and I were wondering if you were up to it.'

'For God's sake, Mum.'

Reggie stood behind his wife and winked at Jenny, 'Don't take any notice of Maggie. She's thrilled really, come in and tell us all about it. How are you feeling?'

'Well, I haven't been sick. I was expecting to; just a bit queasy sometimes.'

'Well that's good,' chipped Maggie. 'Remember pregnancy's not an illness, Jenny. It's a natural thing for a woman. You'll be fine.'

'I can't believe that we haven't you told your mum and dad yet,' Robert said two weeks later. 'I'd have thought that you'd want to tell them straight away, even before mine. You didn't even want to visit them last Sunday.'

How could she say that she was afraid to tell them? That she was scared of hurting her mother; of reminding her of what she had lost.

'Of course I want to tell them. I didn't feel well last week. That's why I didn't go over. We'll tell them on Sunday. I'll be three months then.'

'Mum missed you last Sunday,' Charlie lit another cigarette and continued reading the *News of the World*.

Jenny perched nervously on the edge of the sofa and dug her fingernail into her thumb. 'Oh I wasn't very well last week.'

'Probably that stomach bug that's going around,' Charlie said from behind the pages.

'I don't know why you buy that paper, Dad. It's a load of rubbish.'

'It's for the football results.'

'But you know the results. You always take them down on Saturdays.'

'Leave him alone Jen. Don't take any notice of her Dad.'

'Are you better now Jenny? You haven't eaten your biscuits,' Alice asked as she picked up her knitting.

Jenny bit her lower lip. She couldn't put it off any longer. Anyone would think that she was an unmarried mother. 'Yes, I'm fine. I just feel hot. It's so sticky outside. How are you Mum?'

'Oh you know, just the same, always having to dash to the loo. That doesn't improve. I don't suppose it ever will.'

'I think you've put on some weight.'

'Well I try my best, but I have to force myself to eat, because I know I'll pay for it afterwards.'

Jenny drew a deep breath and stared hard at the Eiffel Tower on the mantelpiece. 'Robert and I... We're expecting a baby. It's due next January,' she blurted.

Colour drained from Alice's face and Charlie's paper dropped across his knees. For a second she glimpsed their conflicting emotions.

'That's wonderful news – congratulations.' Charlie stood up – the sheets dropping to the floor – and went over to the bureau. He pulled the cork from a bottle of sherry and filled four glasses. 'Congratulations to both of you.' He raised his glass.

'Yes, that's lovely news,' Alice added, putting her knitting aside. She stood up, went over to the sofa and gave Jenny a hug.

I could ask them now, Jenny thought, remembering what the doctor had said when he had confirmed her pregnancy. *'Do you have any family history of pregnancy problems?'*

'I don't know; I'm adopted,' she'd replied feeling embarrassed, and had watched as he scribbled on her notes.

She should ask them now if they knew anything about her birth parents. It was the right time. But she couldn't form the words, and the moment passed.

Jenny stood in the toilet cubicle and panicked at the scarlet stain on her knickers. 'Oh no!' she cried and left work immediately. The pains started as she walked alongside the prison walls towards their house.

Later that evening, their doctor stood at the end of their bed holding a kidney dish and examined the expelled contents of Jenny's uterus. 'I'm afraid you've lost the baby Mrs Maynard. I'm so sorry, but you're both young. You can try again in a couple of months. There's no reason to think it will happen again.'

Jenny lay in bed and cried for three days. Robert comforted her by making endless cups of tea, and repeating the doctor's words every time he entered their bedroom. Jenny thought back to Alan's wedding, when she had held her cousin Leslie's baby. At first it had felt awkward as she tried to manoeuvre him into position; and he made her arms ache. But as she stared at him, his eyes scrunched shut, a desire for a child of her own had swept over her like a tidal wave. She remembered wondering if it was a biological trick played on women to make them reproduce once they had caught their man. She had pleaded with Robert for a child. 'Don't be ridiculous Jenny,' he had said. 'We don't want a baby; we've only been married six months. We agreed we would wait two years.' Her desire had vanished with their normal routine, until now.

On the fourth day Robert said, 'Jen, shall I bring the radio in? It's fantastic, Apollo 11's about to re-enter the atmosphere. I've been listening in the kitchen. It might take your mind off things.'

'Things, things, what do you mean things?' she yelled. 'We've just lost our baby, for Christ's sake. Go away – I don't want to listen to the radio. I don't care about a man on the bloody moon.'

5

Summer 1970

'I'm going to die!' Jenny shouted, as she panicked and gripped the nurse's hand. 'I'm splitting apart. Where's Robert? He's left me to die in agony. He should be here.' A circle of light glared down from the ceiling of the delivery suite, obliterating the difference between day and night.

'You're not going to die, Mrs Maynard. Push down hard as you can with the next contraction. Baby is almost here.'

'I can't!' Jenny screamed at the midwife.

'Good, good. Now with the next contraction I want you to pant, don't push. Baby's head is almost out. Don't push.'

She was whole again. New life slithered between her legs and a cry filled the room.

'It's a girl, Mrs Maynard, here she is.' The midwife dangled a squirming grey infant in front of her. She lifted her fob watch and called across to the nurse. 'Ten minutes to midnight.' We're just going to weigh her and clean her up for you.'

'Is she alright?'

'She looks fine.'

'Can you tell Robert... my husband?'

'Yes, the nurse is just going to tell him. Once you've delivered the after-birth he can come in.'

Jenny's earlier accusations melted away as Robert walked into the delivery room. 'It's a girl.' Jenny smiled, 'It's a girl. I'm so happy.'

'I've just seen her, Jen, she's beautiful.' He took his wife's hand and kissed her on the forehead. 'You're marvellous.'

'You can stay until the doctor comes,' said the midwife. 'We're taking baby to the nursery now.'

Ten minutes later a doctor entered the room. Jenny thought he looked as if he hadn't slept for a week. But worse than that, he looked the same age as herself. He hoisted one of her feet, and then the other, into the stirrups, settled himself between her legs and began to sew.

'Wake up Mrs Maynard, wake up, baby needs her feed.' A nurse shook Jenny gently on her shoulder.

Jenny squinted and rubbed her eyes. She turned to where the words were coming from, then closed her eyes and turned over. Who was this? Where was she? She had been in a pethidine-fuelled dream – chasing an old woman down Oxford Street.

'Come on Mrs Maynard, wake up; your baby needs you.' Another shake of her shoulder, more insistent this time. 'You must wake up. Sit up and make yourself comfortable. Place one pillow across your lap to support baby.' The nurse passed her the white bundle and helped the baby to latch onto her nipple. 'Your milk hasn't come through yet, but it's important for baby to suckle. There, she seems to have got the hang of it. I'll come back in fifteen minutes.'

Jenny stared down at the red squashed face. *She's mine. The first person I've seen who's related to me. She just looks like a baby though, any baby.* She had imagined that she would feel immediate love for her baby, but she didn't; just enormous relief. She couldn't lift her eyes from her daughter as she nuzzled her breast. Her heart beat faster as she wondered, *is she alright?* She remembered her miscarriage and how much she had worried during this pregnancy. Perhaps it had damaged her? Suppose she had inherited some abnormality? Did she ask the midwife if she was alright last night? She couldn't remember. Her heart continued to thud against her ribs, as she unwrapped the white hospital cotton that swaddled her child. She counted the number of toes on each foot and then the fingers on each hand. She peered hard at her rosebud mouth, her tiny nostrils. She ran her hand over the soft dark hair until she reached the fontanelles, where she lifted her hand in panic. *Surely it shouldn't be like that.* She turned her baby over, and scanned the tiny body. Satisfied, she swaddled her in the sheet.

'How are you getting on?' The nurse stopped at the bottom of Jenny's bed.

'I think she's feeding alright.'

The nurse peered over and adjusted the position of the baby's mouth.

'That's better, hold her closer to you. Don't be afraid of her, she won't bite – well she might later.' She laughed out loud.

'Nurse, what are those red marks on her eyelids and the back of her neck?'

'Stork bites, we call them. They're nothing to worry about. Lots of babies have them. They'll fade completely in a few months.'

'I'm frightened to touch her head, it's much softer than I expected.'

'That's perfectly normal, you'll get used to it. The bones will gradually close over the next three months, she's fine. Now, you carry on a little longer, I'll come back in five minutes and take her back to the nursery, so you can get some sleep.'

'I've fed her twice already,' Jenny beamed at an enormous bouquet of mixed roses as Robert arrived at the side of her bed.

'I'm so proud Jenny. I've just seen her again through the nursery windows. The nurse held her up for me, she's beautiful.' He bent down and kissed Jenny on the forehead. 'How are you feeling?'

'Sore, I think the pethidine's wearing off.'

'I couldn't sleep last night with excitement. I've brought your mum and dad over with me. They're just giving us some time on our own first. What shall I do with these flowers?'

'Leave them at the end of my bed. The nurses will put them in water later.'

Jenny spotted her father's hair; then the small frame of her mother. She was looking forward to showing them her baby, but this was tempered by the thought that she would always remind them of their own loss, especially when they saw them together. At least they hadn't had a boy, she thought.

'We've been down to the nursery to see her Jenny, she's gorgeous. You forget how tiny they are.' Alice gave her daughter a hug and sat down on a chair by her bed.

Jenny smiled with relief.

'So how does it feel to be a dad?' Charlie slapped Robert on the back. 'We must wet the baby's head, when you come over.'

'I've brought the matinee outfit I was knitting. It'll probably be too large, but she'll soon grow into it.' Alice smiled broadly. 'I've told all the neighbours, Aunt Doris and everyone else. We're grandparents now like them. We'd better not stay long dear, you must be tired.'

'Yes, I am, but there's no need to go, not just yet.'

'It wasn't too long a labour was it?'

'Twelve hours – long enough.'

'Have you decided on a name?'

'Only Nicholas, we were convinced it would be a boy,' said Robert.

'I was named after my mother, she was Alice Beatrice.'

'I don't think we'll be calling her Jennifer, Mum. I'll have a think about it after you've gone.'

Jenny dozed fitfully. When she woke, the nurse suggested that she take a bath. Slowly lowering herself from the bed, she reached inside the cabinet for her wash-bag, and shuffled along the polished floor to the bathroom. She peered into the mirror above the wash basin, and ran a comb through her shoulder-length hair. 'That's better.' Turning the bath taps she inched her nightdress up and over her head. She looked down at the folds of her stomach that resembled a large deflated balloon. *My God, I still look pregnant. I can't stay like this surely?*

At seven o'clock Robert returned with his parents in tow.

Maggie kissed Jenny on her forehead. 'Congratulations dear, we've just seen her. She's lovely, but she's quite small isn't she?'

'She's two weeks early, that's why,' Jenny said.

'I always think it's best to have a boy first. It's the natural order of things. Mind you as long as she's healthy, that's the most important thing.'

'Of course it is Maggie.' Reggie passed a chair to his wife and raised his eyebrows at Jenny. 'What are you going to call her then?'

'We haven't decided yet. We had a name for a boy but not a girl,' said Robert.

'I quite like Lorna,' said Jenny.

'Lorna Margaret. They go well together, don't they Reggie?'

Not if I can help it, thought Jenny.

'We'd better not stay too long Mum; we don't want to tire Jen. She's already had her mum and dad visit.'

'You're not too tired, are you Jenny? Women in Africa have their babies behind a bush and then carry on working straight afterwards, don't they Reggie?'

Jenny thought women in Africa would probably prefer to work after giving birth, if they knew that Maggie was going to visit them.

'We've got something at home for the baby, Jenny. It might be a bit on the big side though.'

'Babies do grow Mum, I'm sure it will be fine,' Robert said.

The sister rang the bell to mark the end of visiting time, and they turned and waved as they reached the end of the ward. Jenny sank down into the pillows. She looked across at the girl in the bed opposite. She was still lying under the bed covers. She hadn't had any visitors all day and there were no cards or flowers on her bedside table. She cried every time her baby was brought to her. Then once the baby was fed, she slipped back under the blankets again. *Perhaps I'll talk to her tomorrow. It must be terrible to be surrounded by happy families,* Jenny thought. *She might not want to talk to anyone, though. She might want to shut everything out.* She wondered if her own mother had felt like this girl – surrounded by families when she had no one. She wondered where she had been born – in a hospital – at home? A hundred years before it would probably have been in a workhouse. She thought of poor, fated Fanny Robin, struggling up the street in Casterbridge to knock on the union door. Tess, sweet Tess, gave birth to Alec's baby in rural Wessex. Both babies had died. In Fanny's case, the mother too – birth, death and loss – inextricably linked. Hardy had known all about unmarried mothers. Most people know where they were born; the time and day of the week – *Monday's child is full of grace* – the rhyme played in her head. She thought of her own newborn daughter lying in the nursery – *a Thursday child* – she felt proud. *Lorna Katharine sounds lovely. I'll see what Robert thinks tomorrow.*

Jenny waited until the girl in the bed opposite had returned from the bathroom.

'Hello, I'm Jenny, from over there.'

'I know, I saw your husband when he brought you those flowers, they're lovely.' She didn't look at Jenny but continued to stare straight ahead. 'I'm Jane.'

'Have you got a boy or a girl?' asked Jenny.

'Girl.'

'Have you named her yet?'

'I've called her Andrea Jane.'

'That's a nice name. Mine's a girl too; but we haven't decided on a name yet. Well I have, I like Lorna, but my husband's got to like it too.'

'I hate it here. I can't wait to get back to the mother

and baby home. The other girls are really supportive, they understand. I'll be there for another six weeks, while they find…' she didn't finish the sentence.

'It must be hard for you in here.'

'Yes, it is, terrible. The other girls said it would be hard, but it's worse than they said. I've just got to get through this week as best I can, like they did.'

Jenny searched for something to say. 'Well, if you feel like talking, come over, any time. I'm here 'til the end of the week too.'

But Jane was already sliding down between the sheets.

The remaining days passed quickly. The new mothers settled into the routine of feeding, changing and bathing their babies. With each day that passed Jenny understood the pain that Jane must be feeling. No wonder she wanted to hide herself away.

'Ready then?' Robert beamed at his wife as she finished dressing Lorna Katharine in her white matinee jacket and bonnet. They stood back and admired their daughter as she lay on her back asleep; her arms above her head. Jenny reached into her case for the shawl that her mother had crocheted, and gently wrapped it around Lorna.

'Are you all packed and ready Mrs Maynard?' the nurse said as she came over to them. 'Let me carry baby for you.'

Jenny looked across the ward. Jane's covers were

thrown back. *She must be in the bathroom*, Jenny thought. She wouldn't be able to say goodbye to her; but perhaps she didn't want her to.

The three of them walked out of the ward, along the corridor, and into the car park.

'If you get in, and make yourself comfortable, I'll pass baby to you,' said the nurse.

Jenny settled herself in the passenger seat. As Robert sat behind the wheel, he turned and kissed her. 'I can't tell you how proud and happy I am.'

'Me too,' Jenny beamed.

The nurse placed Lorna in Jenny's arms. 'Here she is dear, good luck. Don't forget your six week check-up will you?'

Later Jenny wondered why they couldn't have carried Lorna down to the car themselves. Robert had carried her case, so she could easily have carried her. She mentioned it to another mother at the baby clinic who told her, 'The nurses always carry the baby out. It's in case you suddenly get cold feet and abandon the baby at the hospital.'

6

June 1981

The smell of burnt toast wafted into the dining room.

Jenny dropped her pen and ran into the kitchen. She pulled the grill pan onto the drop door and grabbing a kitchen towel smothered the flames that were licking up the sides of the charcoaled bread. 'Too late,' she sighed.

Glancing out of the kitchen window she saw Lorna and Nicky racing around the tent that Robert had erected on the back lawn for the spring bank holiday. Jenny smiled and thought, not for the first time, how much more fun it must be to have a brother or sister to play with. She went over to the bread-bin and picked up another slice of homogenised white bread.

An hour later she looked at her watch and closed the study manual. Two years ago she had decided that being a silver service waitress at the Greyhound Stadium had been fine while the children were small, but she needed more of a challenge. She had toyed with the idea of studying for a degree in travel journalism, but had settled for the more prosaic and cheaper course of accountancy and law. It had proved a good choice. Three days a week, she would drive along the ridge of the Downs towards Ditchling Beacon. Halfway along, at the end of a rutted track, sat a detached pink-washed house – the home of Celia, a reclusive fabric designer. Jenny would spend her first half-hour there, trying to find unopened invoices and delivery notes, which were always stuffed behind cushions, and hidden away in drawers as soon as they were received. She looked on it as a game of hide and seek.

Jenny opened the kitchen door and looked around the garden. There was no sign of the children. 'Can you come in now, wherever you are, it's time to go,' she shouted. Lorna poked her head through the tent flaps. 'Come on, we'll be late. Granny will be waiting. Lorna, if you come, Nicky will too.' *Why can't they ever do anything the first time I ask?* 'Lorna.'

A girl of about ten years ran up the concrete steps to the kitchen, wiped her feet on the mat and looked up at her mother. 'What's for lunch?'

'I told you earlier, we're having lunch at Granny's. I expect she's making her special chicken soup.'

'Can I take my Princess Diana doll?'

'Of course you can. Just go back and get Nicky.' Lorna was the image of Robert; the same square face framed by straight light brown hair, and hazel eyes that always seemed to be judging her. She had expected her daughter to look like her. Nicky, two years younger, had inherited her dark wavy hair and green eyes. *Two miniature Roberts*, she thought, *would be one too many*.

Jenny took her eyes off the road and looked round, 'Stop fighting in the back, will you. Give Nicky his Action Man.' It was a miracle that she hadn't been involved in an accident. However short the journey, it was impossible for her children to sit in the back seat without squabbling. 'Look there's the windmill,' Jenny said in an attempt to stop them arguing. She drove past her parent's flat to where fields met the estate. Turning the Morris Minor around, she doubled back, and parked outside.

'There's Granddad,' Nicky shouted. Her father was on a step-ladder hammering nails into the brick wall that formed a back-drop to the front garden.

'Now go quietly. Don't shout or Granddad might fall. He doesn't know we're here.'

'Granddad, we're here. I've brought my Princess Diana doll to see you,' Lorna shouted as she ran up the concrete path.

Charlie turned, wobbled and steadied himself on the top of the steps. 'So you have. There's my girl. Just let me just finish tying up these roses and I'll be down. The door's on the latch.'

'Go inside and see Granny both of you, I'll stay with Granddad.' Jenny stared at her father's bare arms as he tied green string around the pink papery blooms. *His muscles have disappeared*, she thought, remembering how he used to puff with pride, when he would pull his shirt sleeves above his elbows, so that she could feel the solid lumps that had a life of their own. 'Make them wobble,' she used to say, and would watch transfixed as they danced.

'The garden's looking lovely today Dad, especially those roses.'

'The thorns are little buggers on these climbers. I have to be careful.'

'You mustn't overdo it. I bet you've been down here since nine.'

'Tell Mum I'll be up in five minutes.'

'I can't see the house-martins this year,' said Jenny looking around at the houses opposite. 'They always used to build their nests under the eaves of the house at the end of the road.'

'I don't think they've been here for a few years now.'

'That's such a shame. I loved to see them. I'll see you upstairs then, Dad.'

A few months earlier, Charlie had been admitted to hospital for investigations.

'It's nothing to worry about; everyone's got a bad cold this winter,' he told both Alice and Jenny in turn.

Alice had visited Charlie every other afternoon and Jenny would visit in the evenings. The day before he was due to be discharged, she had strolled into the ward as usual, when the ward sister poked her head around her office door.

'Mrs Maynard?'

'Yes.'

'I was hoping you would come tonight. May I have a word?' She closed the door behind them. 'As you know your father's going home tomorrow. The pleurisy's completely cleared.'

'Yes, that's good,' Jenny said.

'What would we do without antibiotics? There's just one thing. The X-rays showed a small growth on his left lung.'

Jenny stared at her. She had a squint, which Jenny tried to ignore. 'A growth – you mean cancer?'

'Yes, but you're not to worry. We find that in elderly patients it's very slow growing. Your father will probably die of something else before it grows large enough to affect him. It was probably that that caused the pleurisy. He's a heavy smoker isn't he?'

'Does he know?' She couldn't decide which eye to focus on.

'No, as I said it's very slow growing. There's nothing to be gained by telling him, but, as his daughter, you should know. I understand your mother's not a well woman.'

'No, she isn't. Thank you for telling me.'

'Hello Mum.' Jenny planted a kiss on her mother's forehead. 'How are you?'

'All the better for seeing the children; look at them, they love making pastry.'

'You've got more patience than me with them.'

'Granny's made her special soup for us.' Nicky wiped the back of his hand across his nostrils leaving a moustache of self-raising flour on his upper lip.

'I told you she would, didn't I?' Jenny smiled at her son. During school terms she would visit her parents most Sundays. Robert would usually come too, unless there was a model train exhibition within driving distance. She knew how much they looked forward to seeing their grandchildren, and it made her feel good to see them happy. Since the day she had brought Lorna home from the hospital, she had hardly thought about her adoption. Occasionally, she would read an article in a magazine, but her attention was soon diverted. In 1975 she read that a law had been passed that enabled adopted adults to be given information about their birth families. She had read the article with a detachment that surprised her, and promptly used the sheet to wrap up the vegetable peelings.

'Can we get down now?' Lorna was half off the chair already.

'What do you say?' said Jenny

'Thank you for the soup Granny.' Lorna grabbed her doll from the table and ran out of the kitchen.

'Can I see your medals Granddad?' asked Nicky.

'You can see your Great-Granddad's too if you wipe your fingers. He was a soldier in the First World War.' Charlie smiled and led Nicky by the hand into the bedroom.

'I see someone's moved into the flat next door, Mum.'

'Yes, an unmarried mother and her baby. That's council policy now. Once the decent families move away, they put *those* girls and their babies in these flats. We get men coming round at all hours of the day and night. I expect there'll be one in here when we've gone.' Alice's mouth set in a tight line.

Jenny stared at the check tablecloth. She hated it when her mother spoke like that. It wasn't the words, but her tone; it made her feel uncomfortable, as if it was a slight on herself.

'Look what Granddad's given me.' Nicky burst into the kitchen flourishing a brass button, 'It's got an elephant on it.'

'So it has.' Jenny stared at the button.

'It used to be on my uniform. Our regimental badge had an elephant on it too. I've got more, he can keep that one. Where's Lorna? It's time for some capital cities.'

'She's in the sitting room Dad.'

'India,' Charlie's voice carried into the kitchen.

'New Delhi,' Lorna answered.

'Kenya.'

Then Nicky's voice, 'Nairobi.'

'Shut-up, I'm doing this with Granddad not you.'

'Hey Lorna, don't push him,' Charlie said, and started coughing.

'Jenny, I'm just going to lie down for a bit,' said

Alice. 'I'm exhausted once I've prepared lunch, what with this pain in my side as well. I suppose I'll have to go to the doctor.'

'You haven't coloured your hair lately Mum.'

'No, I can't be bothered anymore. It can stay grey now.' Alice put both hands on the table to ease herself from her chair, and disappeared into her bedroom. She returned almost immediately carrying a brown envelope. 'I want you to look after this for me.'

'What is it?'

'It's just some money that I've saved from our pensions.'

'Can't you keep it here? You might want to go on holiday somewhere.'

'Well if we do, I'll ask for it. We're not getting any younger and I don't want anything to happen to it. Put it in your bag.'

'I think Dad's lost some weight. Is he alright?'

'You know your Dad, he never says much. All he says is, "don't worry Gal. Old soldiers just fade away."'

'Does he cough a lot?'

'No more than usual.'

'You go and rest Mum. I'll do the clearing up.'

'Look, what I've found,' Lorna ran into the kitchen holding a book that Jenny recognised from her childhood.

'I loved that book; especially the pictures of the lions and elephants. I haven't seen it for ages.'

'Can I take it home?'

'No – leave it here. You can look at it when we come over then.'

'You know what a cheetah is, don't you?' Charlie had recovered his voice which echoed through the flat.

'Yes, you told me last time Granddad. It's the fastest animal in the world.'

'Good boy. Well when I was in India this Maharaja – that's an Indian prince – had two of them. He would take them for walks on a lead just like dogs. They were so tame. Then one day my bull terrier Major…' Jenny poured the washing up water away and went into the sitting room.

'Come on you two, we have to get back.' Nicholas and Lorna were sitting on either side of Charlie on the sofa. Nicky's eyes shone like polished emeralds as he looked up at his grandfather.

'No, I don't want to go. Why do we have to go back? It's too soon. I want to stay here. I want to hear another story about India.'

'Go on son; do as your mother says. I'll tell you another one next time.'

Jenny stared out of the kitchen window into the garden; she had planned to finish her homework once they were home, but she couldn't concentrate. Lorna and Nicky were careering around the tent pretending to be Red Indians. Lorna usually refused to be drawn into Nicky's games, but was hollering louder than her brother. Jenny hoped that her neighbours were out. A pair of blue tits ignored the noise as they flew to and fro to the nest box that she had attached to the plum tree. Jenny was worried. She was sure that her father had lost weight, and her mother had a yellowish tinge to her skin that she hadn't seen before. She went over to the kitchen chair, reached inside her handbag and felt the brown envelope. She could feel the notes inside. Her mother had said it contained money, but it might also have information about her. She decided she'd better not open it as she might have to give it back. Taking the envelope upstairs she opened the linen cupboard and sandwiched it between two tea towels advertising the charms of Guernsey. Returning to the kitchen she made herself a cup of tea and sat at the kitchen table flicking through a *Cosmopolitan* magazine. "You too can have multiple orgasms". The heading jumped out at her, above the soft focus picture of a glamorous woman with parted lips showing perfect teeth. As she read the article she thought that Robert would say it had been written by a bra-burning lesbian. He always said that whenever he saw the magazine. Perhaps he felt threatened. She wondered why she bothered to buy it – as most of the articles didn't seem relevant to her life.

'Well they are getting on a bit, aren't they?' said Robert.

'Mid-seventies isn't old; not these days.' Jenny cleared the remains of their dinner onto a sheet of newspaper.

'Well they've had their three score years and ten.'

'You wouldn't be so blasé if we were talking about your parents,' Jenny said, thinking that Maggie was never ill. She would probably live to be over a hundred.

'Of course I'm concerned. I'm just trying to make you feel better.'

'Well you're not doing very well, are you?' Jenny turned and shouted as the lid fell on the waste bin. She picked up her magazine, went into the dining room and poured herself a glass of *Liebfraumilch*. She knew what Robert would do now. He would go down into the basement and play – although he would dispute that word – with his model railway. The room resembled an underground version of Clapham Junction. Then precisely one hour later – there was obviously a station clock down there somewhere – he would emerge. Jenny went into the lounge. Shrieks of laughter rippled down the stairs. If she was lucky she would have half an hour to relax before she had to gather all of her strength, and persuade Nicky that it was bedtime. She flicked over the pages until she arrived at the headline "What Men Want". *Why am I reading this?* she thought, after scanning the first paragraph. *Do I care what men want?* She couldn't imagine Robert reading an article headed "What Women Want".

7

August 1981

'Dad's agreed to come and stay with us, so you don't have to worry.' Jenny leaned forward on her chair and patted her mother's hand.

'He says he does himself a meal when he gets back, but I know he doesn't bother. He's always been the same – rather go hungry than cook for himself,' Alice sighed and seemed to disappear as she sank back into the pillows.

On a stand above Jenny's head dangled a polythene bag of blood labelled "A negative", broadcasting her mother's blood group to the ward. Jenny avoided looking at it, thinking that what flowed into her mother's veins was a private matter.

'I'll be out of here soon, Jenny. I felt so much better after the last transfusion.'

Jenny looked across the ward. 'I can't get used to seeing men in here, Mum. It feels – wrong somehow.' Jenny averted her eyes as the man in the bed opposite tried, with some difficulty, to manoeuvre his legs over the side of his bed.

'I'm too tired to care Jenny.'

'It's hot outside. Lorna's going to the Isle of Wight for a week tomorrow with the Brownies. She was up at six today packing. Do you remember when you and Dad took her there for the day? She never stopped talking about it.'

'Yes, it was a good day,' Alice sighed again.

'I've left Nicky at the flat. So when I collect him, I can help Dad pack a few things.'

'It's a good job you had your holiday at the end of July.' Alice's eyelids began to droop.

'Yes, it was,' Jenny had thought the same herself.

'When do they… go back to… school?' Alice's voice trailed.

'Two more weeks yet,' Jenny replied, but her mother was asleep.

'Take a seat Mrs Maynard.' The doctor sat down behind his desk. 'Your mother's done very well. It's been twelve years since her operation?' He looked down at the file on the table, and then peered over the rim of his glasses which had slipped down his nose.

'Yes, I think the grandchildren keep her going.'

'I'm sure you're right. But I'm afraid the cancer's spread to her liver and there's nothing further we can do surgically, but we can keep her comfortable. The transfusions are helping with her anaemia, so she shouldn't feel so tired.' He pushed his glasses over the bridge of his nose.

Jenny wished that she hadn't asked to see him, but there was never a doctor around at visiting times.

'We'll keep her here until there's a vacancy at Copper Cliff. I expect you've heard of it – the nursing home in Withdean?'

Jenny's heart raced, she was no longer listening. Of course she'd heard of it – everyone had – 'You know she's gone to Copper Cliff, don't you?' The news was always conveyed in hushed tones and the response would be a nod and a solemn face.

'Don't worry. We'll make sure that her pain is controlled.' He wriggled his nose in an effort to keep his glasses from slipping back down, got up, walked around his desk and rested a hand on her shoulder. 'I'm sorry it's bad news.'

Jenny's footsteps echoed along the long hospital corridor and reverberated inside her head. Robert was waiting outside. 'She's dying Robert,' Jenny broke down as she sat in the passenger's seat. 'What am I going to tell Dad?' she sobbed.

Robert pulled her towards him and hugged her. 'You don't have to say anything Jen. I'm sure he knows.'

'You think so?' she sniffed.

'Yes, I do.'

Jenny looked up and searched the azure sky. *The swifts have gone*, she thought, wishing that she could just see one – a straggler from up north – but the sky was empty apart from a lone seagull and the vapour trail of a plane.

That's it for another year. They're probably in the South of France now, screaming over the gite we rented. When they're here, everything seems alright with the world, now...

She lingered in the shade of a horse-chestnut tree that fronted Preston Manor House. When they had first moved to Brighton, she had missed living close to the Downs, but now, she couldn't envisage living anywhere else. Stepping back into the late afternoon heat she crossed the main London to Brighton road to a small corner supermarket. Emerging with a bulging carrier bag she decided that as it was still early, she would walk along to the rockery. She sat on a wooden bench in the shade. Opposite, half a dozen stepping stones bridged a large irregular-shaped pond containing at least a dozen overfed goldfish. A small boy was jumping from stone to stone. Every time he landed he turned to his mother and shouted, 'Look at me!'

Jenny wondered what she was going to tell Lorna and Nicky. They knew their Granny was ill, but assumed it was only a matter of time before she was better. They kept asking when she was going home.

'I want to stay here!' the small boy screamed. Jenny stood up, thinking that she had enough screaming children at home. She crossed the main road and passed a hollow elm tree, one of a pair that had seeded and grown for centuries. *They've seen so many things*, she thought, *our lives are so short in comparison.*

Crossing the road from the park, she spotted Nicky

waving at her from outside their front gate. She smiled and waved back. As she walked nearer she heard him.

'Mummy, quick, it's Granddad. He's fallen over.'

Jenny ran towards their gate and dropped her shopping on the tiled path. 'What do you mean?'

'Quick, he's fallen over. Lorna's with him.'

Jenny ran through the open door, along the hallway and into the kitchen. Her father was lying at the bottom of the concrete steps that led down from the side door to the back garden.

'Thank God you're back. It's my leg. It's painful when I try to move it.'

'Well don't move it then. What on earth were you doing?'

'I was going to mow the lawn while you were out. I missed my footing that's all. Can I have my cigarettes?'

'Lorna, go and get Granddad his cigarettes, and the matches. For God's sake Dad, you didn't have to do that. Robert will do it at the weekend. I'll have to phone for an ambulance now.'

'Course you won't woman. There's no need for that. Just help get me up.' Jenny took one arm, while Charlie gripped the railing with the other arm. 'It's no good,' he puffed. 'I can't put any weight on the bugger.'

The accident and emergency doctor strode over to Jenny. 'I'm afraid your father's broken his femur. He'll need an operation. Hopefully, we can fit him in tomorrow.'

Jenny stared at the specks of blood on his white

coat, and hoped they weren't her father's. 'Oh no, my mother's seriously ill.'

'I'm sorry, but he has to stay in. I'll ask the nurse to get you some tea. You can go and see him now. Stay as long as you want.'

'Mummy, why has that girl got bandages around her wrists?' Nicky tugged at Jenny's arm.

'Shh, not so loud, I don't know. Go and get a comic.'

8

September 1981

The nursing home stood in the shadow of a hangar of beech trees. Jenny carried a bunch of orange gladioli up the carriage drive and pushed the doorbell. Alice had been admitted a week ago, and Jenny had visited every day with Charlie. But today she was alone.

Her heart sank as she crossed the polished hallway and climbed the sweep of stairs to the first-floor bedroom. Opening the door she thought that her mother was asleep so laid the flowers on her bed, and stepped over to the large bay window. The manicured lawn was surrounded by neat borders filled with late summer blooms. She thought how her mother would have loved the garden. It was unfair that she was only here when she was too ill to enjoy it.

'Hello dear.'

Jenny turned, 'Hello Mum, I thought you were asleep. I've brought your favourite flowers,' she said picking them up. 'I thought they would remind you of your garden.' She kissed her mother on her cheek, feeling the bone through her paper thin skin.

'They're beautiful.'

Jenny noticed her pupils, they were like pinpricks. *Is that the morphine? Should I tell her about Dad's accident? She must wonder why he isn't here.*

'You look comfortable, Mum.'

'Mmm… I am.'

'You're not in any pain are you?'

'No, not now, they're giving me injections.'

'Good,' Jenny said, thinking that her mother sounded hoarse.

'You can sit on the bed. They won't mind.'

'I'll change the flowers.'

'No, leave them for now,' her voice became stronger. 'Sit here for a moment.'

Jenny's heart raced as she thought she was going to ask why she was on her own.

'You must go and see if you can find your father.'

'I thought I'd give Dad a break this evening,' Jenny said, glad that she didn't have to lie.

'No, no.' Alice moved her head from side to side on the pillow.

What does she mean? I'll have to tell her about the accident now.

'No Jenny – your real father,' she rasped.

'What! You don't need to say anything about that, Mum. I don't want to talk about it.'

'He was from Africa.'

'Africa!' Jenny stared hard at her mother. 'Africa? What are you talking about?'

'South Africa, he was from South Africa. He was a soldier.'

'I'm not interested Mum. I never will be. You and Dad are my parents.'

Her mother's lips lifted at the edges, and she closed her eyes.

Jenny remained seated on the bed, staring at her mother until her heart slowed, then picked up the vase of carnations – their blooms browning around the edges – from the bedside table. She refilled the vase from the wash basin, arranged the gladioli, positioning them so that her mother could see them and sat by the bed for a further half an hour. Her mother's breathing became shallower. At nine o'clock she kissed her on her forehead and left.

Driving home her mother's words ran through her mind. *It must be the morphine. It can't be true?* The only things she knew about South Africa were the cities of Pretoria and Cape Town; Table Mountain and apartheid. She remembered a scrapbook she had when she was a child, and the hours she had spent cutting and pasting pictures of hippos and elephants. She remembered pestering her parents to emigrate to South Africa, saying it sounded so much more exciting and warmer there. Why would she remember that, when she had forgotten so much else? *'He was a soldier. It was the end of the war. Things were different then.'* Her mother's words reverberated in her head. *Why should she tell me to find my father? What about my mother?*

Two days later the phone rang, 'Mrs Maynard?'

'Yes.'

'It's Sister Gillespie here. I'm phoning to tell you that your mother has slipped into a coma, but there's no need for you to rush over.'

'A coma, what do you mean? She was dozing on and off last night, but she knew we were there. I'll come over. I was just about to phone the hospital to see how my father is.'

'Look, as I said, there's no rush. You can go and see your father first, and then come over.'

'Alright,' Jenny's hand shook as she replaced the handset. She stood and stared out of the lounge window. A postman was opening the gate to the house opposite. *I must phone Robert.*

Robert put his arm around Jenny's shoulders as they approached Charlie's bed. She drew a deep breath and pulled the curtain back. The hospital gown had slipped off his shoulder, exposing a white triangle of flesh. His face had collapsed. A pair of false teeth lay in a glass of water. 'Hello Dad, they fixed your leg then?'

'Bit sleepy, but I'll soon be on the mend,' he slurred.

'Well you're bound to be for a while, because of the anaesthetic.'

'Mum alright?'

Jenny bit her lower lip. 'Yes, they're looking after her really well. We saw her last night and we're going up again straight from here. We can let her know that we've seen you; and that you're O.K.'

Robert put a hand on Charlie's bare shoulder. 'Now, you just concentrate on getting better Dad.'

'Tell her, I'll be out of here soon.'

'How long will it be?' Jenny asked at the bottom of the sweeping staircase, thinking it was always dark in there, even when the sun was shining.

'It's hard to say. It could be tonight, or it could be a couple of days. You go up and I'll make you both a cup of tea.'

'If it's a couple of days, my dad might be able to see her. The hospital said they may be able to bring him then, didn't they?' she looked at Robert.

'Yes, they did. But would she know he was here, Sister?'

'Well, hearing is always the last of the senses to go. So, yes, she would recognise his voice.' She placed her hand on Jenny's arm.

Tears welled behind Jenny's eyes. 'I really hope she can hang on a bit longer. At least Lorna and Nicky are back at school, I've arranged for our neighbour to look after them until we get back.'

'Stay as long as you like. I'll be here 'til ten o'clock this evening.'

Jenny gripped the polished curve at the bottom of the banister. 'I don't want to go up, Robert. I don't want to see her.'

'Come on, take my arm.'

They walked slowly up the staircase and into the bedroom. The curtains were drawn, but a gap in the centre threw a shaft of afternoon sunlight across the carpet. Jenny sat down on the bed and took her mother's hand. She stared at her cracked lips; every intake of breath was an effort; and each exhale a relief. She no longer looked like her mother. They stayed until nine-thirty. Before going to bed that evening, Robert moved the telephone from the lounge onto the bottom stair. When the phone rang early in the morning they didn't speak. Jenny sat up and stared into the darkness. She heard Robert's voice, 'We'll come straight over,' and then his feet on the stairs coming closer, 'get dressed Jen. We'd better go.'

A nurse Jenny hadn't seen before opened the door. 'I'm so sorry Mrs Maynard, but your mother slipped away ten minutes ago.'

'You mean we're too late, she's gone?' Jenny cried. 'We came as fast as we could. We should have stayed last night Robert. Then we would have been here. I should have stayed. Why didn't I stay? Now we're too late.'

'It's very difficult to anticipate when it's going to happen. The change in breathing is an indicator, but sometimes, relatives just leave the room for a moment and they go; it's almost as if they wait until they're on their own.'

Jenny turned to Robert, 'I didn't have to go home, it was you who said we ought to go. You could have gone back for Lorna and Nicky, and I could have stayed. I could have slept in the chair. Why didn't I do that?' Tears rolled down her face.

'Jen, Jen, try not to think of that, it's not going to make any difference. As the nurse said, you could have been here and just left the room for a minute, and it could have happened.' He pulled Jenny towards him but she pushed him away.

'But at least I would have been with her,' she cried.

Jenny braced herself as she walked into the ward. She couldn't erase the picture of her mother's body from her mind. She had never seen a dead body before, and it wasn't how she wanted to remember her. They had stayed in her room until the nurse had persuaded them to leave. She could still feel the coldness of her mother's skin on her lips. She took a deep breath and parted the floral curtains around Charlie's bed. Pulling up a chair she reached for his hand and took a deep breath. 'Mum's gone, Dad.'

'She's gone. Gal, gone, you say she's gone.' Charlie gripped Jenny's hand and frowned at her as he tried to make sense of what she was saying.

'She didn't suffer, Dad. Robert and I were with her at the end.'

'Peaceful?'

'Yes, yes it was.'

'She'd put up with enough pain in her life. She was a fighter.' His blue eye moistened.

'Yes, she was.' The sight of his tears released her own. 'I've spoken to the ward sister, and Robert's waiting to speak to the doctor.'

'I saw her at the weekend, didn't I? It was the weekend wasn't it, before my op? She spoke to me didn't she?' Charlie tried to hoist himself up in the bed.

'Yes, you did.' Tears streamed down each cheek.

'Gal, Gal!' he shouted out.

'Dad, Dad,' Jenny rested her hand on her father's arm. I think the doctor's coming over to give you an injection.'

'Injection, I don't want no bloody injection. You tell him.'

'We'll do everything that needs to be done Dad. You just concentrate on getting better.' Jenny pulled a crumpled tissue from her bag and wiped her face.

A doctor carrying a kidney dish parted the curtains.

'Gal, Gal!' Charlie shouted louder than before.

Jenny opened her eyes and felt a giant standing on her chest, pinning her to the bed. She remembered what she had to do. There was no alternative but to get through the day as best she could. She didn't cry until she saw her father being wheeled carefully down the ramp of the ambulance and up the path towards the churchyard gate. 'Hello Dad, you look very smart in your best suit and tie,' she leant over and kissed him on his forehead. Wiping her eyes, she lifted his cold hand and gave it a squeeze in an attempt to reassure them both.

'It was a lovely service; just what your mum would have wanted.' Doris caught up with Jenny as she pushed Charlie's wheelchair out of the west door of the church, and into the autumn sunshine. Her husband George lingered a few yards behind. Jenny noticed he'd put on weight around his midriff since she had last seen him, and now looked less like a Greek god, and more like Aristotle Onassis.

'I chose the readings and hymns myself. I couldn't ask Mum what she wanted when she was so ill,' Jenny whispered. 'As for Dad, well, he always refused to talk about anything like that.' She thought they had never talked about anything important, even when they were well. 'I'm pleased that you could both make it.'

'We flew back yesterday. We're staying with Alan and Jackie.'

'You must be warm in that fur coat?' Jenny said. 'The sun's quite hot.'

'No I'm not. It's freezing here compared to Larnaca.'

Five years earlier, Doris had sold her house in Woolwich and bought a villa in Cyprus where they now spent the majority of the year. Since her marriage Jenny had taken to visiting her aunt regularly, and had found that she missed their conversations. She could talk to her aunt about subjects she felt inhibited about discussing with her mother. Alice always made some disparaging remark when she mentioned she was seeing Doris. When Jenny had told her about her aunt's intended move, and that Doris would have preferred an apartment in Torremolinos, but to please George – who had wanted to return to his roots – she had agreed to buy in Cyprus. Her mother had said that, 'She never wanted to please Jim.'

'Jackie and I are so sorry about your mum. My dad… Uncle Jim always had a soft spot for her. Here, let me wheel him for you?' said Alan.

'Thank you, but it's a bit tricky between the graves. Just let me take those tissues off his lap.' Jenny leant over her father, picked up the box and adjusted the tartan blanket around his legs.

'That's better isn't it Dad?'

Charlie sat erect in his wheelchair and stared straight ahead; his plastered leg jutting out from under the blanket. The wheelchair seemed to diminish him.

A family of jackdaws cackled as the mourners gathered in silence around the open grave. Alice's coffin was slowly lowered into the ground.

'In sure and certain hope of the resurrection into eternal life, through our Lord Jesus Christ, we commend to almighty God our sister Alice, and we commit her body to the ground, earth to earth, ashes to ashes, dust to dust.'

As the familiar words of consolation were spoken by the vicar, Jenny bent down, picked up a handful of earth from the pile and scattered it on the coffin. She passed a handful to Charlie and manoeuvred his wheelchair closer to the edge making it easier for him to perform his final duty.

Alan stood aside as Robert gripped the wheelchair. 'Let's go and look at the flowers Dad.' He pushed Charlie back up the grassy slope to a concreted area by the west door. Jenny followed hand in hand with Lorna and Nicky, both wearing suitably solemn faces. She hadn't wanted them to come to the funeral, knowing that their tears would make her more upset. 'They can stay next door and join us at the house afterwards,' she had said to Robert.

'No Jen, it's best that they come. They're old enough to say their goodbyes.'

The autumnal sprays and wreaths were laid in a row. Jenny knelt down looking at each message of condolence in turn.

A huddle of elderly women wearing dark coats and hats stood whispering as they waited to inspect the flowers. Jenny recognised them as her mother's friends from the Townswomen's Guild.

'It's good of you to come,' Jenny said.

'We were all very fond of Alice. I mean your mum. I saw her the week before last at Copper Cliff. She had a lot to put up with, but I remember she always said, that there was always someone else worse off than her, didn't she?' she turned to the woman on her left. 'We're all going to miss her on Wednesday afternoons, especially me. At least it's a sunny day; nothing worse than pouring rain at a funeral.'

'Yes, that's something I suppose. You're all welcome to come back to the house. Robert will organise a lift for you.'

'No, it's alright dear – we just wanted to pay our respects. You've got enough on your plate with your dad in the wheelchair. He looks so frail. How's he coping, poor man?'

'Well it was only ten days ago that he had his operation, so considering what's happened, he's not doing too badly. The ambulance is bringing him back to our house, and then they'll come and collect him later.'

'It's terrible for him and for you too, dear.'

'Yes it is.' Jenny was deliberately trying not to think about what her father was feeling. If she did, she knew she wouldn't cope. 'Well, you must excuse me, but I must go and talk to the others.' Two of her father's brothers were standing around his wheelchair smoking. She couldn't remember them being in the church. The last time she had seen them, was twenty years ago, at her cousin Leslie's wedding. They hadn't been invited to hers – Alice had seen to that. As Ernie drew on his cigarette she saw that two fingers were missing from his right hand. So it was true then? She remembered her parent's conversation years earlier.

'Cissie said he lost them in a revenge attack Gal. He was bloody lucky that was all he lost from what I've heard about them.

Always flew close to the wind did Ernie. I remember when he was a lad my old man thrashed him with his shaving strap for stealing.' The name Kray had been mentioned, and when she heard the name again on the news a year or two later; she had shivered. As she approached, they simultaneously dropped their cigarettes, grinding them into the path with the toes of their black shoes, then, they both laid a hand on Charlie's shoulders and said, 'You look after yourself, old soldier,' and with a perfunctory nod to Jenny, they turned on their heels and marched from the churchyard towards a grey Bentley. *At least they came to support Dad. It doesn't look as if they're coming back for tea.*

The following morning Jenny stood at the kitchen table and untied the wire from the flower sprays. Robert had returned to the churchyard once their relatives had left and brought the sprays home, saying it was a waste to leave them to rot when they could be enjoyed by other people. As she separated each lily, her tears fell onto the glossy leaves and glistened like raindrops.

9

October 1981

Jenny dreaded visiting her father. He hadn't mentioned the funeral, so she hadn't either. They spoke only of the plans she was making for his discharge at the weekend. Jenny decided that there would be plenty of time for talking once he was out of hospital.

'Mrs Maynard,' the ward sister called her over. 'You're not to be alarmed, but your father has developed pneumonia. We've started him on strong antibiotics this morning, so he should respond quickly.'

'Pneumonia, but he was doing so well. We were only talking yesterday about him staying with us until he feels able to return to the flat.'

'Did he used to be in the army?'

'Yes, for many years.'

'That makes sense of some of the things that he's been saying. So he's an old soldier?'

'Very much so,' Jenny smiled.

'He didn't want to get out of bed after you left yesterday. Then later in the evening he developed a high temperature. But as I've said, you're not to worry, this sometimes happens, especially with older patients. They don't move about as much as younger people. You do know that he has a tumour in his left lung?'

'Yes, I do.'

'That may have had some bearing on him breaking his leg – it may have spread into his bones. But it hasn't been causing him any problems with his lungs until now. You know that you and your husband can visit whenever you like.'

'Yes, thank you.'

'Oh, and thank you for bringing the flowers in the other day, they really brighten up the ward.' The ward sister turned away and started to flick through a pile of medical notes.

Jenny parted the curtains and was overpowered by the fragrance from the lilies on the bedside cabinet. Charlie lay propped up against three pillows and opened his left eye.

'Hello Jenny. Not so good today.'

Charlie's lungs improved over the next three days and a new discharge date was arranged. Jenny returned to work and spent her free time turning their dining room into a bedroom ready for Charlie's return.

'Can I sleep down here?' Lorna and Nicky asked in turn as they bounced on the mattress that lay on the folding bed.

'No, of course you can't. It's for Granddad. You know that.'

'Oh please – I'll be good, I promise. I'll go to bed early and I'll be really really quiet, like a little mouse, you won't hear me, I promise,' Nicky pleaded.

Jenny was tempted, but reason triumphed. 'No, now get off the bed both of you and let me make it up.'

The evening before Charlie's discharge Jenny was in the kitchen revising for her exam while Dolly Parton's longings burst forth from the tape player on the windowsill. Lorna and Nicky were playing hospitals in the dining room. She could hear Nicky pretending to be an ambulance with sirens blaring. *Why are boys so noisy? Can't they ever play quietly?* The hatch doors were open and she heard the phone ring in the lounge. Robert would answer it. He was expecting a call about a cricket fixture.

'Robert Maynard.'

Then silence until she heard him say, 'We'll come up straight away.'

The receiver clicked back on the handset. Jenny sat frozen at the table staring straight ahead. She heard footsteps in the hall, and turned in her chair. Robert filled the doorway; his face ashen.

'He's gone Jen, Dad's dead.'

They passed a nurse pushing a trolley laden with dirty dinner plates along the corridor. The ward sister was waiting for them.

'We're so sorry Mrs Maynard, he just slipped away.

He was sleeping, so the nurse left his dinner on his table and went back after she'd taken the other meals round. She realised straight away that he'd gone. It must have happened in those few minutes. We're as shocked as you are. He was due to be discharged tomorrow.'

'He was an old soldier – he never wanted to make a fuss,' Jenny said, staring at the fully drawn curtains around her father's bed.

Eleven days later there was another funeral in the flint church opposite the windmill. The mourners were the same as three weeks earlier – with the exception of the four ladies from the Townswomen's Guild.

A week after Charlie's funeral when Lorna and Nicky were asleep, Jenny went upstairs to the linen cupboard and removed the brown envelope from between the tea towels. She went into her bedroom and shut the door. Taking a pair of scissors from her dressing table, she slit the envelope open, shook the contents onto the bed and peered inside the envelope; there were no documents. She started to divide the money into piles of twenty, ten and five pound notes.

'Jen, are you alright in there?' Robert's voice came from behind the closed door.

'Yes, I'm fine. I'm just resting. I'll be down in a minute.' She resumed counting. 'Two thousand nine hundred and eight pounds – nearly three thousand pounds,' she lay back on the bed and wondered how many years her parents must have been saving. Five minutes later she sat up, and pushing the notes back inside the envelope, took it downstairs into the lounge.

'Robert, I've been thinking.'

'Be careful,' he said from behind his newspaper.

'Look, Mum gave me this money a few weeks ago.'

'Did she?' he put the paper down.

'Yes, before she went into hospital. I think she knew how ill she was. Anyway, I think we ought to use some of it for a holiday. It would do us both good, and it would be a thank you from me, for all your support. I couldn't have managed without you.' She bent over and kissed him, remembering how he had helped her to arrange the funerals, making numerous phone calls, and finally, supervised the flat clearance, so she didn't have to be there.

'You don't need to thank me Jen.'

'I know I don't; but I want to. It would be in memory of Mum and Dad too.'

'Well, if you're sure?'

'I am,' Jenny went over to the bookcase, pulled out an atlas and lay it on the coffee table. 'We can have a look where we might go.' She turned the pages until Europe and the Middle East were spread out in front of them.

'What about Cyprus? Your aunt lives there. She did invite us.'

Jenny remembered Doris's words after her father's funeral, *Jenny, I'd really like it, if you, and Robert and the children of course, could come over and stay sometime soon. I didn't want to ask before, not while Alice – your mum – was alive. We didn't always see eye to eye, and I didn't want to cause any trouble. George and I would pay the airfares. You only need bring some spending money.'*

'Yes she did. The thing is, I've got my exams soon, and you'll have to get time off. So we probably won't be able to go until after Christmas. It will be too cold in Cyprus then. We can always go there later on. She won't be expecting us to go this soon anyway.'

'Well that cuts out a lot of places Jen. We can't afford the Caribbean, or anywhere in the southern hemisphere. What about the Canary Islands?'

'No, too boring. I don't want it to be just a holiday. I want it to be an experience; something we can remember and talk about for years to come.'

Robert ran his finger eastwards from the Canaries along the line of latitude – 'Morocco; Tunisia; Egypt; Israel.'

'Cairo, Robert, let's go to Cairo. It will be warmer than Europe and there'll be plenty to do if it's chilly,' Jenny said excitedly.

'I don't know Jen. It sounds very foreign. We might pick up something. I've heard everyone gets ill who goes there – gyppy tummy.'

'Well, at least we'll remember it, won't we?' Jenny laughed. 'Think of the Pyramids, and the Sphinx.' Jenny poured over the atlas. 'Look, there's a train line marked to Luxor. We could go there if we don't like Cairo; or it's too cold.'

'Let's see.' Robert moved his finger down the page.

'I suppose we could. But what about Lorna and Nicky? I wouldn't be happy taking them to a place like Cairo.'

The wipers slapped furiously as rain streamed down the windscreen.

'I hope they'll agree to look after them. As you say, they can't really come with us, and it will be term time. Anyway, we're the ones who need a break.' Jenny turned to Robert who was leaning forward trying to see through the glass.

'I'll ask Mum. Don't you say anything, let me do the talking.'

'I don't want to stay with Nanny and Grandpa Reggie,' Nicky shouted from the back seat.

'Stop being a wimp.' Lorna pinched her brother.

'Ow.'

'He elbowed me.'

'Stop it you two. Nicky it's really important that Dad and I have a holiday on our own, so we can come home happy, and remember Granny and Granddad.'

'I want to come; so I can remember them too.'

'Don't be stupid; didn't you hear what they said? Anyway we can't miss school,' Lorna stuck her tongue out.

'Yes we can, I don't care.'

Jenny bit her lower lip as she placed her cup and saucer on the coffee table. She could hear Lorna and Nicky squabbling in the room above. Robert took a deep breath and looked up at Maggie. 'Mum, Jen… I… was wondering if you could do us an enormous favour and look after the children for two weeks in the New Year?'

'What… why?' Maggie pursed her lips and frowned.

'After everything we've had to deal with lately, we… we… were hoping to get away for a break,' Robert stuttered.

'I know it's been hard for you both lately, especially for you Jen. But we've helped out when we could; having them for the odd day, here and there. But for two whole weeks, that's a long time. I never had a break when I was bringing you up Rob, on my own as well. I didn't know what a holiday was.'

'I know Mum, I know, but Jen really feels that she needs to get away.'

'I have just lost both my parents Maggie. If that's not a good enough reason I don't know what is?' she could feel a tear forming.

'Well I think it's a good idea,' Reggie added.

'Suppose it snows? It often does in January. How will I get them to school?'

'I could take them Maggie. You don't need to worry about that,' Reggie puffed on his pipe.

'I might get one of my migraines? They last for days. I'm fit for nothing – certainly not looking after two lively children.'

Jenny noticed the look of surprise on Reggie's face.

Maggie was never ill. She only thought anyone else was when they were on their death-bed.

Robert stood up as if to leave. 'Mum, if you're not willing to help us out just this once, I'm not going to come to David's wedding.' Jenny looked at him in astonishment.

'I wish I didn't have to be there,' Reggie said. 'Mind you, they haven't set a date yet, knowing him they'll never get round to it.' David had recently broken the news that he was going to marry Corinne, a new age traveller with Rastafarian dreadlocks.

'Reggie how can you say that? Corinne's a lovely girl. I know I was disappointed at first, but she has qualities.'

'What qualities? The only thing I've noticed is her ability to avoid working, so they make a good pair,' Reggie puffed on his pipe again.

Maggie sighed, 'Well, I suppose they could stay here.'

10

November 1981

'Those clouds look ominous. It's going to rain later,' Robert said peering out of the kitchen window. He grabbed his anorak from the back of the chair and gave Jenny a peck on her cheek.

'I've got to go to the churchyard later. It's Mum's birthday – she would have been seventy-four.'

'You don't have to go today, do you?'

'Yes, I do.'

Three more graves had been dug since her last visit. Jenny glanced down at the shiny brass plaques, but didn't recognise any of the names. She bent down and placed her rose in front of the wooden cross and whispered, 'Happy birthday, Mum.' Tears streamed down her face, mingling with the drizzle. She wiped the sleeve of her coat across her cheeks and wondered why she hadn't thought to bring any tissues. She sniffed hard and stood up. Moving to the end of the mound, she stared at the light brown soil interspersed with chalk. *'You'll miss me when I'm gone,'* her mother's words that she had dismissed with the casualness of youth; now seemed a just retribution. She would have to decide about a memorial stone soon. Someone, she couldn't remember who, said that you had to wait a year for the ground to settle.

'Excuse me.'

She jumped and spun round, lifting her umbrella. A man stood in front of her, the tip of his jacket collar touching the lobes of his ears.

'I'm sorry if I startled you, but I think you've left your lights on. Is that your Morris Minor outside?' He frowned and looked down at the cross. 'My God, it's Jenny – Jenny Porter, isn't it? I don't believe it.' A broad smile stretched across his sharp features. He held out his hand, but then let it drop by his side.

Is it him? she thought, her heart banging against her ribs. *No, it can't be. Not here.* As the man turned his head slightly, she noticed a mole that interrupted the line of his jaw. 'Martin.'

'I'm sorry, I shouldn't have disturbed you.' He turned to go.

'No, no – it's alright.' Her chest tightened. She swallowed. 'I never expected to see you again. You moved away. You don't live here any more.'

'Yes, we did, and I don't. But my parents moved back about ten years ago. They always liked it up this way. That's their house down there.' He turned and pointed in the direction of a red tiled roof.

'Yes, it is nice. But not today – I mean with the rain.'

She blinked several times to refresh her eyes, thinking how awkward she must sound.

'You were crying the last time I saw you,' he said softly.

So he remembers. It was here by the windmill. But I'm years older now. She flicked her head back and ran her fingers through her hair, pushing it off her face. 'I'd better go – my lights. I'm always doing that when it's dark during the day.' She didn't move.

'Yes, it's easily done.' He gazed at her. 'It's great to see you again, Jenny. I can't believe it.'

'Yes, it's great to see you too,' she said. Words that she had always imagined saying had vanished. 'I must go – my lights.' She drew her umbrella closer and started walking towards the path. She knew he was watching her, and it took all her strength to place one foot in front of the other.

'I'm sorry about your parents,' his words carried across the churchyard.

She turned and nodded. He was still standing at the foot of her parents' grave. A pied wagtail bobbed out of her way as she met the solidness of the path. She shut the gate and, glancing back to check that she was out of sight, ran across the green towards the faint yellow beams. Balancing the umbrella against her body, she leant on the car and fumbled in her coat pocket for the key, her hand trembling as she tried to force it into the lock. *For God's sake, go in. Why won't it go in?* She removed it and tried again, it turned. Relieved, she threw her umbrella onto the passenger seat and sank behind the wheel. *Why is he here? He must have lost someone too*, she thought. *I should have asked. I must go before he comes out. He can't see me – not looking like this.* She pulled the choke out and turned the ignition. The engine groaned. *No, not the lights, please start, come on don't let me down.* She adjusted the choke. On the third attempt the engine fired. She released the handbrake and drove away.

Jenny thought of nothing else for the rest of that afternoon. She now had a new image of Martin. It would take some getting used to; she had been comfortable with the old one. His words replayed in her mind as she stared at Nicky, who sat twirling a sausage around with his fork in a pool of tomato sauce. She slammed her hand on the table. 'Stop playing with your food, Nicky.'

'I'm not hungry. Look, it's a helicopter.'

'You're not hungry because you've been stuffing your face with chocolates,' said Lorna, leaning over the table towards him.

'You said you wouldn't tell.'

'Well, you shouldn't have hit me then, should you?'

'She had some too,' Nicky turned towards his mother.

'But I've eaten all my dinner.'

'For God's sake, stop it you two,' Jenny said, irritated that her thoughts were being interrupted. She glanced up at the clock on the kitchen wall. 'Lorna, finish your pudding, then go and get ready for Brownies. You'll need your coat, it's still drizzling. No pudding for you, Nicky. I should be able to trust you not to eat sweets before dinner.'

'Jen, let it go, what's the matter with you?' Robert stopped eating and looked up. 'He's eight years old. He's going to eat sweets if they're around. Did you do anything today?'

Jenny winced as she spotted a sliver of cabbage stuck between his front teeth. 'I went to the churchyard. I told you I was going. It's Mum's birthday; she would have been seventy-four today.'

'I'm sorry, Jen, I should have remembered.' He reached for the tomato sauce. 'I thought I'd never get home tonight; the A23 was a bloody nightmare.'

'But, Mummy, why did you go to the churchyard? You said Granny's gone to heaven.'

'She has Nicky, and so has Granddad. I go there to feel close to them.'

'Is that because they lived near there? Why don't you go to their flat?'

'Nicky, that's enough. Just get down,' said Robert.

'I miss Granddad.' His lower lip quivered as he slid off his chair.

'I know Nicky, we all do, come here.' Seeing him hesitate, Jenny pulled him towards her and hugged him.

'You must have been the only person there on a day like this,' Robert said as he pierced a sausage with his fork.

'Yes, I was,' she said, thinking that this was the first time she had lied to him.

Jenny tossed and turned all night, until the hands on her alarm clock told her that it was seven in the morning. She was consumed with thoughts of Martin. So his parents had moved back ten years ago. She was sure he hadn't been that tall the last time she had seen him, but he had only been sixteen. She remembered reading somewhere that men continue growing until they're twenty-one.

She arrived at work early, and instead of searching the room for any post that had arrived since her last visit, she sat at her desk staring through the French windows at the bulk of Firle Beacon in the distance. It was only when Celia came into the room that she realised she had forgotten about the delivery of the printing fabric.

'My God, you're here already, I'd better go and make the coffee. I've got to go out soon Jenny, so, if you wouldn't mind signing for the rolls.'

Celia had been commissioned by Colefax and Fowler to print her latest design, and was hoping that it would lead to more work in the future. She had spoken of nothing else the week before. Jenny nodded in agreement and continued staring through the French windows.

Celia returned carrying a tray containing two mugs of steaming coffee. She placed them on the low window-ledge and seated herself on the *chaise-longue* opposite Jenny's desk.

'Celia, I was wondering if I could leave a bit earlier today. I'd like to go to the travel agents and book that holiday I mentioned last week.'

'Of course you can. It would do you both good to get away. I was worried that you came back to work too soon. I thought you were starting to look like your old self again, but you look tired today.'

'I didn't sleep very well last night. But no, it's been fine. I needed to get back to some normality.'

'Are you going to take the children with you?'

'No, Robert's mother has agreed to look after them.'

'Good, so it will be a proper break for both of you. Don't let your coffee get cold, there's some biscuits on the tray.' Weak rays from the sun shone through the windows onto Celia's fine hair, which was held at the back of her head with a large clip. Although she was nearly sixty, the style suited her, accentuating her fine features. She reminded Jenny of Virginia Woolf, who had lived and died not far from here.

She left her car alongside the windmill and noted that no other cars were parked. He must have come by car yesterday, but she couldn't remember seeing one. Why couldn't the weather have been like this yesterday? She might have looked half-decent instead of a drowned rat. She walked over to the churchyard. It was highly unlikely that Martin would be here again – not the next day. She peered slowly over the flint wall — nobody there. She opened the gate and ran down a line of earlier graves. At the head of the final grave stood a large grey headstone. She stared at the black lettering.

IN LOVING MEMORY
OF ELLEN MARY BARRETTI
16th April 1915 to 25th November 1978
BELOVED WIFE OF ENRICO
AND MOTHER
OF MARTIN AND ANNA
Rest in Peace

His mother — so that's why he was here; the day before yesterday had been the third anniversary of her death. He probably couldn't make it on the day. A memory of a slim, laughing, dark-haired woman wearing an apron with a frill flashed before her. It had been his sister's birthday and the first time she had visited his house. She remembered what fun his mother appeared to be, and how young she looked — but then, everyone's mother had seemed young compared to her own. Although, as she rechecked the dates, she realised that there weren't that many years between them. Sixty-three — Jenny calculated; she had only been sixty-three when she had died; she probably had cancer. Her eyes moved to the mound of earth less than ten feet away that covered her parents. In spite of her ill health, her mother had outlived Martin's. *'Creaking boards last the longest,'* her mother used to say. She had been right about that.

Leaving the travel agents Jenny visualised bazaars filled with carpets and leather goods; rows of colourful spices piled in pyramids on top of hessian sacks. She could almost smell the cumin and sandalwood.

Cairo – the greatest city in the Islamic world comprises of half a dozen cities and spreads across the Nile towards the Pyramids at Giza. Medieval trades and customs co-exist with a modern mix of Arab, African and European influences. Its population is estimated at seventeen million, with around half a million squatting in cemeteries – the cities of the dead.

She hurried back to her car. She couldn't wait to tell Robert.

'Jenny, Jenny.'

She was jolted from her middle-eastern imaginings by a breathless voice. She turned around.

'Jenny, it is you.' A woman with short spiky dark hair and wearing an ankle-length floral print skirt over black boots, smiled and panted simultaneously, while Jenny searched desperately for a name.

'I thought it was you. I was at the bus stop, when I saw you coming out of the travel agents. I've been trying to catch you up.'

'Gail, my God – Gail,' Jenny said recognising a chickenpox scar on her friend's forehead. She looked younger than ten years ago, and Jenny would never have recognised her if she hadn't been standing inches away from her face. 'It's been ages, Gail. Do you live around here now?'

'Yes, in Portland Road. You know I left Chris?'

'Yes, I do.' Jenny remembered their last meeting. She had been pushing Lorna in her pram when she had bumped into Gail in Marks and Spencer. She had looked depressed, worse than when she had visited her at her flat. She had told her that Chris's gambling had escalated and that she had taken the children and moved back to live with her parents. 'You look well, Gail.'

'Yes, I am. Once the children were at school I decided to enrol for a mature student's teacher training course at Sussex Uni. Do you remember? You said that I might be able to. Mum and Dad have been marvellous; it was hard for them having the three of us around all the time. And guess what? I'm even back teaching at my old junior school. Would you believe it?'

'That's amazing Gail. I'm really pleased for you. So you got there in the end.'

'Yes, and there might be a new man on the horizon too. I met him a few weeks ago at the local Labour Club. He's thinking of standing in the local elections next year; how about you?'

'Well the last few weeks have been really grim. Mum and Dad died recently.'

'What together?'

'Well, within two weeks of each other.'

'Oh no, that's terrible. I'm really sorry, Jenny. I remember your mum teaching me to crochet, well trying to. I had two left hands. Do you remember? She was so patient with me. So you're an orphan?'

'Well, if you can be an orphan when you're in your mid-thirties. Robert has been marvellous. I couldn't have coped without him, that's what I was doing in the travel agents, treating us to a holiday in the New Year.'

'Well, we always knew he was rock solid, didn't we? I really envied you back then.'

Jenny glanced at her watch. 'Look, I've got to get back for the children Gail. We've got a boy now, Nicky, so I can't stop any longer. Look, why don't we meet up when I come back from holiday? We can catch up properly then. I'd love to hear about your children and the teacher training.' Jenny fumbled in her bag and scribbled her telephone number on a receipt.

'Where are you going?'

'Egypt – in January – I'm really looking forward to it.'

'Wow, how exciting. I'll give you a ring in the February half term then. Have a good Christmas, Jenny. Oh sorry, I shouldn't have said that. I didn't think.'

'It's O.K. We'll still have a good Christmas for Lorna and Nicky's sake.'

'See you soon then?' Gail smiled and walked back towards the bus stop.

Driving home Jenny realised that she hadn't given Christmas a thought until now. It would be difficult this year despite what she had said. She thought about Gail and how her life had changed for the better. She said she lived in Portland Road, so she might know something about Martin.

11

January 1982

Jenny leapt out of the way as a runaway donkey cart careered down the *souk*.

'We were nearly killed just then,' Robert said, mopping his brow.

'Look at that shop. It's packed with semi-precious stones, they're so colourful; I'm going over.'

'Engleesh – Engleesh, come here, come buy.' They were assailed from all sides.

Jenny felt a hand squeeze her buttock. She grabbed Robert's arm.

'I've had enough of this Jen, it's so claustrophobic. Let's go back to the hotel.'

'We haven't been here long, not yet.'

'It's long enough.'

'Let's just see what's around this corner, it might be less crowded.'

'I doubt it. I know what's around the corner – more hassle.'

'But that's what gives it the atmosphere. Look at those spices, piled in pyramids, I'll buy some later.'

'Look at that man leering at you. I know exactly

what he's thinking. I've a good mind to go and punch him on the nose.'

'Don't you dare,' Jenny looked up. A large man wearing a *galabiyya* was grinning at her lasciviously from behind the hessian sacks. 'It's only because we're tourists. I'm wearing a long skirt.'

'It's not your skirt he's looking at.'

Jenny looked down and fastened the top three buttons on her blouse as they were jostled forward.

'Ah, Engleesh, Engleesh, come, come take tea with me. Sit in my shop. Try perfume. No buy – no mind – just drink tea.' A tall young Egyptian smiled at them as he stood up from behind his hookah pipe and beckoned them into his shop.

'Come on, let's go in, he looks nice.' Jenny pulled Robert into the shop where on tiers of shelves stood row upon row of small glass bottles. Every one had a brown label with Arabic writing.

After half an hour of sipping strong sweet tea and Robert discussing the relative merits of Arsenal versus Manchester United with the young man who had introduced himself as Ahmed, they were led over to the shelves.

'In all these bottles – essence – perfumes. This one, roses from banks of Nile.' He lifted one down, removed the stopper and waved the bottle under Jenny's nose. 'You like?' He led her to the other side of the shop and took another bottle from the shelf. 'This one – water lily – smell.'

He then reached up to the top shelf. 'This one,' he didn't name it, 'makes husband big and hard, keeps beautiful wife happy.' Jenny blushed as she sniffed the musky aroma.

After five minutes of haggling, they emerged, with Jenny clutching a small parcel.

'Look out,' Robert shouted as a grey horse bore down on them. 'That's it Jen, I've had enough. I can't stand it any longer, let's get back. That's if we can ever find our way out of this maze. I reckon we paid about ten times more than we should have done for that,' Robert nodded towards the paper parcel.

'That's the first and last time we go in there. It takes four times as long as it should to buy anything. I hate all that haggling.' Robert removed his sandals and collapsed on the bed.

Their hotel room in the *Sharia Ramses* was large and square. A wooden fan spun on the high ceiling. Long wooden shutters opened onto a small iron balcony. Although they were on the fourth floor, they might just as well have been in the street. Whistles blew and horns blared, drowning out the shouts of the street vendors below.

'That's what makes it exciting, it's different. I thought it was amazing, so many stalls, and so many people, I'm going back before we go home.' Jenny was sitting at a rattan dressing table. She started to undo the brown wrapping paper, removed the stopper from the bottle and dabbed some perfume in the hollow of her neck and on the insides of her wrists.

'You can't possibly go back in there on your own. God knows what would happen to you. I'd probably never see you again.'

'Don't be so ridiculous. I'd be fine. They don't mean any harm. They're just trying to make a living.'

'Can you close the shutters Jen? Let's try and have a bit of peace for an hour.'

Jenny went over and pulled the shutters towards her. The room darkened, and the sounds from below muffled to a low blur. She felt her way over to the bed and lay down beside Robert. After a few seconds he turned to kiss her, and began unbuttoning her blouse. Jenny lifted herself making it easier for him to remove her clothes.

'Look Jen, the perfume's worked.' Robert smiled at her as he sat up and removed his shorts. 'He wasn't having us on after all. Mmm, I can't wait.' He fell on top of her, covering her mouth with his own.

'Christ, that was good for you too, wasn't it?'

'Yes, it was.' Feeling his detumescence slipping out of her, she wrapped her arms tightly around his back and started pushing against him again.

'Not just now Jen, later.'

Jenny reached across to the bedside table for the box of tissues.

Jenny dozed intermittently, while Robert slept.

Tiny chinks of light from gaps in the shutters flashed onto the dark wooden floor. They hadn't made love like that for a long time. They'd hardly had sex at all for the past year. She knew he loved her, and after today, she could hardly complain that he couldn't satisfy her sexually. She just wished that they were soulmates; that they had more in common apart from the house and children. He hardly knew a dandelion from a daisy, and she knew that he wasn't excited about being in Egypt – he would rather have had a holiday in England. But it was impossible to have everything. He was a good husband and she must be grateful. Life could be a hell of a lot worse. She smiled as she thought about Lorna and Nicky – their absence ironing out their imperfections.

Robert stirred and flung an arm across Jenny's breasts. 'Why is sex in the afternoon so much more satisfying?'

'It feels decadent I suppose.'

'I've been looking forward to this break for weeks. I was hoping that… you know, we'd get back together again properly, like this.'

'It might also have something to do with the fact that Lorna and Nicky aren't around,' Jenny added.

'Yes, that's true; and we're not worn out. If only it could be like this all the time. Perhaps it will be – now you've got that perfume?' He laughed out loud and rolled her left nipple between his thumb and forefinger. 'I think we ought to make more effort when we get home. It was a good idea of yours to get away. We both needed it, thank you.'

'Don't thank me, thank Mum and Dad; if it wasn't for them, we wouldn't be here.'

'I'm sure that they'd be pleased that we're enjoying ourselves.'

Jenny got up and walked over to the shutters. A *muezzin* was calling the faithful to prayer from a minaret. She blinked as the late afternoon sun blinded her, and then stepped back as she realised her breasts were bare.

'Don't open them Jen, not yet. Come back here.'

The next four mornings followed the same pattern. They visited the Pyramids and Sphinx; had the obligatory camel rides; took a *felucca* trip on the Nile, and then returned to their bedroom for the afternoons. On the fifth morning as they stepped out of their hotel foyer, a cold wind from the north east whipped down the street. They shivered, returned to their room for their jumpers, and booked the overnight train to Luxor.

Their hotel stood on the eastern bank of the Nile at the southern end of the *corniche*. Every time they left the foyer they were besieged by *caleche* drivers, offering their services into town.

'Look we want to walk for a while, go away,' Robert shouted, waving his arms around.

'No walk, you English, no walk, I have good horse.' An elderly man, his head wrapped around with a black and white chequered turban, stood up in his carriage and beckoned them over.

'I think we better take it Robert. He sounds angry. It can't be that much money.'

'Alright then,' he sighed.

They scrambled up into the carriage. The driver cracked his whip and, with them both clutching the sides the *caleche,* careered down the road.

'Luxor Temple, please,' Robert shouted above the sound of the horse's hooves.

The driver dropped them outside the Winter Palace Hotel, tapping his watch furiously.

'How much?' asked Robert.

'Ten pound – English.'

'Not bloody likely – ten Egyptian pounds.' Robert thrust some notes into the man's gnarled hand and grabbed Jenny's arm.

'Horse, money for horse, horse hungry,' the driver shouted after them.

'Can't they just leave us alone? Thieves all of them,' Robert said as they crossed the road, dodging cars and *caleches,* all seemingly intent on not wanting them to see another day. A group of cruise boats sat at anchor below the promenade.

'I think in the future, we must agree a price before we get on. Look, there's a pied kingfisher. Do you see it?' Jenny pointed towards a large black and white bird perched on the anchor rope of a cruise boat. 'Let's sit down here.'

'Baksheesh, baksheesh,' two barefoot boys immediately ran over to them, their hands stretched out in front of them.

'Go away, scram.' Robert waved them away, but they stood firm.

'I might have some pens in my bag.' Jenny rummaged through her shoulder bag and produced two biros. The boys beamed.

'Imshi, imshi,' an old man shouted and limped over to where they were seated, waving his stick. The boys ran off.

Jenny stared at the distant mountains on the far side of the Nile. 'That must be the Valley of the Kings on the other side of the river. Let's book a trip for tomorrow?'

'Yes, we'd better make the most of our time here. Let me know when you're ready and we'll cross back over to the temple. If we stay here any longer we'll be pestered again.' Robert looked around anxiously.

'Have you noticed how all the women are covered in black?' Jenny said as they passed a group chattering amongst themselves.

'No,' he grimaced.

'Well they are, all of them. I wonder why. Are you alright?'

'I need the toilet Jen. My guts were dodgy after breakfast. I thought I'd be alright.'

For two days Robert lay prostrate on the bed apart from

numerous sorties to the toilet. Jenny made drinks of *kakaday* – a tea made from hibiscus flowers – which had been recommended by the hotel reception. She spent her days in the hotel garden, watching the barges chugging up the Nile, laden with sugar cane and livestock. Training her binoculars on the water birds that lurked in the green fringes of the river, she listed them in the back page of her *Birds of Europe and North Africa* book. She relished the jewelled green and turquoise of the bee-eaters, and the pink, black and white of the hoopoes, thinking how exotic they looked, well, apart from the black and white wagtail bobbing about her feet, waiting for titbits. She remembered there had been one in the churchyard the afternoon she had met Martin again. She thought about him every day, but distance made him seem unreal. Here, she could give all her attention to Robert. The distant mountains gradually changed colour – from sandy yellow in the morning, to the colour of mustard around midday, and finally golden, as the sun disappeared behind them. On the third day Robert felt well enough to get dressed and eat a few mouthfuls of hummous. In the afternoon, he walked into the garden and found Jenny sitting on a sun-lounger.

'So this is where you've been hiding yourself. What are you doing?'

'I'm making a note of the birds I've seen. I've seen over twenty just from here. Karnak was amazing this morning, Robert. I wish you'd been well enough to come. Enormous pillars, covered with hieroglyphics; the site went on for ever. I've taken lots of photos, but they won't do it justice.'

'It's a shame we haven't got more time.' He bent down and placed his arm around her.

'Well, we can always come back when the children are grown. We can see the Valley of the Kings then. They'll still be here,' Jenny smiled up at him.

12

March 1982

Jenny couldn't settle. After a perfunctory wipe of the dining room table, she returned to the kitchen to finish scraping the remains of toast from the breakfast plates. She then hovered in the hall before going upstairs. Her ears bristled as she heard the letterbox open. *That sounds like it*, she thought, and rushed back down. A single brown envelope lay on the doormat. She picked it up and ripped the envelope open. A grin spread across her face as she read the flimsy piece of paper, savouring every word. When she was satisfied that she had saturated herself with the good news, she walked into the lounge and picked up the telephone. *You idiot, they're not there, you can't tell them.* Seven – seven – two – five – three – eight; seven – seven – two – five – three – eight. Her parents' telephone number was embedded in her memory. She wondered how many more years would pass before she would no longer be able to recall it. She sat down on the sofa and stared out of the window. The postman on the opposite side of the road was looking intently at the addresses on a bundle of envelopes. *This is when you really miss them*, she thought, *when you want to tell them good news.*

She walked up the stairs to the second floor of the house and into the spare room. It wasn't used as a bedroom as the ceiling sloped too steeply to the window frames at either end. For the past eighteen months they had rented it to an actor for storage. He rarely put in an appearance, and if it hadn't been for his quarterly cheques, they would have assumed he'd forgotten about his possessions. To the right of the door was a built-in cupboard. Manoeuvring her way around the cardboard boxes Jenny opened the white painted doors. Stale cigarette smoke and pheromones were released. She was back inside her parents' flat. She buried her nose in the lapel of her father's check jacket and inhaled. 'I haven't lost you. I just wanted to tell you that I passed my exams,' she said out loud.

Jenny moved the coat hanger along, revealing a plain navy blue dress, complete with a marcasite brooch in the shape of a lily. Her mother always wore this when she wanted to look smart. Hanging next to the dress was her father's best grey suit – a white handkerchief peeped out of the breast pocket – he had worn it at her mother's funeral. Quickly she moved the suit along. There was her wedding outfit, a straight turquoise skirt and jacket. Folded over a double hanger, hung a pair of casual brown trousers that her mother had always worn around the flat. Jenny had visited the cupboard several times since her parents had died. The last time had been when they returned from Egypt. If they had still been alive, she would have called on them, and excitedly explained every photograph. Instead, when Robert and the children were occupied, she had come to this room and told these shrouds instead. She supposed she would have to get rid of them eventually – but not yet.

'I've got some good news.' Jenny grinned as she greeted Robert in the hallway.

'Let me guess – David and Corinne have called off their wedding.'

'No – well at least if they have, we haven't been told. I've passed my exams.'

'Well done Jen, I knew you would.' He leant over and kissed her on the cheek. 'Let's have a drink to celebrate. I'll just go and get changed.'

'I'll get the drinks.'

'Does that mean you'll be leaving Celia?' he said as he came through the lounge door adjusting a maroon jumper over his cords.

'No, I haven't even thought about that. It's too far ahead. I've only just received the results.'

'You're not thinking about working more days are you? I'm not sure that would be a good thing. The children are still young.'

'No Robert – I've just said, I'm not thinking about anything like that. I'm quite happy with my three days at the moment.'

'Good.'

'But, I'll probably want something more in a year or two; once Nicky starts at secondary school. This widens my options. I could try for a job in Brighton then, one with prospects.'

'We can manage – money wise. There's no need for you to work more days.'

'It isn't only about money Robert. Anyway talking about secondary schools I thought we might have heard today about Lorna.'

'I want to go to Varndean. Sarah and Emma are going there and we can't be separated.' Lorna came into the room clutching a dark brown plastic horse which she placed on the coffee table. Nicky trailed behind her.

'Go and lay the table, you two. We'll be in after we've had our drinks. Lorna, don't forget that Emma lives directly opposite the school. We're on the edge of the catchment area here, so you'll just have to wait and see.'

'She'll get in Jen,' Robert said picking up the newspaper from the sofa.

'What's for pudding?' Nicky looked up.

'Do as you're told. Go and lay the table or you won't have any,' Robert sighed from behind the paper.

'I know what it is,' said Lorna, 'I saw Mummy making it – it's Angel Delight – your favourite, and I'll eat yours if you're not having any.'

'Lorna, stop winding him up,' Jenny shouted as they disappeared.

'It says here that there's a model exhibition at Horsham this Sunday, shall we go?' Jenny didn't answer immediately. No matter how much she tried, she couldn't work up any enthusiasm about different sized gauges and bogies. But they'd agreed on holiday they would both make more of an effort, and Robert was always pleased when she did go with him.

'Well, what do you think then?' Robert looked directly at Jenny.

'I'm going horse-riding with Sarah on Sunday,' Lorna said coming back into the room.

'Yes, I'll come.'

'Good.'

'I like it best when you come with us Mum,' Nicky followed his sister.

'If we're going to Horsham, I'd like to stop off at Oreham Common on the way back. The clocks go forward next weekend, so it will be lighter in the evenings. Once I hear the chiff-chaffs, I know that spring's here.'

'That's boring,' said Nicky, going over to the television.

'Well, we can have a game of cricket, while Mum wanders around,' said Robert.

'For God's sake Nicky, how many times have I told you not to switch the television on before dinner?' Jenny snapped.

'Come on son let's go and eat,' Robert placed the newspaper on the coffee table. 'Do you want to come down to the cellar and help me paint the station fence afterwards?'

Lorna lay on the floor in front of the gas fire reading *How to Care for your Pony*, the plastic horse at her side. Jenny sat on the sofa and regretted shouting at Nicky. It wasn't him she was annoyed at. It was Robert. She was irritated that as soon as she had told him about passing her exams, he said that he didn't like the idea of her working more hours. Of course she had thought about leaving Celia, but the present arrangement suited her. Celia was flexible about the school holidays. If she was to leave, they would be a problem; especially now that Mum and Dad were no longer around. Obviously, Robert didn't want things to change, and they could manage financially, but she couldn't work for Celia for ever. She wanted more of a challenge, and to meet different people. She looked down at the coffee table. Her eyes rested on the newspaper headline – "Argentine Flag raised in South Georgia". Moving the paper to one side, she picked up a booklet. She missed the stimulation of studying, and had been thinking about signing up for a four week course. She turned to the page "Habitats and Wildlife", "starts Tuesday April 20th". She would phone the next day and book a place.

'Look Mummy, I've plaited his mane.' Lorna waved the plastic horse in the air.

Jenny bent down and removed a diary from her bag. She thumbed through the pages and pencilled the course in, adding a question mark. She flicked back a page. Friday April 16th. The date had stayed in her mind since she had read the inscription on Martin's mother's gravestone. *That's four days after Easter Monday.* There was a chance that Martin would visit the churchyard that afternoon. He had been there in the afternoon before. She remembered a conversation with Gail at half term. They had been sitting in the bow-window of a coffee shop in George Street. After fifteen minutes of listening to Gail's tales of difficult children, she had said, 'Oh by the way, do you remember Martin Barretti from the youth club years ago? I met him again in November in West Blatchington churchyard, where Mum and Dad are buried.'

'Did you?' Gail looked intently at Jenny. 'That must have been a shock. What was he doing there? I didn't know he lived around here anymore, he moved away – years ago.'

'He told me his parents came back about ten years ago.'

'I remember you were really keen on him weren't you?'

'Oh that was ages ago. We were just kids. I just wondered if your parents or cousin had heard anything about them – you know – living near.'

'No, I haven't heard anything, but Mum might have. I'll ask her. Oh, I must tell you about the parents of this little boy in my class, you'll never believe this.'

Nicky ran into the lounge, jolting Jenny back into

the present. 'Dad's just coming up, we've finished painting the fence.'

A week later another brown envelope dropped through the letterbox together with a sky blue airmail letter. Jenny opened the brown envelope first and gave a sigh of relief that she wouldn't have to deal with Lorna's tears later. "Lorna's place at Varndean School for September 1982 has been confirmed". She took the letters into the kitchen and sitting down at the table opened the letter from Dido. Jenny's eyes quickly scanned the initial pleasantries until she reached the second paragraph:

...I'm sorry that I haven't written for so long but life hasn't been easy here. We had a third boy last year – we called him Ethan Benjamin after Jed's grandfather. He wasn't thriving and tests found he had a large hole in his heart. He's had several ops, and he's doing well now. The problem now isn't Ethan – it's Jed. He's left us, but he couldn't help it. It wasn't his fault, at least that's what I keep telling myself, to stop myself going mad. There's no other woman or anything like that – he just couldn't cope and the worry about Ethan was the last straw. Since he returned from Vietnam he's been a changed man, he explodes at the slightest thing. I've had to be so careful what I said around him, and the boys did too. It wasn't easy, but we got used to his moods. Then he had counselling – they do that for veterans here – and he was

doing really well, he was the old Jed again. But when Ethan was born it was too much, even though Ethan's heart has repaired and he's better. Jed went back to being angry. I got up one day and he'd gone. In a way it was a relief. I went to see his parents – they live here in Wichita – but he wasn't there. They said he might have gone to Chicago – his army friend lives there. Then two weeks later they told me they received a letter from him – they didn't say where he was, perhaps they didn't know – saying that he wanted them to tell me that he was alive, and that he was really sorry about leaving us, but he couldn't come back to his old life here, he couldn't cope and I'd be better off without him – we all would. So, my dear old friend – oh Jenny, it seems a lifetime away now, those days at the ministry, good ol' Dido is on her own with three young boys to bring up, and no choice but to carry on. Anyway enough about me, I heard that Mike has got divorced and now lives in London…

'Oh no – poor Dido, that's awful,' Jenny spoke out loud. She put the letter down and reflected on her own life. What did she have to complain about? Nothing – she had two healthy children and a steady husband. She wished that she could visit Dido – but Kansas – no, it just wasn't possible.

13

April 1982

'I don't think I've seen you wearing that skirt before,' said Celia as she attempted to pull a roll of fabric taller than herself from the pile in the corner.

'No it's new, I thought it was time I bought something new – with summer coming.' Two days before, on the promise of their favourite ice creams, Jenny had dragged Lorna and Nicky in and out of the clothes stores in Brighton. When she could no longer bear their protestations, she bought a tiered cream skirt and matching cowl-necked jumper.

'I hope you don't mind Jenny, but I need you to help me with the printing this morning. I wasn't feeling well yesterday – tail end of a cold – so I couldn't finish that order for Colefax.'

Oh no, why does she have to ask today of all days? Jenny thought, as she searched for envelopes behind the sofa cushions. *But at least that makes it easier for me.* 'No, that's alright Celia, but I was wondering if I worked through my lunch break, if I could leave twenty minutes earlier?'

Celia flashed Jenny a quizzical look. 'Yes, that's fine. You'd better be careful not to get any ink on that skirt though. I'll go and find you some overalls in a minute. I think there's a pair in the garage.'

As she disappeared, Jenny thought how stupid she had been, to wear her new clothes today. What was the point? A fresh north-west wind was blowing. No one would go outside without a coat. But she couldn't have worn her usual work clothes – not today. She looked down at her legs – they would be visible below her coat, she'd have to be careful not to get smears of printing ink on her tights. She glanced up at the studio clock. Five hours to go.

Cotton wool clouds raced across the sky as she negotiated the potholes on the track that led from Celia's house. Reaching the tarmac Jenny sped along the Ditchling Road until she reached the lay-by by a dew-pond. She switched off the engine. Her stomach was churning like the tub of her washing machine. She opened the glove compartment, undid the cling-film and forced herself to eat a sausage roll. She looked towards the red tiled roofs of the farm buildings nestling in a hollow of the Downs. Jenny smiled as two lambs pranced on the ridge that surrounded the pond – their undocked tails swinging like tiny pendulums. Opening her handbag, she took out a mirror and said a silent prayer that she had not succumbed to Robert's heavy cold; that would have been a disaster. *At least I look normal this time, and it's not raining.* She examined her make-up and ran a comb through her hair, then taking a deep breath, turned the ignition.

Her palms stuck to the steering wheel as she waited for the traffic lights to change. Looking across to the green she saw a Land Rover parked outside the church. There were no other cars. Her heart fell. *That can't be Martin's – he works in a bank.* She couldn't remember seeing a Land Rover last November, but then she wouldn't have noticed if an elephant had been standing outside. The lights changed. She parked a few yards down from the Land Rover. Tightening the belt on her coat, she walked purposely across the green, her desire to see Martin again overcoming her nervousness. 'Please let him be here, please let him be here,' she whispered.

She peered over the flint wall. A dark-haired man was bending over a grave at the bottom of the slope. 'He's here,' she said softly, but then thought, *I can't do this. He's bound to realise I've come to see him. But if I don't, I'll always regret it.* Her heart knocked violently against her ribs. She took a deep breath, lifted the gate latch and walked into the churchyard.

'Hello Martin,' her voice quivered as she stood behind him.

'Hello Jenny,' he spoke her name before turning his head.

Jenny's breath came in short bursts. 'I hope I'm not disturbing you?' she brushed back some strands of hair that had blown across her face.

'Of course not, it's lovely to see you again.' He stood up and smiled. 'It's my mother's birthday today, so I've brought these tulips over – they were her favourite flowers.'

'I'm sorry about your mother,' Jenny said, looking at the headstone. 'I should have asked you when I saw you before. The flowers are lovely – very colourful.'

'That's alright. You were upset,' his brown eyes held hers.

'Yes I was. I've got to decide about my parent's headstone soon. I had some spare time this afternoon, so I thought I'd come over and get some ideas.' As soon as the words were out of her mouth, she thought how he must see through them.

Martin bent down again and started clearing up the discarded paper, stems and leaves. 'My mother told me you'd got married.'

'Did she? How did she know? You weren't living here then.'

'She probably heard it from Gail Simpson's cousin. They used to live next door to us, and her mother kept in touch when we moved.'

So, Gail must have told her cousin. 'Are you married?' Jenny felt she had to ask the question, even though she knew the answer.

'Yes, to Marilyn – we've got a son, Daniel. He'll be thirteen next week.'

Marilyn, that sounds quite glamorous, she thought. An image of a pretty blonde-haired woman flashed before her. She disliked her already.

'I've got two children,' Jenny added, and then realised that she had said I and not we.

'I thought you'd probably have children.' He stood up and stared at her.

'Everyone I knew was married by twenty-two – it seems so young now.' She looked away from his gaze.

'A couple of my friends are divorced.'

'Oh, are they?' Jenny reddened and remembered why she had said she was here. 'I'd better look around, get some ideas.' She moved a few feet away, stopping by her parent's grave for a moment, and then walked up a line of earlier graves, looking at each of the headstones in turn, but conscious of Martin's eyes following her. As she reached the top headstone, he was by her shoulder. Her skin tingled.

'Do you see that clump of celandines under the tree?' He pointed to the sycamore at the edge of the churchyard. 'Whenever I see them I know that summer will soon be here.'

Jenny turned, her body almost touching his. 'Yes, I love to see them too. They always look so cheerful. It's strange why so many spring flowers are yellow.'

'It's probably to do with yellow being the brightest colour in the spectrum, helps to guide the insects for pollination.'

Jenny searched desperately for something else to say.

'I'm starting a course next week in Lewes – Habitats and Wildlife,' she blurted out.

'I don't remember you being interested in the

countryside, but we didn't go out for long did we? And I probably had other things on my mind.' He grinned and gave Jenny the wry smile that she had always remembered.

She reached out for the top of the nearest headstone to steady herself. 'I'd better go soon. I've got to pick the children up from a neighbour. She looks after them sometimes, when it's the school holidays.'

'Oh, of course, I'll walk you back to your car. At least you won't have left your lights on this time.' He grinned and walked towards the bin provided by the verger for discarded tributes.

Jenny stared at his retreating figure. He was wearing a three-quarter length brown jacket over dark blue jeans. They weren't clothes that someone would wear to a job in a bank. *Perhaps he has a day off.* Having spoken and seen him once more, she couldn't bear to let him go away again. But what could she say? She cast her eyes down at the grass as he walked back towards her.

'Have you managed to get some ideas for the stone?'

'Yes, a few,' Jenny said, thinking that she would find it difficult to remember anything about the headstones. They walked side by side up the slope towards the path.

'I… I was wondering if we could meet again, somewhere else. I mean, just for a coffee somewhere? We haven't had time to catch up properly. But I'd understand if you felt you couldn't,' he spoke quietly as he closed the churchyard gate behind them.

'No, it's alright. I mean yes, I'd like to – to catch up; that would be good.' Jenny smiled, relieved at his words.

They walked the next few steps in silence while Jenny searched desperately for conversation. 'Is that your Land Rover?'

'Yes, it is. I've had it for a year now, since I changed my job.'

'Changed your job? I remember you worked at a bank in Brighton.'

'Yes, I got a transfer to a branch in Southampton,' Martin paused. 'So, ladies first, you'd better say where and when.' He laughed nervously.

'Well, I work three days a week, but I could meet you before my class, next Tuesday. It starts at seven, so I could meet you at six-thirty – but it's in Lewes.' *It doesn't give us very long,* Jenny thought, *but if it's a disaster, it wouldn't be too embarrassing.*

'That's fine for me. We live just outside Lewes. What about The Pelham Arms at the top of the High Street, it's opposite St. Anne's Church? That's on your way into Lewes, so you wouldn't have to go out of your way. We could still have a coffee there – or a drink – if you'd prefer?'

'That sounds good,' Jenny said, thinking that she didn't care what she would drink. Suddenly they were standing by her car. She searched in her handbag for her keys. 'Sorry,' she said looking up at him. 'I can never find my keys. It's all the junk I keep in my bag.'

'Women and their handbags,' Martin teased. Her

hand trembled as she put the key in the door. He held it open for her.

'Thank you.'

'My dad used to have a Morris Traveller. You know the model with the wood surround. They're very reliable.'

'Yes I've heard they are. This one's a bit old now, but I'm very fond of it,' Jenny said, wishing she could think of something more interesting to say.

'I'll see you on Tuesday then, six-thirty at The Pelham Arms.' He closed the car door with a solid clunk. Jenny smiled and nodded at him through the window as the engine turned over. She released the handbrake and pulled away. Looking in the side mirror, she could see him standing in the road watching her. Once she was below the windmill and out of his sight, she turned into a side road, and pulled over. She relaxed and revelled in the last twenty minutes, re-living every moment. He did come today, just as she'd hoped, and she was going to see him again.

Since the start of the Falklands War, Robert always joined Jenny in the lounge after dinner to watch the extended news. 'Look at those destroyers Jen. We've the best navy in the world. I can't stand Maggie, but you've got to hand it to her, she's a good leader when we need one.'

'Well I didn't vote for her either, but she's certainly a strong woman.'

'You look nice in that skirt and jumper. I don't remember seeing them before.'

'Mummy bought them on Tuesday – it was so boring. She spent ages in the shops.' Nicky was on all fours pushing one of his aeroplane fleet across the carpet.

'You didn't complain when you were eating that gi-normous ice cream sundae.' Lorna came into the room dressed completely in yellow; her favourite colour of the moment. It reminded Jenny of the celandines in the churchyard. She wondered if insects would be attracted to her.

'We had to wait at Christine's today, 'cos Mummy was late.' Nicky looked up at his father for masculine support.

'It was only a few minutes,' Jenny added.

'No it wasn't, it was ages.'

'Don't be such a baby, Nicky.' Lorna pushed her brother over with her foot.

'Ouch.'

'Shut up, both of you, I'm trying to listen to the news,' Robert said.

Jenny stared at the screen, but the pictures going through her mind were of a place much closer to home. Once she had internalised the afternoon's events, a fresh worry surfaced. Supposing she was ill, or had an accident? Or he had? How would they contact each other? He didn't even know her married name. She stood up and went over to a small oak table in the corner of the room and picked up a directory. Finding the page she read, Ballard; Barnard; M.Barretti, 2, Blacksmith Cottages, Lewes Road, Ringmer, alongside his address was the number, Ringmer.3495. *I could phone him*, she thought, but supposing his wife answered – what would she say? No, she couldn't do that. She would just have to hope that nothing untoward would happen. It was only a few days away and she would have to be on her death bed not to go. She slid the directory back on the shelf under the table.

'Jen, did you hear me? I said do you want me to leave the TV on or not?'

'Oh sorry, no, turn it off. By the way, you know that my classes start next Tuesday, for six weeks?'

'No, I'd forgotten. What time do you have to be there?'

'Six-thirty, so I'll get some food ready before I go,' Jenny added, feeling that she needed to preserve their normal evening routine.

'I'd have thought you'd have had enough of studying after finishing your course.'

'This is different. It's not work.'

'It's still a course. I'm just going downstairs for an hour, Jen. Then I'll come up and do the washing up.'

'Can I come down Daddy?' Nicky jumped up, treading on the wing of one of his aeroplanes.

'For goodness sake, what are you doing?' Jenny shouted. 'You must be more careful, look you've broken it.' Nicky's face crumpled.

'Jen, that was a bit harsh. I'm sure it can be mended, if not, it will teach him to be more careful. Won't it son? Come on, no tears.'

The recent shower glistened on the tarmac, as the early evening sun broke through the clouds. Jenny's stomach knotted.

Stopping at the traffic lights by the prison she could see the terraced house where they had lived before moving to Brighton. She looked away, not wanting anything to disturb her thoughts. She parked just beyond St. Anne's church and checked her watch, six-twenty-five. There was no sign of Martin's Land Rover. She opened her bag and squirted some perfume in the hollow of her neck and on the inside of her wrists. Swallowing hard, she locked her car and walked slowly up the hill towards the white washed public house. A westerly wind ruffled her skirt from under her three-quarter length coat. *Suppose he isn't here?* she thought, at least she wouldn't have to feel like a teenager on a first date. No – she wanted him to be here.

She walked slowly up and down – the sign squeaking as she passed under it – unsure whether or not to go inside. On unsteady legs she stepped into the tiled entrance and pushed the door into the saloon bar. She caught her breath. He was standing and smiling at her from behind a small round table at the end of the room.

'Hello Jenny, sit down, I was wondering whether you might have had second thoughts about coming.'

So he had thought that too. Her mouth was parched. She couldn't find the breath to speak, so smiled, and took her coat off, draping it on the back of the chair.

'What can I get you? A drink, or would you rather have a tea or coffee?'

'No, I think I'd rather have a drink,' she gulped to moisten her mouth, 'a lemonade shandy please.'

Her heart slowed and she noticed there were only two other people in the bar. She stared at Martin as he waited to be served. His straight dark hair rested on the collar of his jacket, while a side-parting forced his hair to flop over his forehead. He was slim, not too tall – about five eleven. Under a dark cord jacket, his shoulders were broad and slightly hunched. He had the look of an academic. The more she stared, the stronger her body reacted. It screamed for her to reach out and touch him. It was hard to carry on a normal conversation. She had been attracted to men before – including Robert – but it had a gentler quality, not this frightening intensity. Was that why she had run away from the churchyard last November? Was this love or lust? How would she know? Men always said they knew the difference. As he carried the drinks to their table, she noticed a dark polo-necked jumper and blue jeans. *He doesn't look as if he's come straight from work.*

'Here we are.'

Her hand shook slightly as she took her glass.

'So, where have you got to go for your class?' He sat opposite her.

'Oh, farther down the High Street, at St. Michael's church, where the large clock overhangs the road. Apparently there's a hall there.'

'Yes, I know it. Not far away then.' He started drinking from his pint glass.

'No, I've brought a notebook and pen to make some notes.' *Oh my God, that sounds so childish.*

'That's very industrious of you.' The skin around his eyes crinkled as he teased her. 'I only realised after you'd driven away last week, that I didn't know your married name.'

So he had thought that too. 'It's Maynard – my husband's Robert – Robert Maynard. His family come from Brighton. We lived here in Lewes when we were first married. Then when Robert went to work for Brighton Council, we moved. We live near Preston Village now. What about you? You said that you changed your job.'

'Yes, about a year ago. I'd been at the same bank since transferring from Brighton. Financially life was good. The low staff interest rates meant that we could easily afford a large house. But, my heart wasn't in the job. I didn't want to feel like that for the next thirty years, staying there, just for the benefits and a pension. That would have been a living death. So about seven years ago I started an open university course, studying in my spare time. I'd always been interested in the countryside so, once I graduated I applied to be a countryside ranger.'

'Where?'

'The Seven Sisters Country Park.'

'Oh,' *so that explains the Land Rover*, she thought.

'You look surprised.'

'Well, it's certainly different from working in a bank.'

'Yes, it is. The money's a lot less of course, and our house is tiny compared to our old one. But I'm much happier. I don't work nine to five, and I'm virtually my own boss. Also I was pleased to come back this way. My father's on his own since Mum died, so I can see him more often. Anna – my sister – she still lives in Southampton. Marilyn was marvellous about the move. She comes from the New Forest. Her family are all still down there.'

Jenny winced at his mention of his wife.

'You don't look any older to me, Jenny. I've always thought about you and wondered what you were doing.' Martin smiled and put his glass on a beer mat that advertised a local brewery.

Jenny updated him on her life since leaving school and then added, 'I've just finished a part-time course in accountancy and law at the technical college,' her voice trembled.

'That's good. Is that what you do at the moment?'

'Well, yes, I suppose I do, only part-time though. I'd like to do more once Nicky, our youngest, is a bit older.' Jenny sipped her drink.

'How old is he?'

'He's nine, and Lorna's nearly twelve, she starts high school in September.'

'You know Jenny, I probably shouldn't say this, but I was hoping that I might see you again – in the churchyard.'

Her spirit leapt. She smiled and wondered if she should say something similar, but decided not to.

'Who's taking your class tonight, I might know him?'

'Andrew Jones.'

'Yes, we've spoken on the phone a few times. He works for the R.S.P.B. at Shoreham. It should be interesting.'

'So, you live near Lewes then?' Jenny blushed as she recalled how she had looked in the telephone directory.

'Yes, at Ringmer, on the main road, I cut over the Downs by Glyndebourne. Then it's about twenty minutes to the Country Park. Daniel's at the community college, in the village. We would have preferred the school here, in Lewes, but there were no vacancies. He's doing well though, so we're pleased.'

Jenny bit her lip, she would have to leave soon.

'My sister always does that when she's worried.'

'Does what?'

'Bites her lower lip.'

She blushed as she thought he might know what she was thinking. 'I'd better go.' Jenny lifted her glass and drained the last few drops. She stood up and lifted her coat from the back of her chair.

'Yes, you can't be late for the first class.' Martin smiled sardonically and took her coat, holding it open for her. She was aware of him behind her as she put her arms through the sleeves. She didn't want to move.

They left the warmth of the bar, and met the chill of the spring evening. 'I'll walk you to your car.'

'I'm just over there,' Jenny pointed to her car. 'Where did you park?' she asked, thinking how unnatural she sounded.

'There's a small area at the back. I managed to get a space,' he paused, 'Jenny, how do you feel about meeting up again, same time next week? I'd be interested to hear about your class.'

He does want to, she thought, relieved that he had spoken the words she was unable to.

'Yes, I'd like that too. The time went too quickly, didn't it?' Jenny said as she rummaged in her handbag for the key.

Martin grinned and held the car door open. 'You should be able to park down there, this time in the evening. I'll see you next Tuesday then, same place.'

'What's happening to me?' Jenny asked herself. She whispered the words while washing the breakfast dishes, while driving to work, while cooking the evening meal, and thought it when she sat beside Robert on the sofa and watched the evening news. She wondered how she could prevent her excitement from bursting forth. Jenny had on her own admission, always been a "news freak", thinking that women who didn't take an interest in anything outside their domestic world, were shallow and parochial. Now, here she was, watching the escalation of war in the South Atlantic, men and boys being killed, families mourning their losses, and all she could think about was another man – she was no better than the women she had always despised.

When Jenny entered the saloon bar the following Tuesday, her face dropped. The corner table was empty. Oh, no, what should she do? Leave, or order a drink and wait? Glancing quickly at the barman, who had his back to her, she turned on her new heels and walked towards the door. She would wait in her car until she could see him arrive.

'Jenny, where are you going?' Martin's darkened outline appeared in the doorway.

'Oh, I left something in my car, but it doesn't matter.' Relief flooded through her. She smiled at him, and turned around.

'I'm sorry I was late, there was an accident on the A27. I was worried I'd be even later. The tailback went right back to Firle.' He wiped the palm of his hand across his forehead. 'I could do with a drink.'

'I'll buy them this time,' said Jenny.

'No, you sit down. I'll get them, same as last week?'

'Yes please.'

'So how did the first class go?' Jenny felt his fingers gently brush against her own as she took her glass. Martin stood and gulped a quarter of his glass before sitting opposite her.

'It was good, I enjoyed it. There's about fifteen of us. Andrew spoke a little about the various habitats, and how they were formed. Then he showed us a few slides. He plans to go into each habitat in more depth, it's downland this week.'

'He's bound to mention the Seven Sisters, although he might leave it until he covers the coast.' Martin took another gulp of his drink. 'That's better.' He smiled across the table at Jenny and fumbled in his coat pocket. 'Do you mind if I smoke?'

Jenny was taken aback. She had assumed that he didn't smoke.

'No,' she said, remembering how she had pestered Robert to give up when the children were small.

'I don't smoke a lot, just socially, normally with a drink to relax. Daniel hates it. I've promised him I'll give up soon.' He offered the open packet to Jenny.

She had a vision of a boy – a younger version of Martin – vehemently taking his father to task.

'No, thank you, I don't, not now. I did for a while when I was younger – everybody did didn't they? But I gave up when I was expecting Lorna.'

She thought of her daughter's indignation at anything she decided was an unsuitable activity for parents. She certainly wouldn't approve of her mother sitting here.

'Very sensible, I shall have to follow your example, won't I?' He smiled his teasing smile and flicked his lighter. He inhaled deeply, leant back in his chair and stared at Jenny.

'So what does Robert do?'

'He works in the Highways Office.'

'Is he interested in the countryside?'

'No, not really, but he makes an effort because of me; his main hobby is model railways – there's one in our cellar – and he plays cricket sometimes. He's in the work's team. Is, is – Marilyn interested?' Jenny forced herself to say her name.

'Not really, she's a sporty girl. She represented Hampshire when she was younger – athletics. That's how we met. I used to do some DJ-ing in a pub in the evenings, and she and some others came in for a drink. She doesn't participate anymore, but enjoys taking Daniel to events. He's inherited her sporting ability, so she's kept busy driving him around at weekends. Most Saturdays she's gone all day. You have to do it for them, don't you?'

'I remember when you said you were saving up for a guitar.'

'Yes, I've still got it. I give it a strum now and then.'

'My father taught me the names of all the capital cities when I was young.'

'Capital cities? That's different.' Martin gave her a quizzical look.

'Yes, I know. I've never forgotten them. I've – we've manage to visit a few – Paris; Dublin; Edinburgh; Bonn and earlier this year we went to Cairo.'

'Cairo? That's impressive. You are well travelled. I haven't been outside the UK, Marilyn's never been that keen. I've been to Scotland though, and Ireland. You haven't been to Rome then? My dad's family come from a small town near there.'

'I hope to, in a few years.'

'I'm sure you will.' He gave an amused smile that implied more than the spoken words.

Jenny melted into the moment, she felt invisible. If someone who knew her had walked into the bar, she felt that they wouldn't see or recognise her.

'Were your parents involved in an accident? Only I noticed, on their cross, that they died close together. I'm sorry, I shouldn't ask you.' He suddenly looked solemn.

'No, it's alright; they both had cancer, although my mother was ill for much longer than my father. I think it was the shock of losing her that caused him to die so soon after. But now, I think it was for the best. He would have hated living on his own, he never had. Before he was married he was in the army. He wouldn't even cook a meal for himself.'

'That must have been hard for you.'

'I couldn't have managed without Robert. I don't have any brothers or sisters.'

'My mother died of cancer too. She ignored the symptoms, said it was nothing, so by the time she went to the doctor it had spread too far. She was only in her early sixties.'

'Did your aunt live very long?'

'My aunt?' he looked puzzled.

'Yes, she was seriously ill. That's why you moved back to Southampton, so your mother could look after her.'

'Oh, yes, she did die, but not 'til quite a few years later.'

Jenny glanced at her watch. 'I'll have to go now.'

'Yes, we mustn't dwell on unhappy times, must we? Life's too short. Go and enjoy your class.' He lifted her coat from the back of the chair.

His hand briefly touched her shoulder as he helped her into her coat.

'I don't really need a coat this evening. It's warm for late April,' Jenny said as they crossed the road towards her car.

'Yes, the swifts will soon be here. They usually arrive at the Cuckmere on May 4th.'

Jenny turned to Martin as he walked by her side. 'You mean they arrive on the same day every year?'

'Yes, nearly always.'

'That's amazing. I love seeing the swifts.'

Their next two meetings followed the same pattern. Jenny felt more relaxed in his presence, but still couldn't eat more than a mouthful of food before leaving home, and her heart still wanted to leap out of her chest as she stepped into the pub. But once she glimpsed Martin, it soon returned to a slower rhythm. He would have a drink waiting for her, and ask about the previous week's class, and she would enjoy sharing her newly acquired knowledge. They would discover a little more about each other's lives; each revelation a strand of invisible thread connecting them to each other. Martin told how his grandfather had come to London as a young man with his wife and baby son before the First World War. How he had sold ice creams from a bicycle before buying a café with his cousin. His father, born a year after they arrived in England, had met his mother on a day trip to Southampton just before the start of the Second World War. They married and set up home in Brighton to escape the bombing. Jenny then told him about her parents' early lives, pleased that she could tell him, that they too, had been brought up in London, and later moved to Sussex.

Jenny's happiness spilled over to her family. Every evening she would greet Robert with a kiss, instead of being a passive recipient of his affection. She took an interest in Lorna's enthusiasm for all things horsey and was able to recite each stage of saddling up.

She promised Nicky that they would have a day trip to Duxford in the summer holiday to see Concorde. She didn't analyse her happiness. She was seeing Martin again, and that was enough.

'You're looking really different lately,' Robert remarked, one day in May. 'Blooming, in fact, it must be all those talks about wild flowers.' He laughed out loud at his joke, and Jenny smiled. She knew that in anyone else's eyes it was wrong to continue to see

Martin, but rationalised that she had known him before Robert and so that made it alright. *Anyway,* she thought, *is anyone strong enough to weigh morality against happiness and choose the former?*

14

May 1982

On the fourth evening of Jenny's classes, they sat opposite each other at the end of the saloon bar. Concealed behind her smiles, Jenny wrestled with the question – what would happen now?

'It's my last class tonight,' Jenny said, a few minutes after arriving, not able to hide her thoughts any longer.

'I know,' Martin stared at her, his face suddenly solemn. 'Jenny, you have enjoyed meeting up, haven't you? Because I have.'

How could he ask that? Can't he see how happy I am. 'Of course I have.'

'It will be very hard not to see you again,' he said, still staring at her.

'It doesn't have to be our last meeting,' Jenny said, remembering she had told Robert that there were six classes, not four. 'We could still meet up, next Tuesday?' Time was suspended while she waited for his reply.

'I couldn't ask you that, you understand why, don't you?'

'Because I'm married?'

Martin nodded. 'It had to come from you, to be what you wanted.' He placed his hand over hers.

'But you're married too.'

'I know, but it still had to come from you.'

The warmth from his hand diffused throughout her body. She didn't want him to take his hand away.

'I'd love to show you around the Country Park – it would be like a postscript to your classes – a field trip.' He laughed, the skin around his eyes puckering. 'I could meet you there. It's quite a way for you to drive, though – from Brighton. We could meet somewhere closer, if you'd rather.' He removed his hand, but the warmth remained.

'No, I'd love to see the Country Park.'

'Mummy, I feel really ill.' Lorna's shaky voice carried down the stairs and into the kitchen.

'I'll come up,' Jenny sighed, as she dried her hands.

'My throat's really, really sore.' Lorna's white face looked up from the pillow as she twisted a strand of light brown hair around her index finger. Her resemblance to Robert made Jenny think that she was ill to thwart her.

'Did you take the paracetamol tablet I left you?' asked Jenny.

'Yes.'

Jenny looked at the alarm clock. 'Ten fifteen – I better give Dr Mason a ring. It's best if he takes a look at you. Then I'll go down to the chemist for some more blackcurrant drink – there's not much left in that bottle.'

'I really, really wanted to go to school today. There's a teacher coming from Varndean to talk to us.'

'It can't be helped, can it? You'll hear all about it from Emma and Sarah when you go back. Would you like anything else from the shops?'

'Could you get me a magazine, anything except *Jackie*; I've already read this week's.'

'Alright, but try and go back to sleep. I'll be as quick as I can.'

'Don't be long, will you?' Lorna called after her.

'I'll have to phone the doctor first.'

As Jenny went downstairs, she thought, and not for the first time, why no one ever warned them how often children are ill. People are compelled to speak about sleepless nights, toddlers' tantrums and teenage angst, but there was a conspiracy of silence about the endless rounds of colds, sore throats, sickness and diarrhoea. *Children are virus factories,* she decided. *It wouldn't be so bad if we didn't end up getting them as well. At least it's better now than when they were younger. I'd better phone work first.*

'I'm sorry Celia, but Lorna's not well. I can't come over today. I can come on Thursday instead, if that's alright. No, I can't tomorrow – Lorna won't be well enough for school. I'm sorry to mess you about Celia. I'll see you Thursday then.' Jenny replaced the receiver thinking that even if Lorna was better by tomorrow, which was unlikely, the last thing she wanted to do was to go to work. She wanted to be free all day to linger on her evening with Martin. The anticipation was as delicious as their meetings. 'The surgery next,' she muttered, picking up the phone again.

Jenny tiptoed into Lorna's room. Her daughter lay asleep on her side, breathing noisily. Her eyes were caught by a poster above the dressing table. A group of four blond, seemingly acne free, teenage boys were leaping into the air. She didn't remember seeing it before. She was sure that a picture of a galloping black horse had been on that wall a few days earlier. She placed the bottle and magazine on the bedside table and crept out of the room. Ignoring the bowl of unwashed breakfast plates, she made herself a coffee, took it into the lounge and stood staring out of the bay window. She was deceiving Robert, and he hadn't done anything to deserve it. She remembered he always came home in the early hours after his office Christmas party, but she knew if anything sexual had occurred, it wasn't serious enough to worry about. Perhaps she should tell him that she had met Martin again. Nothing had happened between them. She could say that he was just a friend. Was that possible? She could say she had bumped into him before her class. She needn't say anything about the churchyard. Perhaps Martin and Marilyn could become friends of them both. Then she could see him without any secrecy. She imagined them visiting each other's houses; long conversations over three course meals. But he would be with her. She would have to watch him walk away with her; and he would see her with Robert. No, he wasn't just a friend. Why do we say 'just a friend' anyway? She thought of her friends – they were important to her, not *just* anything. Could she greet Martin with a cheery peck on the cheek and casually wave him goodbye? No – it would be too painful. She didn't even like him mentioning his wife's name. She wanted him.

Jenny forced her thoughts back to Lorna. She was growing up. Her deception about Martin reminded her of a conversation she had had with Robert the other day, as they had driven home from the cinema.

'Now that Mum and Dad have died, I've been wondering if I ought to tell Lorna and Nicky that I was adopted. What do you think?'

'Why on earth would you want to do that?' Robert had said, not taking his eyes from the road ahead.

'Well, it was a terrible shock when I discovered the truth. If I don't say anything to Lorna and Nicky, I'm just doing the same to the next generation, perpetuating a lie. I would never have said anything to them while Mum and Dad were alive. But now they're gone…'

'But it's different, Jen. They're not adopted. They don't need to know, and anyway would you have been any happier for knowing? You might have worried about it, if they had told you.'

'I suppose I might have. Anyway, I don't think I can tell them right out of the blue, that Mum and Dad weren't their real grandparents. But they were their real grandparents, just as Maggie and Reggie are. In fact, thinking about it, it's only your mother who is a blood grandparent.' *And I can't stand her,* Jenny thought. 'No, you're right. They don't need to know – it might spoil their memories.'

'Mmm,' Robert had nodded, still staring straight ahead. Jenny remembered her mother giving her the same reasons for not saying anything. *If we don't tell the truth at the beginning of a relationship, the more difficult it becomes to tell it at all,* she thought. For the first time Jenny understood why her mother had not been able to tell her the truth.

The dark mass of Friston Forest lay below the horizon. In the valley below lay the sluggish meanders of the Cuckmere. Straining her eyes Jenny saw the dark green shape of a Land Rover – like a Dinky car – in the car park beyond the riverbank. He said he would wait for her there. Excitement mixed with fear gripped her as she coasted down the steep hill, and clattered over the wooden bridge.

'Hello Jenny,' Martin said jumping down from the Land Rover. A pair of binoculars bounced against his brown shirt.

'Hi,' she tried to sound casual as she faced him.

'I hope it hasn't taken you too long to get here?'

'No, it was an easy drive,' she said shakily.

'I thought we might drive down to the estuary. It's a bit too far to walk there and back.'

'That sounds good,' Jenny said, reaching back into her car for a jacket. 'I'll probably need this. It's still cold in the evening.'

'Yes, summer hasn't arrived just yet.'

She felt his eyes on her as she locked the car door.

'I haven't seen you in trousers before, they suit you.'

Jenny reddened, remembering how long she had spent in front of her bedroom mirror trying to decide which pair of her three casual trousers would flatter her figure the most.

They clambered into the Land Rover and turned to each other and smiled; silently reassuring the other that there was no need for words. He reversed out of the car park onto a concrete road that edged the downland.

'I've been looking forward to this evening,' she said.

'So have I.' He turned and held her eyes. 'I hope it wasn't difficult for you, coming here?'

She knew he wasn't referring to the traffic. 'No, no it was fine.' She had left Lorna in bed still recovering from tonsillitis, and on the threat of withdrawing his pocket money, told Nicky not to answer the phone or the door, until his father came home.

A pothole in the road surface caused her to lurch towards him. Their shoulders touched. She pulled away.

'Sorry, it's a bit of a bone-shaker,' he said. 'So, what have you learnt about the estuary?'

'That it's famous for its ox-bows, and important for migratory and wading birds.'

'Yes it is. There's a bird ringing station a couple of miles away.'

At the end of the road a rough track led across the salt marsh. Martin drove until they arrived at a bank of shingle that stretched from the east side of the river to where the Seventh Sister cliff bent low and touched the pebbles with white chalk.

'Have you been down here before?'

'Not right down to the estuary. A couple of years ago we walked over Seaford Head to the coastguard cottages. There's a fantastic view from the top. I remember we took some photos.'

They stepped down and walked side by side, their feet sinking into the shingle. Apart from a fisherman casting his line into the sea, there was no one else around. A sharp breeze blew their hair back from their faces. Jenny realised that she had left her jacket behind. At the edge of the salt marsh Martin bent down. Jenny stared at the back of his head. She reached out to touch him, but inches from his head pulled her hand back.

'This is Glasswort. See how it has these fleshy leaves?' He stood up, standing inches away from her and passed her the plant.

'I remember Andrew saying that's how they adapt to the salty conditions.' She put the stem in the pocket of her trousers and looked away. 'I think there's a heron over there. I knew I should have brought my binoculars,' she laughed nervously.

'What's mine is yours,' he said with a sardonic smile,

and looping the strap over his head passed her a pair. 'It's a bit exposed here. You're not cold are you?'

'Yes, a bit, I left my jacket in the Land Rover.' She raised the binoculars to her eyes.

'Here, have mine,' he took off his jacket. She tingled as she felt his hands adjusting his jacket around her. 'That's better isn't it?' His hands lingered on her shoulders. She continued to look through the binoculars, and then turned to face him. He looked away quickly. 'We'd better get back to the car. We can watch from there.'

They sat and stared at the sea through the smeared windscreen.

Martin spoke first. 'How's Lorna and Nicky?'

'They're fine, Lorna's getting excited about changing schools in September. How's Daniel?'

'Fine, he goes to Scouts on Tuesday evenings. Are you warmer now?'

'Yes.' Jenny searched desperately for something else to say, but his presence drove out words.

'I saw a long-eared owl here the other day – over the marsh. I think there's a pair nesting in Friston Forest. That's unusual for around here. If we're lucky we might see it.'

'I saw a barn owl once, it looked like a ghost.'

'Yes, they do,' he chuckled. 'They're much rarer now. Not many old barns left; they're all being converted into houses. I think it's a mad idea. Apart from destroying valuable habitat, they must be freezing in winter, and cost a fortune to heat.'

'I suppose people who can afford to convert them, can afford to heat them.'

'Hmm.'

'I can tell that you really love your work,' Jenny turned to face him.

'Yes, I do, I'm very lucky.' He held her eyes, until she was forced to look away. 'If we drive back slowly we can keep a look out for the owl. I could make you a drink when we get back, if you'd like? I've got an office at the visitor's centre. That's if you don't have to rush back.'

'No, no, I don't.'

'Well we didn't see any owls – or ghosts, did we?' Martin laughed as he unlocked the wooden door to the centre. 'Mind you, it's probably a bit early for ghosts. This used to be a barn, until it was converted to the visitor's centre.'

'I think Lorna and Nicky came here once with the school.'

'They probably did. We get lots of school parties here. I'm supposed to say that I enjoy showing the kids around, but I don't. I like some children individually, but en masse they're a different matter.' Jenny wondered if he would like Lorna and Nicky. She didn't like them herself sometimes. She followed him to the rear of the centre. 'Here we are – enter,' he gave a low sweep with his right hand. 'This is where I spend quite a few hours each week, too many sometimes.' Jenny walked into a small square room. 'Sit down and make yourself at home – tea or coffee?'

'Coffee would be good.' He disappeared into an adjoining room. Jenny could hear him whistling as she looked around. Files covered an old wooden desk, while on a dusty windowsill stood an even dustier spider plant, its many off-shoots dangling to the floor. The walls were covered with posters.

He came back into the room carrying two mugs of steaming coffee. 'I bought some chocolate biscuits earlier. I hope you like them.' He placed the drinks on the table and went over to a cupboard and produced a tin that showed New Forest ponies munching grass on the lid. 'You're not dieting or anything, I hope?'

'No, I'm not.' Jenny laughed as she thought the last thing she needed to do at the moment was to diet. The tension and excitement of the past few weeks were doing a good enough job. She put the mug to her lips, took a sip and placed it on the table. 'It's a bit too hot to drink at the moment.'

'I'll show you around then while they cool down.'

Jenny followed him out into the visitor's centre. The walls were covered with colourful posters showing downland and estuary plants, birds, mammals and insects. Glass cases sloped downwards from the walls. Fossils and flint axes were displayed with labels showing when and where they were found. Jenny lingered by a "Shepherd's Crown". She read "Birling Gap 1979".

'We find a lot of those in the chalk,' said Martin.

'Does anyone else work here with you?'

'Not permanently. I have volunteers all year who help with the management, and a university student comes in the holidays. It's not lonely here, there's always plenty of visitors.'

Jenny ran her fingers along the top of the glass as she walked along, trying to concentrate on what lay beneath. She was aware of Martin inches behind her.

'You've got a barn owl,' Jenny spoke softly as she reached the corner. The stuffed bird looked down at them from a wooden bough.

'Yes, we've got some more birds over there.'

'Where?' Jenny turned. He was almost touching her. The air between them quivered with longing.

'Over there.' Martin looked straight into her eyes.

This is it, she thought, and lifted her hand to touch his hair.

'Come here,' he whispered.

'I suppose this is when I'm meant to say I'm sorry, and that I didn't mean this to happen. But I can't Jenny, because I'm not sorry, and I did.' He lifted his head from between her breasts and kissed her tenderly on her lips. 'Is it uncomfortable for you lying here?'

'I haven't noticed, at least it's carpeted of a sort. I'm not sorry either.' She covered his face with kisses. She had never felt so complete.

'Mmm,' he gave a deep sigh. 'I could stay like this all night, but, it must be getting late. I'll go and make us a drink. The others must be stone cold by now.' He smiled at her, the skin around his eyes crinkling. He sat up and looking around, laughed out loud. 'Look at our clothes.'

Jenny joined in his laughter. 'How did they get over there?'

'I don't remember.' He laughed again.

'Nor do I.' Jenny watched him as he staggered to his feet and found his underpants, then his socks and trousers. She couldn't take her eyes off him. He covered her body with his shirt. 'This will keep you warm.'

Jenny sat up, the ghostly mask of the owl watching as she gathered her clothes.

'Coffee's made. Come and sit in here,' Martin called from his office.

Jenny smoothed her jumper over her trousers and ran her fingers through her hair in an attempt to untousle it.

'We'll try again, shall we?' He smiled sardonically, as Jenny entered the room. He placed two chairs side by side.

The fading light cast shadows across the desk as Jenny sipped her coffee. She was a married woman with two children. Suppose he didn't want to meet her again? She couldn't bear it. But he was married too. He took both of her hands in his.

'I should have done this earlier,' he said. 'I wanted to, but, I couldn't.'

'Yes, I know.' Jenny remembered how she had reached out to him earlier on the beach. It had to be all or nothing.

'If you drive back soon, you shouldn't be too late. You should get home before it's too dark.'

'What will you say?' Jenny said, not adding his wife's name.

'Don't worry about me. I'll think of something.' Martin walked over to a filing cabinet. 'I've got a meeting in Chichester tomorrow, so I need to take a file home with me.'

Jenny stared at his back as he rummaged through the metal cabinet and wondered where they would go from here.

'We'd better go.' Martin shut his office door behind them and they walked past the spot where they had made love. 'I won't be able to forget you now will I? Not that I could before.' He drew her to him and kissed her tenderly. After padlocking the wooden door to the centre, they walked hand in hand in silence across the road. Jenny panicked, as she felt for her car keys in her trouser pocket. *Should she say something?*

'Jenny, do you want to meet here again next Tuesday?'

Do I want to? Do I want to? It's too late for that. 'Yes, of course I want to.'

They kissed again, and tried to draw apart, but embraced twice more.

'I can't bear to leave you,' Jenny whispered. 'Shall I phone you here if there's a problem?'

'Yes, the number's in the book. I'll see you here the same time next week then.' He held her car door open. 'Take care driving back.'

'You're late,' Robert said as Jenny walked passed the open door.

She went into the kitchen and sat down. She couldn't face going straight into the lounge as she usually did. She opened the hatch. 'I'll be in, in a minute. Would you like some tea?' Robert never drank coffee.

'Yes, if you're making one. We've lost some more ships.'

'I'll be in soon.' Jenny felt in her trouser pocket and removed the stem of glasswort. She turned it over in her hand and took an eggcup from the cupboard. Adding a little water she placed it on the windowsill. *Did that really happen tonight?* She hadn't expected it. But what had she expected – a few kisses and a cuddle? She had spent enough time making sure she looked attractive for him. She lingered in the kitchen after she had made the tea.

'Jenny – are you coming in?'

'Yes, just coming.'

'Here you are.' She handed Robert his tea.

'Come and sit here with me.' He moved the newspaper along the sofa.

Jenny sat down in the armchair opposite. 'The class went on a bit longer this evening.'

'It's your last one next week isn't it?' he looked across at her.

'It might not be. Someone asked Andrew if we could go on some field trips, now that it's summer; so they might go on a bit longer.'

15

July 1982

'I hate you having to lie,' Martin said as he lay on his back in the grass.

'Saying I'm going on a field trip isn't really lying. I'm just being economical with the truth.'

The temperature had reached eighty-six degrees earlier that afternoon. The newscaster had said that it was the hottest day of the year so far. They left the Land Rover at the end of the concrete road and walked across the Downs for half a mile to a hollow screened by a trio of gorse bushes. Jenny turned on her side and raising herself on one elbow smiled down at him thinking that she would say anything to be with him. 'You have to be economical too, don't you?' Jenny picked a stalk of grass and ran it up his neck, and down to the edge of his forest of chest hair.

'I do, but I can always say that it's to do with work. You can't go on field trips indefinitely.'

Martin reached into his jeans and pulled out a packet of cigarettes. 'You don't mind do you Jenny?'

'No, of course not.' If Robert has asked the same

question, she would have said she did mind, and start to nag him. That was the difference – she loved this man. It was impossible for her to refuse him anything.

'I haven't done this before. I want you to know that,' he flicked his lighter and drew deeply on the cigarette.

'I should hope not.' Jenny grinned and covered his lips with her own, devouring the tobacco. 'Neither have I. You've made a scarlet woman of me, Mr Barretti.'

'My mother used to say that.'

'What – you've made a scarlet woman of me?' she laughed out loud.

'No, well not exactly that. She might have said it to my father though,' he laughed. 'She always used to call him Mr Barretti when she was cross with him, which was quite often.'

'Well I'm certainly not cross with you.' She covered his face with kisses. 'I remember your sister being angry with you at her birthday party, that day you invited me round. She accused you of taking something from her room. I can't remember what.'

'I can. I took some of her birthday money. I wanted to buy you a record. I owned up the next day, and paid her back.'

'I remember wishing my hair was straight like hers, instead of wavy and unmanageable.'

'She's blonde now – it doesn't suit her, but she won't have it. She thinks she's one of Charlie's Angels. Anyway I love your hair wavy and unmanageable. I can bury myself in it.' He pushed her back on the grass, rolled on top of her and pressed his mouth hard against hers. 'Look what you do to me. If we stay here any longer I won't be responsible for my actions for the second time this evening, and you'll be very late home.' He stood up, fastened the belt on his jeans, reached out his hand and pulled Jenny to her feet. 'We've got quite a walk back. I was tempted once. It was a girl at the bank; we were on a course. It's usually at work where these things happen, isn't it?'

'I wouldn't know. It certainly couldn't happen at Celia's,' Jenny said, fastening the buttons on her blouse.

'But I didn't want to risk my marriage.'

But you are now, she thought. She didn't know whether to feel pleased that he felt so passionately about her, or jealous that he had once considered someone else. He must have fancied Marilyn too. *Does he still?* The question lingered. He had confided in her though. That brought them closer. Perhaps she could confide something too? The sun was still high as they walked down the chalk path.

'You look deep in thought, the way you're biting your lower lip. Are you worried about something?'

Jenny's ankle twisted on a large flint. Martin reached out to steady her. 'Careful, are you alright?'

'I was adopted – as a baby,' she said.

'Were you?' he smiled at her. 'My best friend at school was adopted. Dave, David Warlow – I don't think you knew him. He didn't come to the youth club.

We were at junior school together, but lost touch after we moved. Men aren't very good at keeping in contact. He was always boasting that his real dad was a G.I. We all thought he was lying, but it was probably true. His birthday was at the end of 1944. He was always playing cowboys and Indians. Mind you we all did back then.'

Jenny remembered her cousin Alan as a boy, wearing his Indian headdress.

'Does it worry you?'

'Not now. It did when I first found out.'

'You found out. Your parents – didn't tell you?'

'No.'

'So did they say who your parents were?'

'Only that my father was a soldier from South Africa, and my mother was a young girl. That's enough for me. I don't want to know anymore than that. I loved my parents.' Jenny brought the topic to an end. They had both confided in the other. They were equal.

'South Africa, so we both have foreign roots then.' Martin put his arm around her shoulders. 'We better get a move on if we're going to have time for a drink.'

They clambered over a stile and quickened their pace across the short turf. 'There's a badger's sett on the other side of this field. There were some youngsters there the other evening, we might see them if we're lucky.'

16

July 1982

'I'll think I'll have an early night. What about you Jen?'

... *Cape Town occupies one of the world's most stunning locations. Take the cable car to the top of Table Mountain, where to the south you can see Cape Point and look across to Robben Island in Table Bay...* 'I'll just finish this chapter first.' She knew the code. An early night meant only one thing. Initially, when she had thought about it at all, she had decided that seeing Martin didn't have to threaten her marriage. They could carry on meeting, sharing their lives, her joy spilling over into everyday life. One of Lorna's friends had remarked on it just last week, on a day trip to London.

'Your mum's so much more fun than mine,' she had heard Sarah say as they had waited for an hour in the queue outside Madame Tussauds.

'Yeah, she has been lately,' Lorna had replied, and cupped one hand over her mouth and whispered something to her friend. They had both burst into fits of giggles.

Two weeks earlier she had taken Nicky on a day trip

to Duxford, enthusing with him every time they clambered up into the metal bodies of the planes and were shown the controls. The previous weekend she went to a cricket match – in Croydon, of all places – to watch Robert play. All these things she had done willingly. The problem was sex. It had been easy in Egypt, where there were other distractions and the distance from home liberating. They had returned home full of Middle-Eastern promise. For a few months the promise was fulfilled. Even when she began meeting Martin, her happiness ensured a generosity of response when Robert reached for her in bed. But once they had made love, everything changed. A few weeks ago, they had invited some friends over for Sunday lunch; they had just left, when she noticed Robert staring at her.

'Have you changed your hair Jen? You look different lately. I can't quite put my finger on what it is about you. More confident perhaps, that's it; you're more confident. It's very sexy.'

He had been right. She had changed. Everything that had been an effort before was easy; except for one thing.

Robert had come over and pulled her towards him, running his hands up and down her back, and whispering in her ear, 'I'll do the clearing up later, let's go upstairs? The kids are in the garden. We can lock the door just in case.'

'I'm expecting a call from Celia.'

'Let her ring back.'

'No, it would spoil it if she rings.'

'I'll take the phone off the hook then.'

'No.'

Robert's face dropped. The tone of her voice had been enough. He sighed, walked out of the room and opened the cellar door.

'Are you coming up?' Robert's words booming down the stairs returned her thoughts to the present.

Jenny put a bookmark between the pages describing the Cape Winelands, and with a heavy heart walked from room to room, checking that all light switches and sockets were turned off, and that the front and back doors were locked.

'What on earth have you been doing down there?' Robert sat naked on his side of the bed, splashing aftershave across his evening stubble. The small bedside lamp on Jenny's side threw a beam of soft light across their bed.

He's so predictable, she thought as she slipped between the sheets. *No, that's unfair. He doesn't deserve that. He's a good man. He's never done anything to hurt me, but I don't want him.*

Sliding alongside his wife, Robert ran his hand up Jenny's thigh.

'No, I'm sorry Robert, I've got my period.' She pushed his hand away.

'You said that last week. You can't still have it.' He pushed her nightdress up over her hips.

'It's been lasting longer lately.'

'Well, it can't be that bad now. It was nearly two weeks ago. I'll just lie on top of you.'

She knew what he was thinking; that once he started to arouse her she was bound to respond – period or not. He rubbed his penis against her stomach and moved slowly downwards. *He was right,* she thought, as she parted her legs, and turned her head to avoid his kisses. As Robert thrust against her, she thought of Martin and imagined him and his wife in bed. Jealousy surged like a tsunami. She couldn't bear the idea of him with anyone else. What did Marilyn look like? Her chest tightened at the thought of her. She gasped for breath.

'See, you're enjoying it too,' Robert muttered breathlessly, then groaned and collapsed, pinning her to the mattress.

17

July 1982

Jenny parked on the narrow road that encircled the green. Cricket stumps bent towards her as a gust of wind blew. She walked back towards the main road that separated the two halves of the village. *I'll cross over and walk towards Lewes first*, she thought. She passed a line of detached houses that lay back from the road, Sunnyside; Holly Tree Cottage; Well Cottage. *Why on earth do they call enormous houses like these cottages.* At the end of the row a post box edged the footpath. Behind it was the Post Office and general store. Alongside stood a Victorian detached house divided into two; the bricks advertising its age. No. 1 Blacksmith Cottages was written roughly on a wooden gate. Beside the second semi was a low wooden building. A sign hung from the guttering, B. Goble – Hand Made Furniture. *That looks as if it was the forge*, she thought, picturing shire horses waiting patiently to be shod. *At least these are proper cottages.* Checking that there was no sign of Martin's Land Rover, Jenny approached until level with the gate. She stood and stared. The house had two floors, with a dormer window poking through the roof. The paintwork was a freshly-painted sage green. The rooms looked small. *It must have been strange for them moving here after a large house.* A pair of muddy wellington boots stood in the porch. She turned round. There was a lane opposite, tunnelled by overhanging trees, she decided to drive there and wait.

Jenny raised her binoculars. A dark-haired boy on a bicycle skidded to a halt by the gate. Leaning his bike on the hedge, he rushed up the brick path and opened the front door. *That must be Daniel.* Five minutes later the boy emerged. Jenny raised her binoculars again, and staring hard, took in his every feature. He was a miniature version of Martin – the same straight floppy hair – she felt that she knew him already. He had changed from his school uniform into jeans and a black tee-shirt. He held a can of coke in one hand and was biting on what appeared to be a chocolate bar. There was a screech of brakes. A fair-haired boy on a bicycle shouted something to Daniel. She heard him reply, 'Let's go.' He threw the can on the grass and, leaving the gate open, whipped his bike around, stood on the pedals and chased his friend up the road. *It's strange*, Jenny thought, *how Martin and I talk about our children, but never our partners. That's too painful.*

She checked her watch – four twenty. Marilyn should be home soon. She rummaged in her handbag and found a piece of ginger cake in a plastic bag. She was about to bite into it when a small blue car stopped in the middle of the road and turned into the gap between the old forge and Martin's house. Jenny dropped the cake. Crumbs of gingerbread fell over her skirt as she grabbed the binoculars. A woman stepped out, wearing a pink blouse. *She's got blonde hair, blonde straight hair*, Jenny thought. She appeared tall – taller than herself – and well built. The woman stared at Jenny's car as she walked to the back of her car. *She's attractive, but why wouldn't she be? Martin married her. What was I expecting – some harridan?* The woman removed her shopping from the boot and walked towards the small gate. She stopped to pick up the coke can and stepped inside the porch. Jenny wondered about the nature of attraction. *Everyone says that opposites attract; but that article the other day said we're attracted to people like ourselves. She certainly doesn't look like Martin. Perhaps the opposite theory is correct? Perhaps he really fancies blondes, and is only seeing me because I'm so keen. He wouldn't turn it down, would he?* She brushed the crumbs from her skirt and started the engine. It would take at least thirty minutes to drive back. She felt a stab of guilt. It was Lorna's first day at her new school and she wouldn't be back in time to welcome her home.

'Where's my clean white shirt?' Robert's voice carried down the stairs.

'Oh, the interview,' Jenny muttered, as she stopped searching through the bookcase. She went upstairs into the spare room and rescued a shirt from the bottom of the washing pile.

Robert was standing in front of his open wardrobe, swishing coat hangers to and fro.

'It was in the spare room drying. I'll iron it for you now.'

'I wanted to get to bed early. You know how important tomorrow is for me; for all of us. If I do well I could be in line for promotion. You know what that would mean.'

'Yes, I know what that means; your mother's mentioned it enough times; bloody private school. To hear her talk anyone would think we're sending them to a remand home. It's a perfectly good school that gets excellent exam results. Lorna's happy there, she doesn't want to change schools.'

'And what about Nicky?' Robert said, facing her.

'What about Nicky? We can't send one without the other. It wouldn't be fair. Anyway it's all academic, if you'll excuse the pun. You haven't even got a promotion yet.'

'I'm not likely to get it either, if I don't get any support from you,' Robert raised his voice.

'I've always supported you. You know I have.'

'You used to.'

'I still do. I've come up to iron your shirt, haven't I?'

'I reminded you earlier, it's a bit late now.'

'For God's sake, of course it isn't. I'm going to do it, aren't I?' Jenny yelled as she dragged the ironing board out from the side of the wardrobe. 'I saw a job in the Argus last week that I thought I might apply for,' she hadn't meant to tell Robert yet, but couldn't resist saying it.

'What on earth are you telling me that now for? Anyway, what would you do about the school holidays?'

Trust him to say something negative, she thought as she bent down and slammed the plug into the socket. She had told Martin about it the evening before as they were walking back to the visitor's centre. He had encouraged her to apply.

'Well I'll worry about that if I get the job. I'm sure something can be worked out. It isn't a full week anyway, just a few hours more than I'm doing now. The job sounds interesting, and it has prospects.'

'Prospects – what do you want prospects for? You won't have time, especially now your class is carrying on. You're always saying how tired you are – especially at bedtime.'

'I can fit everything in.'

'Everything except me,' he snapped.

'What's that supposed to mean?' Jenny stopped ironing and turned to face him

'You know bloody well what I mean. I'm fed up with your excuses. Mum said how fed up I looked at the weekend. You hadn't noticed. You don't notice anything anymore. You're so sodding distant.'

'That's a miracle, her noticing, she's usually only concerned about herself, or David of course.' She knew she had struck a raw nerve.

'Don't speak about my mother like that.'

'She's a selfish cow.'

'And you're not, I suppose.'

'Mummy, Daddy, why are you shouting?' Nicky stood in the doorway rubbing his eyes.

'Ask your mother.'

'I hate it when you argue.'

'Go back to bed Nicky, it's nothing,' Robert said ushering him out of the door. 'See what you've done now.'

'I'll go to him.' Jenny stood the iron on the metal arm. 'Nicky it's alright. Get back to bed and I'll tuck you in.'

'Daddy doesn't like me.' His serious face looked up from the pillow.

'That's not true. Of course he does. He's not angry with you. He's angry with me.' Jenny smoothed her son's tousled hair.

'But he shouted at me yesterday, when I asked to help him with the railway. And he didn't kiss me goodnight. He's never missed before.'

'Daddy's got a lot on his mind at the moment; to do with his job. It's nothing to do with you Nicky.'

'Simon's dad doesn't live at home any more. He said his parents are getting a diverce.'

'A divorce.'

'He hit me in the playground, and he doesn't ask me to his house any more.'

'He's probably upset about his parents. That's why he hit you. You could ask him back here. I'm sure he still wants to play with you.'

'Will Daddy leave us?'

'Come here.' Jenny reached over and lifted her son into her arms. She buried her face in his hair, and breathed deeply. It smelt of lemons. 'Daddy isn't leaving.'

18

October 1982

'They offered me the job,' Jenny said grinning at Martin as she opened her car door.

'Well done. I knew you'd get it,' he said, bending to kiss her. 'Let's go over to the Golden Galleon for a drink to celebrate. I could do with a burger. I didn't have time for much earlier.' He locked the Land Rover and they began the short walk across the Cuckmere valley.

'So where's this job again?'

'In central Brighton, with a firm called Wiley, Smart & Lyneham; I'll be helping the cashier to start with, so I can get to know how their system works. Then, later, I can have my own probate cases. It will be a mixture of accounting and law; four days a week, nine thirty to four. I can even choose my days – not Tuesdays of course,' she added, 'and I can reduce my days in the holidays if I want to, without pay, of course, but I don't mind that, brilliant, isn't it?'

'Yes, it sounds fantastic.' Martin put his arm around her shoulders and pulled her towards him. 'Congratulations.'

'The only downside is I've got to tell Celia.'

Later that evening as they sat in his office, Martin reached for her hand.

'I can't meet you next week Jenny. It's half term, I always take a week off then, and in the spring half term. It's too busy for me to have any time off in the summer.'

'Are you going away?'

'Yes, we're going to Cornwall. We'll call on Marilyn's parents at Fordingbridge on the way down, and again on the way back, so Daniel can see his grandparents.'

Jenny winced.

'Marilyn's booked this hotel in Bude. We're thinking of arranging some windsurfing lessons for Daniel when we get there. I'm hoping it might improve his behaviour. He's been bloody hard work lately. He won't do anything we ask him. It's his age I suppose.' He stroked her hand.

Jenny winced again. She didn't hear his concerns about Daniel. She heard only the words 'Marilyn' and 'hotel'. She saw them relaxing, with time on their hands, sharing a room, sharing a bed. Blood rushed to her head.

'That's nice for you, plenty of time with your wife.' She pulled her hand away.

'Jenny, Jenny, you know how I feel about you.'

'No I don't,' she said. 'I only know you like doing… what we've been doing here.'

'That's unfair; you went on holiday with Robert in August, didn't you?'

'That's different. It's different for me; you don't understand.'

'I love you.'

'Not enough to leave your wife for.' She had said the words that she had promised herself she would never say to him.

'Jenny, the only reason I haven't asked you to be with me all the time is because it's too important. I didn't think you wanted that – to leave your marriage. I couldn't ask you to do that; to do that for me. I could only take what you've been willing to give me.'

Jenny felt calmer and reached for his hand.

'Well, do you then, want to leave Robert?' He stared at her, his eyes glistening like coals.

'I'm not sure, Martin.'

'So, I was right then.'

'Hope you didn't mind coming into Brighton,' said Gail, as Jenny met her at the entrance to the Imperial Arcade.

'No, of course not, it's easier than Hove for me. I'm sorry it was a bit short notice.'

'That's alright; it's just that I have to squeeze all my clothes shopping into half term week. I'm going into Marks after we've eaten,' said Gail.

'We've got a good hour to spare. I've left Lorna and Nicky at the ice-rink in Queen's Square.'

'Let's go into this café then. They do good lunches. You're looking amazing, Jenny, have you lost weight?'

'Yes, that's one of the reasons I asked if we could meet up.'

'One of the reasons?' Gail's face dropped. 'You're not ill are you?'

'No, thank goodness; at least, not in the way you mean. Anyway, tell me about you first. How are you?'

'Tired, but good, I'm always exhausted by the end of half term. It takes me at least three days to recover, but I love teaching. I'm still seeing Gerry, my new man. I did tell you about him, didn't I? It's been nearly twelve months now; how about that? And he gets on with Mark and Vicky.'

'That's brilliant Gail. I'm really pleased for you.' Jenny cast her eyes over the menu as the waitress approached, 'I'll have the leek and potato soup and a brown roll, please.'

'Same for me, only with a white roll,' Gail leaned across the table. 'So, come on, tell me, I'm intrigued, why have you lost weight?'

'You know the last time I saw you, I mentioned that I had seen Martin Barretti again.'

'Oh, I asked Mum if she had heard anything about them coming back. She said she hadn't – thank you,' Gail unwrapped the paper napkin from around her spoon as the waitress placed the bowl on the table.

Jenny did the same but instead of dipping her spoon in the soup took a deep breath. 'I've been seeing him.'

'Seeing him – what meeting up?'

'Yes.'

'On your own?' Gail's soup spoon remained suspended in mid-air as she digested Jenny's words instead of her food.

'Yes.'

'What, you mean you're having an affair?' Gail's eyes doubled in size.

'Yes.'

'My God, I'd never have thought that. What about Robert? You are still together?'

'Yes, but things aren't good. That's why I needed to talk to you.'

'Go on then.' Her spoon was still halfway between her bowl and her mouth.

'Gail, I really love him – Martin – I mean. I've never felt this way about anyone before. I'm so attracted to him physically. The sex is fantastic, but it's not only that, if it was, I could say it's just lust, wonderful of course,' she laughed, 'but after a while it would burn itself out and we would realise we had nothing in common. It would still rock my marriage, but I would see sense. But I feel so close to him in every way. He completes me. If he has a pain, or a worry, I feel it too. It's getting harder and harder to leave him after we meet, and I'm really jealous of his wife now. I hate being like that. I used to despise women who were possessive, but now I understand, because I'm just the same. It's affected my marriage. I don't want Robert – physically – anymore.'

'Yes, I suppose it would.' Gail's mouth remained slightly open.

'I want to be with him all the time, but I can't leave Lorna and Nicky. I can't do that to them. They're everything to me – but in a different way to Martin.' Jenny had never told Gail about her adoption, and didn't want to complicate matters by mentioning it now. She remembered how twenty years earlier, a tearful Gail had asked her for advice.

'Does he want to be with you all the time, or is he happy to keep things as they are? You know what men are like. Having their cake and eating it. They can do that.'

'I know, but he feels the same. I try not to mention Robert, and he doesn't mention Marilyn – that's his wife. But last week he told me they were going on holiday. It's stupid really. I mean we went on holiday in August. But something snapped. I said something I regretted. I couldn't help myself. But he understood why I said it. He said he loved me and would leave her, if that's what I wanted. If it was just her and Robert to consider I would leave. I don't feel guilty about them. Perhaps I should, but I don't. It's Lorna and Nicky, and he's got a boy, he's thirteen. The thing is, I know that if I carry on meeting him, it will destroy us. I can see that clearly now. I must have been really stupid and naïve not to have realised that. But even if I had, I don't think it would have stopped me. I wanted him so much, and that overrode everything.'

'Oh my God Jenny, I don't know what to say.' Gail finally lowered her spoon into her soup.

'Yes, I'd better eat mine before it gets cold.'

They ate in silence for a minute. Then after wiping her mouth, Gail said, 'All I know is that, half, no more than half now, of the children in my class come from broken homes. I know it's common these days, but it does affect them; some more than others. One little girl refused to speak for a whole term. I can't talk though, can I? Excuse the pun. I left Chris didn't I?'

'Yes, but you had good reason to leave. I don't. Robert's a good husband and father. If it wasn't for Martin we would still be rubbing along fine.'

'That doesn't sound very exciting – rubbing along.'

'Well that's what married couples do, don't they, after several years together?'

'If it hadn't been Martin, it might have been someone else?'

'No, I don't think so. I'd have flirted with an attractive man, of course I would. Perhaps it would have gone further. But it would have been under control. Perhaps it's because I knew him from years ago. Perhaps it's because I've just lost my parents, sometimes these things affect you in ways you don't expect.'

'I don't know what to say. Jenny, I can't advise you. It's too important. It has to be your decision.'

'I know, but just talking it over with you helps. You're the only person I've spoken to about it. Anyway enough about me, is Gerry still going to stand for the council?'

'Yes, and guess what, so am I. Gerry is really supportive. We've talked about buying a house together in the New Year. We're taking it slowly because of the children. I can't risk another mistake. At least I know what I'm letting myself in for this time.'

'Older and wiser, eh, that doesn't seem to apply to me.'

19

November 1982

'Come in Jenny.' Martin pulled the window blind down to shut out the night sky. 'I've put the electric fire on, it's chilly this evening.'

'Did you enjoy your holiday?' Jenny said, sitting down. She had promised herself that she would be reasonable.

'Well, the weather wasn't up to much, but Daniel loved windsurfing. He's been a changed lad since we got back. I've brought some cakes back from Cornwall for us. I'll go and get them.'

'Did you get to see much wildlife?' she called after him.

'Yes,' his voice echoed. 'Puffins, guillimots, gannets, even seals. There were some good walks along the cliffs. I went out most days.' He poked his head around the door, 'I kept wishing that you were with me, but you were in spirit.'

Jenny took a deep breath. 'And Marilyn, did she enjoy it?' *So far so good*, she thought as Martin returned with a plate of scones and clotted cream.

'She said she did. She played tennis with Daniel a few times when it stopped raining. God, how I missed you, you don't want to know what I thought about on those walks.'

'I've a pretty good idea,' she grinned.

'No you don't, it wasn't pretty, come here.' He pulled her up and pressed his mouth hard against hers.

She tried to pull away from him, but he held her tight. 'Let's eat first Martin, I want to say something...' her voice trailed off.

'Later, later,' he whispered, as his mouth explored her neck.

His smell overwhelmed her. She pulled his jumper over his head, undid his shirt buttons, trouser belt and zip. His jeans fell to the floor, and they each tore off what clothes remained on their bodies. Martin kicked both chairs out of their way and they fell to the floor.

Kneeling together in front of the fire, he bit each of her nipples in turn. She flinched. His hands pressed into the small of her back, and then reached under her buttocks and between her legs. She ran her hands through his hair, covering his face with kisses. He pushed her back; his tongue moving continuously over her skin. 'I could eat every part of you,' he whispered, burying his mouth between her legs until she cried out with pleasure. She moved and sat astride him, caressing his chest with her lips. She moved lower, her hand between his legs, cradling him. She took him into her mouth until he moaned, 'Stop, stop.' Pushing her back he fell across her and slid inside, his climax immediately washing against her womb. She tightened herself around him, wanting to absorb all of him; his seed, an embryo, a child, his child. Yes, she wanted that.

They lay exhausted with arms and legs entwined; their skin glistening in the glow of the fire. There had been an edge to their love-making tonight, she thought, both of them wanting to imprint themselves permanently on the other.

'How can you go back to him after this?' Martin was the first to speak.

'I can't, I can't go back, not just yet.' She kissed his forehead, his nose and his lips.

'I'll make us a drink, when I feel strong enough to move. You know Jenny – my reality is here in this place, with you. I know we could be happy. We could go to Rome together – to see my relatives – that would be another capital off your list. When I go home now, it's as if I'm a visitor, calling in; looking in on someone else's life.'

'I know, it's the same for me. That's what I wanted to tell you. I love you and want to be with you. But I can't do this any more Martin.'

He looked stricken as he stared at her. 'What – you mean you don't want us to meet anymore?'

'No, I don't want that, of course I don't. But I must try to make my marriage work, for Lorna and Nicky's sake.'

'What about your sake?'

'Perhaps what I want isn't so important at this time. Later on – then we can be together. This is what I wanted to say, before we did this, but I wasn't strong enough.'

'So it is for the children?'

'No, not completely; it's for my sake as well. If we carry on as we are, we will destroy what we have. I can see that clearly now, and I couldn't bear it.'

'We could still meet; in a pub with other people around, like we used to. We could just talk, nothing would happen then.'

'No,' Jenny said, with a strength born from self-knowledge. 'That would be impossible, at least it would for me, and I think it would be the same for you. It's all or nothing for us, Martin. It always has been. I realise that now.'

'You know I'm willing to leave my marriage for you Jenny. So just promise me one thing,' his eyes blazed at her, 'that you'll phone if it gets too hard for you. I won't contact you. I'll give you a chance, even though…' He shook his head as he sat up and reached for his clothes. 'I had something to tell you too, but it doesn't seem important now.'

'Yes it is, everything you say to me is important.'

'I've given up smoking.'

20

December 1982

Lorna grimaced and whispered, 'Mum, I hate celery,' as Maggie placed a plate of cold turkey and ham, edged with green sticks and tomatoes in front of her.

'Just try and eat some with the tomatoes. Nanny's been very busy preparing a special lunch for us.'

'Yes I have young lady. Don't you know it's rude to say you hate something,' Maggie said as she continued placing plates and serviettes on the table. 'Your father had to eat what was put in front of him when he was your age, and so did I. There was none of this faddiness then,' she added as she took her place at the head of the table.

'Come on you two, get up off that sofa and come and eat,' Reggie directed his words at David and Corinne. They had finally married at Brighton Registry Office on the winter solstice, with two friends as witnesses. Corinne's dreadlocks formed a grey curtain around her head, parting in the middle to reveal eyes, a nose and a mouth. Reluctantly they unwound their arms from each other's bodies.

They're really happy, Jenny thought – remembering, not for the first time that day, her final evening with Martin. Every cell in her body ached for him. She knew how someone could die from a broken heart.

'Well, Happy Christmas everyone,' Reggie raised his glass of Cava.

'Happy Christmas,' they chorused.

Jenny picked up her knife and fork and started to pick at the turkey slices.

'When can we pull the crackers Nanny?'

'After we've finished eating, Nicky.'

'How do you wash your hair Corinne?'

'With difficulty and not very often,' Reggie muttered under his breath.

'Nicky, stop staring at Corinne, and start eating.'

'Leave the kid alone, Rob, he's excited. It's Christmas for God's sake.' David winked across the table at his nephew.

'Uncle David, I've brought my Darth Vader light sabre over. Can we play *Star Wars* after lunch?'

'I will destroy your world,' David spoke in a deep deliberate voice.

'Is that a new jumper Rob?' Maggie asked.

'Yes, Jen's Christmas present to me.'

'That bottle green colour suits you. What did Rob buy you Jenny?'

'A watch,' she pulled back the cuff on her blouse to reveal a thin black strap and chrome dial.'

'That's lovely, isn't it Reggie? I hope that new job of

yours isn't too much for you, Jenny? You don't seem your usual self.' Maggie peered over her pink-framed glasses.

'No it isn't. It's only a few more hours than what I was doing before, and it's quicker to get there. It's the dark mornings and evenings, I always feel a bit down at this time of the year. I'll feel better once January's over.'

'Well, there's a while to go yet. Mind you, I don't hold with all this talk about nerves and depression, I was listening to this programme on the radio the other day. What have people got to be depressed about these days? A few days hard work would soon cure them. They'd be too tired to feel depressed then.'

'Yes, David, did you hear what your mother said?' Reggie looked down the table at his son.

'I'm not depressed, nor's Corrine. Once we've finished kitting out the van, we're going to Scotland. We can get casual work up there. We'll probably call in and support the steel workers on the way. Being a wage slave in a capitalist society is enough to make anyone depressed. We'll never get rid of Thatcher now that we've got the Falklands back.'

'There's a girl at work who suffers from depression and she works really hard,' Jenny added.

'There you are. What did I just say?' David said, as Corinne's dreadlocks bounced in agreement.

'I don't know why you stopped going to your ecology classes, Jen. You really enjoyed them, didn't you?' Robert spooned a large portion of pickle onto his plate.

'I told you, they weren't as good as before, and I

started my new job. I can always go to some more later on, and when the weather improves I'll go out more.' Jenny stared at her plate.

'I can come with you Mum,' said Lorna.

Jenny turned and smiled at her. 'That would be nice, I'd like that.'

'I'd find being unemployed depressing,' Reggie said. 'There are a lot of people losing their jobs at the moment. A man's not meant to hang around the house all day. Luckily I'm O.K. on the buses. You're alright at the council aren't you Rob?'

'Of course he is Reggie. He's just been promoted, not before time either.'

'Yes, thanks for reminding me Mum,' Robert threw a look at his mother. 'There's going to be some reorganisation next year, Reggie, but it's not going to be middle management. So I'll be alright.'

Jenny pushed her chair back. 'I'll collect the plates up for you Maggie.'

'I thought you liked turkey,' Maggie said.

'I do, it was lovely. It's just that I had quite a lot to eat yesterday.'

'I was worried you might be thinking of becoming a vegetarian. One in the family's quite enough.' She looked down the table at Corinne.

'I couldn't eat the celery Mum, I did try,' Lorna whispered.

'Think of all those starving children in Africa, Lorna,' Maggie said, passing her plate to Jenny. 'Can you bring in the trifle and the pudding bowls, please? There's also some Christmas pudding steaming for those who would prefer something more substantial. Rob, I think you should think again about sending Lorna to St. Mary's Hall. You can afford it now, what with your promotion, and Jenny earning more. The discipline's so much better in the private sector; and you get a better class of girl there. It's so important who they mix with at Lorna's age.'

'But I love it at Varndean, Nanny,' Jenny heard Lorna's voice from the kitchen.

'That's as maybe, but girls your age don't always know what's best for them.'

Jenny wondered what Martin was doing for Christmas. His father probably goes to their house, or they might all go to Southampton to his sister or parents-in-law. It couldn't be any worse than here. Jenny looked at her watch and wondered if Robert had given her it on purpose; as if time didn't pass slowly enough now. She picked up some spoons and carried the large bowl of trifle decorated with hundreds and thousands into the dining room.

'From what I've heard about the girls at St. Mary's Hall, they're either the daughters of dodgy antique dealers or even dodgier businessmen. That's how they can afford to send them there,' Jenny said.

'There may be a few like that, but there are a lot of professional parents too. All three of Dr Quigley's daughters go there.'

'I think it's up to us how we spend our money, Maggie, seeing as we're the ones earning it. In fact we're all going to Cyprus at Easter to stay with my aunt. She invited us a while back.' Jenny's face was scarlet as she placed the trifle in the centre of the table.

Robert looked up open-mouthed, 'Jen, Jen, calm down. Mum's only saying what she thinks is best for Lorna.'

'Yes, exactly – what *she* thinks.'

'Sorry, Mum, Jen feels strongly about this.'

'You don't have to apologise for me Robert.'

Maggie pursed her lips as she looked at her daughter-in-law.

'I didn't know you were a comrade in arms; solidarity with the workers, eh, Jen?' said David, grinning at her, while Corinne's dreadlocks covered her face.

Reggie picked up his cracker and pointed it at Nicky. 'I think we'll pull the crackers now.'

21

May 1983

Since last November Jenny never drove eastwards; whenever she needed time on her own to reflect, she either drove north, or turned the nose of her Morris Minor west, along the A27.

Leaving her car in the lane, she took the footpath alongside Clayton church and climbed steeply to the pair of windmills that crowned the hill, known as Jack and Jill.

Halfway up she sat down by a patch of cowslips to recover her breath. A cuckoo advertised its presence from a horse chestnut tree, heavy with candles. She stared into the distance. The weald stretched to the rise of the North Downs. The flint cottages of Clayton that had stood for centuries, gave way to small towns that had wrapped themselves around the main London to Brighton railway line. She felt the warmth of early summer on the back of her neck, and leant back into the tall grass and closed her eyes.

Robert had taken Lorna and Nicky to the Bluebell Railway. Nicky had been keen, but it had taken a

Herculean effort to persuade Lorna to join them. As for herself, she had abandoned feigning interest in Robert's model exhibitions. In March she had said that she didn't mind going to watch him play cricket occasionally, but she was damned if she was going to anything to do with trains. Robert's jaw had dropped as he listened in silence to her outburst. He didn't ask her again. Instead, she went out either on her own, or with Lorna. Robert was going to drop the children back home later, and then visit his grandmother in hospital. The unaccustomed heat made her eyelids heavy. After a few minutes she woke to the screaming of the swifts, twisting and turning above her. *God, I wish Martin was here. I miss him so much. I never thought it would be this hard. This time last year...* she recalled their walks and lovemaking. *Perhaps he has the hardest part, surrounded every working day by tangible memories of their closeness.* He had kept his promise not to contact her. She wondered if he still thought of her when he was at home, or whether her physical absence had made it easier. Not an hour went by when she didn't think about him. To lessen the pain she forced herself to think about their holiday to Cyprus. They had decided to leave their visit until half term. The children were excited, and she was looking forward to it.

Nicosia – divided since 1974 – became the capital in 11th century AD. The northern part now functions as the capital of the Turkish Republic of Northern Cyprus. Venetian walls dating from the sixteenth century encircle the old city with world famous Ledra Street in the middle.

Aunt Doris had said in her letter that they couldn't wait to show them around, and that she had something important that she wanted to talk to her about. Robert said that she was probably going to leave them some money in her will, but Jenny thought that unlikely, as they seemed to be the last of the great spenders, anyway, she had Alan and his family. She had already decided that she would mention her adoption to Doris while they were there. She no longer wanted it to be a family secret. She sat up and reached in her bag for an apple. A colony of ants scurried at her feet. As she bit into the flesh, she watched them weaving between the blades of grass; intent only on survival.

Jenny threw the core under a small hawthorn bush, stood up, brushed herself down and continued her climb towards the windmills.

'*It's a Knockout's* coming on Mum,' Nicky shouted from the lounge.

'I'll just be a minute,' Jenny shouted from the dining room.

'I want this one, there's a stream in the garden,' she heard Nicky say excitedly.

'No, that one's better, it's got some riding stables nearby. Quick hide them, she's coming.'

As Jenny walked into the lounge, she saw Nicky stuffing papers between the sofa seat and the arm. 'What are you looking at?'

'Nothing,' Nicky said, turning bright red.

'It must be something. Whatever it is, it sounds fun.' She reached into the gap and pulled out a bunch of crumpled papers. Straightening them, she frowned as she looked at each one in turn. *Why on earth have they got these, they're Estate Agent's details – houses in Guildford; Shalford and Godalming.*

'Where did you get these from?' Two pairs of eyes stared up at her.

Lorna was the braver of the two. 'Daddy showed them to us them this afternoon, after we'd been on the train. He asked us if we liked any of them. He told us not to say anything to you as it was going to be a surprise. You've spoilt it now Nicky – you stupid dolt.'

'No, no it's alright. I'll forget I've seen them. You better put them back before Dad gets back. Were they in his desk?'

Lorna nodded, 'But it's not a surprise any more.'

Jenny handed the sheets back to Nicky. He ran out of the room.

The three of them watched the programme in silence from the sofa. As giant padded penguins danced on the screen, Jenny was wondering when she and Robert would next be alone in the house.

'For goodness sake stop doing that,' Jenny said, as Nicky absentmindedly kicked the kitchen table leg. 'Why don't you phone Simon, he might be able to play this afternoon?'

'I've already told you. He goes to his dad's on

Sundays. Anyway, Lorna promised me she would come to the park with me. That's just like a girl to break her promise.'

'But you know she always goes to the stables on Sunday afternoons.'

'I don't see why she has to go every single week.' He started kicking again.

'Look, just give Simon a ring. He might not have gone. If you don't ring, you won't know, will you?'

With a deep sigh, Nicky slid off the chair, and left the kitchen. Jenny opened the oven and removed a tray of sponge cakes. Hearing Nicky speaking she went into the hall. 'Brill, I'll be round in half an hour then.' At the click of the handset she hurried back to the kitchen.

'Well?'

'Yes, he's there, they're just finishing eating.'

'There you are then, what did I tell you?' Jenny said, placing each cake onto a wire rack.

'Yummy, can I have one now?'

'Alright then, take two with you, then Simon can have one.'

'I'm off then.'

'Be careful.' Since his tenth birthday earlier that year, Nicky had been allowed to cycle on his own to his friend's house, but Jenny didn't stop worrying about him until he returned.

'Don't fuss, Mum,' Nicky said. He threw the cakes into a plastic bag and rushed out of the back door. Jenny went into the lounge and watched through the window as he cycled along the pavement and turned the corner. She could hear Robert moving about upstairs. He was taking three days extra holiday before half term to tackle and hopefully complete at least two unfinished projects. First on his list was to re-fix the front panel that had fallen off the bath, leaving a gaping black hole. Lorna was refusing to go in there, crying hysterically that she could see gigantic spiders lurking there. Jenny walked into the study, opened the top drawer to Robert's desk, and sprinted upstairs. Robert was dressed in a pair of dark blue overalls, and lay on his back attempting to push the panel into place. Tools were strewn across the floor.

'Wretched thing never stays where it's supposed to.' He raised himself slightly. 'Have you come up to see how I'm getting on?'

'What the hell are these?' Jenny waved the house details under Robert's nose.

He sat up. 'What are you doing with those?'

'What am I doing with them? What are *you* doing with them? That's what I want to know.'

'How did you get them? I told them not to say anything to you.'

'They didn't say anything, at least, not until I saw them looking at them. They weren't going to say anything, because you said it was going to be a surprise. Well it's certainly that. Why have you got them?'

'Oh, bloody hell, Jen.' His blue eyes stared up at her. 'I wanted to tell you, but you've been so damned moody and snappy lately, I just couldn't. I thought... oh it doesn't matter now. I thought it would be best to wait until I knew for sure.'

'Knew what for sure?'

'That I'd got the job.'

'Got the job, what are you talking about? You've already got a job,' she shouted.

'No, I haven't, at least not for much longer. That's why I couldn't tell you, not until I knew I had another one. It's the re-organisation. My job's going at the end of July.'

'You mean you've been offered a job in Surrey?' she emphasised the last word.

'Yes, with Waverley Council. They offered it to me on Thursday, at the second interview. That's when I went to the agents.'

'You mean you accepted a job in Surrey, without telling me,' she shouted. 'Well you can't take it, can you? You'll have to tell them,' she lowered her voice.

'Don't be ridiculous Jen. I won't have a job at all, if I refuse it.'

'Well, you can always re-train for something else. Transport isn't the only job in the world you know.' She thought of Martin giving up his secure job in a bank.

'Transport's the only job I know that I'm good at, and interested in; and it pays a good salary.'

'What about my job? I haven't been there five minutes, and I enjoy it. I can't commute from

Guildford, can I?' her voice rose to a crescendo. 'I can't believe you accepted without talking to me about it.'

'I couldn't tell you, at least not then. But it wouldn't have made any difference if I had told you. We'd just have had this argument a week earlier. I can't turn it down. It's for all of us, Jen. I'm getting more money, for God's sake. I'm sorry about your job, of course I am, but you can always get another job up there, when we're settled. We won't be short of money.'

'Money's not everything you know,' she thought again of Martin. One of the things that made their separation bearable was that they still lived and breathed the same county air, and that she hadn't upset Lorna and Nicky. 'What about Lorna? She's just settled at her new school, she has friends there. That's important at her age.'

'She'll soon make new friends. Nicky seemed keen, when I mentioned it.'

'Yes, he might be, but I bet Lorna wasn't. I'm not going Robert.' It was one thing to carry on with their life and remain where they were. But to move away, to give up her job – no – if her life was going to change it wouldn't be like this. 'I'm not going.'

'Don't be ridiculous, Jen. This is exactly why I didn't say anything earlier. I wasn't sure how you'd react. Can't you see it's really good news for us.'

'Good news. Good news – what, that I'll have to

leave my new job, and Lorna leave her school. What's good about that?' Jenny shouted.

'You're completely over reacting. We can have a good life in Surrey.'

'I don't want a good life in Surrey, I have a life here.'

'Not without me and the children you wouldn't.'

'I might.'

'What do you mean, you might? You're not going to stay in Brighton on your own, are you? We can't afford two houses,' he gave a deep sigh. 'For God's sake, any other woman would be pleased that I'd had the gumption to find another job and be accepted.'

'Well, I'm not any other woman.'

'No, you're not. You're moody and unpredictable. You're not the girl I married; a change would do you good.'

'Do me good, do me good, it wouldn't make any difference, because I don't love you,' she screamed.

He stood up and faced her, his face drained of colour. 'What the hell are you talking about?'

She smelt onion from lunch on his breath. 'I don't love you. I love someone else.'

'You love someone else – who?' A sliver of spit landed on her cheek.

'It doesn't matter who, does it?'

'It does to me.'

'You don't know him.'

'So that's alright then, is it? Oh I get it. It's someone at work isn't it? That's why you don't want to leave. You think you can go to him. Well, who says he wants you. You've been bloody moody ever since you started there.'

'You're wrong. It's no one at work.'

'I don't believe you. You would say that, wouldn't you? Who the hell is it then? You don't go anywhere else.' Jenny saw the truth dawning on Robert's face. His upper lip curled. 'Of course, that's it isn't it? It's a man you met at those classes you went to last year. You went out on those so-called field trips in the evenings, and you go out when I go to the exhibitions. Are you still seeing him?'

'No, I'm not,' she shouted.

'Did you sleep with him?' His eyes bulged.

Jenny turned her head slightly so as not to see those eyes.

'I'll take that as a yes then.'

'You're not whiter than white, are you? What about those office parties? You never came home 'til the early hours.'

'What the fuck are you talking about?' He shoved her back against the bathroom wall, kicked his hammer out of the way and marched out of the room.

Jenny's heart hammered against her ribs as she stood staring at her reflection in the mirror above the wash basin; her lips apart as she breathed heavily. The floor was covered with tools, and the panel hung loosely from the bath. Five minutes later she heard footsteps on the stairs. Robert stood in the doorway.

'Look I'm sorry Jen. I've been thinking, we've both

made mistakes. I can forget about this afternoon, if you will. This is a good reason for us to move, don't you see – we can start again – somewhere new.'

Jenny took a deep breath. 'No, I can't Robert. That's what I've been trying to do here. I'm sorry, I really am.'

'Well fuck you then – bitch.' He slammed the bathroom door in her face. Jenny stared at the paint work and began to shake. A few minutes later she heard the revving of a car engine as Robert screeched away from the house.

The next morning as she was getting ready for work, the telephone rang. 'Hello,' she answered.

'Oh, it's you.' Jenny froze, as she recognised her mother-in-law's voice.

'Do you want to speak to Robert?' Her heart raced.

'Well, I certainly don't want to speak to you. Robert told me what you said. How could you do that to him? Those poor little children.'

'He's no angel himself, you know.'

'It's different for men.'

'Oh, is it? At least I made him happy once; which is more than he can say about you.'

'How dare you speak to me like that, you little slut; blood will out in the end, that's what…'

Jenny slammed the phone down; her hands trembling. She sat in the chair by the window and felt a pricking at the back of her eyes. A tear teetered on the edge of her eyelid and trickled down her cheek.

Another formed and dripped onto her lip, she removed it with her tongue thinking how salty it tasted. Outside a young mother was pushing her child in a buggy. Jenny watched until she was a dark speck at the end of the road, and then stood up, walked over to the corner table and flicked through the telephone directory. She picked up the receiver and dialled the number. She felt strangely calm. 'Martin, it's me. Can I come over?'

PART THREE

1

September 1984

Toby sat expectantly at the door of the cottage, his tail sweeping the floor.

'Alright, I'm coming,' Jenny bent down and attached the lead to his collar. She pulled down the door latch and stepped out onto the brick path that led to the lane. Once past the old school she removed his lead. Toby rushed to the edge of the pond and barked at the ducks waddling on the baked mud. Startled, they retreated and paddled furiously towards their island refuge. Jenny stared at the water level. It was low, but not as low as she remembered it had been in the drought of 1976. Wandering past the disused village pump, she turned right alongside the church; the morning sun warming her bare arms and legs.

She had been living with Martin for over a year, and they were renting a small flint knapped cottage in Falmer. It was cramped, but in a strategic position; Martin said that his journey took only five minutes longer than it had from Ringmer, and Jenny could drop Lorna at school on her way into work. She bent down and threw a stick for Toby. It had been her idea to buy a dog; to help distract Lorna and Nicky from the inevitable fall-out from her separation from Robert. Last December, she had taken Lorna to the R.S.P.C.A. kennels, where a wire-haired fox terrier cross had immediately decided they were going to adopt him. The cross part of Toby had been the subject of much discussion since, but with no determinate conclusion. Toby had been a great success. No one could fail to raise a smile in his presence. Both Lorna and Nicky – when he came to stay for the weekend – vied to be the one to take him for a walk. At the southern edge of the churchyard, harvested fields, prickly with stubble, stretched into the distance. Jenny turned right alongside a line of alders, and picking up another stick threw it onto the grass. Toby hurtled towards it, skidding to a halt and returned to her triumphantly.

'Only a short walk today, Toby.' Usually, she would take the narrow path that led to the footbridge over the A27. They would walk past the village stores and almshouses, and along the lanes of the northern half of the village. The walk would take at least half an hour, and Toby would return exhausted. Today, he was still lively as she walked up to their cottage door and stepped into the sitting room. A wood burning stove sat in a tiled recess. By the side was a wicker basket filled to the brim with logs that Martin had collected ready for autumn. Picking up a writing pad and pen from a side table, Jenny walked through the kitchen and out onto a small brick patio. Sitting at the small wooden table she began to write.

Dear Dido,

I hope this letter finds you and the boys well, and I'm sorry it's been such a long time since I last wrote, but you'll see I'm not at the same address anymore. You remember I told you that Robert and I were separating. Well, here I am, living with Martin. I don't know if you'll remember, but Falmer's just outside Brighton. We're really happy, but the last few months haven't been easy, and still aren't, because of Lorna and Nicky, and Martin's boy – Daniel. The children have been the hardest part – I feel permanently guilty. We plan to stay here, at least until our divorces are finalised. Lorna lives with us, it's a bit cramped, and Nicky lives with Robert in Surrey. He's settled at school there, and Lorna goes up once a month – for the weekend – and Nicky comes here on another weekend. Anyway, enough about us, I'm really pleased that you've got a job, and things are a bit easier now the boys are older. I can't believe that Mike's chucked his job at Lloyds and is travelling around South America. Has he gone on his own?

Jenny put her pen down and stared along the narrow garden which faced due west. The sun was prevented from reaching her by the walls of the kitchen extension. The hum from the dual carriageway formed a background to her thoughts about the children. The phone rang in the sitting room.

'This is a nice surprise,' Jenny said, recognising Martin's voice.

'Daniel phoned today.'

'Oh, good, I'm so pleased.'

'Apparently, he had a bad cold at the weekend, and Marilyn didn't want him to go out and make it worse. He said he wasn't that bad, and still wanted to see me, but didn't want to upset her.' Martin had planned to meet Daniel on Saturday, but after waiting one hour, he had given up and returned home with disappointment written over his face.

'Is he better now?'

'He's still a bit croaky, but he said he's better. What are you doing this morning?'

'I've just walked Toby round the pond, and I'm in the middle of writing to Dido, you remember, I often mention her?'

'Well, enjoy the peace while it lasts. I'm just off to that meeting I told you about, so I might be a bit late.'

'Take care – love you.'

Jenny replaced the handset, went into the kitchen and filled the kettle. She smiled as she imagined Martin in his office, his elbow on the desk as he told her the good news. *At least Daniel's phoned him at work*, she thought, *even if he doesn't want to phone here*. She knew he felt guilty about Daniel; she felt the same about Lorna and Nicky. They only had to be unusually quiet; say they felt ill, or have trouble with their friends, and she would immediately blame herself. *At least we can sympathise with each other.*

She sat and stared at the trees on the skyline beyond the university, and again recalled last Saturday afternoon. Robert had met her as usual at the petrol station on the A23. With a nod of his head and a curt hello, he had opened the car door to let Nicky out. She had been surprised to see Nicky dressed in school uniform.

'Why are you wearing your uniform?' she had asked.

'I have school now on Saturday mornings. Dad's just collected me.'

'Oh.'

'It's O.K. Dad's brought a change of clothes for me.'

'That's not the same uniform you had last term, is it?'

'No,' he had quickly looked away, watching Robert's car as it disappeared down the slip road. 'Mum, can I have a Cornetto?'

'Alright,' she opened the glove compartment and gave him some coins. 'Don't be long. Lorna's looking forward to seeing you, and so's Toby.' As he disappeared into the garage, she had realised that whatever they had agreed about their son, now counted for little. She recalled their conversation from the day before, Martin was standing at the end of the kitchen table carving slices off a leg of lamb, when Nicky had said, 'We had lamb chops on Friday.'

'Did you? That's good,' she had replied, pleased that at last Robert was cooking decent meals. 'Does Dad often do those for you?'

'No, I think he did it because Louise came round.'

'Louise – is she your new friend?' Lorna had asked.

'No, Dad said she was a friend from work. She cooked me sausage and bacon before school yesterday.'

'You better watch out, or you'll be getting too fat to play in the football team,' Martin added quickly with a nervous laugh.

'I prefer rugby now.'

She had felt an unexpected pang of jealousy, and wondered what Louise looked like. Looking across the table she saw Lorna had stopped eating and was staring at her plate. Later that evening she came into the kitchen.

'I don't want to go to Dad's on Saturday. I'd rather stay here.'

'Why's that?' she had spoken without thinking.

'I just don't.'

'You'll feel differently at the weekend. Could you get an apple from the fruit bowl for me please?'

'Get it yourself,' Lorna had yelled, slamming the door behind her. She hadn't spoken to her since.

Ancient elm trees lined the right side of the road that led up to West Blatchington windmill. *It looks strange without its sails, an armless torso*, Jenny thought. *They must be down for renovation.* She flicked the indicator switch, and turned left into the crescent.

'It's on the right, in the middle,' Martin said, 'the one with the red roof tiles.'

Jenny swallowed several times as she followed Martin up the shared drive to the semi-detached bungalow. Dandelions sprouted from cracks in the concrete and marigolds multiplied haphazardly in the flower beds. It was the first time she had accompanied Martin to visit his father. She decided that she couldn't put it off for ever. They had spoken several times on the telephone, he had been polite, but she always passed the receiver to his son.

Martin pressed the doorbell. He was about to press it again when the door opened, and a grey-haired man of medium height stood before them. Replicas of Martin's eyes stared at Jenny.

'You look as if you've seen a ghost, Dad. We told you we were coming today,' Martin said.

'Yes, I was expecting you. It's just that… Oh, it doesn't matter. Come in, come in.'

The aroma of freshly made coffee wafted around the hallway. Jenny held out her right hand which he immediately lifted to his lips. 'So you're Jenny?' His eyes glinted. 'Ricco, call me Ricco.'

Martin embraced his father, kissing him on both cheeks. 'How are you now Dad?'

'Could be better, could be better, but it's good to see you both. Go through to the lounge and I'll bring the drinks through. No one makes coffee like us Italians.' He ushered them into a small room that looked out onto the road.

'Dad – for God's sake,' Martin raised his eyebrows

at Jenny. 'Don't take any notice of him. He plays on the fact that he's half Italian; thinks it makes him more attractive.'

Jenny bit her lower lip and looked around the room. A gas fire was set into a tiled 1930's fireplace. Beside the sofa in an alcove was a sideboard covered with framed photographs. Martin and his sister in junior school uniforms smiled at her. Martin's tie was skewed to the left. Another photo showed them at about fourteen. Behind stood a black and white photo of Martin's parents arm in arm outside a church on their wedding day, beside that, a coloured picture of them seated together at a restaurant table several years later. Jenny was reminded of her own memory of Martin's mother. A young man in uniform, who Jenny assumed was Ricco, looked proudly from another frame. At the back were two sepia photographs of groups of people.

Martin removed a newspaper from the coffee table as his father entered the room. 'We can't stay long Dad. We've got to pick up Lorna from her school at five.'

'She's been camping for the weekend; Duke of Edinburgh Award scheme,' Jenny added.

'Martin told me that you have two children, Jenny.' He placed the coffee cups on the table and sank with a sigh, into a chair under the window. 'This old body of mine is not what it was – everything's an effort since my Ellen died. Anna and Martin are good to me, but it's not the same.'

Jenny nodded and sipped her coffee.

'Family are very important. I can't say I was pleased when Martin told me he was leaving Marilyn. I liked the girl. But now I see you with my own eyes, perhaps I understand a little. You make my son happy, so perhaps I should be happy too.'

Jenny detected a slight accent as he spoke.

'Dad, that's enough. We're going to get married as soon as we can, so we can be a proper family.'

'Is that you in the uniform?' Jenny asked, nodding towards the photograph.

'Yes, that's me. I was good looking then. My father and Paolo, my brother, were interned on the Isle of Man. They were born in Italy, you see – enemy aliens – that's what they were told when Mussolini declared war; even though the only weapons they had were ice creams,' he laughed. 'But I was born here, so I joined the air-force.'

'My father was in the army,' Jenny said. 'He served for over twenty years as a regular soldier. He lost an eye in India, so he spent the war as an instructor.' She gave a little smile as she remembered his yarns.

'I was part of the Italian campaign – I suppose they thought I would be useful because I spoke the language. I even saw my papa's village near Roma. You see those two photos at the back, they were taken in Palestrina – they're my aunts, uncles and cousins – nearly all of them moved away after the war; to England or America. The older ones and some of the younger ones are dead now. Roots you know – they're important – always a part of you, they keep you strong, grounded as they say these days. My papa used to say "A man with shallow roots is like a tree, he doesn't grow strong. He falls over when a strong wind blows". Have you any brothers and sisters Jenny?'

'No, I'm an only child.'

Ricco gave her a pitying look. She looked over at the photos of his relatives. 'Do you mind if I have a closer look?'

'Of course not, bring them over to the light.'

Jenny lifted the two photographs and took them over to the window. She scrutinised each one. There were about twenty people in each photograph. The older ones stood at the back – men with thick black moustaches, and old women with covered heads. Mothers nursing babies sat on chairs in the front row, while the children sat cross-legged on the ground. She could see a family resemblance in the shape of their faces. The photo looked as if it had been taken in a village square. A church stood in the background.

'We're thinking of going to Italy at the end of October, aren't we Jenny?'

'Yes, we're planning to go to Rome. I've got this thing about capital cities. We hope to visit Palestrina, so Martin can see where his grandparents came from.'

'Good, good, I'm pleased. It makes me sad that I never took my Ellen back to visit my relatives. But there was no money for that back then. We were going to go when I retired, but then, it was too late.' He brushed a hand across his eyes, 'But at least we moved up here, she always loved it, especially the view, better than where we used to live. You going to visit your mama while you're here?' Ricco pulled a handkerchief from his trouser pocket and wiped his eyes.

'No, Dad, not today. As I said, we can't stay long. I visited Mum's grave just a few weeks back. Jenny's parents are buried there too. That's how we came to meet again.'

'You lived near here then?' he sniffed hard and stared at Jenny.

'Yes, just beyond the windmill. But that was a long time ago.'

'A long time ago, yes, I was hot-blooded back then.' He nodded towards the sideboard. 'Now the fire has gone, but sometimes, when I see a beautiful woman, a flicker returns.' He smiled at Jenny.

'Dad, that's enough.' Martin finished his coffee with a gulp and stood up.

'Come and see your old papa again soon, bring Jenny and the children if you can, so I can feel young again.'

'Of course I will.'

Jenny followed Martin towards the door. She turned, smiled at Ricco and offered her hand. He lifted his arms to embrace her.

'He's sweet,' Jenny said as they drove back along the crescent.

'He's alright. Goes on a bit. He was very jealous years ago, his latin temperament I suppose. He didn't like Mum going out. He was always asking where she was going, and who with. Yet he had girlfriends. I didn't realise it then, but I do now. There were some terrible rows. He's forgotten about all that, gone sentimental in his old age. Perhaps when you lose someone, you only remember the good times.'

'Yes, I think that's true,' Jenny said, remembering her parents. 'You're not like him, only in your face and eyes.'

'No, I take after Mum's side of the family, in temperament and height. Anna's more like Dad.'

Many times during the following week Jenny thought of Ricco's words, and the two Italian photographs. On Saturday morning she drove into Lewes and approached the library desk. She was about to speak when a man came up behind her. Not wanting to be overheard she walked away and browsed through a guidebook on Rome. After checking that no one was about, she approached the desk again.

'Just this book, please,' and then added, 'I know that a few years ago the law changed so that adopted people could trace their relatives, and I was wondering if you have any information about it?'

The woman looked over her glasses. 'Yes, I think we do, I know that the person has to be over eighteen years of age. Is it for yourself?'

Jenny reddened and nodded. The woman bent

down and searched through a box under her desk. She waved a leaflet in front of Jenny. 'This will tell you the procedure.' Jenny saw the words "Access to Birth Records". She grabbed the leaflet and left.

A raindrop fell on Jenny's cheek as she stood outside the ringing hut.

'I think we'll call it a day. We're not going to catch many birds in the rain.' Martin looked at the ominous clouds building from the west, and placed an arm around Jenny's shoulders.

'Let's go and have some lunch in The Golden Galleon,' Jenny said.

'Good idea. I'll just thank the others, and tell them we're off. Looks like they've already decided they've had enough.' Martin walked across to where three members from the local Ornithological Club had started to fold up the netting.

'We finished just in time,' Martin said, as heavy rain washed like waves against the windscreen of the Land Rover.

Jenny peered through the wipers as they bumped along the track. 'Be careful, there's a large flint in the centre of the track.'

'It's O.K. I've seen it.'

'It was a good morning wasn't it?' Jenny said.

'I'm glad you enjoyed it. We've ringed quite a few. I hope it was worth getting up at the crack of dawn for?' Martin turned and smiled at Jenny, his hand stroking her thigh. 'I thought you seemed a bit quiet on the way over?'

'Well, I'm never at my best first thing in the morning, and I was thinking about something.'

'That sounds ominous. Do you still want to go to Rome at half term? We don't have to, you could go and see your aunt in Cyprus instead, I don't mind.'

Jenny remembered when she had written to her aunt to tell her that her marriage was over, and that they weren't able to visit as arranged. To her surprise, Doris had replied sympathetically, saying of course they were disappointed, but that she understood that she wouldn't have taken such a step lightly, and had suggested that she visit on her own, when she was ready.

'No, it's not about that. I'm really excited about going. It will be lovely, just the two of us. I'll visit Aunt Doris early next year. It's about me.'

Martin frowned.

'It's nothing for you to worry about. I'll tell you when we get to the pub.'

'I'm intrigued.'

Martin steered the vehicle over the final ruts in the track, and turned onto the coast road. Ten minutes later the wheels rattled across the wooden bridge across the Cuckmere; the rain falling like pebbles into the river beneath.

'I don't know about you, but I'm starving.' Martin parked as close to the entrance to the bar as was possible.

'It's absolutely pouring. We'll have to make a run for it,' Jenny said as she jumped down and held her coat above her head.

Martin placed their drinks on a table by the window, and sat opposite Jenny. 'I've ordered our food. It shouldn't be long, there's hardly anyone here.' He took a long gulp from his glass. 'What is it you've been thinking about then?'

'That I want to find out about my parents – my birth parents.'

Martin looked askance at Jenny. 'What's brought this on?'

'I've been thinking about it on and off since the summer I suppose. But it was visiting Ricco the other day that finally decided me.'

'Dad – what's he got to do with it?'

'It was the photographs of his family in Italy, and him talking about his roots and how important they are. It's funny, but I never wanted to know anything before. The thought never entered my head when my parents were alive. Perhaps it's only now they're dead, that I can allow myself to think about it without feeling disloyal. It's purely curiosity. I'm not looking to replace Mum and Dad; I don't need another mother or father. I just need to know who I am, and why I was adopted. I can't go to my grave not knowing.'

'Well I hope you're not going there just yet?' he laughed and covered her hand with his.

'When Lorna was born, I couldn't stop staring at her, she was the first person I'd ever seen who was related to me. Everyone else sees people like themselves all the time, but I never had. The funny thing is that Lorna looks like Robert. I remember years ago, I was going out with this boy, and when I met his father I was amazed that their voices sounded exactly the same. I've always remembered that.'

'I think there must be advantages to not knowing who you are, or who you look like. It means you're completely free to be yourself – there can be no family expectations.'

'Yes, I think you're right about that. I've never felt pressurised to do anything other than what I wanted to do, or to be like anyone else.'

'I'm glad.' He stroked her hand. 'Your parents did tell you something though, didn't they? I remember you saying.'

'Yes – Mum did.'

'Well, it was just after the war, wasn't it? I'm sure lots of girls had babies they couldn't keep back then.' Martin stared into his half-empty glass. 'Can you do that anyway? I mean trace them. I thought adoption was final.'

'It is – but the law changed in 1975 to allow anyone who was adopted to be given information about their parents; only the children, not their birth mothers, or anyone else. I picked up a leaflet about it in the library yesterday.'

'Well, as long as you're sure that you want to know, and it won't upset you.'

'It's the right time for me now. I'm happy and settled.' Jenny smiled and squeezed his hand.

2

October 1984

Jenny fingered the letter as she spoke into the phone, 'I've filled in the Access to Birth Records form and I've got a letter to say that I should contact you.'

'You'll need to make an appointment with Mr Golding for Section 51 counselling. He's the Children's and Adoption Officer, but I'm afraid he's out this afternoon,' said a woman's voice over the phone.

'Oh, when shall I ring back then, any particular time?'

'He's usually here tomorrow until midday.'

'Tomorrow morning, I'll ring back then, thank you.' Jenny replaced the receiver, wondering where she could find an unoccupied room at work. 'Wednesday,' she said out loud, and remembered the manager's meeting at eleven the following day.

Jenny reached under her desk and pulled back the zip on her bag. For the third time that morning she felt the sharp edge of the letter. 'I need to take an early lunch today Moira, if that's alright with you?'

A grey-haired woman of around fifty raised her eyes from the ledger. 'That's a good idea; beat the lunchtime rush. There's a sale starting today at Vokins. I saw it on the way in. That's the third this year. That never used to happen; sales were only ever after Christmas. I suppose it's the recession.' She rubbed her lips together as if in anticipation of the bargains to be discovered. Jenny enjoyed working with Moira, but found her nosiness irritating. She was always asking how she and Martin were coping, 'Especially with the children,' she would always add, reminding Jenny of precisely what she came to work to forget.

'Yes, that's right, beat the rush,' Jenny said. 'I'd thought I'd go in about five minutes. I'll finish the bank statements when I come back.'

'Good, you can tell me what's there then.'

Jenny picked up her bag and left the room. She knocked gently on the door to the office opposite. No reply. She pushed it open slightly. The room was empty. Mrs Janaway had left for the managers' meeting. They always lasted until one o' clock, when trays of pre-ordered egg, cheese and ham sandwiches covered in cling-film would appear; compensation, Jenny thought, for the previous stultifying two hours. Seating herself behind a desk piled with ziggurats of probate files, she pulled the letter from her bag, unfolded it, and dialled.

'Hello, may I speak to Mr Golding please?' she recognised the girl's voice, 'It's Mrs Maynard, I phoned yesterday.' Jenny cleared her throat of the lingering remains of a head cold. 'Hello, Mr Golding, I was told to call today. I've filled in an Access to Birth Records form, my name's Mrs Maynard.' Jenny's heart thumped as she stared at a calendar view of the Highlands – complete with rampant stag in the foreground – that brightened the wall opposite.

'You know that you need to arrange an appointment?'

'Yes, I understand that. Your receptionist told me yesterday that I wouldn't be given any information until I came to see you.' She listened intently for any sounds outside the door. 'It will have to be a day when I'm not at work.' She stared at the heavy black numerals on the calendar… yes, that sounds fine… Tuesday next week at two… No, I don't, but I can find it. I'll see you then, thank you.' Excitement rippled through her as she replaced the receiver. She remembered Aunt Doris's latest letter, when she had mentioned again that she had something important that she wanted to talk to her about. Although her mother had said otherwise, she was sure that her aunt did know about her adoption. Jenny imagined various scenarios; from her mother being an aristocratic girl who having had a passionate affair with a soldier, had been forced to relinquish her baby so as not to disgrace her family; to herself being the unwanted end product of rape. She pushed the last thought from her mind.

'This must be for you. There's a Cypriot stamp on it.' Martin handed Jenny a blue airmail letter.

'That's quick. I haven't answered her last letter yet. I can't look at it today; can you put it in the letter rack?'

'You must be nervous?' Martin asked as he bit on a slice of buttered toast.

'Yes, but it's tinged with excitement. It's like going into labour for the first time. You don't really know what to expect, but you hope it's going to go well, and there's the excitement of seeing your baby at the end of it all.'

'I wouldn't have put it quite like that.' Martin grabbed his lunchbox from the worktop and gave Jenny a lingering kiss. 'Well, I'm off. You can tell me all about it when I get home. I'll be thinking about you.' As he turned around he tripped. 'Toby, get out of the way; you're not coming with me.' The dog whimpered and skulked under the table. 'Lorna, you better get a move on or you'll miss the bus,' Martin shouted up the stairs on his way to the door.

Jenny peered at her daughter as she grabbed an apple from the fruit bowl. 'What have you got on your eyes? Go and take it off. You know you're not allowed mascara at school.'

'Everyone wears it. Anyway, I can't, I'm late. I'll miss the bus.'

'Well, you shouldn't have put it on then, should you? Take this and wipe it off on the bus.' Lorna grabbed the sheet of kitchen roll from Jenny's hand.

Jenny sighed, *I bet she doesn't. I'll have to watch her tomorrow, or I'll be getting a letter from the school.* She walked into the lounge, opened the cupboard under the stairs and pulled out her coat and Toby's lead. They left the cottage and turned left, onto the path that led to the footbridge. It was wet underfoot, but too early in the year for the path to be covered with slippery leaves. She bent down and released Toby, who bounded ahead across the bridge. She looked down; the rush hour traffic had reduced to a trickle. The gaps between the struts reminding her nerve endings of the agoraphobia that had never completely vanished. She gripped the handrail as sweat began to ooze from the pores on her forehead. Most days she focused on Toby to mask her anxiety, and managed to cross the bridge. But today, as her heart hammered, she hesitated and panicked. She took a deep breath and let her shoulders relax. The sign of The Swan swayed on the wall of the public house at the end of the bridge, and she thought, *so near, yet so far*. She looked down at the cars speeding below. No – she couldn't do it – not today. 'Toby,' she shouted. He was already on the other side, but had stopped and was looking back at her, his tail wagging. He sniffed the air, and hurtled back across the bridge. Stepping back onto the path her heartbeat slowed. She bent down and patted Toby's head. 'Sorry, old boy, we'll go twice round the pond instead.'

The brick built house stood on at the northern edge of the council estate. It overlooked a pre-fabricated junior school built at the end of the war. At one time the detached house would have been occupied by a family, but it had been converted in the early seventies into a social services office. Jenny glanced at a plaque on the wall that stated the opening hours and pressed the bell. The door was answered by a ginger-haired woman wearing a calf-length skirt and an even longer cardigan.

'I'm Mrs Maynard – I've got an appointment with Mr Golding.'

'If you go through into the waiting room, he won't be long.'

The girl ushered Jenny into a small square room with painted cream walls. She sat down on a padded bench under the window. On the wall opposite was a cork notice board covered with leaflets held on by brightly-coloured pins. Jenny eyes fixed on one, *'Your rights if your child is removed.'* An open trunk filled with toys stood under the board.

'Mrs Maynard.' A tall fair-haired man, of about thirty, stood in the doorway opposite. A moustache covered his upper lip. He walked towards her and gave her hand a weak shake.

'Do come through. I'm Ross Golding, the Children's Officer for this patch. Please call me Ross. May I call you Jennifer?'

'Jenny,' she said.

Ross directed her to a melamine chair, pulled a similar one out from behind his desk, and sat a metre away from her.

'It must seem strange, coming here?'

'Yes, it does a bit.'

'If I can just explain the procedure; you've applied for access to your birth records.'

'Yes.'

'You know that the law changed in 1975. Before that date, as an adopted person you were not entitled to any information about your original family. Neither would any member of your original family be entitled to any information about you. This was done to protect yourself and your adoptive family. To give everyone involved a new start. Your birth mother knew when she gave her consent to your adoption that it was final, and that she would never know your new name, or where you lived. She could get on with her life knowing, that herself and any new family she might have, wouldn't be disturbed by her past. But, more importantly, your adoptive parents had the reassurance that all links with your original family were severed. But times and attitudes change, and we now think that must have been particularly hard on the birth mother; but any contact has to be initiated by the adult adoptee.'

Jenny nodded, thinking as she looked at him that she had never been attracted to men with fair hair, especially ones with moustaches.

'Anyway that's why you have to have this meeting. Section 51 counselling we call it; so that you are aware of the implications for everybody involved.' He picked up a thin beige folder from his desk. 'Are your adoptive parents still alive?'

'No, they both died two years ago,' Jenny said.

'Is that when you decided to find out about your birth family? It's a common reason.'

'Well, I certainly never thought about it while my parents were alive. I didn't want or need to. It seemed disloyal.'

Ross nodded and smiled sympathetically.

'I'm not looking to replace Mum and Dad, nobody could. I don't even want to meet my birth mother. I just want to know who I am. I'm settled and happy with my life at the moment, so it seems the right time.' Jenny couldn't take her eyes off the beige folder that lay on his lap.

'I'm glad to hear it. We don't encourage people to act on the information they're given if their lives are not going well for one reason or another. They may invest too much in the person. Some people think that by finding their birth mother, or birth father, it will make everything better for them; it might do. But it will also cause complications, and could make the person feel worse, especially if the birth mother doesn't want to know them. That does happen. It could remind her of a difficult time in her own life. She probably married and had other children, and has never told them, or her husband, so I have to warn people of that.'

'That's doesn't apply to me. I'm just interested in the information,' Jenny said, wishing that he would hurry up. She didn't need all this spiel.

'So, how are you feeling at the moment?' he stared at Jenny.

'I'm fine.' *For heaven's sake, this isn't a doctor's consultation, just get on with it.*

'I want to warn you that when people hear their original name and their birth mother's name for the first time, it can be a very emotional moment.' He finally opened the folder and Jenny was surprised to see that it contained just one form. He cleared his throat, 'I can tell you that the name your birth mother gave you was Georgina Ann, and you were born at 11B, Cannon Place, Brighton.' He paused and looked at Jenny.

Her head spun as she repeated, 'Georgina.' *That's not me,* she screamed inside. *I don't feel like a Georgina. I don't even like the name.*

'Are you alright Jenny?'

'Yes.'

'Your mother stated that she was a housewife, living at the address where you were born.'

That's not what Mum told me, she thought indignantly. *She said I was born in a hospital and that my mother was a young girl.*

Ross continued, 'Jenny, your mother's name was Helen – Helen Barretti.'

The wall opposite shifted to the side. Had there been an earthquake? Ross's lips were moving but there was no sound. His face, large and blurred around the edge moved towards her own, and back again, several times. She felt herself slip in slow motion to the floor. His lips were still moving but she couldn't hear any words; his face was almost touching hers, so close that she could see each blond hair of his moustache; his blue eyes; and then nothing.

He was squatting beside her, holding a small glass to her lips. His face gradually came into focus; the moustache, and then his eyes and tight curls. 'Sip this slowly,' he smiled and said softly, 'I don't often have to produce the office brandy.'

'It's alright, I can get up now,' Jenny muttered.

'Take it slowly, I'll help you.' Ross gripped her arm and helped her back onto her chair, He gave her the glass, 'Just carry on sipping. A few people have burst into tears on hearing their own and their mother's name, but you're the first to faint on me.' He sat back down.

'Sorry, could you tell me my mother's name again please?'

He reached for the folder. 'Yes, of course, it was Helen, Helen Barretti.'

'Not Ellen?' her voice trembled.

'No, Helen.'

'Is there a middle name?'

'There's not one written down here. She was a married woman, because her maiden name 'Neale' is shown. When a married woman has a child, her husband is usually stated on the certificate as the father, even if he doesn't attend the registration. But there is no name here, so it appears that her husband wasn't your father. That was probably the reason you were adopted.'

She must be some other Barretti, Jenny thought, *a relative, Brighton's a big place.*

Ross stared at her. 'Are you feeling a bit better now?'

'Yes.' She wanted to be away from him.

Ross lifted the phone. 'Sue, would you mind making Mrs Maynard a strong cup of tea? Thank you.' He replaced the receiver and looked down at the file. 'There doesn't seem to be any information about the agency that arranged your adoption. Often they have more information, perhaps about your father. But sometimes in these older cases there wasn't an agency involved. Yours may have been a private adoption, arranged by your mother's family doctor. So, I'm afraid that's all the information I can give you.' He closed the folder. 'Just one more thing; now we've had this meeting, you can order a copy of your original birth certificate. It will have on it the information I've just given you. If you feel that you need to talk about any aspect of this, you can always make an appointment with me, or there's an organisation that's very good. They can also help with tracing your birth relatives, if you decide that's what you want. I can give you their number.'

'No, no,' she said. There was a knock on the door and Sue with the long cardigan was standing in the doorway holding a cup and saucer.

'Go back into the waiting room, Jenny, and stay as long as you need to. If you're lucky Sue may even make you some more tea.' He smiled at Sue who glared back at him. 'I'll bring the form for the certificate out to you; you'll need to sign it.'

***

Jenny lay on top of the bed; stared at the sloping ceiling and digested the information she had been given. *It must be a different woman, the gravestone definitely said Ellen Mary.* Her head throbbed with the effort of trying to recall the day she had met Martin's mother. She could remember the argument between Martin and Anna clearly. But the only memory of his mother was of a dark-haired woman wearing an apron with a frill around the edge, pouring out glasses of cream soda. Her face was the same as the one in Ricco's photograph, blocking any earlier memory that she might have had. So much had happened to her in the years since Anna's party, she would have to undergo hypnosis to recall any further details. Photographs – that's what she needed to see. She remembered when she was separating from Robert, how carefully she had divided up their photo albums, and other acquisitions of their years together. It was as if, by being scrupulously fair, that would compensate for leaving him. She got up, went over to a chest of drawers and swallowed two paracetamol tablets with the cold remains of a mug of tea. She went back to the bed, slipped underneath the duvet and closed her eyes.

'Lorna said you were up here. What are you doing in bed? You look as white as a sheet.' Martin stood in the doorway, his head almost touching the wooden lintel.

Jenny rubbed her eyes, pulled herself up and leant against the pillows. 'Oh, I had a terrible upset stomach after you left this morning.'

'Probably nerves, how did you get on at the meeting?'

'I cancelled it. I can always make another appointment; there's no rush, not after all this time.'

'You cancelled it! I came home early. I thought you'd want to talk about it.'

'That's really sweet of you.' Jenny stared at him; his shape, his dark hair. Was that why she had been so attracted to him, and he to her; a recognition of the same, a genetic connection? Her eyes were green though. 'Can you come a bit closer?' He moved to the end of their bed.

'Why are you looking at me like that?'

'Like what?'

'As if you're seeing me for the first time.'

'You don't regret leaving Marilyn do you? I know it hasn't been easy.'

'Of course not; we deal with problems together, don't we? I love you. I've never been happier.'

'Me too,' she smiled, noticing a thickening around his waist. He had mentioned it last week, telling her that it was because he was content. 'Did your father have a sister or sister-in-law?'

'He only had the one brother, and as far as I know, he never married. Why are you asking?'

'I was just thinking back to the photos he has on his

sideboard. I was interested. Do you have any of yourself and Anna when you were young – and your mother?'

'I think the ones I had are still at Marilyn's. I didn't have many. Most of them are with Dad or Anna. You don't want them now surely?'

'No, not this minute, but I'd like to see them sometime.'

'Well, I'm starving, so I'll go and get something on for dinner. Lorna's in her bedroom, supposedly doing her homework. Do you fancy anything?'

'No, I don't want anything. Just do something for yourself and Lorna.'

'Are you coming downstairs later?'

'I might do. Martin – was your mum always called Ellen?'

He gave her a puzzled look. 'I never heard Dad call her anything else, apart from when he lost his temper with her. He didn't call her by her name then.'

'He never called her Helen – always Ellen?'

'What's all this about? No, always Ellen, look I'm off downstairs.'

Jenny remembered Ricco had said 'my Ellen' when she had met him the other week, but he did have a slight accent. She waited until she heard Martin in the kitchen, and then reached for the ball of tissue under her pillow and blew her nose. Music that she couldn't put a name to bounced off the wall that separated their bedroom from Lorna's. Turning on her side, she pulled the pillow over her ears and shut her eyes.

Her birth certificate arrived nine days later. She took the buff envelope to her bedroom and pulled the bolt across the door. The more she had thought about her meeting with Ross, the more she wondered whether he hadn't said Helen Barretti at all, but Helen Barretto, or Helen Barretta, and that in her heightened emotional state she had heard only the familiar.

Sitting on the unmade bed she ripped the envelope open and pulled the certificate through the torn edges. She saw her name Georgina Ann, written in small black handwriting in the column next to her date of birth. Her eyes focused on the writing in the next column – Helen Barretti formerly Neale of 11B, Cannon Place, Brighton. She stared at the cream painted wall, and decided that her first reaction must be right after all. There must have been another women with the same surname, especially as the certificate didn't show any middle name. *Yes, that must be the answer,* she thought, in a large town, of course there could be. There are lots of women called Smith, Walker and other surnames. It was just a weird coincidence. She poured over the rest of her certificate. A single black line was drawn under Name and Occupation of Father. Her mother had put 11B, Cannon Place as her usual place of residence. So, she had been born at home, and her birth registered two weeks later. In the space at the end of the columns – as if an afterthought – was the word "Adopted" and signed H. Wade, Registrar of Births, Deaths and Marriages.

She read and re-read every single word.

'Jenny, Jenny, what are you doing? You've been up her for ages.' The black latch was moving up and down. 'Why have you locked the door?'

'Just coming,' putting the certificate back in the envelope, she stuffed it under her pillow and walked over to the door and released the bolt. Martin stood facing her.

Jenny took a deep breath and ran her fingers through her hair. 'I'm just about to make the bed. I'll be down in a minute.'

'I came up to give you this. I found it in the letter rack unopened.'

'Oh, I forgot all about it,' Jenny said, taking the letter from him.

'You've seemed a bit distant lately, as if you're worried about something. You would tell me, wouldn't you? It's not about that appointment you cancelled is it?'

'No, no, I'll make another this week.'

'Don't forget you're taking Lorna over to meet Robert. I hope we're not going to have a repeat of last time, it was terrible.'

'Has she said that she doesn't want to go?' Jenny asked, avoiding his eyes.

'No, but she's hiding away in her bedroom. You better go and speak to her. I thought we could talk about our holiday when you get back.'

Jenny nodded. 'I'll speak to her in a minute. Can you get some salad ready for lunch?'

Hearing the clatter of his feet on the wooden stairs, she took her birth certificate from under the pillow and slid it inside her handbag. She picked up a nail file from the chest of drawers, sat on the bed and opened her aunt's letter...

Dear Jenny,
I know I've only just written to you, but I've got to ask your advice about something. I was planning to chat to you when you came over, but something's happened. This may come as a shock to you, and I didn't want to tell you in a letter, but years ago I had a daughter that I had to have adopted. I won't go into all the details here. But I've received a letter from someone, not her, saying that she's traced me and would like to contact me. So I thought with you being adopted yourself, you could tell me what she would like to hear...

The letter slipped through Jenny's fingers onto the floor. Normally, with news like this, she would have rushed to tell Martin about it – but not now. She didn't even want to read any more. She picked the letter up, walked over to the chest and stuffed the letter at the back of the top drawer.

The early morning rain had passed, leaving behind a blustery wind. Jenny fought her way across The Steine and into Royal York Buildings. Passing an oblong mirror set in green and amber tiles she followed the sign along a corridor. On either side the walls were plastered with wedding banns. She pushed through the swing doors, and walked up to the counter.

'I've ordered two birth certificates,' she said to the bespectacled clerk.

'What name?' the clerk responded as he had done many times before.

'Maynard, Mrs Maynard.' He strolled over to a wire tray.

Jenny's middle fingers on her right hand beat an urgent rhythm on the top of the counter that corresponded to the thumping inside her chest. She watched him flick through about a dozen buff envelopes. *He looks bored stiff. How can he be bored by something that has so much significance for me?*

'Here you are.' He handed Jenny an envelope.

'Thank you,' she whispered, suddenly regretting her decision and thinking that she should hand it back. She could say it was a mistake and she didn't want them after all. It didn't matter to him. He would just think she was crazy and go and eat his lunch. Why does she want to be certain? Surely uncertainty is preferable? But she couldn't give the envelope back. She pushed through the swing doors and sat down on a seat in the corridor. The envelope was unsealed. Her hands shook as she removed the first birth certificate. It was Martin's. Her eyes went straight to the name of his mother – Helen Mary Barretti of 11B, Cannon Place, Brighton, maiden name Neale. Her stomach heaved. She swallowed hard to stop herself from retching. So there was only one. It would be too much of a coincidence if there were two women of the same surname and maiden name, living at the same address. Written in black ink under the heading – Name of Father – was Enrico Guiseppe Barretti. She saw Martin's birthday, 2nd February 1944. She opened the other certificate – Anna Veronica, born at the same address in July 1947 to Helen Mary Barretti. Again, Enrico was entered as the father. *So, Ross was right about her husband not being my father.*

Jenny sat heavy as stone. The certificates hung from her hand as she stared at the marriage banns on the wall opposite. She tried to decipher the names, but was too far away. From the corner of her eye she was aware of a couple walking towards her. The woman was carrying a baby wrapped in a blanket. The father's mouth moved as they stood at the end of the seat. Jenny stared at him not hearing his words. They sat down. Jenny felt the pressure of the woman's body against her own, but didn't move to make room for them on the bench. She continued staring straight ahead. Then she realised she was alone again, but couldn't remembering them leaving. She sighed, put the certificates inside her handbag and left the building.

'Could you put me through to Moira please?' She leant for support against the door of the phone box.

'Hello Moira, it's me. I'm sorry, but I won't be back after lunch. I don't feel well, so I'm going home. No, I'm sure I'll be fine by Wednesday,' Jenny replaced the receiver. She imagined Moira's concerned face peering at her, as she probed into her personal life, thinking correctly for once, that it was making her ill. Jenny took a deep breath and walked slowly northwards, to where she had left her car earlier that morning.

Traffic was light, and high waves pounded the shingle as she drove along the seafront and turned into Cannon Place. It had been one of many regency terraces in the centre of Brighton, but a shopping centre now graced the top end. A few of the original houses remained on the left hand side. Jenny parked and walked up to the one numbered 15. A dirty half curtain and a banner hung across an upstairs window. 'Squatters,' she muttered. 15B was a basement, and Jenny assumed that 11B, when it existed, would have been the same. She stared at the shabby exterior and remembered the day of Anna's birthday. Had her birth mother recognised her then? No she couldn't have. Had she said something to make her suspect that she was her daughter? She couldn't remember, it was too long ago. Was that why they moved away so suddenly? Martin said his aunt hadn't died until a long time afterwards. *Perhaps that was just an excuse to stop us being together. 'My sister always bit her lip when she was worried about something'* and *'my mother always called my father that,'* Martin's words replayed in her mind again and again as she walked back to her car.

Jenny drove past the Peace Statue that marked the boundary between Brighton and Hove, and turned northwards until she saw the renovated sails of the windmill above the rooftops. *Nearly there*, she thought.

Jenny parked and stared at the fields at the end of the road. Milk chocolate furrows stretched to rough grassland, too steep to be ploughed. A ribbon of tarmac divided the fields from private housing on the right-hand side. The afternoon sun shone blinding rays of light onto the rear windows of the cars as they crept to the summit. Crisp orange and yellow leaves twirled in the gutter in front of her car.

She wondered what she should do now. Why did she have to find out? She wished she had left well alone. A Pandora's box. Was this her punishment for leaving Robert? If she told Martin the truth, everything could change; his feelings towards her might change. He might leave her. She couldn't disrupt Lorna and Nicky's lives again. *But, he doesn't have to know. He would never find out, nobody could.* It was only herself who could be given this information. She would never be able to tell anybody, but she wouldn't want to. She would have to live with the truth, she had done that before; she could do it again.

Turning her head, she saw a dozen rusty nails scattered across the red brick wall that formed a backdrop to the front garden. Some of them still held fragments of her father's frayed gardening string. Tears flooded down her face, as she sat mesmerised by them.

Ten minutes later she wiped her cheeks with the sleeve of her coat, and walked up the garden path. She passed the flaking front door, and opened the low gate that led to the back garden. The triangular vegetable patch had been cemented over. Only the gnarled apple tree remained; its stubby trunk rising from a postage stamp patch of earth encircled by concrete. Jenny recalled the acid sharpness of the fruit, remembering how she loved to dip the slices in sugar when her mother wasn't looking.

In front of the dividing trellis had been a well-tended lawn. Now, tufts of tall grass sprouted from rough brown patches that stretched uneasily to the broken wire fence that separated the houses. Locked into the ground were two climbing frames – forgotten skeletons in an open air museum – their bones chipped and fractured. Jenny felt uneasy; she was trespassing in someone else's life. She walked back to her car, and sat staring at the fields. So, her birth mother hadn't been a young girl at all, she was a married woman, neither was she from far away, she was from the same town. Too close for comfort. It certainly was now.

'Get a fucking move on will you.'

Startled, Jenny looked behind her. A heavily pregnant young woman was dragging a coffee-coloured toddler up the path to the front door. The girl's face was framed by a straight blonde fringe and shoulder-length hair. A large gold hoop hung from each ear. The boy screamed and more expletives followed as the girl urged the reluctant child forward. She glowered at Jenny, who looked away. A door slammed and Jenny looked round. They had disappeared inside the flat. Jenny sat and stared straight ahead until her right leg cramped, making her face twist with pain. She stretched her leg to release the muscle and then turned the ignition key.

She braked as the traffic lights changed, and looked across to the church and windmill. *Not now,* she thought. *I can't visit the graveyard today. My two mothers lying feet away from each other. I need to be stronger for that.* Her stomach rumbled like distant thunder and her nausea returned.

Jenny parked in her usual space and ran into the cottage. She threw her handbag and coat onto the sofa and opened the back door for Toby. Grabbing two plain biscuits from the tin she looked up – four o' clock – Lorna would be home soon. She picked up a box of matches and took a newspaper from the top of a pile on top of a chair. Returning to the sitting room she opened the glass door to the fire, took a bundle of thin pieces of wood from the basket in the hearth, and layered them with torn newspaper inside the stove. She struck a match, and then reached for her bag that lay beside a travel guide to Rome. She pulled out Martin and Anna's birth certificates together with the letter from the General Register Office and ripped them into pieces. The flames burst into life as she fed them, carefully turning the wood with the poker. She then pulled out her own birth certificate and tore it into shreds.

There was a squeal of brakes, and a familiar clunk.

Jenny dashed over to the window. Martin's Land Rover stood outside. 'What's he doing back now?' Her heart hammered against her ribs as she ran back to the fire and slammed the door shut with her foot. She fell onto the sofa, and opened the book… *Rome lies along the banks of the River Tiber and is one of Europe's most continuously occupied cities, dating back two and a half thousand years. It is also known as The Eternal City*… In her clenched fist she held the remnants of her certificate. The door latch moved upwards and Martin filled the room.

'I've had enough for today. There was a bunch of school kids mucking about all morning. One of them must have opened the display case as some of the exhibits are missing. I suppose I'll have to phone the school tomorrow. You've lit the fire already?'

'Yes, I felt cold when I got home.' She continued to stare at the pages of the book… *traditional stories explain the earliest history of the city in terms of legend. The most famous being the story of Romulus and Remus, the twins suckled by a she-wolf…*

Martin stepped towards her and bent down. She closed her eyes as she met his lips.

'You're reading up on Rome, that's good. It's not long now before we go. Do you think Lorna's O.K. about staying with Robert?'

'Yes, she's fine about it. Could you put the kettle on for some tea?'

'I'll make you a cup, but I need something stronger.'

As he left the room, Jenny dropped onto the floor

and opened the glass door. She unclenched her fist, threw the remains of her certificate into the fire, leant back on her heels and watched as the flames leapt higher.

04670